ROUND THE BEND

OREGON HISTORICAL BOOK 1

RAIN TRUEAX

ROUND THE BEND

OREGON PIONEER ROMANCE
BOOK 1

The Stevens Family Saga Begins

An original work of Rain Trueax.

Copyright © 2015   Rain Trueax
Reformatted June 2019

ISBN 13: 9781943537617
ISBN 10: 1943537615
Paperback
Comfortable Reading

Prepared and presented by:
Seven Oaks
Monmouth, Or.

061820-113017 392 bask 0 -2

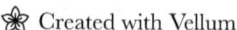

Taopi tawote,
Wound medicine, the Lakota call it.
Yarrow, the English call it.
Strong of scent, herbal healer,
born of the earth...taopi tawote.
Men's souls need wound medicine.

Some hurts go so deep only the strongest of medicines can heal them.

Love is such a medicine...

This is the story of such a love...

CHAPTER 1

Independence, Missouri-- spring 1851

"You don't seem at all excited that finally we're on our way!"
"You think that, do you?"

"Matt, don't you feel it? Like we're geese and heading north or the first who came to this land. Finally, it's us heading for adventure and excitement." Amy tugged on the rough cotton of his rolled up sleeve, demanding his attention, which seemed to be wandering to a robin calling from a nearby oak.

His blue-gray eyes finally looked down at her, the gleam in them belying the serious set of his lips. "Is this one of those questions that needs an answer or you're just talking to be talkin'?"

She decided to ignore the sarcasm. "My point is you aren't taking me or the momentousness of this moment seriously—at all."

"I take you serious-- enough."

They began walking again. For Amy, the day was pure magic. Overhead, large oak trees provided a canopy of protection from the hot Missouri sun. Down the path she heard a small stream bubbling across rocks. Tall grasses were intermingled with wildflowers. It was a world apart, almost peaceful enough to make her forget the noise of the large encampment of wagons and people less than half a mile to the west.

She had talked Matt into taking this stroll with the hope she could share her excitement with him as she had so much in the past. Her best friend had been pulling away. Time for just the two of them would bring him back around to her.

"Why aren't you more thrilled? That's what I want to know." She didn't wait for an answer. "Tomorrow we'll be starting on the first leg of the Oregon Trail. It's something we've talked about, dreamed over for years, a real adventure. Mr. Jones is going to say go, and hundreds of us-- people we know and ones we don't-- we'll all be heading west to the promised land." Her voice rose, quickening with her zeal for all that lay ahead.

"Big doin's for sure," he agreed good-naturedly, stopping to turn and look at her as he reached for a long blade of grass.

"Me, my family. You, your family. All of us."

She saw the shutter drop across his face as though a cloud had passed over. She was used to that response when she mentioned his family. What she didn't understand was the stony expression whenever she tried to talk about the trip. There was no one with whom she so wanted to share her exhilaration. He was shutting her out.

"We don't know what we'll find along the way, Matthew. Excitement, exploration... new experiences, meeting new people."

"That's a plumb lot." There was cynicism in his voice.

"You know that it is." One way or another she would lift his mood. Playfully, she swatted at his chest. "It could be like a novel."

"You'd be the one to know," he acknowledged putting the long blade of grass between his lips, "readin' like you do."

"Not just reading, Matt," she corrected him. "Someday I'll write books."

"A real bluestocking, huh?"

She had taught him the word. It irritated her that he seemed to be using it to make fun of her. "You are teasing me."

"Would I do that, Amelia."

"You would and have." She had to admit, at least to herself

2

that his teasing had a modicum of truth in it. Although she was widely read and loved a variety of authors, her favorites were less famous female poets. These women showed by their words and lives that a woman could be more than wife and mother. They wrote about political ideas, social issues and put to verse the unique problems of women.

Their intellectual and social gatherings had drawn even the lettered men of their time and not for the usual reasons--food, flattery or feminine beauty. They were not geishas trained to please a man but rather women who could use logic and hold their own discussing philosophy and even science. For whatever reason, and Amy had heard several theories, the women at these gatherings had been dubbed bluestockings, at first jokingly but later derogatorily.

"You don't like my thinking so much." It wasn't as question.

"I didn't say that," he drawled. "Look, you want to write. I say write. You want to go around giving talks like that... whoever it was you were telling me about last week, that's fine too."

"It's my dream." When she thought he might say something, he was silent. She looked at his face, trying to get past the enigmatic expression. Distracted she watched a squirrel skitter up a tree. Not looking at him, she said, "You're the only one I've read my poems to."

"Your folks'd like to know you write things. That one you read me about travelin', always wantin' to see what's over the next ridge, that was good."

"Did you really think so?" She was unsure. Was he teasing her?

"Wouldn't say it if I didn't."

She smiled. "You always see past what I say... to what I mean." She shook her head. "I don't think my parents would feel that way about my poems or my goals. They'd be afraid I'd end up like Helen Maria Williams, arrested for political writing... or worse." She laughed. "Involved with a divorced man. No, I don't think they'd be pleased if they knew."

"Well, they'll have to know sometime. Unless you just keep talkin' about it and never do it."

"That wasn't very nice."

She frowned. His moods were shifting directions as fast as the wind on a mountain. He turned and again led their way down the path.

Matt wore his blond hair longer than most men, tied back with a leather strap. They had been friends since childhood, which made it hard for her to see him as anything other than Matt. He was tall, a head above her own height and she taller than most women. Even through the worn, cotton shirt, she could see large muscles move as his arms swung loosely at his sides. Muscular and well-shaped though he might be, he was nothing like the heroes described by Miss Austen. Those men had a cultured elegance, a slenderness of form, their grace not leonine like Matt's, their words filled with urbanity and droll witticisms not his mixture of hill folk and Southern wisdom.

She didn't have to see Matt's face to know the planes and hollows, the strong chin, the way his eyes glinted, turning almost blue with humor or darkening to steel gray in anger. Was he handsome? To her he was just Matt--her best friend. She had seen him in sorrow and laughter, pain and joy. Yet, as well as she believed she knew him, he had always closed off a part of himself. He knew her better than she did him.

"You done?" he asked without glancing back.

"With what?"

"Figurin' out whatever about me has got you bothered now."

She shrugged, tossing long hair behind her shoulders. "I am most decidedly not done. I want to know why you're not stirred with excitement. Trembling with fervor." She laughed. "Matt, the prairie grass is greened up, and we're heading west to a new land, new exploits!"

She pushed ahead of him on the trail and stood blocking his path. Putting her hands on her hips, she threw back her head in a challenging manner. "You tell me what is going on in that blond head of yours. Right now!"

He reached out, lifted her off her feet, put her aside, and continued down the path. On the bank of the small stream, he threw himself on the ground, looking up at her with a lazy grin that irritated her.

"You think you're more mature than me," she protested.

"Just because you're three years older. I'm almost eighteen, Matthew Kane."

"Real grown up."

"You are making fun of me."

"I'd never make fun of you, Miss Stevens."

She wrinkled her nose at him."I wanted us to share what it'll be like when we get to Oregon, about the trip." She allowed her voice to take on a disappointed sulk, glancing out of the corner of her eyes to see what effect that might have on his stern demeanor. "It's a place where people can have anything they want. There are tall trees, meadows, flowers, water. They say the land will grow just about anything."

"That so? Here I was thinkin' you wanted to be a writer, and instead you're turnin' into a farmer." His voice hardened as he added, "Or you met a farmin' expert."

"Are you implying I'd have to get my information from someone else... a man for instance?" She rose to stand above him. Just what she was attempting to dominate she wasn't certain.

One hand under his head, he moved the other in front of his chest into a mock-defensive pose. "No ma'am. I'd never imply nothing about a lady." His grin left open the question of whether or not he saw her as a lady.

Turning away with a swish of her skirt, she walked to the bank. Drawing her skirt back from the edge, she knelt, dabbling the cool surface with her fingertips. "The water's a pleasing temperature. Let's wade," she suggested, plopping onto the bank and beginning to pull off square-toed, leather shoes.

She glanced back. He had propped himself up on one elbow to watch, chewing on that stem of grass. All right, let him miss the fun. She rolled down white, cotton stockings and threw them on the bank. Cautiously she edged her way into the shallow stream, grasping her skirts and slips high above the water, revealing more than a little of her calves, which might not have been considered proper, but then after all, Matt was just Matt. It didn't matter if he saw her legs. He'd seen more than that when they'd gone skinny dipping as children. She smiled, remembering, until a slip on a smooth stone forced her attention back to the stream.

"This is wonderful. Come on in."

He didn't respond. The large oaks cast shadows on the water, providing a changing interplay of light and dark as the breezes moved the branches. The small stones felt smooth under her feet. She was reluctant to leave, but Matt had lain back on the grass, no longer watching her. The blade of grass was gone. It wasn't as much fun without him. She stepped from the stream.

To Amy the air was full of the nervous energy she had often felt when around huge flocks of migrating birds. It wasn't just going to Oregon. That was the beginning but beyond was the Pacific Ocean, the Sandwich Islands, the Orient. Who knew where the trail would lead her.

He had to be feeling some of her anticipation, but for some stubborn reason, he denied his feelings. She grumbled to herself wondering again what he was thinking. A telltale muscle, beating a rhythm in his jaw, was the only indication he felt anything.

She didn't bother to dry her feet before she pulled back on stockings and shoes and tromped over to stand above him. Closed eyes, not withstanding, she knew he wasn't asleep. She debated what he would do if she splashed him. That wouldn't work. I'd end up in the creek--all the way in the creek. She'd experienced Matt's reactions to such provocations before.

Plucking a stiff blade of grass, she plopped down on the ground beside him, not earning so much as a raised eyelid for her trouble. She traced the blade of grass along his face, tickling his closed eyelids, then moving it down to glide across sternly set lips.

He kept his eyes closed, not reacting as she had hoped with laughter. Determined to force a response, she delicately and then not so gently began tickling along the side of his ribs-- in the one area she knew he was helpless to resist. This earned at least a limited reaction. He reached up, grabbed her wrist and held it against his side. She brought her left hand into the game. Leaning across his chest, she launched a fresh attack.

6

Matt was forced to apply more of his strength in defense. She never for a moment thought hers would be enough to overcome his, but she used other stratagems, quick maneuvers and, when required, psychological attacks. He had twisted up and over her, leaving her wrists pinned above her head. "Give?" His body half covered hers.

"No!" she gasped, laughing and out of breath. She pushed upward, trying to roll him from her. There was no smile on his face as she became aware of how his hard body pressed against her breasts, his face only inches from hers.

Before she could open her mouth to question the mood she saw in his eyes, he bent even closer. His lips inches from hers, his breath warm on her face. She felt his breath become part of her own. For a moment, his gaze met hers. He hesitated, and then his lips came down, soft, moving, demanding.

No man had kissed her on the lips. His hard, masculine body made her aware of her feminine softness in a way she'd never imagined. For a moment, she was caught in the claim he was staking to her very being. She felt the muscles of his arms as he pulled her against him. Surprise and something she didn't understand held her motionless. His tongue teased against her lips, forcing them apart, making her want--

With a strength that came from panic, she shoved against his chest. He didn't resist, and she easily rolled him from her.

Jumping to her feet, she smoothed her skirt in one fluid motion before she put her hands on her hips. "Why did you do that?"

"Maybe I'm tired of the games you're playing."

"What are you talking about?"

"Are you really that much of a child?"

She glared at him. "Say what you mean!"

"I mean-- you lay all over a man and then act surprised when he kisses you. What did you think was gonna happen?"

"You're not a man. You're Matt," she retorted before she realized what she'd said.

He snorted. "You got part of it right."

"Is this going to be one of your moods?"

His smile was cold, remote. It was an expression she'd seen

7

on his face, but never turned on her. She could still taste him on her lips and felt infuriated. She wanted to fly at him, claws bared. He had taken her first kiss, something to which he had no right.

She made an effort to keep her voice composed. "Why did you do it?"

He laughed without humor. "You show off your legs in front of me, lay against me and then expect me to be a log. Hell, what did you expect?"

Her hand tingled with the urge to slap his face, wipe that ugly smile from his lips, but she'd be a lady. She'd remain calm at all cost. He wasn't making it easy. "Well, I didn't want that," she said finally making an effort at finding composure.

"You sure?" His smile was almost too much. She couldn't believe the hard tone to his voice. He wasn't even apologetic.

"You treated me like--" She stopped, tried to think of the word and realized she didn't have one she dared use. "Well, not like a lady."

He shook his head, the smile on his lips not reaching his smoke gray eyes. She tried to read the expression in his narrowed gaze. This was not the boy, with whom she'd grown up.

She tried again. "Matthew... We're friends, almost like brother and sister. It's always been that way."

"I'm not your brother, and you said it yourself, you're not a girl anymore even though you act like it sometimes. And I'm sure as hell no boy. Life changes."

"But... I don't want them to change."

He rose to his feet in one cat-like motion. When she recoiled, his smile was cold. "What'd you think I was goin' to do, attack you?"

"Of course not," she said although she was unsure what she had feared.

"You're lying. That's exactly what you thought."

"You're... different, and I don't like it. I want things to be like they've always been."

He shook his head. His eyes changed to a stormy gray, the darkness a portent of what lay within, of the depths she'd never been able to plumb, the part of him he'd never let her see. The muscle throbbed in his jaw.

"You that sure you know what you want?" he asked finally.

"Of course. I want us to be friends."

His laugh was anything but humorous. "Well, then reckon we'll neither one get what we want out of this day."

"Matt, that's not fair. Just because I don't have… a romantic feeling for you doesn't mean we can't be friends." Tears filled her eyes. She felt a renewed anger at their cause. She glared at him. She was sure. She couldn't feel romantic love for Matthew, not the kind that was described so rapturously in the books and poems. He would always be her friend, but not the man of her dreams, not the dark-haired prince, the dashing man who would someday sweep her off her feet and carry her to his world.

Matt's narrowed eyes told her he didn't need words to know what she was thinking. "I'd rather have nothin' at all from you than how it's been."

That was the last straw. Anger flooded through her until she felt as though the top of her head could not contain it. "That is the most pig-headed, arrogant, selfish--" She stopped as she struggled to think of more adjectives to describe the rage she felt.

"After all the years we've been friends! After all we've been through, how dare you say that! You stand there with that smug look on your face and tell me friendship isn't enough without... without kisses and whatever else it is that you think is worth more. That makes me so angry, Matt, I could slap your face!"

He shrugged. "If you think it'd make you feel better, but I never saw it help much."

"Why does it have to change now?" She reached out, pulling on his arm, trying to force him to look into her eyes, to see things her way.

When he met her gaze, she saw firm determination in his eyes. "I won't stand around watchin' you makin' eyes at some other man."

"Other man? What are you talking about?"

"I saw that scout, Stone, comin' around. The two of you

9

laughin', him wantin' to be with you the way I do-- I saw it this mornin'. It was in your eyes when you looked at him."

"How dare you say that! I'm not looking for any man."

His smile was disbelieving.

"You're not being fair."

"Maybe not," he drawled. "but at least I am being honest, which is more than I can say for you."

"I am honest."

He snorted. "Fine, so be it, but friendship with you isn't enough. I'd rather not see you at all than keep pretendin' it is."

She felt a cold fear. "Does that mean you're not going with the wagon train to Oregon?" Something was being yanked from her heart. She crossed her arms over her chest as though to hold it back.

"It's too late for changin' that. Everything I got is into this trip. If it wasn't too late--" He stopped for a moment and then shrugged. "But it is."

"Then you are going to Oregon," she repeated. If he stayed with the train, he would change his mind, see that their friendship was too special to lose. She couldn't help putting words to her thoughts. "Maybe you'll change your mind, see things the way you used to. I want us to be friends, Matt. I want what we had. Just because new people or things come into our lives, it doesn't have to change what we have."

"Life changes, Amy, and sometimes, there's no goin' back." He reached out and touched her cheek. "I'm sorry I hurt you. Sorry I kissed you that way." His smile turned back into the cold one as he dropped his hand and stepped back. "No, that's a lie. That's the one thing I'm not sorry about. I'll walk you back to camp."

They made the walk in silence. At the edge of the encampment, he turned, and left her without another word. She watched him stride off-- still convinced he would change his mind. When she no longer saw him, she felt a pain in her heart, as though a part of her had been ripped away.

CHAPTER 2

M att held the tethers for the oxen in his right hand. With his left he resettled the yokes more securely onto the stubborn beasts' necks. He glared at the closest of the two as he began to tighten straps. "You could end up stew. Four mules'd be less trouble," he growled. With mock innocence, the big head looked back at him, dark eyes reflecting no thought of rebellion, while the heavy body leaned against his. "Keep it up," Matt muttered, slapping the brute on the flank and pushing him back into line.

It was the hour before dawn, the blackness fading away, the rays of the sun lying just below the horizon. From where he stood, it seemed to Matt the wagons formed an endless column, their light canvas covers gleaming in the dim light. While men made last-minute adjustments to buckles and straps, their women and children stood beside them, staring toward the west.

When he had finished yoking his oxen, Matt saw the bearded wagon master, St. Louis Jones, ride his horse to the front of the column. Matt walked forward, standing at the edge of the crowd gathered to hear last minute instructions. Jones dismounted, stepping onto a wagon to get above the people. Matt had assessed the man to be, although not a big man, a strong one, a man to be respected not just for his position or authority but also for the character that stood behind all that.

Jones pulled off his hat, rubbed his hand over a balding head. He raised his arms over his head, his voice carrying across the crowd. "In a minute here, we're aheadin' out, three hundred strong."

As the people's voices hushed, he lowered his arms and looked up to the sky before he went on, "You folks represent just about every kind of folks there be. The oldest we got travelin' with us admits to seventy-five. The youngest is six months. You are farmers, storekeepers, tradesmen. All different, but ya got three things in common-- enough money to outfit a wagon, the want for a better life, and the courage to reach out and make it happen. Ya are the future of these here United States. No matter how different ya be, it's time ya come together like a community and get along for the next months."

An almost unnatural silence settled over the people as they listened to a few of the problems that potentially lay ahead. Matt didn't understand their apparent awe any more than he'd understood Amy's excitement of the day before. He saw the road ahead as a hard one, one he had known would be difficult, but had chosen anyway. For him, it was not romantic or awe-inspiring.

"What I already told ya, the books ya read, they don't tell ya what lays out there for each of ya. Only livin' can do that. At night, you'll be tired. Walk all day, drive a team of mules or oxen and then at night repair yore wagon and cook a meal. Never enough rest.

"Tempers get short. There's no privacy. By the time we get to Oregon, we're goin' to know each other better'n we knew anybody where we come from. Secrets... Wal, there won't be none. Ya got trouble in yore marriage, we'll know it. Ya hit yore kids, we'll know it. Privacy's somethin' ya used to have."

He pointed to two men, one driving the wagon on which he stood, the other holding the reins of a horse. "Tom Ackerman and Clem Johnson are my right hands. They'll be there to help ya, but they ain't goin' to be enough. You'll have to reach out to help each other. Ya will be needed like ya ain't never been needed."

As St. Louis talked, Matt looked at the two men. From what

he could tell of Ackerman, he was soft, not a man to depend on. He had heard him already lamenting the length of the trip ahead. The old one, Clem, was harder to read. Skinny as a rail, he seemed to know what he was about. His pale blue eyes were alert and intelligent.

"Our scout," Jones pointed toward a tall, dark-haired man in buckskins, leg looped over the pommel of his saddle, "has been across the prairies near as many times as me. He might look young, but he's a man to count on in trouble."

The wagon master's voice was powerful, his tone deep with emotion as he pulled off his hat and told the people, "I always believe in startin' out with prayer to the Almighty. Jest like the Israelites headin' out behind Moses, goin' to the Promised Land, we're headin' for a promised land. Each of us maybe believe a little different... but we can agree on one thing. We need somethin' more than us watchin' over and a goin' along."

After his prayer, St. Louis chuckled. "Now, get to yore wagons. We can't spend all day here lollygagging."

On his way back to his wagon, Matt saw Amy in the distance, her sister, Loraine, at her side. He wondered if she'd seen him, if she was still angry. Matt stopped at his own wagon. Damn, why'd she have to be so beautiful? And so far out of his reach? If only she'd been born without that glossy, black hair, if her skin had less of that soft ivory sheen, or if she hadn't those dark, doe eyes, or such a full kissable mouth. If she hadn't been so kind, so intelligent, and full of vitality, less any or all of it and maybe then it would have been possible to be what she wanted —just a friend.

His dreams had been born so long ago; he no longer knew from what they'd been spun. He didn't need to list the reasons love wasn't possible between them-- even if her feelings had been different. He should not have kissed her—except, he wasn't sorry he had. He wanted that memory.

Twisting his thoughts away from what he couldn't have, he ran down the list of supplies and equipment he'd purchased. There'd be few places to get it right if he hadn't already. Too much weight wasn't a problem for the Kane outfit. With just his father and brother, there'd been no woman to argue over taking precious family heirlooms—if there'd even been any. Their big wagon carried hundreds of pounds of flour, almost a hundred of bacon and cured hams, jerked beef, sugar and coffee, sacks of rice, beans, dried fruit, pans, matches, salt, baking soda, medicines and a little medicinal whiskey. He snorted, knowing how much more than a medicinal amount, his father, Nathan, had probably squirreled away in secret niches.

The wagon was equipped with spare parts, extra chain links, harness repair equipment, ropes, hammers, a mallet, an axe and enough resin to keep the wheels lubricated, hopefully all the way to Oregon. Barrels and canvas bags hung on the outsides, capable of carrying water for some distance when needed, and they'd been assured it would be needed.

Matt's prize possession, worth more than anything else he had with him was his Sharps rifle in the boot of the wagon with spare cartridges in a box in the back. He'd worked for an old man in Missouri, Jason Thomas, who liked the idea of Matt going west.

"Yo're gonna need a good rifle though," the old timer had said.

"Not in the budget," Matt had said continuing to nail shingles on the old man's roof.

A week later, Thomas had come to him and handed him a long rifle wrapped in a quilt. When Matt unwrapped it, it was a Sharps. "What's this?" he asked.

"Yuh're takin' it with ya."

Matt had handed it back. "I can't afford this."

"Ya already own it. Look at the stock." On the stock was engraved Matthew Kane. "I bought it for ya and ya are takin' it West. By golly, I can't go, but something is goin' with ya that I give ya."

Matt had felt warmth at the unexpected generosity. "I'll use it well," he promised as he had run his hand over the stock and barrel.

"Let's take 'er out and see how ya do with 'er." They had spent that afternoon sighting it in and taking turns hitting the target they had created.

"Dang, Matt, but you got the eyes of a hawk," Thomas had said with a cackle. "Ya get me some injuns with it, yah hear."

"The word is there won't be that kind of trouble this trip anyways."

"Then a buff'. But ya use it, and I'll be happy just knowin' where it went. Maybe it'll keep ya alive sometime."

Matt had reached out to hug the old man who at first resisted and then heartily hugged him back. "Ya been dang good to an old man, son. Hope the trip is all ya hoped."

Matt knew it wouldn't be. He had known it then, but he was going. He rested his right hand on the handle of the Bowie knife in the scabbard on his belt.

His brother, leaning against the wagon, was chewing on a plug of tobacco. Matt looked down at him, not surprised to see animosity in those cold blue eyes. "We ready, little brother?" Morey asked with sarcasm.

"Yep."

"I'm waitin' for our leader-- our fearless leader-- to tell us to head out." He spat onto the dusty ground not far from Matt's booted foot.

"Head out," Matt said through tight lips.

Morey laughed and started to turn away. "You handle the team today," Matt said, stopping him in his tracks.

"Me?" Morey turned back with shock. "Now why should I do it when a big man like you is right there to take care of it?"

"We're trading off," Matt said through his teeth. "You're goin' to pull your end of the load on this trip, Morey. That was the agreement."

"I don't remember any signed agreement." Morey laughed.

"I told you when you asked to come-- you're not lying around all the way to Oregon."

"You're wrong. Want to know why? First one." Morey began to count on his fingers. "I'm oldest by seven years. The oldest tells the youngest what to do. You do remember that... don't you, Matt?" He laughed. "Number two. Well, I don't think I need to remind you of what number two is, do I, Matt?"

Matt took a deep breath to get control of his anger. Morey was digging at an old wound, one he never let alone long enough to heal. Their father standing at the back of the wagon couldn't have missed a word of the argument, probably took subversive pleasure in it, but the skinny, little man said nothing.

There had been a time when their father would have intervened, would have ripped off Matt's shirt and taken a belt to his back, but those years were behind them. When Matt had grown tall and strong, when he towered over brother and father, they no longer were able to play the games they liked so well. Now battles were of words. Not an area where Matt always won, but at least it didn't leave bruises or broken bones.

He should have left them behind. He should have ignored their pleas and promises. Too late for should haves.

The wagon master rode up, stopped and leaned forward in his saddle, his smile warm. "Ya'll be eatin' dust today," he said, acknowledging the Kane wagon's position of nearly last in line, "but ya'll have yore turn up front."

Matt nodded. The ox beside him moved, tried to put one large hoof on top of Matt's boot. Matt slapped the big bovine hard, forcing it back in line.

"Cantankerous critters," Jones said.

"So I've noticed."

Jones' gaze moved past Matt to his family. "Good ya got three to help," he said with a smile barely visible through the beard. "Don't forget the meeting tonight."

"I didn't see there was much point in me coming."

"I'd like ya to be there. I want all the men there. We'll be electin' a council."

Matt almost laughed. Only politeness prevented him. "You weren't figurin' I'd get elected, were you?" he drawled, leaning against the ox and studying the bearded man's face, wishing he could read his expression.

"Why not?"

Matt laughed. "If you have to ask, maybe you don't know the people on this train as good as you figured."

Jones' eyes were assessing. "Or maybe I do. You come tonight."

∾

Amy trudged alongside her older sister, Loraine, trying to adjust her pace to that of the mules. It was possible to ride in the wagon, but she had already learned, on the short journey from their farm, that it was bouncy, cramped by boxes and chests-- in short, uncomfortable. Walking was better, even with the dust already heavy in the air.

She had been inspired listening to St. Louis Jones talk about the trip. Hopefully, she had scanned the crowd to see if Matt was there. Disappointment dampened her enthusiasm when she didn't see him. Was he still with the train?

She'd written of her feelings in her leather-bound journal. 'Why did he have to be that way? Ruin everything, by what he did? I can't tell anyone. Would they even understand? Would they have been angry at Matt or me for somehow encouraging him? I didn't encourage him. Really I did not.'

She had stopped then, angry at what she had written. The journal was to record the trip West, not... She scratched out a damn. 'He disappoints me. He would have disappointed Pa and Mama too. They always said...' She had stopped writing again. Had they seen something in Matt years ago, something she hadn't. She remembered hearing their warnings-- subtle though they were. He's a good friend for you but don't fall in love with him. It wouldn't work. He's a good boy, but his family... Well, you know... The conclusion was vague, as though they were uncertain how much they were comfortable saying.

Amy understood her parents wanted a good life for her, marriage to a man with no serious problems, a man who could give her all the things they thought she deserved. She didn't want marriage at all. They wouldn't like hearing that either.

The sun lightened the sky to the east as they topped the low ridge west of Independence and finally were on the trail. Amy heard laughter and a few curses as the animals felt out their masters, forcing determinations as to who was boss. Cattle bawled, hooves struck the ground with a constant cadence, people murmured about the day ahead or of what they'd left behind. Beside her was the creak of the wheels as they rolled over the ruts in the road adding a reality to the trip that had

been missing in the first pre-dawn moments. We're going...
We're going...

By afternoon Amy's enthusiasm for walking had waned. Adam
Stone rode by their wagon, wheeled his horse and slowed its
pace to match the mules. "How's it going today, sir?" he asked
Amy's father who was sitting on the wagon seat.

"Just fine." Amos laughed as he tweaked the whip over Blue,
their lead mule. "We've been establishing who's boss again."

Adam laughed. When he glanced toward Amy, his cool,
deep blue eyes seemed to be appraising her. Two could play at
that game. He was a tall, broad shouldered man. Black hair
curled around the collar of his leather shirt, and he sat his horse
as though one with the animal, like the dashing hero of a fairy
tale or a knight of the round table. She forced her mind back to
reality. She didn't want any man. Men ended a woman's
options.

"If I can help," Adam was saying, "just give a yell."

"Sure will," Amos said. "Stop by after supper for a cup of
coffee if you'd like."

"I might do that." Adam's white teeth flashed against his
swarthy complexion as his gaze traveled back to Amy. She
looked away when she saw her mother, who was not far from
her, was watching the exchange with a look of amused speculation.

As Adam rode down the line of wagons, Loraine said, "That
is a fine looking gentleman."

Amy nodded, remembering Matt's words about the scout.
Had he been right? Was Adam Stone interested in her that way?
As a further complication, one she hadn't noticed before, she
saw how intently Loraine watched the handsome scout ride
away. She frowned-- exactly which of them the scout was
coming around to see?

The blonde Belle, who at eleven was the baby of the family,
danced away from her mother and back to her older sisters.
Giggling, she teased, "I think somebody's in love." Faced with
fierce glares from both sisters, she jumped up into the moving

wagon, peeking back out just long enough to stick out her tongue before she disappeared behind the protective canvas to play with her dolls.

~

The sisters fell into a routine for setting up the nightly camp. Belle gathered smooth round stones to edge the campfire while the older girls went to a nearby stream to bring back water, and find firewood to avoid using what they had brought.

Although Martha Stevens was an accomplished cook, cooking over a campfire with cast iron skillet or Dutch oven was a new experience. She greeted it with the expected grumbling as well as a few surprising curses. Some families had brought small stoves with them. They'd been told those would most likely would be left along the road, when the road became steeper and the stock more exhausted. Martha had decreed they might as well learn to cook over the open fire. Smoke curled in their faces, stinging their eyes, as they struggled to keep the fire banked to the right heat for the coffee to perk and the food to cook but not burn.

Amy's father returned from caring for the livestock just in time to eat the roughly prepared meal. Amy was amused as she heard him generously praising the food, even that which had been a bit burnt. She had watched her father smooth over more than a few rough waters with such compliments. He was doing it again as her mother smiled, her beautiful dark eyes warming with his words.

Perhaps because of beginning a new life, she found herself looking at her family through eyes that were newly sensitive. Her father was a tall man, not so much as Matt, but his knees were poked into the air as he sat at one of the stools he had had constructed for the trip west. Her parents exchanged smiles that had her realizing she hadn't really seen them as mates. It felt strange to have that awareness.

· · ·

Amy was just putting away the last of the washed dishes when Adam Stone strolled into their circle, his impressive height dramatically enhanced by the shadows cast from the firelight. He smiled at Amos. "So, how was your first day?" He thanked her when Amy's mother offered him a cup of coffee.

"About like you'd expect. I've got things to learn. We're all stiff. The wagon load shifts. I've some re-rigging to do, but we'll be ready tomorrow—even though it's four females and only one male."

Adam flashed a smile. "Well, it's a lovely family you have, Mr. Stevens."

Amos grinned. "I have thought so."

Adam glanced at Belle. "Where'd you get that blonde one though?" he teased.

Belle said nothing but gave him a look of disgust.

"My mother was blonde like Belle. Amy, of course, has her mother's hair and that red, Loraine can blame on me."

"Well you are a fine looking bunch. If you don't mind my saying."

Amos laughed. "You are a plain talking man, but no, I don't mind, and I agree."

"Have you been across the Plains many times, Mr. Stone?" Amy's mother asked, drying her hands as she moved back into the circle. Amy lingered by the box holding their dishes, strangely reluctant to join them.

"A few," Adam said, smiling, "and please call me Adam."

"How many?" questioned Loraine who was standing a little behind where her mother settled onto one of the small stools.

"Well, the first time was when I was fifteen. I made that trip with buffalo hunters and only went so far as Fort Bridger. Next time I went with a surveying party, which was the most difficult. When I got back east, I signed on with my first wagon train. That was eight years ago. I've been with trains crossing four times since."

"My!" Amy's mother gasped, "You seem so young to have been across so many times."

"I'm twenty-seven, ma'am. It's not the years sometimes but the miles."

"Don't you ever want to stay somewhere?"

"Crossing the prairies can get in your blood. The land stretches forever, miles of grass, buffalo and antelope herds that can run for days. It's a big country, Mrs. Stevens. The word big doesn't do justice to it. The sky gets larger every mile west. The clouds never the same two days running. Hawks and eagles soar free on the wind. That's the way I feel when I'm out there, like I am part of something too big for a man to comprehend." He stopped, his eyes distant as though he were caught up in a vision they couldn't see. Shaking his head, he smiled. "I can't explain it, but you'll feel it yourself, I think."

There was a moment of silence, then Loraine asked, "Where did you come from originally, Mr. Stone?"

"Ohio, and the name's Adam."

"How did your parents feel about your leaving home so young and flying off like an eagle that way?" Amy's mother asked.

"Actually I left home at fourteen, ma'am. I don't suppose my folks were overly happy, but I come from a big family. There were lots of mouths to feed, and one less was probably some-what of a relief."

"Tell us about Oregon," asked Loraine.

"Mostly I know the Willamette Valley where I've spent time twice... Once for a winter."

"Is it all we've been told?" Amy moved into the circle, sitting on the ground, her arms wrapped around her knees.

He smiled. "Well, I don't know what you were told, but it's pretty country, rich land, some of the soil almost black and will grow anything. A big river flows right down through it with trib-utaries coming out of the mountains on both sides. Hot springs... and the fish, you ought to see the salmon when they go up the rivers. A man could almost walk on them. There are huge cedar and fir trees, lush meadows, snow covered peaks to the east."

"Tell me more about the farmland," Amy's father requested, a gleam in his eyes.

"I'm no farmer but looks to me like a lot of water, good soil and with mild winters, that it'll be easy to raise crops. Winters are mild. Mostly the snow only lasts a few weeks, a month at the most. The year I was there, it only snowed one time and melted almost right away."

"With the Homestead Land Act passed last year, are you thinking of staking a claim yourself this time?"

"Man has to stay on it four years to claim it. I used to think no place was worth staying that long. I have been thinking though... Maybe I might want to do that." Adam's gaze settled on Amy.

Amos smiled, nodding his head.

"They told us there'd be no Indian problems," Amy's mother said, as she pushed a wayward strand of hair behind her ear.

"No trouble in the main valley, the country near Portland and Oregon City."

"You hear stories about scalpings... savages attacking peaceful settlers. For instance, there's what happened to the poor Whitmans," she said, a worried frown crossing her beautiful face.

"The thing with the Whitmans was a tragedy based on misunderstandings. It wasn't in the Willamette Valley though, and it was with Eastern Oregon Indians, the Cayuse—not the same at all."

"Why do you say misunderstandings?" Amy's father asked.

Adam shrugged. "I'm not fond of second-guessing people, what they do or don't do, and I didn't know the Whitmans. I hear they were good folks, but too many times the missionaries come to the Indians unwilling to learn anything about their customs and determined to change their way of life. They talk but don't listen," His voice grew hard as he continued, "When the Indians fight back, everybody wonders why."

"That's a severe condemnation of those doing God's work." Amy's father's expression had turned thoughtful.

"Maybe so. I'm not the best man to judge," Adam said, his dark blue eyes saying he'd prefer to discuss something else... anything else.

"What about the Indians along the Trail?" Amy asked. "Like the Sioux."

"St. Louis knows more about them than me. I've traveled by their villages, done some trading, but don't speak their language."

"How about in Oregon?" Amy found him more interesting than she had expected.

He nodded. "Some Chinook and sign language. Enough to get by. And back to the question about trouble as we head west, I don't expect it. It can be a matter of luck, of course."

"And that means?" Amy's father asked.

"Conflicts there have been are mostly the fault of the whites. The Indians were generally friendly to begin, helpful. Most had worked with trappers who weren't meaning to change the land. Now it's looking different. Treaties have been broken. Strangers attack their villages, rape their women and we wonder why they fight back."

"You sound like a lover of the Indian," Amy said.

"I'd call it a respecter. I can understand their frustration. That is not to say that Indians have never been wrong. They have their troublemakers like any peoples."

"Are there broken treaties and killings in Oregon?" Amy's mother asked, her tone sounding unconvinced.

"If I was going to list all the skirmishes, I'd have to admit I did hear there was some trouble brewing down in the Rogue country. You know about the Cayuse, but in the Willamette Valley, we've done the Indians more harm than they could ever do us."

"What do you mean?"

"Twenty years or more now, white men, beaver trappers and traders brought a new disease into the valley. Epidemics took nine-tenths of the Indians living in that area, wiped out whole families, clans and tribes."

"What disease would do that?" Martha asked.

Amy saw her father grimace as her mother found a new bone to worry.

"It didn't hit the white men the same way. Some think it was malaria. Whites got sick, but most didn't die. Natural immunity perhaps or a different way of treating the illness. It was a tragedy for the tribes, but probably lucky for you."

"That's a harsh statement." Amy's father's tone became reproving.

"Maybe, but true. If all the Indians that had lived in the valley still lived there, there'd be little room for incoming settlers. There might have been fighting. As it is, well I suppose some of you Christians would call it an act of God."

"If we were to call that an act of God, we'd be blaming Him for everything that went wrong anywhere," Amos said. "It leaves a bitter taste in my mouth when people blame God for what is clearly an act of nature."

"Maybe," Adam said with a small smile. "I don't believe so much in acts of God."

"What do you believe in?"

"Myself, my strength. I believe in taking care of ourselves."

"We can't take care of everything." Amy's father added, "Of course, I believe in taking action where required."

"I can agree with that." Adam rose. "Might I take action and ask one of your daughters, Miss Amy Stevens, for a stroll around the camp?"

"I would approve of that—if Amy does, of course." Her father grinned.

CHAPTER 3

W alking through the camp at Adam's side, Amy readjusted her shawl around her shoulders at the chill of the night air. She felt uneasy, unsure of what to say, of what she wanted to hear him say.

"And what do you want from life, Miss Stevens?" Adam asked, smiling down at her.

She laughed, a little surprised at his directness. "Would you like my answer in ten words or less?"

He smiled. "Of course."

"Existential, prosaic or religious?" she asked with a laugh.

"Religion is decidedly out. I'd never understand existential; so how about prosaic?"

"Ah that it will rain just enough for the grass to grow. The storms will all be ahead of where I am or behind me. And it will sunshine at least some every day."

"Eden in other words?"

"I suppose so. Perhaps Oregon will be like that."

"I hope you won't be disappointed. It's a land like any other."

"Well, for me it's not just Oregon. It's what lies beyond. All the possibilities of adventure that I know nothing of."

Adam laughed. "Sounds like you don't plan to homestead."

She raised her eyebrows. "As an unmarried woman, I am

not old enough to file on land, but someday, I might. Part of it for me though is traveling, and up until now the farthest I've been from Missouri was one trip to Philadelphia to meet our great-aunts."

"Thus Oregon might be a stopping off place."

"Possibly."

"To where?"

She shrugged. "The Sandwich Islands, Hong Kong or maybe San Francisco. I don't know. It doesn't matter so much where I'm going, but more that I am."

"So, you're like me, or rather as I've been, a searcher of new places."

"A lady doesn't easily have that option," she reminded him, feeling a touch of resentment.

"It would take an unusual woman to reach out for such a life."

"I suppose or to claim a homestead for that matter."

"Of course. You might be just the lady to do either."

Amy lost track of what Adam was saying. Ahead she saw a tall man walking toward them and knew, though his eyes were hidden by the brim of his hat, that it was Matt. She felt guilty that he would see her with Adam. Then she felt irritated that she felt guilty.

She saw the moment Matt became aware of her and then Adam. His jaw tightened, his muscles tensed. As he neared, his cold gray eyes were visible beneath the hat brim, the expression in them dark. Passing, he tipped his hat, but it was as though he didn't know her.

She realized she had clenched her fists and felt a surge of resentment. Friends-- ha. They'd never been friends, or he wouldn't be doing this. He had no right to ignore her. She had expected him to stop and at least say hello. She had an urge to turn around and give him a piece of her mind, a piece he wouldn't soon forget.

"Where'd you go?" Adam asked, forcing her attention back to him. "I know I'm not the most exciting man in the world, but women don't usually fall asleep when they're walking with me."

I was daydreaming. Sorry."

"About what?"

"The trip west," she lied. "What else?"

"I can see you're excited about going."

"Of course."

"And you daydream?"

"It's one of my many character flaws."

"Many, huh? Is that supposed to scare me off?"

"Does it?" she asked, looking up at him.

He smiled again, white teeth flashing. "No, it intrigues me. A traveler, dreamer. Are there other surprises you hide, Miss Stevens?"

"If there were, I would be foolish as to reveal them to you," she said, flirting a little and enjoying it. She's show Matt.

"More and more. A woman with secrets. I guess that's a challenge for me to find out what they are."

"You will be disappointed."

"I suppose you're one of those women who doesn't know her place."

"I'm not sure what a woman's place is, Mr. Stone. Why don't you tell me."

"You don't think you'll trap me so easily, do you, Miss Stevens. A woman's place is wherever she wants it to be."

"Why would you think I want to trap you?"

"Perhaps I was hoping," he said, stopping and pulling her back into the shadow of a wagon. His eyes glittered in the reflected moonlight. The expression in them was too fresh in her memory for her not to know he was thinking of kissing her. She wasn't ready for that and turned away before her maneuver could be taken as a rejection.

"If we were back in Ohio, I'd take my time about this," he said, his tone serious. "I'd come to your house, ask you to a social or two. Might even ask your father if I could court you, but we're out here, Amy Stevens, and it's different. There's not the time for all the little niceties. Things move fast."

I'm for sure being made aware of that. She turned back to face him. Must be something in the air-- or water.

"I'd be wanting to court you," his voice went on evenly, the words smooth and easy. "It won't be possible out here on the trail. I should've been at a meeting to select the council tonight. I'll have to answer to St. Louis, but I wanted to talk to you, to make sure you understood my thinking."

She knew it was foolish, but she asked the question anyway. "And what is that?"

"I want to spend what time I can with you. I'd like you to get to know me better, but my time's going to be limited. I don't want to lose the chance to tell you now how I'm feeling, what I'm hoping you will feel... before somebody beats me to it."

Someone already did. Amy remembered another voice, a soft drawl, telling her how he felt and how if he couldn't have her he would not stand by and watch her with another man.

"Is it impossible for you to see me in that light?"

"Of course not," she retorted perhaps too quickly. "It's just a lot for me to think about. I hadn't expected..." She tried to block Matt's face from her mind.

"Then may I court you, Miss Stevens, as best I can while I'm scouting? I'll ask your father, of course. Just want to be sure it meets with your approval first."

"I would like to get to know you better," she said knowing she had evaded his question. She hoped her answer would satisfy him. "And please call me Amy."

He grinned as he tucked her hand into the crook of his arm. "You have a small hand, Amy," he observed as he put his own long fingered hand over it.

"It's strong though, Mr. Stone. You might be surprised."

"I like the length and shape of your fingers, and it's Adam."

She laughed. "I don't think anyone has ever complimented me on my fingers before. Are you an expert on lady's hands?" she was all too aware that he had not freed hers.

"Maybe a little." He turned her hand over and traced a line across her palm. "You have a long life line, and I see a line there that says you'll love fully and once. A very strong, deeply etched line."

"I don't believe in palm reading. It's from the devil."

"You think? Well, I don't believe in it either-- except I'd not mind being the man that line is waiting for."

"Perhaps it's Papa," she suggested, taking her hand from his.

"That line is for a passionate love for one man, one lucky man."

"What about your own hand? Does it show so much loyalty?" she teased.

He put his hand behind his back.

"I showed you mine."

Reluctantly, he brought his hand forth, allowing her to grasp it. It was a large hand, heavily calloused from hard work. When she looked for the love lines, she laughed.

"You were right," he said with a grin, drawing his hand away. "The whole business is from the devil himself."

She laughed. "Was there a girl at home? Is she that line?"

"There were many girls at home," he teased. "I have sisters."

"I mean a special girl."

"There hasn't been anyone. I've been on the move too much for that."

She wasn't ready to have their conversation become so serious, but she could think of no way to deflect his blunt statement into the safer earlier bantering. Turning toward her own campfire, she said, "I see Mama has company. Do you want to join us?"

"Not tonight."

She smiled up at him, trying to take away some of the doubt she must have given him. She felt confused. She had believed she never wanted to marry. Is that why she had wanted to slow down Adam? If she had wanted to be a wife someday, he was so much the man in the books—except...

By the time Matt arrived at St. Louis' meeting, most of the men had gathered in a rough semi-circle. He found a place to the back and leaned against a wagon, his arms crossed over his chest, his mood dark. On the far side, he saw Amos Stevens, knew the older man had recognized him. He looked away, not eager to talk to Amy's father.

The wagon master raised his voice and the men stopped talking to listen. "I always like to wait 'til we're on the trail to have this talk... kind of give you all a little taste of traveling. I figure to remind ya of a few things tonight. One bein' that we're under military law out here. That's different than what ya knew back where ya come from. Signing the articles though, you agreed to be bound by that code for the safety of us all."

There were nods of agreement.

"We'll start with election of a council, who'll be a jury and help with decisions when need be," Jones explained. "There'll be times we'll meet as a group, but that ain't always practical. I need eight men, and when I call up the council, you will come without no more discussion. The rest of you won't argue with decisions made by the council. There's no time nor benefit to fightin' with each other. Where it comes to when we stop or camp, that'll be Adam and me decidin'. It might seem to ya sometimes that the day was too short or too long, but we'll have our reasons. This is not a democracy but a dictatorship."

St. Louis went on, explaining about setting up night guards, only one man at a time for now, but more when they reached Indian country. "It's kind of a game to 'em," he explained, "they steal each other's horses or mules, and we come along... they steal ours. It don't mean nothin' except, o' course, we don't want our animals stole, and so we got to play the game along with 'em. Ya miss out on a little sleep on the nights ya do guard duty, but then ya sleep a little better on the nights ya don't." Understanding chuckles greeted his words.

Matt noted with satisfaction that Amos Stevens was nominated to the council and voted for him when it came his turn. Although Amos didn't look pleased at the responsibility, Matt knew he would be a reliable man for important choices.

"Now I got a list of all the men here and yore supplies, how many breech loaders ya got, how much ball and shot. This way if somebody gets into trouble, we'll all know what's available. I won't ask nothin' of no man he can't give."

"Wait a minute. You mean we might be asked to give what we've brought to others who didn't bring enough?" questioned a big, aggressive man from the back.

"Wal, I'll tell ya, Mr. Hall, like I jest said, ya won't be asked to give nothin' ya can't spare. And ya won't be forced to give

30

what ya're asked, but yeah... ya might get asked. Then again, ya might be the one doin' the needin'. Things happen out on the prairie and crossin' the rivers. Folks lose their wagons. Accidents happen. We got two thousand miles of rough country ahead. Might jest be you'd be the one gettin' sick, or have a wagon break down, or an animal die. We help each other."

He raised his voice for emphasis. "We'll have days when everybody's dog tired, ready to fight. By the time we get to Oregon, some of ya'll be wanting to kill each other. Travelin' in a tight group this way, tempers fly. Cooperatin', keepin' things cooled down, will be a help to me. When we do have a problem or disagreement or somebody breaks the articles, the council will help me decide appropriate punishment.

"Clem and Tom are here to help with stock, drive a wagon if someone's sick, fix wheels, just generally do what's needed. Come to one of them first. If you have more serious trouble, ya can come to me or Adam Stone." He stopped looked around the crowd. "He's goin' to be here for ya too, but he ain't just now."

Matt felt a surge of irritation as he remembered just where he'd last seen Stone. He flicked his gaze toward Amos, saw the older man was watching him again, concern in his eyes. Matt turned away.

One of the men spoke from the back, interrupting Matt's gloomy thoughts, "What about Injuns, Mr. Jones. You said you expected no trouble, but I've read--"

St. Louis cut him off with a loud guffaw. "If you read any of them little paperback books with the grisly covers floatin' around the country, there ain't nothin' in 'em but make believe. Yore baby daughter could write as close a story to the truth as most of them got."

The man's laughter sounded nervous.

"When do we get to Indian Territory?" another uneasy voice asked.

"Officially, we're in it, but don't start worryin'. What ya're askin' about, we don't hit 'til we come to the Platte, then we pass through country belongin' to tribes that have been known to get a little feisty. Up north ya got Sioux, Cheyenne, Arapaho, Crow... beyond that, in the Rockies Shoshoni. In Oregon there are the Cayuse and Paiutes. But for the most part, Injuns'll leave ya alone if ya leave them be. Mostly they ain't lookin' for trouble."

When there were no more questions, at least none voiced, the men headed back to their wagons. Matt cut out the back, making certain he meet Mr. Stevens. He had nothing to say to the man much as he liked and respected him.

As he walked back toward his own wagon, he tried to think about what St. Louis Jones had said but found himself instead remembering seeing Amy with Adam Stone. This trip west was promising to turn into a trip into hell, and they had barely begun. Glumly he didn't want to consider what the rest of the days might hold.

~

Stepping into the circle of campfire light, Amy looked beyond her mother and sisters to two women she didn't know, one holding a baby.

Her mother smiled as Amy sat down beside her. "This is Amelia, although we call her Amy. Dear, I want you to meet Agatha Collins. Her wagon is just behind ours." Agatha Collins was a pinched, older woman, her hair drawn tightly back from a thin, lined face. Amy greeted her politely. "And this is Jennette Porter and her baby, Eliza."

Amy's smile was more genuine for the girl holding the baby, a girl who looked to be younger than she was.

"Everyone calls me Jennie," Jennie Porter responded with shyness. Her pale blonde hair was in a braid tightly clipped to a finely shaped head, her wide eyes a soft blue.

"We were speaking of the difficulty we had in fixing our suppers tonight," Amy's mother said.

"I burnt everything," Jennie said as she cuddled Eliza on her lap. As the baby slept, she made soft sounds, her tiny fist in her mouth.

"Injuns was meant to cook outdoors. Not ladies." Mrs. Collins' voice was thin and reedy.

"Meant to or not, we're going to learn. It's that or go hungry."

"Man that asks a woman to do such an unreasonable thing deserves to go hungry," Mrs. Collins barked. "I wanted to bring a little bitty cookstove, didn't weigh hardly nothing, but Mr. Collins flat out said no."

"The cast iron," Amy put in, "even if it seems small, would be heavy in the wagon, and I've read we'd have just ended up leaving the stoves someplace along the trail."

"Books ain't always got all the answers in 'em, and it'd made my work a heap easier." She sniffed loudly.

"Might have prematurely worn out your team," Amy added to the disapproving frown of the older woman.

Mrs. Collins turned to Amy's mother. "I hear you folks are rich," she said abruptly.

Martha gave a little laugh. "Where did you hear such nonsense?"

"Yore outfit and all. Just talk. Seems like I heard you sold a couple of stores afore heading out."

"Goodness, gossip seems to be flying."

"Strange you'd leave good businesses like that and head off to the wilderness."

"Is it?" Her mother put tea in a pot and filled it with hot water.

Apparently seeing she would get nothing more on that end, Mrs. Collins continued enumerating all her problems and the losses she'd incurred in traveling West at her husband's insistence. "I had a beautiful garden in Kentucky. Not going to have it in Oregon," she finally concluded.

"Why not?" asked Amy's mother. "I brought seeds with me from my favorite flowers and herbs, rose cuttings, and one from my Rose of Sharon. There's no reason not to have pretty things around us out there."

"Probably lose the seeds. Won't nothin' grow the same in Oregon. You mark my words."

Hoping to avoid more complaints from the old woman, Amy turned to Jennie. "How old is your baby?"

"Six months-- yesterday."

"She's beautiful. Look at that sweet little nose. She looks a lot like you."

Jennie's rosebud mouth broke into a broad smile. "She's just starting to crawl, which I'll have to admit is a bit of a trial with us traveling and all. Keeping her out of harm's way and still getting my work done-- it's not easy."

"Try harnessin' her," suggested Mrs. Collins.

"Harnessing?" Jennie asked, horror written on her smooth face.

"Well not like a mule or somethin'," the older woman said succinctly, obviously out of patience for having to explain a simple thing. "Jest cut a sheet into wide strips, fasten it around one ankle, gentle-like, and she cain't get too far. Don't hurt her a bit."

"It might work," Jennie said, frowning.

"Don't be afraid of limitin' her freedom a bit," Mrs. Collins went on. "Better limited freedom than a dead baby, caught under some critter's hoof or grabbin' a snake or some such thing. Children get too easily spoiled as it is."

To stop the disturbing litany of potential disasters, Amy tried to come up with a distracting question. "How many children do you have, Mrs. Collins?"

"Raised six. Lost three."

"I'm so sorry." And that she had asked.

"Tweren't all babies. One was born dead. Another got took by the cholera, and the last-- he drowned."

"How did you bear it?" asked Jennie, hugging Eliza more tightly to her own thin body.

"The help of the good Lord, I figure. And I had the others. Tweren't easy. I'm not saying it was, but we bear what we have to... We're women. It's always been our lot to bear. That's what the Good Book says."

"You're acting as though the Bible gives nothing but curses to women," said Amy's mother.

"It starts it out with pain. God told Eve she'd bear her children in pain. He weren't just a talking about the birth. That's painful enough, God only knows-- no man does. But He meant our whole lives with our children. Them that can't have 'em, they weep for 'em. Them that can, they weep too. It's the lot of women to weep." She shook her head regretfully at the sad facts of life.

"That's a depressing way to look at life," commented Loraine, who was sitting back watching the other women from the shadows, Belle asleep with her head on her lap.

"It's not the only part of the curse," Mrs. Collins went on, clearly enjoying the attention, the looks of dismay on the younger women's faces. "Woman does the same thing with wantin' a man. God cursed us good on that one." She cackled. "He give women a yen for wantin' a man, no matter how shiftless or no count. A yen that drives women plumb crazy... and then what? He puts the man to rulin' over the woman. It tain't fair. We got to be always wantin' somethin' that's gonna take away all our freedom."

"It is not like that," Amy's mother protested.

"Are you goin' West because you're awantin' to?" asked Mrs. Collins.

"Not exactly..."

"Well, there you have it. You had a right good life in Missouri but here you are. You're under a man. He makes you do it. It's the curse of the Lord-- that's what it is."

"I'm going because I love my husband. I wanted him to have a dream that while I didn't share, my dream was to make him happy. If I had said no, we'd be in Missouri."

Mrs. Collins snorted. "Believe it if you want, but I say you'd be doin' just what you're a doing. It's just the lot of women."

"You make being a woman sound dismal," said Amy, thinking of the two men who had most recently set out to court her-- each in their own but equally stubborn way.

"All that might have been true in the Old Testament, but it isn't now," her mother said recovering what Amy knew, from experience, to be rapier debating skill. "If there was a curse, it ended with Jesus."

"Believe what you want," Mrs. Collins said, not hiding her frustration at Scripture being turned against her.

"There's more," Amy's mother went on, clearly enjoying herself now. "In the writings of the Apostle Paul, he said women were to obey their husbands, but husbands were to take care of the women as though they were God themselves. I'd say that curse business was put away completely. When a man treats a woman right, what difference does it make who does the ruling?"

"Hmph." Mrs. Collins settled back into the shadow, obviously searching her mind for another scripture to bring forth in this war of holy verses.

Amy grinned. Seeing her mother's skill in an argument turned on someone else was a pleasure.

After a few moments of silence, Jennie said, "While I did want to go to Oregon. We had nothing and there is hope when we get there, the free land, we can build a better life for our baby. I worried though about taking her into the wilderness."

"I understand, but as Mrs. Collins just said," Amy said, "tragedies can happen anywhere."

"That's true," Jennie said with an uncertain smile. "We're hoping for so much when we get to Oregon."

Mrs. Collins turned to look at Amy. "Was that Adam Stone I saw you with earlier?"

"Yes, ma'am."

"Fine looking man that one. So polite. Too bad there aren't more young men like him. Wish my daughters had married ones half so good." She squinted. "There a wedding in the wind here?"

Amy straightened up and looked down at the tiny woman. "I barely know the man."

"Looked like spooning to me. Don't take a man like that one long to go after what he wants," Mrs. Collins chortled.

"I expect you were quite the expert on men... in your younger days, that is," Loraine said with a grin as she deflected the conversation once again. For the life of her, Amy couldn't imagine Mrs. Collins having younger days, of course, she had.

The older lady turned red for once at a loss for words.

When Jennie used the moment of silence to say goodnight, taking Eliza home to bed, Mrs. Collins left too.

"I can't believe it," Amy said, trying to whisper, almost successfully. "You actually shut her up... not that I imagine it will last long. She's probably gone home to study her Bible for more damning of women quotations."

"Girls," their mother said but laughed with them.

~

The moon still shone through the narrow opening of the tent, where she and her sisters slept, lighting up the area, making it hard to sleep. At best Amy slept restlessly when the moon was full. Tonight, her thoughts were bursting. She gave up and by moonlight wrote in her journal.

'I left things in Missouri home, friends, all the life I knew but that was nothing to me. What lies ahead will be opportunity, adventure, new ideas, new places, new friends, new freedoms. Leaving my books was hardest when Father said I could only bring four. How does one narrow all beloved books to four? I chose small volumes by Wordsworth, Tennyson, Browning, and Shelley. Can anything soothe one's soul better than poetry?'

Restlessly, she bit on the end of her pen before she added, 'More than my books, I realize I left my childhood there.' There was another thing she'd left there, one she refused to write about, as it would make it real. Only in Missouri was her friendship with Matt. The tears the laughter, all gone. He had ruined everything.

Although her own ambivalence over marriage and the limitations it would entail didn't leave her eager to accept the courtship of any man, if there had been a man, Adam Stone would have been the perfect one. He was Lancelot and Apollo rolled into one. Mentally she listed his qualities-- his confident way of talking, kind manner with people, the square jaw, the black curly hair, the soft buckskins, which emphasized his muscular frame. He was a man who would fit any girl's dreams. He had told her what he wanted. Why did she feel so miserable?

There was one reason. To be happy, she had to make peace with Matt, make him see their friendship was more important than his silly ideas of... well, something else. She'd grown up believing there was nothing she couldn't do by confronting it directly. It was intolerable to have someone she loved angry with her.

She put away the journal and lay back on her cot. She did love Matt-- like a brother. She would talk to him, and it would be all right. After that, she could consider Adam's courtship more seriously... Matt could find a girl to love and— She stopped at that thought, unable to finish it, unable to face her feelings if that did happen.

CHAPTER 4

The boom of the sentry's wake-up shot, startled Amy awake with the feeling she had not slept at all. She pulled on a plain cotton dress and hurried out to help with breakfast while Loraine with Belle's help took down the tent. They had arranged a system of chores that gave each of them a week of one thing, then a week of another.

Shaping biscuits, Amy put them in the pan and then over the fire. There was little talk as they cooked the meal. Everything had to be prepared, eaten, and cleaned up by seven o'clock when the train would pull out.

The noises around them increased as the men brought the stock to the wagons and began harnessing them in their traces. Ox-rings working in steeples, the jingle of chains, a dog barking, and the complaints of the oxen, horses and mules filled the early morning with sound.

In the distance a man yelled at his wife. Somewhere a child wailed. Farther down the line, children laughed as they played. Confusion hung as heavily as the dust in the air around people struggling to get everything ready to pull out.

The country they passed through was lovely, filled with rich grass, wild roses, and colorful wildflowers. It was a succession of rounded, grassy hills with water in many of the hollows. Amongst the beauty, there were already a few grave markers along the roadsides. They were stark reminders of the dashed hopes of the travelers who'd passed before them.

Walking beside their wagon, Amy looked around for the Kane wagon with the hope one evening she'd have enough energy to find Matt and convince him he had been wrong. Maybe he'd already changed his mind.

Adam made himself available to her family and her as often as possible. Amy appreciated his kindnesses and even more the fact that he wasn't pushing anything on her. Sometimes he came to talk with her father. Now and then he and she walked in the evenings. When a bouquet of wildflowers appeared on the wagon seat, it had the opposite effect that had been intended as it brought tears to her eyes at the memory of another bouquet.

～

Sitting at the Porter campfire, sipping a cup of tea, Amy came to attention when Jennie said, "He's frustrated with me."

"Who?" She hoped it wasn't trouble with William. She didn't want to hear about problems between a wife and husband.

"My husband. You must have noticed he's never here at night. He escapes as soon as possible after supper. I guess he plays cards 'til bedtime... at least that's what he says."

Amy considered the possibility that the mysterious, floating card game, only hinted at by the women, was where Matt had been. She'd certainly had no luck in finding him after dark. After a moment of waiting for Amy to say something, Jennie went on, "I just don't do things the way he likes... the way his mother did."

Amy smiled at that. "Does anybody ever do anything the way their mother did?"

"I suppose not. It's frustrating though to always fall short... not even knowing exactly what it is that I'm falling short of. I've burned the dinner-- every night."

"Every night?" Amy repeated a little surprised. She and her mother had mastered the open fire cooking quickly.

"Either burnt or not done. I don't know. Sometimes I'm just so tired."

This obviously was about marital problems, and Amy unhappily realized if she wanted to be a friend to Jennie, she had to listen.

"The trouble is," Jennie went on, "I'm only eighteen, and he's almost thirty. He's so much wiser than I am."

Amy pictured the small, unattractive man who was Jennie's husband, then looked at the delicate blond girl sitting beside her. She wondered what could hold her in awe of him. It didn't make sense. William Porter's hair was light brown and thinning, his squinty eyes half hidden behind narrow wire-rimmed glasses. He looked like a man who would be totally out of his depth if he was called on to do more than hitch his wagon. Yet Jennie saw him as far above herself.

"How did the two of you meet?" Amy asked.

"We never really met. We just always knew each other. I grew up in this little community in the hills-- more a crossroads than a town."

"Were you friends before he asked you to marry him?"

"He didn't really ever ask me. It just happened. My parents and his mother, they thought it would be good for us. I guess it was assumed. Now he's not happy and neither am I."

"You don't love him?"

"I don't even know what love is."

"Couldn't you have refused to marry him?"

Jennie sighed and looked into the darkness. "Unless you understood my family, I guess it would be hard to explain. They had made up their minds. They always made me feel I was too stupid to do anything right. They said I'd be happy married to him. But I wasn't. He doesn't seem to even like me."

"Oh." Amy wished she had words that would help, but what did she know of marital problems.

"I am sorry. It's just I needed to talk to someone. William is never interested in anything I say, and I guess you seemed like you cared."

Amy realized words were needed. She hoped they would be the right ones. "We're all different; if we fail in one thing, prob-

41

ably we're good at another. I'm sure even with Mr. Porter's mother, there were things about her that weren't good."

Jennie gave a small laugh. "I don't think so."

"Jennie, you need to believe in yourself. You're gentle, kind, helpful. You're a loving mother to Eliza. So what if you burn a meal now and then."

"All the time."

"All right, all the time. Do you think that's what Eliza will remember when she grows up, or will it be the times you cradled her in your arms?"

"But..."

Amy shook her head at Jennie's timidity. "If you let someone else run you down long enough, you'll start to believe what they're saying."

Jennie's smile was faint. "It's just hard to imagine telling William he was wrong about anything."

"Don't start by telling him. Start by telling yourself. You have dark circles under your eyes. I'll bet part of your problem is you're too tired. Taking care of a baby, doing all that needs doing every night, you probably aren't getting enough rest."

"I do feel tired all the time."

"We could keep Eliza for you sometimes, let you get in a nap." Amy felt a twinge of fear that Eliza would be thrust immediately into her arms. Caring for a baby had never been something she'd thought much about. In a safely remote place, mistily shrouded in the future, she supposed she might someday have children. Most women did. It was on no life list, however.

"I never thought anyone would be willing to do that. I never even left Eliza with anyone. William's mother said she wasn't up to caring for a baby, and my parents were always too busy."

"Well, you do it." Amy stiffened her spine. She could take care of a baby. It was such a tiny being. There shouldn't be that much to it. "One more thing. William Porter is lucky to have you for his wife. Don't you forget it."

"You're good for me, Amy," Jennie said with a smile.

"Maybe I'll see if I can write a poem about women believing in themselves."

"Can you do that?" Jennie asked, her eyes wide, obviously a little awe-struck at the idea.

"I'm not sure," Amy admitted. "Poetry doesn't come just when I want it. A lot of times the ideas come out of something negative, from times when I'm unhappy."

"But you write poetry, real poems?"

"I've put them down in journals, on scraps of paper. I've never really gotten them together in a book or anything, but someday I might." Amy laughed. "Some are terrible. I ought to destroy them. Some are... kind of funny. They help me get through things. You might think about trying it yourself."

"I'd never have the talent to do something like that," Jennie said.

"You won't know if you don't try. Poetry flows out of living, kind of like music. You think about something, write it down, think about it some more, change it, look for words that sound right together at the same time they carry the idea, even hum a melody and the next thing you know, you've got a poem."

"I'd love to read yours."

"They're not that wonderful, mostly just about little things around me." Amy smiled. "I do have one you might like. It's about cooking over the campfire." She felt a little nervous sharing it. "Don't expect something like Wordsworth or Blake here."

"I won't," Jennie said.

"All right." Amy hesitated again and then recited from memory. "O Muse of the Campfire, answer my plea. Keep the smoky pyre burning clean and free. As I watch and weep, smoke assails my sight. O Muse, earn your keep. No burnt offerings tonight!"

Jennie laughed. "Maybe I could post that one on my pan box."

"It came to me one day while the smoke was making me cry. Poetry isn't so much a talent as it is a letting something in."

"You even talk like a poet. I hope you do get a book published someday, I'd love to read it. Have you written any poems about Adam Stone?"

Amy frowned. "Why would I?"

"He's handsome, and I know he's been courting you. Everybody knows that."

"It seems people know too much."

Jennie laughed. "I suppose everyone feels sorry for me because William leaves me alone so much, but at least he doesn't beat me like Mr. Jacobs does his wife."

"Papa said the wagon master tried to talk to Mr. Jacobs about it, but he and she both denied anything happened. How can they think people don't hear?"

"Canvas covers don't hide much."

"I suppose it's also difficult to..." Amy stopped, unsure if she was treading into an area too private to discuss.

"If you were going to say something about the sounds of the... marital bed," Jennie said with a sigh. "It might be a problem for some, but not William and me. We haven't... done that since... well, before Eliza."

Amy was curious. Her knowledge of sexual matters was from novels, which didn't reveal practical information. Although her mother had explained basic biology, she knew there was more to it. But what exactly...

"Frankly," Jennie said before she could find an excuse to leave, "his having no interest has been a relief to me. I didn't... Well, maybe I'm not built right for it."

"You didn't like it?"

"It... hurt and well, there just wasn't much to it. It might be different if a man and woman loved each other."

"I have no idea." There was a lot she didn't know.

"Do you think you could love Adam, someday?" Jennie asked.

"I haven't thought about it."

"Is there someone else, someone you do write poems about?"

"No. Well... just a friend."

Jennie's blue eyes widened with surprise. "Is he back in Missouri?"

"No, he's traveling with the train."

"But, I've never seen you with anyone but Adam."

"It's mixed up. He's not a... He's just a friend." Glumly, she corrected herself. "Or at least he was one. He was born in Missouri, but his family had left, moved to Georgia, before I was born. When they came back, I was seven. He became like my big brother."

"If he's like a brother, I'm surprised I haven't seen you with him."

"We had an argument. Actually it was more than an argument. We had a major falling out." Amy stopped and looked around the campsite, trying to put her feelings into words. "I used to think I knew him so well, but lately I don't think I ever knew him."

"That sounds familiar. I'm beginning to think no woman can know a man. They just don't think the same way." Jenny shook her head, staring at Amy, a mixture of frustration and amusement on her face. "You sure you don't love this brother who isn't a brother?"

"I'm sure. Of course, despite having read hundred of poems and books about the ecstasies of love, I also don't have the faintest idea what it's really all about."

"I know what it's like to love my baby. It's like she's a part of me. I'd do anything for her. If it weren't for Eliza, I'd say I'd made a terrible mistake in marrying William, but I have Eliza and nothing can take that away." Jennie smiled down at her daughter, who had fallen asleep, diapered little bottom in the air and button nose wormed down into the blanket.

"Was her birth very painful? I remember when Mama had Belle, but I don't really know, if you understand what I mean."

"It hurt real bad, but then she was there, and all I could think was how beautiful she was, and she was mine. Really, truly mine, like nothing else ever had been."

"I haven't thought of having children or... well, you know. Several of my friends in Missouri are married. To be honest I hadn't thought I wanted to marry."

"Maybe it'll just take the right man to come along."

"Perhaps," Amy said not believing a word of it.

A blonde, buxom girl walked up to the wagon. Smiling and saying hello, she plopped herself down between Amy and Jennie. "Have you two met?" Jennie asked. When Amy shook her head, Jennie introduced her to her cousin, Bernice McDowell.

"Where do you come from?" Bernice asked, looking Amy up and down.

"Missouri. No town you'd have ever heard of, just a place to go through."

"I didn't much like Missouri."

Amy was determined to be polite. "Did you live near Jennie before the trip?"

"Oh, heavens no! I come from Chicago."

"After living in such a big town, the rough conditions on the trail must be a little difficult for you."

"Unbelievable. So primitive. No stores for things I forgot. Actually I wasn't going to come with my parents. My grandparents said I could stay with them." She began to smile as she added, "Until I heard the ratio of men to women in the West. It's incredible. It's going to make every woman worth her weight in gold." Bernice smiled again, a pale imitation of Jennie's authentic smile. "I've seen you before, Amy, although you wouldn't be likely to remember me. You were with that handsome scout, Adam Stone." She licked her lips. "At the time you weren't looking at anyone but him."

"Oh."

"He's just too good looking, but then the wagon train seems to be filled with wonderful looking men."

"You think so?" Amy asked with no real interest in the answer. She began casting through her mind for an excuse to leave.

"Yes, I always notice handsome men. You mean, you don't?" She looked at Amy as though she might be some new sort of creature, unknown until now. She shook her head and went on, "Adam is a fine looking man, but there's another one. He's like a god, a Roman sculpture or something, sooo gorgeous." Her voice rose with her enthusiasm. "I'd give practically anything to meet him... and of course, I will."

Amy lost all interest in the conversation. After a few moments of polite conversation, she excused herself and headed back to her own wagon.

As she walked, she thought of Adam. Even Loraine seemed to be interested in him. He was obviously the catch of the train... unless you counted the god, whoever he was.

In no hurry to get back to her own campfire since she had seen gossipy Mrs. Collins talking with her mother and sisters, Amy strolled through camp. She stopped, looking off at the black prairie, awed by the vastness of the flat space before her eyes. It was so dark out there-- no flickering lights, no small houses, a black void of nothingness. High above her, she heard a keening cry-- a nighthawk. In the distance, two killdeers swooped low over the grassland, their cries echoing. The bird calls made her think of Matt, and all the nights they'd spent listening to the sounds of the night. He had explained each one to her.

With a sense of resolution, Amy patted her hair, making sure each strand was tucked into the bun pinned high on the back of her head. Swallowing hard, she started through the wagons. She would confront Matt. This had gone on too long.

By the light of a flickering campfire, she saw him sitting on the tailgate, bare-chested, his shirt in one hand, a threaded needle in the other. Her first thought was that he'd lost weight, her second that although she had seen Matt without his shirt when he was a boy, she never had since he'd become a man. Good Lord. That broad, masculine chest was ridged with muscles all the way down his belly. His body, outlined by the flickering firelight, was so blatantly masculine that she felt a quiver of what felt like fear.

Although the air hadn't seemed cold a moment before, she hugged her shawl more tightly to her shoulders. Shy now to approach him, she watched for a moment from the darkness as he stabbed the needle into the shirt and gave a mild curse when it stuck his finger.

She moved out of the shadows and into the light. She had no idea when he became aware she was there, but he didn't look up until she was a few feet away. His gaze met hers, but he said nothing.

"Lose a button?" she asked, even though she could clearly

see he held one against the front of the rough cotton shirt, the needle plunged into it.

His eyes were a stormy gray. "What's it look like?"

She smiled at his ill temper but chose to ignore it. She sat on the tailgate beside him. He began again to try to work the needle through the button and fabric, stabbing his finger in the process.

"Let me. Before you get blood all over that shirt." She reached out, took the shirt and needle from him. Their fingers brushed as she grasped the needle. Matt yanked his hand back as though he'd been burned. She tried to ignore the nervousness she now felt at being beside him. Worse was the tingle in her fingers where his hand had brushed against hers.

He said nothing as she secured the button and handed the shirt back. "There," she said, "don't bother thanking me."

"What do you want, Amy?" he drawled as he slid off the tailgate and shrugged into the shirt, not bothering to button it.

"You haven't come to visit us," she said, beginning with the obvious, making the effort to look at his face so she didn't look at that muscular chest.

"No." He looked into her eyes, the gray of his drilling into her, making her aware in a strange way of his proximity.

She tried to steady her breathing. "I-- I thought you would change your mind."

"I haven't."

"You're being foolish."

His smile was hard. "Thanks."

"You know what I mean." She got off the tailgate and moved to stand near the campfire. Uncomfortable, she wrapped her arms around herself.

"Don't reckon I've ever known what you mean by anythin'." Matt didn't follow her. He stood back, almost in the shadows.

"You've thrown away our friendship," she snapped. "None of this makes sense. All because--"

"Because," he finished for her, "I'm not goin' to stand there watchin' you make calf-eyes at some other man."

"Calf eyes?" she repeated, half insulted, before she remembered she wasn't going to let this turn into an argument.

"There've been fellows around before. You never seemed to mind."

"I didn't like it, but they didn't mean nothing."

"What makes you think Mr. Stone does?"

He ignored her question. "You got every right to be with him, but I'll be damned before I'll be there too."

"But…"

He clenched his jaw, seemed to consider for a moment, before he reached out and pulled her into his arms. He drew her against his long, hard length. When she tried to push away, her hands were trapped against his bare chest. He bent and brought his lips down on hers.

Amy pushed against his chest, feeling his smooth skin under her fingers, shocked at the reaction of her body when, with his mouth still hard against hers, he pushed his tongue against her lips, forcing them apart and delving within. The kiss seemed to draw the very breath from her soul. His hands stroked her back. For one wild moment she almost threw her arms around his neck. Stopping herself, barely in time, she shoved hard against him.

When he released her, she almost fell, saved by his quick grip on her arm. Heaving for breath, she saw his tight smile. With all the strength she possessed, she let fly, slapping him so hard it snapped his head back.

The smile never left his face. "Now do you understand?" He made no move to touch her again or wipe the trickle of blood from the corner of his mouth.

"I hate you!"

"I know."

"I…" She turned away, her hand stinging from the force of the blow she'd landed. Rubbing her wrist, she muttered, "I shouldn't have slapped you. I'm sorry. I don't know what made me do it. I just got so angry at you taking what didn't belong to you."

She swallowed and moved to stand on the other side of the campfire. "You've always been able to make me madder than anybody else on the face of this earth, Matthew Kane. But you never made me mad enough to hit you."

"So stay away."

"But--"

"From all accounts, I hear Stone's a good man. I'm glad for you. At least I want to be. It never could have been between us anyway."

"You wanted my friendship once," she whispered, hating the pleading tone that had come into her voice, hating even more her growing feeling of emptiness.

"We can't always have what we want." He stalked off leaving her standing alone by the dying embers of the campfire.

CHAPTER 5

Matt stood in the darkness, watching Amy walk away. Damn! He wanted to hit something, preferably something he could splinter to pieces. When it came to Amy, he had very little will power. What she wanted from him, she usually got. But not this time. He had been forced to leave or see his resolve break. Next thing he knew, she'd be asking him to hold Adam's coat when he came sparking.

When she had gone, he walked back and slumped down beside the wagon. The ache in his gut felt as though he was being torn in two. He had fought against the feelings that surged through him as he had watched her grow into a graceful, beautiful woman. He'd tried to stifle the sensual thoughts, to not see the fullness of her breasts, the slimness of her waist, to not lie in the darkness of his room wondering what it would be like to stroke that satiny skin, peel away the blouse from her shoulders and bare her breasts to his touch and taste.

His dreams had rested on her and with them his hope that this trip would give him something to offer. Life in Missouri had offered no such possibilities. Until Independence, he'd nursed a flicker of hope that things could change.

Closing his eyes, he couldn't shut away the memory of watching Adam Stone ride up to the Stevens wagon. Not that the scout's admiration had surprised Matt. He'd seen how men watched her, the warm appreciation, and sometimes lust in their eyes. But with Adam it had been different. This time he'd seen an answering glint of interest in Amy. His dreams had crumbled with her returning look, one she'd never given him.

Dreams were for fools. He'd had one once. He'd worked for this trip in a way few would, holding down two jobs, fighting to keep the money from being drunk up by his father or stolen by his brother. Each step along the way had been a milestone. Where for others the eighty dollars for a wagon or fifty dollars for a team of oxen had meant only a trip to the bank, for Matt it had meant months of back-breaking work, plowing other men's fields, lifting heavy sacks of grain, digging ditches. It had been worth it... until Independence.

The laugh was on him. He was going to Oregon all right, but instead of the tenuous hope that someday the woman he loved just might be his wife, he had the living hell of watching her with another, seeing her hands touch that man in a way she would never choose to touch him... knowing that in the darkness, another had those beautiful lips.

He opened his eyes, stared up at the dark sky. He didn't need an answer from heaven as to why it would not be him. He understood all too well the attraction of the tall scout. Adam Stone talked smoothly, used words in a polished way that Matt envied. The scout was a tough man, knowledgeable about the land, strong, confident in himself. Matt knew, except for Amy he would even have liked him.

Staring grimly out at the black sky, the dark hills, he saw himself reflected back, a Missouri farm boy with no education, tied to a backwoods, hard-living, drinking family. He should have never let them come with him. He had stupidly found it impossible to say no to their hope for a better life, but it had been as big a mistake as thinking there could ever be anything between him and Amy. There were dark things in his past, things about which he didn't want to think.

He took his blanket from the wagon and, wrapping himself in it, lay down on the hard ground. Across the prairie, he heard a coyote howl. Another respond. The lonely cries echoed his own.

. . .

Matt rose before dawn starting the fire and putting the coffee pot on the edge of the flames. The smell of it perking finally roused his father from the wagon. Scratching his stomach, Nathan Kane stepped into the light, the sour smell of whiskey permeating the air around him.

"Mornin' air's bad for my rheumytism. Makes it act up somethin' fierce." He poured himself a cup of coffee and sat by the small fire, hunched against the morning air, his deeply lined face scrunched into an expression of misery.

Matt held in his feelings as he'd learned so long ago to do. His brother, Morey, came from the edge of the camp, having slept only God knew where. Wordless, the three of them sat around the fire, nibbling on cold, hard biscuits and sipping the black coffee.

When Matt glanced at his brother, Morey was watching him. In his eyes was the same expression Matt had seen all his life. The only time it had seemed any different was when Morey told him he wanted to go with them to Oregon. Matt had had a glimmer of hope it might change. It hadn't. Morey's resentment and anger showed along with the sly smile.

Seeing Morey stroke his small mustache, Matt thought tending to that mustache was only constructive thing his brother did. As a child, Matt had been helpless under the taunting and tormenting, at least until he was big and strong enough to stand up to Morey and demand, if not respect, at least to be left alone. He should have left them both in Missouri.

Striding off to the makeshift corral to get the oxen, Matt brought them back to the wagon to yoke up. Even after the week and a half they'd spent on the trail, they were still a difficult team to work. It took all his strength and will to move them into position.

The day proved to be hot for spring, soon almost unbearable. The alkali powder hung heavily in the air, stirred up by animals and wagons. Clouds of dust settled around Matt and his team, making the air almost too heavy to breathe.

By evening, he was soaked with sweat and coated with dust.

With a dry camp, he could wash off only the worst of it. His father came to stand beside him as Matt shrugged back into his shirt.

"Anything to drink, Matt?" the old man questioned, looking into the box of supplies.

"Water in the barrel," Matt suggested between his teeth.

"Ya know what I want. Don't be givin' me a bad time, son. I couldn't find my bottle tonight. Ya ain't seen it, have ya?"

"Nope, but I'd try lookin' where you passed out last night." Matt had only a thin leash on his temper.

"That's no way to talk to yore pa."

"Pa? If you're lookin' to use that as a way to get what you want, I think it's a little late."

For a moment Nathan looked at him, then reached out to slap him across the mouth. Matt stepped back and laughed. "Maybe you better think about givin' up the booze. Your best shot ain't good enough anymore."

His father stared at him dumbfounded. "What's got into ya?"

Smoldering with anger, Matt brushed past Morey, shoving him aside as he strode from their circle into cleaner air. Matt felt Morey's glare follow him, but he never looked back. At least the trail dust had settled.

With no destination in mind, only the need to get away, Matt stalked along the perimeter of the wagons. He had no refuge from the feelings within. At the edge of the encampment, he leaned against an oak, still seething with frustration. After a few moments, he became aware of another presence. Looking up, he saw a blond woman, likely a little older than he, boldly looking him up and down, her gaze coming back finally to look into his eyes. She sauntered toward him.

"Hello." She stopped in front of him, her lips curved in a smile of encouragement.

"I know you?" he asked, knowing he didn't.

"I doubt it." Her voice was soft, girlish. "But I know you."

"You do?"

"Your name's Matthew Kane. You travel with a brother and

father. You come from Missouri, and you're twenty or thereabouts."

"How'd you find all that out?" He knew few people on the train, and those he did wouldn't have been likely to encourage her to seek him out.

"One of the men who works for St. Louis," she admitted with a coquettish smile. "They have a list of everyone. I even know how many guns you carry in your wagon."

He felt a faint amusement at her bluntness. "Since I don't know your name, am I goin' to have to find that fella with the list?"

"Not unless you want to. I'm Bernice McDowell. I don't suppose you ever even noticed me." She pouted full, red lips.

"If I had, I'd remember."

"Flattering, but it'd be more flattering if you'd noticed me. I've been watching you."

"I've been busy."

Laughing, she said, "Surely you have some time for... something that isn't work." She moved closer to him, batting her big blue eyes as her body almost but not quite touched his, her ample breasts poised near his arm.

He straightened a little, backed against the rough bark of the oak tree. "Always work to do." He wasn't widely experienced with women, but he'd known a few like this one-- women, who'd offered more with their eyes than, he had ever intended to take.

"It was a nice day," she was saying, "although a trifle hot. Didn't you think?" She lifted her blouse away from her breasts, as though allowing cooling air to caress her flesh.

"I reckon."

"It would be a nice night for a walk," she murmured, moving even closer, still not quite touching.

"Sorry but work isn't done."

He felt her fingers move to the front of his shirt, pulling it away from his chest and then letting it return, as she buttoned and unbuttoned one button. The moving air touched his heated skin and might have been seductive if he'd been remotely attracted to the buxom beauty. He wasn't.

"Are you sure you have to do it right now?"

The only way around her was into the brush behind him. He smiled wryly at the image of that. Before he come up with the right words to get away, two other people had walked up to them-- Amy and Adam, with smiles of greeting on their faces. Amy's gaze was on him, a strange, unreadable expression in her eyes before she turned to face Bernice.

"Hello, Bernice," she said with a polite smile, her gaze dropping to the hand still playing with the front of Matt's shirt.

"Amy," Bernice responded with scant enthusiasm.

"Have you both met Adam?" Amy looked back at Matt.

"In passin'." Matt replied, resigned to the unnatural situation into which he'd been thrust, when he did not want to be with any of them.

"We were talking about what a lovely night it would be for a walk," Bernice said.

"So you were talking about a lovely night for a walk?" Amy asked Matt.

"It appears you thought so," he said gritting his teeth.

"Adam invited me to walk. No one else did." Her tone was cutting.

"I've been busy."

"Matt and I have been friends for years," she told Adam before looking back at him with a tight smile.

"How delightful," Bernice said inching closer to Matt, her hip now pressed against his.

Adam looked as uneasy at the situation as Matt was. He shifted his weight from one foot to the other.

"How have you been, Bernice," Amy inquired.

"Fine. Of course, the day was hot, but I've certainly been enjoying the evening air." She beamed up at Matt and took a possessive hold on his forearm. A heavy silence descended upon them that no one seemed able to break.

Matt's mind had gone blank as he tried to think of an excuse that would get him away from where Adam had slid his arm around Amy's waist. She was evidently content that it be there.

Adam broke the increasingly heavy silence. "Looks like we'll have a little rain tonight. Might even get a thunderstorm."

"You think so?" Matt said glad for an excuse. "I better go

check our stock. Thunderstorm might make them jumpy." He disconnected Bernice's grip, smiled down at her and then toward Amy and Adam, and made his escape.

At the stock corral, he felt a wave of relief followed all too quickly by a numbing pain. It had been even harder than he had expected to be so near Amy-- to watch Adam put his hands on her. Worse was to think of later when Adam would be holding her in his arms, kissing the soft lips she had denied him. Matt grimaced, knowing he had to stop tormenting himself. He had to let it go.

~

Two days later, Matt woke in the moments before dawn to the sound of angry voices. Barely awake, he pulled on his shirt, trying to make out the words. Scurrying past his wagon Matt saw an old woman, her thin, gray hair hanging down her back, her narrow face pinched with fear and pain. When he heard what she was screaming, he understood the uproar. "We've been robbed. Robbed. Someone had to have been in our wagon and... our gold coins, they're gone!"

Keeping alert to the complaints ringing down the line of wagons, Matt got his oxen and hitched them to the wagon. As the people hurried to check their own belongings, more thefts were reported. "Grandma's broach is missing!" "Somebody took our money!"

The hysteria built as the people became a united force, a mob, running from wagon to wagon, frantically checking and then congregating in a group to share their losses. Matt didn't bother to fix breakfast. Whatever was building wouldn't take long to get to his wagon. It never did.

St. Louis Jones' voice boomed out calmingly. "Don't get yoreselves in a dither now, running around like a bunch of sheep. Ya ain't goin' to gain nothin' by scarin' the stock and younguns."

The final report was that six families had lost money or jewelry. "Now, stop to think. When was the last time ya seen yore stuff?" St. Louis Jones asked again the voice of calm in a storm.

As they talked it over, it was decided it had been Saturday night. Not everyone, but two had checked on their valuables then. The more they talked, the more convinced they were that someone had to have entered their wagons on the only occasion they had all been out of their wagons. Sunday morning, St. Louis had offered them a rare opportunity to have a time together to sing and pray. Most had gone to the meeting.

"It had to be then," one man said, shaking his head with anger. "But who'd take advantage of folks goin' to worship the Lord?"

St. Louis raised his arms. "Wal, we can start with who didn't go to meetin' if you're sure it was the only possible time. Nobody's left the train. So rest yore minds a bit while we check the wagons of those not there that mornin'."

When they got to his camp, Matt stood to one side. "Go ahead, look. We got nothin' to hide."

Two men entered the wagon, rummaged around for what seemed a short time, and came back out with a yelp of excitement. "It looks like it's all here."

"Which one of you thieving Kanes took it?" Ralph Hall, a large, surly man, demanded as the bag was thrown onto the ground. Gold coins and jewelry tumbled out. The people rushed forward to claim what was theirs.

"That there's my broach," said an old, gray-haired crone, crucified Matt with her hard glare.

Matt's father stood off to one side, seemingly unaware of what was happening. Morey, who had been standing behind the wagon, came forward, smiling as he stroked his small mustache. "Let me see that bag."

Matt didn't need to hear the words to know what they would be.

"I hate to have to say this," Morey stated with feigned sadness, "but that is my brother's."

Matt took a deep breath as he looked at Morey.

Jones's eyes were stern. "That true, son?"

58

"It's my bag." He met the wagon master's contemplative gaze. "I have never seen any of those things."

"Yeah, sure, and my grandma's an Injun," one man scoffed.

"If it's his bag, means he took it," another voice snarled.

"Always did wonder how one like him got that fancy Sharps. Must've been stealing right along."

"What are you going to do about this? Scum like this needs to be punished. Where's justice?" asked the old woman, her finger spearing viciously toward Matt's chest.

"Calm down, Mrs. Collins," St. Louis said. He turned to Matt. "What do you have to say?"

Matt shook his head. There wasn't anything to say. No proof he could offer. "I said it already. I haven't seen any of that before and took nothing." It wouldn't matter what he said. He couldn't prove what he knew had happened. The people crowded around him as if to make sure he didn't run for it.

"You folks stand back," St. Louis demanded. "This here's a situation for the elected council." The unhappy people moved to stand in clusters, remaining close enough to hear all that would be said.

Matt understood his situation. There wasn't much hope these people would find him innocent. He didn't know if he would have, given the evidence.

When the council members came from their wagons, St. Louis said, "Most of ya already heard what happened. The stolen items were found in the Kane wagon."

"So it was one of the Kanes," one little man contributed. Under his breath he added, "No surprise in that."

St. Louis raised his hand, "We'll do this orderly like. We ain't got time for a real trial and are too far from any judges; so we make the sense out of what happens as best we can. He glanced down at a list in his hand, "Nathan, Morey, Matthew Kane, Any of you have anything to add to these proceedin's?"

"I don't know nothin'," said Matt's father. "Cain't figure no way it'd be here, exceptin--" His eyes shifted from one of his sons to the other as he slammed his mouth shut.

Morey stepped forward, his voice smooth as he stated, "I

know it sounds like I'm accusin' my brother, but like I said before, that is Matt's bag."

"That so?" St. Louis asked Matt.

"It's my gear, but I did not put those things in it."

"Who else could have taken it and put it in his bag?" Mr. Collins asked from the cluster of on-lookers.

"Ya wanta say anything in yore defense?" questioned St. Louis his eyes hard on Matt. Matt shrugged his shoulders. Nothing he could say would change this, and he'd learned a lot of years ago that begging availed nothing. If you can't fight your way out, you take what is coming.

St. Louis and the eight men formed a small cluster away from the others as they argued over what was to be done. Matt didn't need to hear their words. He had no doubt as to who had taken the valuables, or why it had been put in his bag. He glanced at Morey and saw smug satisfaction written on his fox-like face.

When the men came back, St. Louis spoke for the group. "According to the articles that ya signed when ya joined this here train, ya accepted martial law. The rules say that a thief is to be punished. Justice comes with and from us. Do ya accept the decision of the council?"

Matt nodded.

"The verdict of the majority is guilty. You got anything to say before we tell ya the sentence? You could confess now, might go easier on ya."

"No."

"The penalty for first-time theft, where the goods are all returned, can be either twenty lashes with the bullwhip, or banishment from the train with either yore own wagon or since there's three of ya on this trip, enough supplies to get ya to the nearest settlement if yore folk wanta stay on the train. Since to the best of our knowledge, ya ain't never caused no trouble before and because some of the men have expressed doubts about whether ya are guilty, the council's decided it's to be yore choice."

Swallowing hard, Matt felt his skin crawl at the thought of a whipping. He'd seen what a whip could do to the back of an animal-- the blood, the gashes in the skin.

He closed his eyes a moment, thinking about leaving the train, never having to see his family or Amy again. He'd be free. Would that be freedom? Somehow, despite the ache it caused him, he wanted to make it to Oregon. It was the only thing left of the dream.

A rustle of skirts interrupted his considerations as Amy ran to his side. Her hands reached out to cling to his. "This is all wrong, Mr. Jones. It has to be. Matt's never stolen anything. He'd never take even a nickel that didn't belong to him. Tell them, Matt."

"Look, Miss," St. Louis started to say.

Matt interrupted him. "Amy, you got no part in this."

"I want to help," she cried, trying to pull him to her even as he resisted the tug. "There has to be a way to prove you didn't steal anything. This is all wrong."

"I don't need your help, and I want you out of here. Now!" The muscle in his jaw twitched as he struggled to hold himself together, to hold onto his control and pride. She wasn't helping.

"But Matt--"

"I mean it. Out of here." Roughly, he pulled his hand from hers. He knew she wanted him to change this, but there was no changing it. Finally, she walked away, but not before he saw the tears in her eyes.

Matt gritted his teeth. He could endure whatever came at him. He'd learned that lesson years before. He shrugged his shoulders. "I don't want to leave the train."

St. Louis nodded. "Get some rope," he ordered one of the men.

"No!" The wagon master turned back to look at him. "Nobody's goin' to tie me up."

"What'd ya have in mind?" St. Louis asked as several others snarled their resentment at his daring to think he had a right to any choices in this.

"You said a whip. I can stand and will stand for it." At the increasing rumble of disapproval from the crowd, he knew he'd made more enemies, but he didn't care. He would not be bound like an animal.

St. Louis studied him, and then nodded. "I reckon we'll see about that. If ya try to get away before the whole sentence's been carried out, I'll tie ya to the spokes myself."

Matt nodded taking off his shirt and laying it aside trying to keep his hands from shaking as he walked to the wagon wheel. The bright, morning sun warm on his bare back, he turned to face the wheel. He grasped rough wooden spokes, settled his mind on what he had to do, and waited.

CHAPTER 6

A my stood back, not willing to leave. As though through a
fog, she knew some were moving forward to watch.
Bernice stopped at her side. "What are they doing?" she asked,
pulling on Amy's arm.

"What does it look like?"

When the long, black whip snaked up into the air, then
whipped down onto Matt's bare back, Amy saw his muscles
tighten as he was thrown forward against the wheel by the force
of the blow. She felt a surge of pain deep in her stomach. She
wanted to rush forward, throw herself between him and the
lash. Nothing in her protected life had prepared her to witness
such a savage event.

She heard people talking, laughing, some of them yelling
encouragements to make the blows harder or offering raucous
suggestions. How dare they? How dare some seem to be
gloating over this travesty of justice?

At her side she heard Bernice gasp. She glanced over and
saw the blonde's gaze was fixated on Matt. The blonde stared,
looking almost lustful as Matt's lean frame was again thrown
against the wheel by the force of the whip. Was she enjoying this
spectacle?

Matt's body twisted under the whip, but his hands never left
the spokes. This time when the whip lifted, it left blood. Soon,

welts and bloody marks striped his back from shoulder to waist. She had lost count, was no longer certain how many times the whip had descended. How much longer could this go on?

When St. Louis finally stepped back, Amy rushed forward, determined to be at Matt's side. During the whole ordeal, he'd never let out a sound. Now, his hands gripped the wheel as though bonded to it. When she looked into his face, he didn't appear to recognize her. His pupils were so dilated his eyes appeared almost black.

"Matt," she said, trying to make him hear her as she put her hand over his and pried his fingers from the spoke. When he let go, his whole long length crumpled, carrying her to the ground with him. She twisted as she went down, keeping his wounded back away from the dust, protectively cradling him in her arms.

"Is he alive?" Bernice had moved to stand behind Amy, pulling her own skirts back.

"Of course," Amy snapped.

"I-- I can't stand..." The blonde blanched. "Blood makes me sick." She ran from the circle of onlookers, hands clasped over her mouth.

Amy was aware her own dress was now smeared with Matt's blood and sweat. All that mattered was getting him to shelter and treating the wounds on his back. Her father knelt beside her. "He'll be all right, honey."

Tears rolled down her cheeks as St. Louis Jones knelt beside her. He felt of Matt's pulse, looked into the eyes that although open weren't seeing anything. "I seen something like this before." He didn't say where. "We need to get him into his wagon." Her father and a man she didn't know came forward to help him.

"You can't put him in there." Morey sputtered. "There's not enough room."

"We'll make room. Ya figure he'd be up to walkin' right away," Louis snapped as Amy hurried ahead. In the wagon, St. Louis shoved aside a box with his foot, clearing a spot to lay Matt. As soon as she threw a blanket down, they put him on his stomach.

"I got a salve," St. Louis said, giving his back a cursory

examination, "heals wounds right fine. I'll bring it to ya after I get the train movin'."

Amy looked at him with disbelief. "You just whipped him. Why would you help now?"

A faint smile showed through his bearded face. "Ya don't think I enjoyed doin' that, do ya?" He jumped down from the wagon and strode off.

Her father put his arm around her shoulders. "Come away now, Amy. Mr. Jones will be back to take care of him."

"No! I won't leave until he's himself again." Someone had to stay with him. It would be her.

Her father looked at her for a long moment. "I'll check on you later."

At a sound at the opening of the wagon, Amy turned looking into Morey's face. "What are you doing here?" she asked, her voice cold to hide the fear his presence caused her. "Haven't you done enough damage?"

"You think?" He shrugged with a faint smile. Running the fingers of one hand lightly over his mustache, he said, "He doesn't look so good." He had an odd glitter in his eyes; then she recognized it as excitement.

"He'll be fine. No thanks to you."

"Me? Whatever do you mean, Miss Amy? I'll be back later. That is if you're sure there's nothing more I can do for him." With a tuneless whistling, he left.

Matt didn't seem to be unconscious and yet he said nothing. His eyes were open, blinking but he didn't respond to anything she said. As Nathan Kane started the team moving, Amy balanced herself against the sway of the wagon. "Take it easy," she cried, trying to hold Matt steady despite the wagon's rocking back and forth.

Looking at Matt's lacerated back, a rush of protectiveness overcame her. Fingertips shaking, she brushed his blond hair aside and bent to press her lips against his neck. His skin was so hot.

"Miss Stevens."

She swung around, her hands closed into fists before she realized it was St. Louis Jones who was at the entrance. The man would think her mad. She managed a tentative smile as the wiry wagon master entered the moving wagon.

"Didn't mean to scare ya, Miss. I brought that salve. Some liniment too. Ya know much about treatin' wounds like these?"

"Only a little. His eyes are open but it's not like he's really here. What... Does this seem normal to you?"

St. Louis looked at him. "He'll come around in a bit. I seen the Lakota do something like he done. He went somewhere to get away."

That sounded frightening. "Will he come back?"

"Shore." He studied his back. "Nothing looks too bad. The big thing is to keep the cuts clean. Pour the liniment over the open wounds. Might bring him around. It'll hurt like hell. After his skin dries, use this salve. I know it don't smell good, but it'll ease the pain and speed the healing." He nodded with satisfaction. "Kept it clean when you held him when he went down. I kept the whip high."

"I didn't expect you to want to help him at all."

"Looky here," he said firmness in his tone. "On a train like this, punishment's got to be sure and swift. I don't expect there's anything you, me, or even Kane himself could've done to prove he didn't steal. I know from experience, that justice had to be delivered for us to go on. It don't mean I enjoyed doin' it or even that I figured he was the thief."

"He's not," Amy snapped. "Mo-- Well, never mind. Just Matt's no thief."

He nodded. "I never seen no sneak thief take a whippin' like this man of yore'n did. Not a whimper out of him."

"He's not my man, Mr. Jones. He's my friend."

"Oh-- Wal, ya take care of yore-- of this here fella. He's young and strong. He'll do." Grinning, he backed out of the wagon and was gone.

Hating to hurt him, Amy poured the liniment over the open cuts. As St. Louis had guessed, Matt began to move, possibly to try and get away from the pain. In a moment, he cursed, a few words she hadn't heard before.

"Lie still," she ordered. "I have some salve I have to put on the open cuts."

"You stayed." It wasn't said with pleasure.

She ignored that. When his skin seemed dry enough, she dipped her fingers into the jar, wrinkling her nose at the pungent salve. She hoped she was doing the right thing. As she worked, she felt the tension in his muscles. She was too aware of his skin, the hard muscles. It became almost hypnotic, the feel of his skin beneath her fingertips, the dipping back into the jar, then stroking and soothing along the welts, ridges and open cuts.

As she worked down his back to the narrowness of his waist, she became aware of a strange feeling surging through her body. She had doctored Matt before, but his body was no longer one she knew. It was the body of a man, a strongly built, well-muscled man. Her face flushed with embarrassment.

When she finished, she sat back. "Can I get you some water?" He didn't answer, but she reached into the water barrel with a ladle, and helped him get his head to where he could drink from it. "Is the pain bad?" she asked, knowing it to be a foolish question even as she helped him lie back down.

"I've had worse."

"You scared me. Just now, it was like you were not here, had left your body almost."

He sucked in a breath. "I'm fine now. Go on back to your..."

She put her fingers over his lips. "I am staying for now." She remembered Morey, and how he had looked at Matt. Until he was more himself, she would not leave him.

"So," he retorted, "you get to play at being an angel of mercy?"

She smiled at his less than subtle attempt to offend her. "To the hilt," she agreed with satisfaction, "and I'll be the most proficient nurse you've ever had."

"Ignorin' the fact I ain't never heard that word before-- pro whatever it was-- I never had a nurse to compare," he murmured, his voice breaking as pain shot through his back, shattering his resolve to show nothing of what he was feeling.

"Oh yes, you have. Me."

"Other than you."

"Well I wasn't so good at it back then, being so much

younger. I remember letting you tell me what to do. This will be different."

"I can see that," he groaned.

"Matt," she whispered, jostled to one side by the rocking wagon, "we've been friends too long for you to not know when I make up my mind to something I'm going to do it."

He closed his eyes with resignation. "You don't give up... on anything."

"Since I'm going to be here anyway, can I do anything for you?"

His back felt like flames were eating his flesh, and he couldn't make her or the pain leave. He wished he could go back to the place he used to escape pain when he couldn't avoid it. But he couldn't, not now. He needed to stay.

He tried to smile and found the effort wasted. "More water," he finally mumbled. Even with what she'd given him, his mouth was too dry to swallow, and he was unsure if he had the strength to sit up and get it for himself.

She brought the dipper to his lips, lifting him enough to drink. "Sleep for awhile," she whispered, stroking his hair back from his damp forehead.

"I am fine. You can go."

"Not yet, I have to stay for awhile. I have a question though."

"Ask it."

"Why didn't you tell them Morey was the thief? What made you stand there and take his punishment?"

"It would have changed nothing if I had." He closed his eyes, wanting her to think he was sleeping so there'd be no more questions. He felt her fingers in his hair, stroking, soothing. She loosened the tie and brushed the hair back into it again. Her tenderness eased the pain in one way but in another made it all worse. He needed to convince her to stay away, to escape the stigma that was sure to settle on him in such a closed community, but he had no words. The pain left him weak, too weak to fight her or anything else. He let sleep claim him.

. . .

68

Amy stayed in the wagon as he slept through the day. Remembering the expression on Morey's face as he'd looked down at his brother, she couldn't leave him. Still, the train had stopped for the night. Matt was sleeping, or pretending to, not truly helpless. He'd made it clear he didn't want her there. St. Louis came before she could make up her mind to go.

"Figured I'd look in on him," he said, stepping into the wagon. While St. Louis examined his back, if Matt was awake, he gave no sign. When he finished reapplying the salve, he smiled. "Closin' up good, no infection. Salve does it every time."

"I guess I should leave," she said with reluctance. Outside, she had seen Nathan was sitting by a sputtering campfire. She doubted he would look after Matt, but Morey didn't appear to be nearby.

"I'll stop by through the night, keep an eye on him. Don't worry about a thing. Ya go get somethin' to eat. Ya're lookin' a mite peaked, Miss Amy." She nodded with no excuse for staying. The trouble was-- she didn't want to go.

Walking back to her own wagon, she ran almost literally into Adam before she saw him. He smiled as he looked down at her, but she could see the perplexity in his eyes. "Can I walk with you?" he asked.

"Where?" She tried to smile but knew the effort hadn't been successful

"Wherever you're going."

She thought about the lecture her mother would be likely to give her and was in no hurry to get back to her family.

He seemed to read her mind. "How about a stroll. Let's pretend we're someplace else. Someplace where the air is cool and the grass is green." He took her hand and tucked it into the crook of his arm. Her steps fell in with his, and she let him lead her away from the main body of wagons toward where the livestock was tethered and corralled.

They had yet to reach their destination when Bernice McDowell caught up with them, seemingly breathless from running a few steps. "How is he?" she asked without waiting for a greeting.

"He'll be all right," Amy responded, irked at the blonde's interest.

"He was so brave," Bernice simpered, clasping her hands together over her full bosom. "Can you imagine anyone taking a beating like he did... and not making so much as a sound. I just never thought anyone could be so brave." She rolled her eyes skyward as she talked, accentuating her statements with expressive gestures.

"Yes," Amy agreed, hoping she would leave, "he was brave." She didn't need to hear more accolades about Matt. If she kept on, she'd be talking about how beautiful his body was. That made her feel like ripping that blonde hair out.

"I don't think he stole anything, do you?" Bernice looked questioningly from Amy to Adam.

"Matt's no thief."

"Can he have visitors?"

For a reason she couldn't fathom but didn't attempt to resist, Amy said, "Not yet. He's sleeping. All he needs is rest. St. Louis is going to look after him."

"Maybe tomorrow?"

"Possibly." Remembering Bernice's aversion to blood, Amy added, "He's still not a very pretty sight, from the beating and all."

"Really," Bernice recoiled. "I'd have thought bandages--"

"No, the wounds have to be left open to the air. There's only the salve-- a bad, vile smelling stuff that covers them."

"Oh my! Perhaps I should wait a few days."

"I'd wait at least that long," Amy said with a smile. "He might not be vomiting by then either."

Bernice all but stepped back in horror. "Oh, my goodness. I mean I had no idea he was so sick. Well, thank you." For the first time that day, Amy felt a genuine urge to laugh as she watched Bernice walk off, her ample hips undulating with a practiced sway.

"What was that all about?" Adam asked.

"I'm not sure." Amy remembered the day she saw Bernice and Matt together, Bernice leaning against Matthew. She recalled Bernice's comments, about a god on the train, a man of sculptural beauty. She knew whom she had meant-- her Matthew. The very idea sent a surge of anger coursing through her veins.

Adam took hold of her shoulders and turned her to face him. His fingers were light against her cheek. "You and Kane been friends a long time?" His gaze locked onto hers.

"Since children." How could she describe their relationship even to herself anymore?

"I haven't seen him with you... except that first day."

"Things change."

"You are a loyal friend. Clem told me what happened when I got back this morning from my scout. From what he said, you stood up for him in front of everyone."

"He's not a person to steal."

"Clem said he didn't try to prove he didn't." Adam's expression was thoughtful.

"He said it would do no good. He's proud-- too proud for his own good."

Adam was silent a moment, staring out at the hills in the distance. "If he's innocent, how do you think the things got into the Kane wagon?"

"His brother." She remembered Morey's face, the frightening expression as he had looked at Matt lying unconscious. What was that about? She pushed it aside. "At home, if something was missing, you always knew who'd taken it, even if you couldn't prove it. I believe Morey wanted it to look like Matt did it this time."

"Framed him?"

"There's something awful between them. Their family is the opposite of what one should be. Mr. Kane is a drunk, but maybe you already knew that." She wrinkled her nose with disgust. "I don't know why Nathan and Morey even came with him... except maybe they wanted to keep leeching off Matt."

"Quite the family. What makes you think Matt Kane isn't like his tribe?"

She wheeled on him. "If you knew him, you'd never suggest that. Matt's hard working, always helping people."

Adam grinned, putting up his hands in mock surrender. "Whoa, I didn't intend to make you mad."

"I am sorry too. I shouldn't have gotten upset. It's not your fault." She didn't meet his gaze. "It's just been a long-- a horrible day. You don't know him. It's logical you'd wonder." She felt tears again.

Adam touched his finger to the corner of her eye, lifting away a teardrop. He studied her face as though trying to decide from where it had come.

"Matt's been like my brother." Even as she said the words, the words she'd said so many times, she wondered if she was being honest with anybody—including herself.

Looking up at the tall man in buckskins, so handsome in his doubt, he was all the man any girl could want. Strong, caring, traveled, and maybe open to more. Except, why was it all she could think of was Matt, the feel of his lips against hers, the texture of the skin on his back, his hard muscles? She shook her head, trying to clear it.

They began walking again, to a quieter place just beyond the wagons. They stopped at a grove of scrub oaks. Birds were making their quiet, night sounds overhead.

"I'm glad you're the kind of woman who can be a friend like you were to him." Adam tilted her chin up. She knew he intended to kiss her. She had managed to divert that in the past, but now she needed that kiss. Perhaps it would take away the memory of another's kiss, unwanted but oh so hard to forget.

She lifted her hands up around his neck. His arms went around her, pulling her against his body as his lips came down on hers, soft, tender, caressing. Where Matt's last kiss had been angry and demanding, Adam's was soft, gentle.

As Amy walked into the circle of firelight, her mother asked, "Where have you been?"

Mrs. Collins was sitting on one of the narrow stools, gingerly sipping her tea, talking and gesturing with her free hand. It was obvious from the tired expression on her mother's face that the same conversation in one form or another had been going on all evening.

"Just now-- with Adam," Amy answered, hoping that would forestall further questions.

Mrs. Collins was a help in that, for she went on with nary a pause. "Why that whole family is shiftless no-counts. Should never of allowed 'em to join this outfit with good folks like us. That boy got what was comin' to him. Why I seen that from the first time I laid eyes on him. He's the worst of the lot. Them eyes of his are plumb shifty."

"Matt was innocent," Amy snapped. She knew all the moods of those blue-gray eyes, and not one of them was shifty.

"By cracky, he's got the looks of a crook-- that kind of innocent way of gettin' folks off their guard." She wrinkled her nose as she demonstrated a shifty expression to the limit of her theatrical ability. "Handsome face like that one'll fool folks every time. That long hair, that along tells a body what he's up to. That man deserved every lash of that whip. Should've whipped and then kicked him off the train. That's what they should've done. Or to tell you the truth, iffn I'd of had my way-- they'd of hung him. One less crook to deal with in Oregon!"

"Hung him?" Amy felt enraged. "He was not the one who stole your precious property—and you value things more than human life?"

"Amy," her mother interrupted, "you're forgetting yourself. Mrs. Collins has had a traumatic experience. She's not feeling well because of it."

"It's been worse for Matt."

"I can't believe you're so gullible as to believe he was innocent." Mrs. Collins snorted. "For land's sake, missy, he had the goods right on him. We won't know a safe night so long as he's with us. And I'm not the only one what thinks he should've been kicked off the train. You jest mark my words and remember you heard it here. That boy'll be in trouble again."

Amy was too flabbergasted to think of a fitting reply.

"Matthew was punished," her mother said, a tone of anger

in her voice that Amy rarely heard. "It's over. It's time to quit talking about it."

"How could I do that?" shrieked Mrs. Collins. "I was violated, I tell you!"

Feeling exhausted and confused, Amy wanted to continue arguing with the old woman, but it would do no good. "I'm going to bed."

"I put aside some dinner for you."

"I'm not hungry."

She undressed in the darkness, assuming Loraine and Belle were already sleeping. When she was finally lying in her blankets, Loraine whispered, "How is he?"

"I'm not sure. Her thoughts were going beyond his wounds. "St. Louis said he'll be all right. He has some special salve--" At the words, she dissolved into tears.

Loraine climbed from her own cot and, sitting on Amy's, took her into her arms, letting her cry it out, patting her shoulder. "I haven't done this for a lot of years, little sister," she crooned.

Amy's tears stopped. She sniffled, "I don't know what's gotten into me. I think it's knowing he's alone, suffering. He didn't want me with him, Raine."

Belle's childish voice cut through the darkness. "I wanted to go, but Mama stopped me. Said it was no place for a child, but I am not a child anymore, and I wish people would remember that."

The two older sisters agreed that at eleven she was very grown indeed. "Mama was right," Loraine said. "I left when most of the women did. I couldn't stand watching someone beaten that way especially when I knew them."

After they settled back down into their quilts, Amy lay awake, trying to make sense of the turbulent day. Adam's kiss should have been one of the most important moments in her life. She had put him off, waiting for... She wasn't sure for what she had been waiting. Then when he had done it, the kiss had been fine. Just fine. Only it wasn't. Even with him kissing her, she had been unable to stop visualizing Matt, alone in his wagon with no one to hold and soothe him.

She drew her quilt around her shoulders and tried to work through her tumultuous feelings. Matt was hers. It was in some way she didn't understand. Her friend, yes, but... When she saw him at risk, she wanted to defend him. to fight for him as a mother bear fights for her cubs. Friendship. That's what it was— or was it?

The years they'd shared together came flooding back in memories, in images as clear as though they were happening again.

She was almost seven and he ten, the air hot and humid, thunderstorms in the sky to the south. They had been standing by one of the larger pools in the river that flowed past their homes. "Let's go swimming, Matt."

"What'd we wear?" he'd protested. "We go home with our clothes wet, and we'll get a lickin' for shore."

"Silly, we take them off," she'd reassured him.

"All of ' em? he'd asked, horrified but tempted by the cool water.

"Sure. You scared?"

"Course not."

"Well then..."

They'd done it, and everything would have ended there because they had both been children, and the whole thing had been innocent-- except, Loraine had seen and told. She had received a parental talking-to warning her of the risks of such behavior..

When Matt had finally returned to school, she saw the bruises and asked what his father had done to him. He didn't answer.

She remembered the small school they'd attended, Matt two grades ahead of her, when he'd still been able to attend, before adult jobs took his life away from education.

. . .

Ivan Jamison had decided that picking on Amy would be fun. He began using recess as a time to grab her long braid and pull her around the school yard.

"Quit that," she'd shrieked.

"If I don't?" he'd dared, pulling on her braid hard enough to bring tears to her eyes.

"But you will." Matt had come up behind them, grabbing Ivan's wrist and twisting it until he'd dropped the braid. Fists flew then, with the result of Ivan, older and bigger, lying on the ground, crying.

The schoolmaster had come up just in time to see the end of the fight and blame Matt for everything. He'd grabbed him roughly by the ear, dragging him to the corner where he'd sat him, despite Amy's tears protesting his innocence. It had taken her own father coming down to the school to make things right.

Always, it's been Matt defending her, trying to fix things for her. She didn't know what went on in Matt's home, who was the one hurting him. He told her nothing about how he ended up with bruises or once a black eye. Sometimes he made an excuse that she didn't believe. Ignoring any of her arguments, he had kept her away from his home.

Fear clenched her stomach into a knot. She knew why the whipping had happened. It wasn't to steal for money. Morey had wanted to hurt Matt. What he had done was unlikely to be enough to satisfy what had to be a sickness. Was there ever enough for someone who desired to cause others pain? The thought of Matt being hurt caused her stomach to clench. It was as though someone was clenching her throat.

For the first time she looked within for why she felt as she did. Was what she felt for Matt really just friendship? A more recent image pushed its way forward when she had seen Bernice leaning against Matt. Amy had watched for a moment, heard Bernice's simper. A surge of a strong emotion had surged through her.

Dragging Adam forward by the arm, she had done what was required to put an end to the blonde's aggressiveness and halt whatever potential that little moment might have had. Except, what was that about? Wasn't Matt finding someone exactly what she'd said she wanted? She'd recognized the first twinges of jealousy that night.

She squeezed her eyes, trying to shut out the memory of Matt's half-naked body, of sunlight on broad shoulders, a lean muscular torso, sinewy arms. She felt a quickening in her stomach when she thought of touching that body, as when she applied the salve, only imagined it differently, stroking her fingers down his flat stomach, caressing his muscular chest, voluntarily touching his lips with her own. She frowned at her thoughts. She had known Matt as a boy, but she was only coming to know the man.

CHAPTER 7

Having slept most of the day, Matt found the night offered only wakefulness. Lying on his stomach, he tried to dismiss the pain, not to think about what had happened, about the humiliation, most of all not to think about Amy. He'd been unfair. She'd tried to stand up for him. And what was her reward? Sarcasm and anger. She gave it all, and he held back because he couldn't have everything he wanted. It's not like a person can choose who they love. He well understood the truth of that.

The passion he'd felt for her had grown into a fire that wouldn't let him be. He'd thought maybe a kiss, just a kiss, and he'd be satisfied. He could release his feelings. Except, a kiss had been his undoing. From the moment he'd pulled her into his arms, there had been no peace. He had to quit thinking about what he could not have.

Pushing himself upright, he sat waiting for his head to clear. He wondered for a moment where his pa and Morey were sleeping, but then he didn't care. Feeling for his shirt, he threw it over his shoulders, wincing at even that much weight against his bruised and lacerated back. He struggled to his feet, glad and a little surprised to find he could maintain his balance.

The air in the wagon was stuffy and hot. He felt a need to sleep outside. He grabbed a blanket and made his way to the tailgate, sliding carefully to the ground. For a moment, the world seemed to tilt.

Leaning against the wagon, he looked up at the sky, grateful to see stars overhead instead of canvas. Here on the plains, no hills or trees to block the sight, when the campfires died down, the stars shone brighter than any he'd ever seen. Looking up gave him a perspective that eased everything wrong below. He stood for long moments, emptying his mind of all but the feeling of vastness above.

When he began to shake with cold, he wrapped the blanket around himself. He lay on the ground, on his side, forcing pain from his mind, but not going where pain could not reach him. He knew that place. Oh, he knew it all too well.

He wanted to turn over, to move, but every movement sent a pain across his back. He had to content himself with lying quietly, while he fought through the battle of letting go of Amy.

She deserved so much better from him. He'd claimed he loved her but hadn't shown it. If he had been half the man he wanted to be, he'd have let her go long before. He wasn't worthy of her. He was a man who could barely read and write. Nothing was really possible between them, even before he had been branded a thief, with the marks on his body to prove it. He could almost convince himself to be grateful she had rejected his love-- almost.

With black humor, he thought about his new situation, about the reaction he could expect from the people. If he'd had a lick of commonsense, he'd have left the train rather than take the beating. Folks had looked with suspicion at his family before. That suspicion would be a full-blown hatred now. He felt more alone than he ever remembered.

When he awoke to the blackness before dawn, he realized with surprise he had slept. Rising, he stoked the campfire. By the time coffee was perking, St. Louis Jones stepped into the flickering circle of light.

"Up and about, huh?" the older man questioned. If he saw

Matt's uneasiness, he didn't pay it any mind. "Let's see that there back of yor'n."

"It's fine."

"I said, let me see it."

Jones gave Matt no choice but to pull off his shirt and allow him to examine his wounds.

"Hmmm, ya're a tall un. Bend over here. Get down near that there light." Matt knelt. The bearded wagon master probed along his back. "Not bad. I reckon though a little more of my salve'll be good. Looks to me like you're gonna get through this with no infection. Although," he pressed on a sore point, "if this swells up, we might have to lance it." The salve was soothing as St. Louis applied it to his back, soothing as it soaked into the wounds. "Don't smell like much, but it does its job."

"What's in it?" Matt asked, not sure he wanted to know.

"Buffalo fat, nettle, yarrow, chamomile, yucca, a couple other things not worth mentionin' but e-ssential to its workin'. Injun medicine. Bother ya?"

"Should it?" Matt studied St. Louis for a moment before he poured the wagon master a cup of coffee along with his own.

"I got a question for ya. Ya ever been with Injuns, I mean lived with 'em?"

"No."

The wagon master rubbed his jaw but didn't ask more.

When they'd both taken a healthy swig, Matt said, "I figured you'd leave me in the dirt alongside the road."

St. Louis smiled. "Not that I would have; but if I had wanted, I'd have had to leave that little gal of yours."

"Amy's not my anything. She's made it clear how she feels."

"I'd say so."

"Pity brought her to do what she did yesterday."

"I ain't here to argue with ya," St. Louis said, grinning as he drank the last of his coffee and held the cup out for a refill, "but I'd like to see the man could've made her leave ya. She's one determined gal when she makes up her mind."

Knowing the truth of that, Matt let the statement stand. "So, why are you here now?" he asked. "You got no reason to help me anymore than you already have."

"Ya figure I helped you when I whipped ya?"

"I had a choice. That was a help. You didn't force me to be tied. You could have."

"I was curious about ya."

"About what?"

St. Louis chuckled, his eyes gleaming in the firelight. "Tell me straight now, when nothin' more can be do to ya. Are ya a thief?"

"I told you the answer to that yesterday. It hasn't changed."

"I want to hear it again."

"I've never taken anything that wasn't mine." He looked the older man in the eyes, his own gaze unwavering.

"All right." St. Louis took a sip of his coffee.

"You believe me?"

"A certain kind of man's word's always been enough for me."

Matt snorted. "That's not how I remember yesterday."

"Yesterday was official, like a court of law. What I, as a man, felt in my gut, couldn't figure into it."

Matt sat back a moment, letting the words sink in as the ointment soaked into his back. "You have much luck trusting in your gut?"

The older man laughed. "A lot." He studied Matt a bit. "Something about you makes me curious."

"Well don't expect me to satisfy that," Matt said jolting his back as he straightened too quickly.

The older man studied him a moment. "Ya could have tried harder to convince folks ya were innocent."

"And how would I have proved that? It'd have been the same in the end. It was easier to take what came than--"

"Beg?" questioned St. Louis.

"I don't beg," Matt said; then voice hardening, he demanded, "You're here for a reason. What is it?"

"I got another question. You any good with that Sharps of yores?"

"Good enough."

"Ya didn't steal it did ya?"

He could have taken offense, but he didn't. "It was a gift."

The older man smiled into his coffee cup. "I started out this trip with two hired men, wranglers, all around help. The older I get, the more I need that. I still got the brains and experience but I need young muscle to keep things movin' smooth. One of my hired men is old, like me. The other, the no account, he took off two days ago. Don't know why they can't never figure it out afore we leave Independence. So, I need another man. It'd mean helpin' folks, drivin' a wagon sometimes, repairin' gear, helpin' Adam, maybe using that rifle. It don't pay a lot."

Matt waited a moment saying nothing, until it dawned on him what St. Louis was suggesting. "You want to hire me?"

"To be honest, I had my eye on ya earlier. Three men, one wagon, one of ya could be spared. Yesterday wal, naturally I had to rethink it on a couple of counts. I done that and am offerin' ya the job if ya want it."

Matt just looked at him, too surprised to answer. He stood up and walked slowly away, then back. "Damn this is one I never figured. How's that going to go over? I'm not goin' to be popular with the others."

"Likely true for awhile at least, but ya know how folks are-- always runnin' this way and that, gettin' all het up about some- thin', then forgettin' what it was."

"I just can't see them takin' help from me, not after this."

St. Louis grinned. "When a wagon's broke down or a man's too sick to drive, or we're fordin' a swollen river, folks take help from anybody who knows what's he's doin'. They might not be thinkin' they will, but they will. Ya heard the meeting how folks begrudge helping each other—some anyways. My worry was findin' a good man, one who'd be up to givin' the help. You are actually more than I expected. It'd give ya a meal a day. It'll mean some extra money when ya get to Oregon."

That part sounded good—the meal especially since nobody in his family was much of a cook. Matt still hesitated.

"I seen how you handle your animals, like the look in yore eyes. I need ya, but the decision's yours."

"I can't see folks goin' along with this."

St. Louis's eyes narrowed. "I took on a lot of responsibility when I agreed to lead this train. It's me makes the choices, and it's me has to do what's right. They paid me for my judgment."

Matt shook his head with lingering disbelief even as he put out his hand. "All right then. It sounds crazy but I'd like the chance."

The older man grinned as they shook hands. "Come on over to the wagon after we get settled tonight, I'll take another look at yore back, put more salve on it and introduce ya to my scout and Clem."

Of all the conversations he might have imagined, this had been the most peculiar. Why had the man asked if he'd ever lived with Indians? It was singularly odd that a man who opened his back with a bullwhip one day would offer him a job the next. Life took some weird turns was all he could think-- that and when a turn seemed to be a good one, he should grab on.

Nathan Kane came out from behind the wagon. "Kind of strange," he mumbled, pouring himself a cup of coffee. "Him offerin' you a job like that after..."

"Why's it strange?" Matt asked, ignoring that he'd thought the same thing only moments before.

"Wal, you got yore own wagon for one thing."

"You and Morey can manage it. You're not an invalid, Pa."

"I'm not well, ya know how my rheumatism acts up."

"It'd be better if you drank less."

"I don't drink all that much."

Matt, chewing on a stale biscuit, said nothing. It was an old argument, and his father wasn't going to listen to anything he said.

"Matt," his father said after a moment, "I know I drink a mite too much sometimes, and I ain't been much of a pa to you boys, but... I jest don't know what comes over me. It's like there's a feelin' inside me, kind of an ache. I don't expect ya to understand, but the whiskey helps. It... wal, I just need it."

"It'll be the end of you."

"You been a good boy, and I ain't been much of a pa."

His father became lost in his self-pity, his litany of sins and failures. Matt stopped listening. Self-pity led to drinking. Drinking led to more failure and self-pity. There didn't seem to be a way out of the cycle once a man got into it. When Matt could stand no more, he said, "Quit drinkin'."

"I know son... I know. I'll try to quit... I really will."

No matter how many times he'd heard his father say the words, he always had a tiny hope that maybe this time would be different.

The reaction of the people was as tough as Matt had expected. It was no surprise, but it didn't make it easier to have faces turned away as he passed, whispers behind his back, and insults to his face. Only two men on the whole train seemed willing to talk to him in any kind of normal manner, St. Louis and Adam Stone.

The other hired man, Clem Johnson, a skinny old man, nearly balding, made it plain from the start that he had no use for him and knew him to be a thief to boot. "Dangnabit," the old man grumbled as he went about his chores, "never figger the way folks figger. Plumb crazy... No sense atall."

Matt took what Clem said with a grain of salt, because despite the insults, he began liking the old timer. For the life of him, though, he couldn't have explained why. Clem did nothing but find fault with his work and tell him what a lowlife he was. When Matt laughed off the insults, the old man went off, mumbling and muttering.

St. Louis' acceptance was a lifeline for Matt. The only other man who'd ever talked to him, encouraged him, had been Amos Stevens, and he'd always believed Amos did so because of Amy. The wagon master had reached out to him at the worst period of his life—there was nothing he would not have done for him, no job so dirty that he wouldn't smile and head off to take care of it.

At the corrals, St. Louis asked him, "You any good on horseback?"

"I can stay on." Matt knew he was a good horseman, but it usually paid to underplay his abilities rather than overplay them.

St. Louis led a sturdy brown gelding over to him. "This here's Dartan. He'll be yores for the trip. Sometimes ya might need to ride out with him. From now on, take care of him and make sure you keep that Sharps with ya when you do ride out."

Matt nodded rubbing the nose of the horse and meeting his gaze. The gelding nuzzled him. Putting his hand on the horse's neck, Matt leaped onto his back and rode him at a quick gallop out of the encampment a few hundred feet and back. "I think we can get along," he said patting the animal's neck as he slid off.

"Shore does look like it. Use the saddle next time." St. Louis chuckled and walked off.

The nights had a new element as the four men from different walks of life sat around the campfire talking of the day's problems. St. Louis would list off the tasks needed doing, Clem would list off Matt's mistakes, and Adam would listen and laugh at them all.

As the sounds of the other people slowly faded away, and the night noises from the prairie became dominant-- a hawk crying, coyotes howling, St. Louis said, "It's a night like this, work done, everythin' quiet. It's times like this I get to thinkin' about the good Lord and the strange ways of this old world."

His reference to God didn't surprise Matt as it might have before he came to work for him. Comments about God permeated St. Louis' day in little ways.

"We've had this discussion before," Adam said with a smile, "but I got nothing better to do tonight. You really believe some god made all this? The way I see it is there are so many different ways of believing that I don't know how any man can know for sure one way or the other."

"There's them that believes that way," St. Louis said, nodding with a smile as he refilled his coffee cup.

"I've been among some of the Indian tribes," Adam went on as he pulled a bag of tobacco and papers from his pocket. "Had a pretty good Crow friend who was scouting for the military at the same time I was. They think just like you that they got it all figured out, but none of them agree on much of how things got started, between magic arrows and pipes." He rolled the cigarette and lit it.

"It's true tribes have different beliefs."

"See."

"But," St. Louis added with a grin, "they believe God, whatever they call Him, created this all too."

"Exactly." Adam snorted. "Some of their myths are as far fetched as you believing in an historic Garden of Eden."

Matt sat listening as the two men argued their points back and forth. He'd never been with men who discussed and argued spiritual matters so openly and with no rancor.

"How do you see it, Matt?" asked St. Louis, his face dim in the dying light from the campfire.

He was uneasy in discussing his personal creed. "I can't speak for anybody but myself, but I believe in God."

"Ya see there," St. Louis waved his hand at Adam. "Matt believes in God."

Adam laughed and took a long draw on his cigarette. "Is that supposed to be a proof or disproof?"

Ignoring Adam's sarcasm, St. Louis asked, "Ya don't have to answer this if ya don't want but was it believin' that got ya past the whipping that day?"

Matt wasn't ready to reveal the secrets of his life. He shook his head. "If you mean praying, no, I don't do that."

"But you believe in god?"

"I do, but don't want to lead you wrong on this. I am no churchgoer. Oh I'd go with the Stevens sometimes." He smiled as he remembered how often he'd gone just to sit next to Amy in the pew, their knees sometimes touching, their hands holding a common hymnal, and maybe if he got lucky, brushing her fingers against his. Not exactly a spiritual reason for going to meeting.

"You being a believer in God and all," Clem interrupted, pushing forward, a sarcastic smile on his thin face, "how is it you would steal?" He chortled as he brought home his point.

"I wouldn't," Matt said. Getting up, he threw the remains of his cup of coffee into the edge of the fire. "See you in the mornin'."

The sun had been hot, its beams relentless but most of the day the train had wound its way above a small river. One thought had kept Matt going. At day's end, he would grab his rifle, razor, soap and walk upstream, find a hole deep enough to wash his hair and get the dust off his skin.

In most places the banks were choked with cottonwoods, wild roses and brush, but he kept going until he found an opening and a deep enough pool. Walking to the edge of the river, Matt began stripping off his clothing, throwing them onto the grassy bank beside him. He untied the rawhide thong that generally kept his hair back and strode naked into the water. He welcomed the coldness, the clean feeling of water rippling against his naked skin. The opposite bank was barely thirty feet away. He dove deep before swimming across, enjoying the loose feeling in his muscles as he eased the kinks from his body, the water a soothing, buoyant world, one that let him forget the frustrations of working all day with people who barely spoke to him.

The feminine voice seemed to come from nowhere. "Water feel good?"

He stood now chest deep, swept his hair back, and looked to the shore where his clothing was piled. "How do you come to be here?" he asked suppressing his surge of anger at Bernice standing on the bank. Maybe it was coincidence. Not only he might've wanted a bath.

"I followed you, of course," she said with a giggle. "I wanted to talk to you. Wondered what you were doing going out here alone. I didn't expect to catch you like... well, like you are." She laughed again as she moved to stand by his clothing.

"How you caught me is buck naked."

"I know. I watched you undress."

"And didn't say anything?"

"If I'd said something, you wouldn't have taken off your clothes, would you?" she asked her blue eyes wide with anything but innocence.

He moved toward shore but stayed waist deep in the water, the fading light some covering but not enough. "You mind if I get dressed now?"

"Of course not."

"Then leave."

"Then I wouldn't get to watch again," she said with another giggle. "You have a magnificent body. It should be enjoyed by someone."

He looked at her speculatively. The water was getting cold. Matt didn't like the idea of knowingly being exposed to her gaze. He didn't have much choice. If she had to wait for morning, she would wait. He didn't have the patience to outwait her, and so he strode out of the water and headed straight for his clothing. She barely stood aside while he pulled on his pants.

"We both want it," Bernice said, moving closer, running her hands down Matt's wet belly. "You know we do."

"When I want a woman, I do the askin'," Matt drawled, sitting on the ground to pull on socks and boots.

"You need a woman." She knelt beside him, her expression demanding, a little cold with calculation.

"Might be you know a lot about men, but you're wrong about me."

Her smile turned angry. "If I was to scream right now, to say you tried to rape me, who'd believe you didn't—especially if I ripped my blouse?" He knew she was right. Nobody could stop it. Not many would want to

Bernice stood up, looming over him. He reached out for his shirt, but she put her booted foot on it, holding it down. If he touched her ankle, so much as pushed her away, she would scream. Taking a deep breath, he stood up.

"What do you want?" he asked, holding back an angry retort.

"Maybe nothing." She bent and retrieved the shirt, handing it to him. "Maybe, who knows." She shrugged her shoulders, the movement emphasizing her thrusting breasts.

"We playin' a little game here?" Matt drawled, shrugging into the shirt, buttoning it, and tucking it into his pants. Any such games were likely to see him the victim, and he'd had a belly full of that. He tied his wet hair back with its leather thong.

She shook her head. Her gaze did not leave his chest. "I wouldn't really do anything to get you into trouble. I was only teasing."

"Bad joke."

"I want us to be friends." She pouted. "I saw the scars on your back just now. I wanted you to know I was sorry when that happened. I wanted to come see you then, but Amy said it might not be a good idea, you being so sick." Matt raised his eyebrows at that but said nothing.

Her fingers lightly brushed against his arm, a heady fragrance of some strong perfume assaulted his nostrils. He stepped back. She took a firm hold of his forearm and began stroking his wrist, as though unaware of what she was doing— except she clearly knew exactly what she was doing.

"Don't seem like such a good idea." Matt smiled. "Ever hear Bible stories, Miss Bernice?"

"Some." She frowned, obviously trying to decide what the Bible had to do with what she'd been suggesting.

"Well, they talk about folks called lepers—unclean, diseased. Nobody has nothin' to do with 'em or with anybody who has anything doin' with 'em."

"But I don't see how--"

"Right now, it's like that with me. St. Louis, him offering me a job, that was different. He's a man, a man who knows what he's doin', but Miss Bernice, you bein' friends with me would cause you to lose friends other places."

"Well," she admitted with a coquettish smile, "I must admit I've thought of that. I felt we could see each other in secret. Meet where nobody would see us. It would be exciting, don't you think?" Her eyes promised just how exciting that would be as she shifted her grip from his forearm to grasp the front of his damp shirt.

Matt nearly laughed at her audacity, which would have been his first genuine laugh in some time, but it would encourage her. He could ill afford that. He swallowed his second impulse, which was to tell her what he really thought of her. That still might see him hung for attempted rape. All she had to do was scream. He needed to get her a long way from him and sooner than later. She was proving as dangerous potentially as Morey. Then he thought of something—a truth that might work.

"I didn't want to be talkin' about it, but I'm in love with someone else. It wouldn't be fair-- meeting you."

"But--"

"There's no way I'd let you waste your time, make enemies and all for something that ain't goin' to go nowhere."

"Who is this woman?" Bernice questioned, dropping her grip on him and stepping back a pace to study his face in the dimming light. "I've never seen you with anyone."

"I don't wanta talk about it."

"She's dead?" Bernice asked hopefully.

Matt stared at her for a moment, almost-- but not quite-- shocked at her reaction. "No," he drawled, "not dead, but she's in love with somebody else."

"Well then? I could help you get over your loss," she suggested, moving to again take a grip on his shirt as she batted her big blue eyes.

"No," he said, disgusted with her and afraid if he stayed any longer, it would become obvious. "I got to get back."

"You're sure?" she asked in a plaintive tone.

"I am." He took hold of her hand, disconnected her grip from his shirt and walked away, grateful to have escaped, wondering if he had.

Striding away from the animal enclosure, his mind on his unpleasant encounter with Bernice, Matt didn't see Ralph Hall until he'd bumped into him. "Watch where you're going," the big man snarled.

Matt shrugged as he stepped back to look at the agitated man, "Sorry."

"Clumsy, no account. I don't like you. I never liked you."

"Hell, I don't remember. When did I ask you to like me?"

The man was built like a bull. Although not so tall as Matt, he probably outweighed him by fifty pounds and outreached him by several inches. It was easy to imagine what those ham-like fists could do in a barroom brawl, and barroom brawls were probably all Ralph Hall had known.

"You snot-nosed kid. I think it's about time you learned some manners," Hall snarled, as he stood spread-legged in front of Matt, the altercation attracting a crowd of onlookers egging Hall on.

Matt knew St. Louis wouldn't much like him getting into a fight. Suddenly he didn't care. "Clumsy man like you ought to be on the look-out for others on the trail ahead of you," Matt suggested, smiling.

The big man began to smile too. "You know, I never liked you. Even before," he said as he came forward, his fists raised.

"Can't believe how much that disappoints me." It made no sense, but he was eager for this fight, eager for the chance to let out some of the pent-up energy. The work had provided some outlet, but from experience, a fight would be more effective-- whether he was beaten or whipped the big man. Either way, tomorrow his mood would be better-- even if his body was left bruised. He balanced on his toes, distributing his weight lightly, ready for whatever came at him, bull rush or fists flying.

"Give it to him, Ralph," one of the men suggested with a loud laugh.

"Now the kid gets what he deserved the day of the whipping. It didn't teach him nothin'. He was up the next day. He won't be up tomorrow," crowed another. Obviously the thought their champion could lose never occurred to any of the crowd who had gathered to watch the fight.

"Guess I'm elected to be the one who teaches you some manners." Hall advanced.

"I'm waitin'," Matt said with a wry grin. "If... that is you ever stop talkin'."

Hall lunged. His right fist, aimed at Matt's chin, missed completely as Matt swiftly sidestepped, countering with a solid blow to Hall's stomach. He was not encouraged when his fist seemed to bounce off muscle. Matt grunted as he dodged another flying fist, only to be knocked backward a step by the third.

Still grinning, Matt stepped into the fists, landing blow after blow to Hall's chin and midsection, but taking a battering of his own in the process.

The stocky man smashed a hard slam to Matt's face and tried to follow up with one to his stomach, but he found his efforts blocked as he was hit again and again, staggering backward under the onslaught of swift jolts.

Matt absorbed blows to his abdomen, while landing his own against Hall's chin, then his stomach again. Beginning to heave for breath, he heard the big man wheezing. Hall stumbled, shaking his head to clear it. Both were bleeding now from abrasions and cuts, Hall's nose sprayed blood as Matt's fist again landed hard.

Matt heard the crowd around him screaming for his blood, urging Hall onto new mayhem. It was something Hall was slower and slower in delivering. Matt kept his fists up, delivering blows where he could, but concentrating now on protecting himself. He wasn't out to hurt Hall, only to end the fight with the bigger man on the ground and himself still standing.

After what seemed forever, but in reality could have been only moments, Matt landed a hard left that sent Hall to his knees and then flat out, unable to rise.

Swallowing hard, trying to catch his breath, Matt kept his fists up. There were others in this crowd eager to try to finish what Hall had started, especially with a man obviously worn down.

A wiry farmer stepped forward, his belligerence obvious in the way he held his fists, in the angry line of his mouth, but before he could say anything, before a new blow could be landed, Adam's voice cut through the din, "It's all over, boys!" He stepped into the circle, pushing aside onlookers until he stood between Matt and his new opponent.

Matt felt a surge of relief. Even if he'd been able to knock this man to the ground, he would have been replaced by another. The crowd reluctantly began dispersing, still angrily muttering to themselves as two of them helped Ralph Hall to his feet and then to his wagon.

When they were alone, Matt met Adam's level gaze.

"I know who ended it, but who started it?" the scout asked as Matt wiped the blood from his mouth.

Matt thought a moment. He could have avoided it. It had felt good even while the jolts were being landed against his body. In some way, he'd needed the violence, and he didn't know how to admit that to this man who was the one Amy preferred over him.

"It was a case of what you might call common dislike," Matt said, then added, "but I could've walked away."

Adam shook his head, looking away and then back with what appeared an attempt to suppress a smile. "You fond of getting beat up? Hall had you by fifty pounds if not more."

"Not overly bright," Matt admitted as they walked back to St. Louis' wagon. He felt the beginning of stiffness that, from experience, he knew would be worse tomorrow.

"And you thought a fight would help?"

"Some," Matt admitted with a rueful smile, examining a bloodied knuckle.

"It won't make you more popular."

"No," Matt agreed, trying to act sheepish but still feeling the rush of adrenaline that had given him a sense of satisfaction for the first time in what seemed weeks.

"What would've happened if I hadn't come along?" Adam asked as they reached their own campfire with St. Louis and Clem sitting around it.

"I'd of got beat into the ground," Matt admitted.

"You knew that?"

"I'm no fool. I might've even taken the next one, but I wasn't goin' to take them all."

Clem looked up at him. "What'd ya do now?" he asked sourly.

"A difference of opinion," Matt said, wincing as St. Louis, who had been repairing a harness, rose and came over to them, examining his face for scrapes. He went for his salve, pushing him to sit as he examined and then put some on a cut over his eye.

"With Ralph Hall," Adam added.

"Ralph Hall!" Clem whistled with amazement. "A fight and

you get there in time to break it up then?" he asked, eyes bright with interest.

"I got there in time but chose not to break it up."

"Why not?" St. Louis asked.

"It was a fair fight."

"This boy oughta have his face beat in if he had a set-to with Hall, not be walkin'."

"Possibly but it's not how it was," Adam said with a smile.

"You sayin' he beat Ralph Hall in a fair fight?" Clem repeated the question to himself as no one answered him.

St. Louis sighed, apparently deciding there was no serious damage done to Matt's face. "Next time, I don't want there to be a fight."

"I'll try," Matt agreed. Having gotten this one out of his system, he felt less inclined to there being a next. "But I won't run from one." He met St. Louis' gaze.

"Might be the smart thing."

"Maybe." Matt didn't disagree. As he walked off, in the background, he could still hear Clem asking Adam. "Ralph Hall? You shore it was Ralph Hall and not the Mrs.?"

CHAPTER 8

The large wagon lumbered in front of Amy. Although the sun was barely risen in the sky, dust already hung heavy on the air. Amy turned to Loraine to comment on the prospect of another horribly hot day, when her heart skipped a beat. Matt was riding down the line of wagons, heading toward her. It had been so long since they'd talked, since she'd even seen him. She was torn between wanting to push stray ends of her hair back into the bun at the back of her neck, think of something to say that would heal the breach, or an urge to cut him with a caustic comment, which would let him see how foolish he'd been, how much he'd hurt her.

She had no chance to do either. Hat brim tipped low, shielding his eyes, his broad shoulders set, she caught only a glimpse of grim lips before he was past. Cold and remote, he was as removed from her as though by a thousand miles rather than mere feet. With narrowed eyes, she watched as he kicked his mount lightly in the side and headed across the plains, away from the wagons.

She gritted her teeth. Cutting comments leaped into her mind, but none seemed sufficiently barbed.

"What are you thinking?" Loraine asked, interrupting her inner stream of vitriol.

"Nothing. Why?"

"You looked ready to kill someone. What's wrong?" Loraine's voice reflected genuine concern, but Amy was in no mood to discuss her thoughts with anyone not even a sympathetic sister.

"I'm just hot," she said, lifting the bodice of her dress away from her breasts. "It's going to be a scorching day, Raine. I can feel it."

"I'm sure you're right, but there isn't much we can do about it."

"Look," Amy snapped, "you asked what I was thinking."

Loraine whipped her head around to look at her, her own gaze considering. "You are spoiling for an argument. Is it with me... or someone else?"

Amy stared off to the horizon. She could no longer see Matt, only a faint trail of dust remained, marking the way he'd gone. Where was he going? She felt tears in her eyes, but she didn't want Loraine to know that either. She shook her head. "I'm being testy. Don't pay any attention to me."

"You know, whenever you want to talk about it, I'm here."

"You always have been." Amy wanted only that it be night where she could lie in her cot and cry, with no one to witness her weakness. She didn't want to think about the reason that seeing Matt brought about an ache in her stomach and a yearning in her heart. Why did her whole body come to life whenever she caught sight of him? The repercussions of what she was slowly beginning to realize seemed dangerous-- threatening her happiness, her plans, her whole concept of herself.

She tried to force her mind away from the uncomfortable conclusion to which she was being forced, but it was useless. Delaying facing reality was gaining her nothing except to tear her apart.

With a sigh, she surrendered to the truth. She wanted Matthew Kane. Wanting him would ruin all the plans she had thought she had, but she wanted him in a way she would never want Adam Stone or any other man. With her acknowledgement came a kind of relief. She didn't know what she would do about it, but she at last knew what she wanted.

~

Nearly a mile from the trail, in low, brushy hills, Adam waited for Matt, his leg crooked over the pommel of his saddle, his black hat resting on his knee. As Matt reached him, Adam said, "You're late."

"Palmers needed my help. One of the wheels on their wagon was rubbing. I had to pull them out of line and then took a few minutes to find the problem." He reached for his canteen, taking a swig of the tepid water to give him a moment to clear his head.

To see Adam so soon after Amy only served to irritate the thorn already thrust into his flesh. Much as he enjoyed his time out on the prairies with the scout, the feelings were tainted by jealousy. He'd seen Amy and Adam together too many times to deceive himself as to what was happening. Time and again he'd had the misfortune to come around a bend only to see the two of them walking, her dark head coming barely to Adam's shoulder, laughter carrying back on the air. Adam Stone was friendly enough, had stood between him and a beating, but how could Matt like the man who held Amy in his arms at night?

Interrupting his thoughts, Adam said, "Let's get to it." He dropped his leg down around his mount and kicked it into a fast trot.

With feel of his gelding between his thighs, the creak of saddle leather, the smell of the sage and grasses, the power of the wind in his face, Matt felt his internal strain drop away. He'd never known the kind of freedom or satisfaction he felt riding free, hard, and sometimes fast across the plains.

Adam stopped now and then, taking a good natured, big brother approach to teaching Matt about the things around them, for what to watch, to expect. There was the knack to choosing a campsite for their large party. It had to be analyzed for water, forage and enough level space. There were ways of determining whether others were ahead of them on the trail, and if so, how far. Were they friend or foe? How many? Little things like a bent blade of grass told Adam something. Which direction was it bent? Whether it was broken or leaning.

Adam put up a hand, stopping Matt. He leaned forward and pointed at the dusty surface of the ground broken by tracks. "Deer."

"Good sized bunch." Matt kept his voice low.

"See those split hearts, maybe two, three inches long, no dirt back of the track, bent grass. What's that tell us?"

Matt smiled. "Neat deer?"

Adam chuckled. "White tails. Not too far ahead either. How about us getting some fresh meat?" Since they'd been living on dried meat, there was little doubt as to Matt's response. They pulled their rifles from their scabbards. Matt checked to be sure his had a shell in the chamber.

"You any good with that Sharps?" Adam asked.

"When the motivation is right."

"Most likely they'll all be does," Adam said in an undertone. "The bucks aren't usually with the herd this time of year."

They rode cautiously, watching the horizon keenly, eyes sweeping the brush beside the trail. The smell of sage was strong in the draws through which they rode. "Wind coming into our faces," Adam murmured, "ought to keep our scent from getting to them. We ride a little ahead, stop, then ride again. If they do hear us, it'll keep them off guard, make them think we're just other grazing animals. You go straight after them, and it spooks them."

As they topped a ridge, Matt saw the herd, feeding on shrubs at the mouth of a draw. Five in the bunch, the animals had yet to see the two hunters a hundred feet and a little above them. Matt brought his rifle up to his shoulder, easing it into position as he kept a light rein on his horse. This would have to be a shot from horseback if they were to get the skittish deer, which now began to look around, their ears erect. He wondered how his gelding would respond to the shot going off so near its head.

One of the does heard something and pricked her ears. The others reacted, their tails raised in warning. In an instant, they were off, bounding across the rough ground, heading slightly away and to the left of where the men sat their horses, waiting for a clear shot. "You take the first one," Adam hissed.

Matt sighted in on the large doe. Aiming to the front of her shoulder, he squeezed the trigger, watching as the beautiful animal staggered, lurched, then fell. Almost at the same instant, Adam fired, and another deer somersaulted to the ground.

Riding over, as they reloaded their rifles, they saw both animals had been killed with clean shots. They dismounted, blooded out and gutted the animals.

"I'll go back to the wagons," Adam said, "and bring out a pack animal. You stay here and keep the scavengers from enjoying our luck."

Alone on the plains, only the wind for company, Matt savored the peace. He took the canteen from his saddle and drank deeply. Untying his scarf, he wiped the sweat from his brow. Gutting the deer had not been easy work. It never was. Matt had never been fond of that part of hunting, but it was an essential skill. A man who couldn't shoot or hunt was a man who couldn't provide for his family. Growing up in the hills, he'd done his share and then some of both jobs. He had taken blood responsibility onto himself as part of the cycle of life.

The day promised to be a hot one. Matt ground-tied his horse and settled himself against a rock to wait. In the distance he watched a hawk swoop and then scale the heights in search of prey. A cooling, breeze picked up as the sun rose in the sky. Already the buzzards had started circling high above. "It's ours," he yelled with a faint smile. "Be patient, and you can have the guts-- later."

He had enjoyed the day. He'd learned again from Adam. Some things, having grown up in the woods and in a family where money was scarce, he'd practically been born knowing; but if it was satisfying to the dark-haired scout to play teacher, it suited Matt to let him do so. There was always more to learn.

As the days passed, opportunities to escape from the wagons disappeared. A sick driver, an ox that had strained its leg, wheels and wagon parts that dried, cracked or broke--always something demanded Matt's hand, preventing him from so much as a night on the prairie by himself. Working side-by-side with a man to repair a wagon wheel made it impossible to ignore the scorn with which he was regarded. Loneliness would definitely have been easier to take. He remembered the lone morning in the canyon as a brief point of light in a pattern of darkness.

With unfriendliness his expected, daily dose of social life, Matt was surprised by the change in Clem's attitude. The old man still found something to pick apart with his work, always telling him a better way to do a job, but he actually smiled at Matt a time or two. He made sure supper was kept hot no matter how long Matt was held up. When Matt came to the campfire, he was quick to offer him coffee. Matt could only attribute the improved treatment to bringing in the game and the fist fight. Clem routinely asked questions about both but didn't seem resentful when Matt chose not to discuss the fight.

Unexpectedly, the hardest times he faced were random taunts from children. Walking past a cluster of boys, throwing sticks into a pail, they turned from that game to another, showering Matt with dirt clods, laughter and taunts. He'd never experienced social acceptance, but he'd never had this kind of ostracism to deal with either. He had been right in what he had told Bernice. To the people, he was a leper, but St. Louis had also been right. People would use him, but refused to be touched by him in any way.

He'd thought he didn't care what others thought, but he'd been wrong. He cared. There was just nothing he could do about it. He'd learned as a small boy that some things you couldn't change. What you can't change, you accept and keep your head high through it.

His work gave purpose to his days, left him tired enough to sleep through the nights, but couldn't keep away the nightmares. Threatening visions, of being attacked, violently wounded, beaten, would wake him with a jolt, covered with sweat, full of fear of an unseen enemy. His other dreams were equally disturbing-- hot, erotic dreams of Amy, where he touched and kissed her all the places he'd could imagine, and she responded with equal passion. He woke from them his body aching with need.

~

Matt watched from his horse as the wagons wound down a gentle, grassy slope to a grove of tall trees-- oaks, cottonwoods, walnuts and sycamore. Lush grass and wildflowers filled the hollow. From the scouting he and Adam had done, he knew a short distance away, a natural spring gushed from a ledge of rock, forming a waterfall and filling a wide basin with cold, sparkling water.

St. Louis had decreed that even though it was only noon they would stop. The springs provided one of the most favorable campsites Adam had said they would find for weeks. A free afternoon would give everyone a break from the monotony of constant travel, a chance to do washings, cook a special meal, repair equipment, or rest.

St. Louis told only Adam and Matt that he was counting on the early stop to soften some of the tension in the air. The fraying of nerves and fist fights had been plaguing more than Matt. There had been some sort of angry confrontation every day. Some of that would settle down as men adjusted to the exigencies of traveling so closely together, but St. Louis said that over the years he'd learned an unexpected break soothed a lot of edginess. "It's like the rain that comes with a thunderstorm," he told Matt. "It eases things considerable."

In the early evening, St. Louis stopped by the Kane wagon. Squatting and watching as Matt worked on repairing a broken strap, he sipped a cup of stout coffee. Matt's fingers worked the awl through the leather, preparing the holes for stitching a replacement piece.

"Reckon ya heard Abe Bennett's goin' to play his fiddle down in the meadow after dark. Young folks fixin' to have a bonfire and a dance from what they tell me."

"I heard."

"You goin'?"

Matt smiled as he looked up. "Suggestin' it might be better if I don't?"

101

"Just the opposite."

"I don't think there's many that'd agree with you."

"I'm sayin' ya oughta go."

"Why?"

"It's the natural thing. You're young, oughta be havin' a good time with other young folks."

"There won't be any down there wanting to see me."

"Maybe one."

He couldn't mean Bernice. "You are not making much sense tonight."

"Folks need to see ya ain't got nothin' to hide. Ya got every right to go down. Might actually ease things."

Matt shook his head. "I don't see how."

"Listen here, if ya keep to yoreself, folks'll get to thinkin' there's somethin' strange about you, somethin' unnatural. If ya come, they see ya for what ya are."

"And what's that, St. Louis?" Matt laughed. "Who knows though. You might be right. The last time I stayed home, I had to take a whipping."

St. Louis chuckled. "See, it's the right thing for ya to do."

"I'm thinking."

"Is it because ya don't want to see Miss Amy?"

Tightening his jaw, Matt said, "She has nothin' to do with it." He lied badly and knew St. Louis saw right through him.

"Ya don't avoid her?"

"What makes you think I do?"

"Maybe the way ya shy away when her name is mentioned like ya just did now."

"You got a tall imagination for a short man."

St. Louis laughed again, sitting back and watching Matt, his expression thoughtful. "Ya know I like Adam. I've come to like him a lot, but where it comes to that little gal, he's blind, or he don't want to see. She don't love him."

"Yeah right. I suppose somebody makes her go walkin' with him!"

"So ya do keep an eye on what she's doin'."

Shrugging his shoulders, Matt took a square of leather, laid it on the ground, and pulled his knife from its sheathe. "Think what you want."

"I usually do. Like in this here case with three stubborn people I see things the rest of ya don't."

"You are doing a lot of daydreaming in your aging years." Matt measured the leather with the breadth of his hand, determining how long a piece he needed to cut for the repair.

"Maybe, but like I told ya before, I read people pretty dang well. I see the way that little gal watches for ya when ya been out scoutin'. She don't watch for Adam thataway. And there's a soft look on her face when she sees ya ride in. It ain't there for Adam. He might like to think it is, but it ain't. My bet though is ya already know what I'm tellin' ya, because I seen ya watchin' for her too. Ya know right where she is without even lookin', just feelin' her, like a cougar would a deer."

Unable to stop St. Louis, Matt felt the muscles in his stomach clench. When St. Louis finally stopped, Matt managed a smile. "Sounds like a fairy story. You got a monster for this yarn you're making up?"

"Most likely one is pride—on all three sides." St. Louis smiled, his expression uncomfortably aware.

"I don't want to talk about this." Matt threw down the piece of leather he had ruined when his hand slipped with the knife. Luckily, it was all he'd sliced.

"One more thing. I seen her when ya was hurtin'. A woman can hide a lot 'ceptin' when them she loves is hurtin'."

"Even if I'd been a stranger, she would've done the same thing. Hell, she's done it for dogs. She was always taking in some stray or feeling sorry for some poor critter. That's her way."

"I'm not talkin' about her nursing ya, Matthew. I'm talking 'bout--" he waited a moment-- "her kissin' ya."

Matt felt as though he'd been kicked in the gut. "What!"

"Ya was lyin' there, not knowin' nothin', but she was kissin' and whisperin' to ya. That weren't pity."

Matt studied the knife in his hand. "She wants me to be her brother."

St. Louis laughed. "Shore she does."

"Why didn't you tell me this before?"

"I didn't figure she'd like me sayin' nothin'. It wasn't really my business. Kind of felt like I'd seen somethin' I wasn't meant to, but now I'm not so sure. I don't need no more tension on this train-- not when it's somethin' can be fixed. There's three of ya mixed up in this. I figure it's you needs a kick in the pants."

"You must've read what you saw wrong. I told her how I felt before we left Missouri. She turned me down flat."

St. Louis smiled, a soft reminiscent look in his eyes. "Ya live a little longer, ya'll learn somethin' about women, Matt. Sometimes they plumb don't know what they want. Other times, takes 'em a spell to figure it out. That's just the way them critters is."

"What makes you such an authority?" Matt scoffed. "Even if you were right," he added, not willing to consider that possibility, "it's too late now."

"Son, when it comes to love, it ain't never too late 'til one of you is dead," St. Louis bristled. "When somethin' special happens between a man and woman, ya grab on, thank God, and don't bother askin' why or how it come to you. Don't no man deserve it when it's a good woman comes to love him, who offers him everything. No siree. No man alive does."

"How is it you know so much about this anyway? You ever been in love?" He saw he answer in St. Louis' eyes.

"What'd ya think? I was always a bearded old man? Think love's only for the young? Shore, I been in love."

"But, it didn't work out." Matt shook his head. Love was transitory and painful at best. The destructive aftermath appeared to be eternal, the closest to hell on earth that Matt could imagine.

"It's too long a story for tonight. But I'll tell ya this much. It worked out. Now you jest think on what I been tellin' ya. You reach out with both fists and grab onto what ya are given. Sometimes a body don't get as long with it as they hope."

Matt smiled. "I tried grabbing. The lady wasn't buying."

"Anything' worth having is, worth fightin' for."

"Too much has happened."

St. Louis shook his head. "Ya are lettin' that pride of yours get in yore way."

"Sometimes it's all a man's got."

"I think ya got somethin' more." He stood up and looked back down at Matt. "Think on what I said, and tonight, well I got a feeling about this. You come on down." With that, he was gone.

As darkness settled over the camp, the music drifted up from the meadow to where Matt sat beside his lonely campfire, pride a cold companion. He could see a large bonfire with people around it and hear the sounds of laughter. He had the slim comfort of knowing he'd been right not to go.

Sitting back and closing his eyes, he imagined Amy waltzing around the circle, in and out of the light of the flames, wrapped in Adam's powerful arms, a smile on her lovely face, her black hair swirling around her like a cloud, her gaze looking up at Adam with love. Matt opened his eyes, trying to erase the images he'd created, wondering if what he was inflicting on himself wasn't worse than the reality he would see if he did go down.

Listening to the faint melodies became too strong a temptation. Just to stand in the darkness at the edge of the gathering, there was no reason to deny the small pleasure of listening to the music. There would be pain at seeing Amy with Adam, but suddenly he knew it would be worth it. Talking about her to St. Louis had made him long to see her, to see those big eyes framed by dark lashes, the way her lips turned up in that secret smile of hers, as though she knew something, something he hadn't even guessed at. Leave it to St. Louis to stir up an ache he'd hoped he'd buried.

Drawn against his commonsense, he found himself walking toward the bonfire, then standing in the shadows. Almost immediately, he saw her. Across the campfire, Amy was a vision of loveliness, her head thrown back, thick black hair falling in a cloud, high cheekbones illuminated by the flickering firelight, her eyes black as midnight. A simple, pink dress clung softly to the rounded curves of high, young breasts, darting in to emphasize a slender waist before the petticoats filled it out to flounce around her as she moved to the music.

Adam wasn't at her side, but there were two young men, standing, talking and laughing. It looked as though they were trying to coax her to dance. Maybe she was waiting for Adam. Whatever words they said, they were making her laugh. It was a mixed blessing for Matt. He smiled, with irritation at himself, as he realized how much he was enjoying watching her in secret. Maybe St. Louis had been right, not about confronting her and facing her repeated rejection, but about relaxing, shaking off some of the tension that had been his daily companion.

Unexpectedly, she looked in his direction, her gaze seeming to peer past the others and into the darkness. She couldn't really see him in the shadows, but it was time to leave. He turned, trying to get past the people who were filtering down from the wagons.

A hand was on his biceps, a soft hand, holding him, pulling him back. Reluctantly he turned, then felt caught by her beautiful, warm eyes.

"How long have you been here?" she asked.

"Just got here," he lied

"Ask me to dance, Matthew," she whispered, the corners of her lips barely turning up in a faint smile. "We haven't danced together in a long time-- too long."

"Not a good idea."

"Why not?" She moved to grasp his forearm just below where his shirt was rolled. Her touch was warm against his flesh, her fingers making him aware of his body and hers in a way he remembered, a way he had tried to forget.

"I gotta leave," he managed. "I'm not welcome here."

"You are by me."

"Don't go telling others that." He forced a smile as though making a joke.

"And you think I care what others think?" She was closer now, her body nearly but not quite touching him, her proximity lighting a fire, threatening to consume his ability to resist whatever she might ask.

"I care, and besides-- what about Adam?" He felt as though he'd run a race, his breath coming short and jerky. He realized she was breathing fast too. He turned away, not waiting to hear her answer, wanting only to get away, when he felt a different grip on his arm, and roughly swinging him around with a violent force.

"Not very polite to the lady!" Matt recognized one of the young men who'd been standing with Amy when he first saw her. He looked past him and saw the other, both with belligerent stances as they blocked his way.

"Is this your business?" Matt drawled, his eyes narrowing.

"We're making it ours," one of the youths retorted, his voice raised.

Matt wanted nothing so much as to be left alone, to get away from other people. St. Louis' words echoed in his head-- 'I don't want no more fights.' Swallowing hard, he tried again to leave, but the taller of the two youths poked his chest, pushing him backward.

"Look, I just want what you do—for me to get out of here," Matt said.

Amy tried to place herself between Matt and the youths. "Please, leave us alone."

Matt took hold of her arm and pushed her behind him just as the first youth swung his fist, colliding with Matt's jaw and knocking him back half a step.

"All right," Matt invited, smiling now, "You want it. I reckon you're going to get it." Both came at him at once. The taller of the two lashed out and found his fist met only air as Matt came in under his guard and landed a solid punch to his stomach, doubling him as he gasped for air and collapsed. The huskier of the two stepped back, but it was too late as Matt's right fist connected with his chin. His left lifted the young man almost literally from the ground to collapse beside his friend.

In the few moments it had taken, a crowd had gathered. A woman's voice snarled, "Disgraceful! You bully, coming in here, picking a fight, ruining our dance."

"Get outa here. Stay away from decent folks. You're nothing but riffraff!" The voice came as though from many rather than one.

"We should've strung him up. Picking on boys thataway."

The words and accusations ran together. Matt'd heard them

all before, too many times, too many ways. Roughly shoving a man from his way, he tried to break through the circle that had formed around him.

St. Louis' voice cut through the confusion. "That's enough! I saw what happened. These so-called boys of yores got what they asked for. Let Matthew be, or answer to me!"

Able to break free, unable and unwilling to face St. Louis or Amy, Matt strode into the darkness, aware it was where he always seemed to be heading. He had no idea where he was going, or what he'd do when he got there—except he needed a place to hole up and lick his wounds.

CHAPTER 9

Beyond the light of the campfires, Matt realized someone had followed. He stopped abruptly and whirled, to hear a decidedly female oomph when Amy ran into his chest. "Whoa, where do you think you're going?" he asked.

"With you."

"Turn around. You are not."

"Wrong."

"God damn it, girl. This is no place for you."

"It is the only place."

He sucked in a breath. His thoughts were scrambled. It was all coming too fast. "It's not safe out here."

"Then why are you here?"

"It's different."

"All right, want to go back and dance?"

"No."

He turned and increased his pace. With barely enough moonlight to find the faint path, he was sure he'd leave her behind. He didn't. When he got to the little pool, he stopped, staring into the dark water and not looking at her, as she came to stand beside him.

"Matt, what happened wasn't your fault."

"I know you're trying to make it better, but you're not helping."

"Because you aren't letting me." She reached out. Her hand brushed his cheek. "Don't shut me out."

"It's not your problem." Unbelievably, he heard her laugh as she moved to stand in front of him. Her fingers went from his cheek to his neck, around the edge of his shirt. Hell, what was she doing? "I know you are trying to be a friend," he said fighting to ignore what her touch was doing to him. She'd kill him is what she'd do, touching him that way and expecting him to stand like stone.

"So I want to be a friend, do I?" she asked as she shifted to both hands now around his neck. "Not long ago, you wanted more than friendship."

He kept his arms stubbornly at his side. He would resist the temptation to put them around her. "I've been wrong a time or two."

"Ah, good you can admit that. I'll remember it for future reference, as I'm sure I'll need it. Except in this case, there's a bit more to it. I've thought about what it was quite a lot these last weeks."

"I admitted you were right. Don't go askin' for more than that." There'd come a time he could congratulate Adam, genuinely wish her happiness with him, but it sure wasn't there yet.

"Thinking about that day in Independence kept me awake for more nights than I'd like to count." Her fingers dropped to begin playing with the top button on his shirt before she slipped it from its hole. "When I've seen you, riding someplace, when I've known you were avoiding me, when I've realized you might never be a part of my life again unless I did something about it, I've thought about it. I've remembered."

"Amy, I'll try to be a friend to you. I know I haven't been fair."

She moved to push the second button through its hole. "Remember that day I saw you with Bernice? You don't need to answer. Well, that day, I got mad at seeing her touching you." She moved her fingers down to the next button, which she also unfastened. God, where was the naïve girl he'd kissed when they began this trip?

"I didn't know why, but then I realized what my problem was. I wanted to be the one touching you--" Before he could protest again, she reached up to put her fingers over his lips. "You weren't wrong at all, Matthew. I was the one wrong that day."

He took hold of her wrist, gently pulling her hand from his mouth, resisting the temptation to kiss each finger. She had been so sure. So positive. She had dreams. They did not include him. He didn't want her out of pity.

She shook her head now smiling more broadly. Her eyes, almost black in the moonlight, had determination written in their depths. "We're not just friends. Well, we are but so much more. I'm only slowly learning all I want from you, Matthew Kane. I need you to teach me the rest."

He swallowed hard, looked away from the beautiful temptation. He tried to get control of his voice. This was changing too fast. Even after what St. Louis had told him, he had been so sure there was no way. "You were sure. You knew what you wanted. I wasn't it."

"I was so wise that day, so very definite, and so wrong." He could hear the smile in her voice. "I didn't know why it was I always wanted to touch you, to play with you, to be near you, to hear your voice. I wasn't a quick learner where it came to this, but I know now."

"Even if I let myself believe you, it's too late," he said trying to get control of all she was making him feel. Things had died in him these last weeks. He didn't want them coming to life, making him feel again, destroying him when they were snatched away. And they would be snatched away.

"Why? What's changed? Have you changed how you feel about me?" Now she was the one with uncertainty in her voice.

It would have been easier to let her think that, but he couldn't lie to her about something that mattered so much. "Not that."

"Then nothing matters except how you and I feel."

"You think that now, but other things do matter. Besides, I know what's goin' on with you now." He hesitated, hating to voice it, but he couldn't accept her this way. "What you feel is pity, for what happened, for how folks see me, and I don't want that-- not from you."

She laughed and enclosed him in an embrace as tight as any he had ever dreamed of giving her. His arms, with a will of their own, traitorously went around her slim body.

"Is this pity?" she asked, as her lips moved against the skin on his chest that she had bared. "I might be new to all this, but I know it's not pity I am feeling. I want something from you." He bent to kiss her hair. The scent of her filled his nostrils.

"I've missed you, missed talking to you, seeing you. I've missed hearing about your day... and do you know something else, Matthew Kane?" She didn't wait for his answer. "I've missed your kisses."

That was it. He lost it. The kiss he meant to be light and barely brushing her lips changed when her mouth opened for him. Her arms tightened around him. Whatever control he had was gone, and he delved his tongue within her warm mouth. Feeling her tentative and then more passionate response, he felt his hands going down her body to her buttocks, as her hands moved down his back.

He exercised a strength he barely knew he had and broke it off, dropping down to sit at the edge of the pool and catch his breath. "I have to be dreaming," he muttered as she knelt beside him.

"We could test it," she purred. She took his hand, turning it so the vulnerable inner wrist was against her lips. Slowly, sensually, she nipped the skin. Her gaze met his, the promise within her dark eyes tender. "If it's real, you should have felt that." She bent and kissed the flesh she had so lightly bitten.

"I felt it, all right," he admitted, knowing he'd felt it all the way to the tips of his toes. His whole body was on alert for what she might do next.

"I don't know," she teased, "maybe to really put this to the test, you should bite me." She offered him her own slim wrist.

"We do much more of this, and I won't be responsible for the result," he retorted as he lightly kissed the offered fingers. She moved to shift onto his lap, wrapping her arms around him. Her tongue darted into his mouth. They fell back onto the grass, entwined in each other's arms as their lips sought again and again for what had long been denied. Her fingers tangled in his hair as she gave of herself, responding to his kiss, initiating her own.

Her passionate response kindled a flame that was demanding more fuel. His hands stroked down her slender back, back to the curve of her buttocks. "Oh, Lord," he groaned, as he awoke to his hard arousal. There was no doubt in Matt's mind, with that small part that could still think, that in another moment there would be no turning back for either of them.

He was not going to take her like that, with no thought for the consequences. He pushed himself away and sat up, feeling as though he needed to gulp air, as though that could put out the fire inside. "Reckon that's about all I can take," he drawled when he had command of his voice.

"Why?" she asked, still lying back on the grass.

"Because, just in case this is not a dream, I don't want to do somethin' we'd both regret tomorrow."

"Maybe we wouldn't be sorry," she suggested, sitting up and coming back into his embrace.

This was all shifting too fast for him. Leave it to Amy for those quicksilver changes. "You will be sorry tomorrow," he said.

"I wouldn't rely on that if I were you," she teased. "This is heady stuff. If I'd known this was what they were talking about in those books, you'd have had to fight me off years ago."

He groaned as she pressed herself against him again, almost, but not quite, taking away his ability to say no to himself and her.

"There is a solution to the problem, you know." Her breath was a whisper against his cheek. "I mean, I have been thinking about this more than you obviously. We could have a trail wedding tomorrow. Mr. Jones can marry us."

"You can't mean that."

"Isn't it what usually happens when two people feel as we do? Don't you want to marry me?" She traced a pattern with one slim finger on his chest as she waited for his answer.

"Amy, this is too new for you to be thinking that way."

"I love you."

"What about all those dreams, the Sandwich Islands, San Francisco?"

"What is this really about, Matt? Is it you who have the doubts about us?" Her eyes, black in the moonlight, demanded an answer.

"It's not about that. I do love you," he said pushing the words out. "I don't remember a time I haven't."

"I was a little girl when we first met," she reminded him with a smile.

"Pretty little thing too-- big eyes, dark hair, always followin' me around."

"You'll notice I'm still doing that," she retorted. "Oh Matt." She tightened her arms around him. "I love you so much. Why can't we just get married-- now?"

"Not long ago you didn't want to be married to anybody."

"I've changed my mind."

"I can tell. Well, it's not possible."

"I know what I want. Don't you?"

His stomach twisted as he thought about having her for his wife, about nights spent with her in his arms, and then another thought came into his mind, a fear he couldn't name, but it sent a shudder through him. It couldn't be. "And whose wagon would we live in? Your folks or mine?" He wouldn't have her anywhere near Morey.

"Oh, you're going to be practical," she complained. Moving to her knees, she was a little above him.

"Somebody's got to be." He fought against the warring impulses in his body that were telling him he was a fool to turn away from this chance with her, even if it was only for the moment.

"It does take the fun out of it." She ran teasing fingers along the opened edge of his shirt

"You're tryin' to tempt me," he drawled knowing it didn't take much.

"I think I'm trying to seduce you," she admitted, "but it doesn't seem to be working like it does in the books."

He laughed at that. "Just how far do those books you read carry it, baby?"

"Well, not too far enough obviously." She smiled.

"So how do you know it's not workin'?" he asked with a rueful grin, aware it was working all too well as he could demonstrate if he put her hands on his groin; but if he did that, this was decided. He'd not have the will to turn it back. "You know, if you'll have me, I want to marry you-- someday."

"That has the ominous ring of a long way off."

He smiled. Now that she knew what she thought she wanted, it had to be immediately. She had never liked waiting for anything, even Christmas. The question he had was would she change her mind if she got it and decide it was not what she wanted after all? That had happened also.

"I still can't believe you'd marry me, but if you mean it, and still feel that way when we get to Oregon, we will be married."

"Matthew," she protested. "I don't like it, but since I can't think of a better plan, I'll agree-- for now." It didn't fool him. She had only qualified her submission to his will while she tried to think of a way to convince him to become husband and wife immediately.

"You haven't been sure of this for very long. Give yourself time to know it's what you want," he argued still finding it hard to believe this was happening.

She laughed. "I've known it all my life; but how I feel now, that I've known for weeks as we've traveled, but I just couldn't find a time to talk to you. You are so busy. There's so little privacy with people around all the time."

He had his doubts about that, but one thing he had no doubts about. "Nobody can be told about this between us. I won't have you gettin' tarred with the same brush that's got me marked. There's a brand on me. The folks here won't be forgetting it, and anybody near me is going to be treated bad."

"People forgive and forget. You know I wouldn't care anyway."

"You're an innocent. You don't know what it'd be like not to have any friends. To have yore own turnin' against you."

"They won't do that."

"It's a chance I'm not lettin' you take." She wouldn't wind him around her little finger on this. It was too important.

115

"Just exactly," she asked, her voice growing cool, "what are you suggesting? That we not be together until we get to Oregon?"

"It's not what I want, but it's how it's got to be."

She was silent a moment. "Maybe we have to compromise. I want to get married right now. You want to wait. All right, we wait. I am sure of my feelings. Maybe you need time to be sure. You say we can't see each other until we get to Oregon. I want us to be together-- if not openly then in secret. You get your way on the first. Mine on the second."

He didn't like that idea at all. "That wouldn't be easy on the train, everybody so close."

"We could manage it."

"By sneakin' around." They moved apart, not touching.

"I can't be apart for months, not like it's been. I can't and won't not see you, and I won't agree to anything that means us being estranged."

"There you go with those words again. Who do you think you're talking to here?" He laughed.

"You know what I meant. Don't you want us to be together?"

"You think I like the way it's been? All I could see was you runnin' around with Adam, which come to think of it--"

"Don't you go harrying off on a wild goose chase, Mr. Kane. We are going to settle the first issue. It wouldn't be sneaking. We'd just be discrete." She smiled innocently at him.

"Whatever that word means," he drawled with amusement, his fingers reaching out to caress her cheek.

She bent her head slightly, trapping those fingers between her cheek and shoulder. "It means," she whispered, bending to kiss his fingers one by one, "that we will be careful where and when we come together that no one sees, but we will have time together." He shook his head, but took her back into his arms.

When she nipped his earlobe, he shuddered. He felt a mix of pleasure and shock at how quickly she had shifted into a lover. For a moment, he wondered if Adam had taught her. He pushed the jealousy aside.

"Don't you like having me in your arms? Don't you need

to see me, touch me, kiss me?" she questioned, running her lips along the edge of his jaw. "Have I ever told you how much I love your face, Matt? You have such strong, defined bones."

She ran her tongue along them. He sucked in a breath but lost the will to fight what she was doing to him. After long, passionate kisses, he again forced his better self to pull back. It took long breaths before he felt in control of himself.

"You know it has to be that way," she whispered in his ear. "We just have to arrange things. You'll see, Matt. It has to be like this, us together. You don't know how it's been for me."

"I don't?"

"If you did, you would know this is the right thing."

"Yes, but--" She kissed him again. When he could finally breathe, he said, "I reckon you know you've won. I never could say no to you about much of anything."

She giggled. "Aren't you rewriting history here just a bit. Didn't I ask-- no, beg a certain man if we couldn't just be friends? Don't leave me alone, I cried. And what did this cold-hearted personage do?"

"I couldn't be around you when you were with somebody else."

"As I admitted, I'm not so fond of the feeling myself. I got a vivid lesson the day I saw that woman clinging to you."

"All I was thinkin' that day was how to get out of there." He decided it was better not to tell her about the episode at the river, to which she would be unlikely to react well—maybe even blame him. "And there you were with Stone, his hands on you-- after the way you'd slapped me."

"Ah yes," she sighed, her lips soft against his cheek. "I did slap this didn't I?"

"I can't say I didn't deserve it."

"Well, you got your revenge when I saw that brazen hussy hanging all over you."

"She wasn't hanging all over me."

"She was. And what was worse, I knew her intentions. She had told Jennie Porter and me about this man she'd seen, a blond, gorgeous, veritable god, whom she intended to meet.

When she went on about this fellow, I never dreamt she meant my gorgeous god!" She finished with a very feminine growl.

He laughed and shook his head. "You didn't think I was so gorgeous then."

"Oh yes, I did. I was angry at you, but I wanted to claw her eyes out. I'd never felt jealousy before then."

"Poor thing," he drawled as he considered what she'd said. "All right, we'll try it your way but just keep anybody from knowin' anything's changed between us."

"So long as we can find times like this, and I know we can. I need you, Matt. You are the last piece of a life puzzle for me. Now I feel… well complete just knowing it's you."

"Baby, you think too much," he teased.

"It's one of your travails that you must put up with."

He laughed again at her choice of words. "Are you that sure Adam isn't the last piece of that puzzle?"

"I admit I thought he might be. He seemed like that story-book hero, but then I found out… my heart had already been taken."

CHAPTER 10

Amy turned from side to side but could not sleep. Giving up, she pulled out her journal, then was in no mood to write. She set it on her knees and stared through the tent flap at the gradually lightening sky. Because she had snuck into her cot after everyone else was asleep, she had evaded the questions she knew awaited her with morning. She didn't want to think about that. She only wanted to savor her memories.

When she had first seen Matt standing in the shadows-- so tall, so alone, his mouth a grim set line-- her driving impulse had been to get to him, to stand at his side. When trouble had exploded, and he had stalked away, she had no choice but to follow.

Perhaps their time apart had not been all bad. Out of that period of loneliness and estrangement had come something solid-- the certainty that what she felt for him was real and enduring, not a flight of fantasy. The passion had always been there, lying dormant, needing only his kisses and words to stir it to life.

Amy thought of her girlish dreams of love, the poems and tales of romance she'd read, and knew this one night of reality with Matt had more than matched any fantasies she might have harbored. Yes, he was her friend. She had been right about that, but he was so much more. She understood now all the times she had playfully wrestled with him, not realizing what her body had been seeking. Shivering, she touched her lips, treasuring the memory of his against hers, his passionate response as he'd held her in his arms, pressed against his body.

It was as though her body had been lying dormant, like a fallow field. Now it was alive with sensations and feelings. Her breath came more quickly remembering how he assaulted her senses, not just with the touch of his lean fingers, but also the male scent of his skin, the texture of his hair, the sensation of hard muscle under silky skin.

Realistically, she understood the difficulties they would face. Matt had complicated things with his desire for secrecy. What could she do about the persistent Adam Stone? Since she'd realized her feelings for Matt were not what she'd thought, she'd discouraged Adam, maneuvering never to be alone with him. Her efforts had been less than effective. How could she discourage Adam without telling him the truth? She felt a twinge of anger with Matt. He was making something complex, which should have been simple.

When she thought over what Matt had said-- and not said, his reluctance to talk about marriage, about a future together, she felt disturbed. Was this a result of his natural protectiveness, which had driven her to distraction in the past, or was it some deeper problem?

Amy remembered a poem by Helen Maria Williams, which she had always liked but never fully understood. It spoke of a woman who loved a man but could never convince him that his love was all she needed. He left her, constantly facing danger, leaving her alone, all to provide her with the material things he thought she wanted--except all she had really wanted was him. Was that man Matt? Was it what she had taken on? Matt was determined to protect her, to give her everything--except the one thing she most wanted, which was to be with him openly, no matter what the cost.

When she awoke at first light, Loraine whispered. "I covered for you last night by lying and saying you had already gone to bed, but Amy, you better think what to tell Mama and Papa this morning. They know you went off when he did."

"I know." She dressed and helped her sister take down and put away the tent. By the cook fire, Belle kneaded dough that would spend the day rising in the wagon while their mother stirred the morning's oatmeal.

"How you folks be?" Mrs. Collins asked, looming out of the dimness and plopping her bony frame onto a small stool.

"We're fine." Amy's mother poured a cup of coffee and handed it to the old woman.

Mrs. Collins blew on the surface. "My rheumatism was somethin' awful last night. What'd you say that stuff was you give me before?"

"It doesn't have a name. It's just something my mother used to make, a mixture of dried wintergreen leaves and yellow dock root."

"It did help. You wouldn't have more of it, would you?"

"You used it up so quickly?" Amy's mother asked frowning now. "You were only supposed to take two or three teaspoons of the infusion before meals. How much did you take?"

The old woman shrugged. "Maybe took a mite more than that."

"I can give you a little more, but I couldn't bring all that many of each herb with me, Agatha, and with the way livestock eats down the land alongside the trail, I haven't found more to gather. I'm afraid that until I get to Oregon and find new supplies, you'll have to husband what you have. Are you watching your diet the way I suggested, drinking lots of water?"

Looking guiltily away, Mrs. Collins grumbled, "I think it most likely was worse last night because I got so upset over that lordly Matthew Kane, having the nerve to go down where the young folks was dancing. Quick as you'd figure, he started a fight. Beat up two fine young fellas." She shook her gray head. "It's disgusting, that's what. I don't see why Mr. Jones don't do something about him!"

Amy, who had poured herself a cup of coffee, started to protest but stopped when she heard her mother. "What would you suggest, Agatha?" There was coldness in her voice that Amy rarely heard.

"Wal, give me a minute to think." Amy saw the old woman hesitate, considering options that would be vile enough. "Kicking him off the train would be none too good for the likes of that one."

"Perhaps then he could starve to death out on the prairie," Amy's mother suggested. "Of course, we wouldn't want to give him any supplies. I mean he has worked for this train, helped one family after another with repairs, driven wagons, worked until he had to be falling into his blankets exhausted, but the proper thing would be to turn him out-- perhaps not even let him take a horse."

"He's been paid to help folks. Although just why Mr. Jones would have been so foolish as to hire one like him is beyond me. We'll never know a moment's peace 'til we get rid of him-- not a moment."

Again Amy was stopped from retorting by her mother's angry snort. "I have a suggestion, Agatha. Of course, we have to find some Indians willing to help us out. Since dying quick would be too easy for Matthew, we need to turn him over to the savages. They could tie him to a stake, torture him and-- if we're fortunate, burn him alive. Now, wouldn't that be just the thing for a useless, no-account man like Matthew Kane!"

Amy gaped at her mother as did Agatha Collins. Although on occasion she had heard her mother raise her voice in anger, it had usually been when she didn't think she was being over-heard. This time, she saw her struggle for control and then give it up.

"Frankly, I've heard all the condemnation of Matthew I want. From what I heard about last night, and I heard about it from Amos who was there, Matthew was not the cause of the trouble. He was attempting to leave the gathering-- which by the way, he had a perfect right to attend-- when hooligans attacked him. According to Amos, he didn't start it, but he did end it-- and quite appropriately." She stabbed her spoon viciously into the oatmeal. "I don't want to hear another word against him-- not while you're at this campfire!"

Mrs. Collins appeared dumfounded. She sat for a moment before she put her cup down with a slam, added a loud harrumph, and was gone.

"Good riddance," Amy heard her mother mutter under her breath. Unfortunately, in the next breath, she remembered the rest of what had transpired. "And now, Amelia, you did follow him, didn't you?"

"Excuse me, but will somebody please explain to me what happened," Loraine interrupted. "I missed the whole thing because of sitting with Eliza."

Amy frowned, remembering her anger and frustration. "Matt did nothing. Brick and his friend attacked him, told him that he didn't belong there, and then, yes, he did defend himself."

Turning to the dish box, Amy's mother brought out the cereal bowls. "It's an unpleasant situation," she said, spooning out the oatmeal, "but I don't want to think you're seeing Matt behind our back. After everything he's been accused of, rightly or wrongly, it would not do your reputation any good to be meeting him clandestinely."

"You know he didn't steal anything," Amy countered, jutting out her chin. "If you didn't, you'd never have defended him to Mrs. Collins." She began halfheartedly nibbling at her cereal.

"That isn't what concerns me about this, Amy, and you know it."

"It's hard enough to listen to others criticize Matt-- without it coming from you."

Amy's father walked into the circle, the mules behind him. "Amy's right about one thing," he said, as he moved the team into position with practiced ease. "Matt's no thief. I tried to convince the others, but it was no use. They didn't know him, and there was no way to prove they were punishing the wrong Kane."

"He has certainly gotten handsome," Loraine said changing the subject. "I mean Matt was always cute as a boy, but have you seen how he looks as a man? All muscle and those broad shoulders." She rolled her eyes expressively. "It's enough to turn any woman's head to see him walking by."

Amy laughed shortly. "Sounds like you're the one with an interest in Matt."

"A woman can appreciate male beauty without wanting to own it." Loraine grinned.

"Both of you girls, get your heads on straight," their mother ordered. "Honestly, I can't believe such talk from my own daughters. I thought I raised you to be ladies. Such foolishness." She began vigorously scrubbing the pan, keeping her head down, but she was unsuccessful in hiding her smile.

Amy watched her mother glance over toward her father where he was stretching to move the mules into their traces, the muscles in his arms bulging with his effort. Amy saw their gazes meet, the blush on her mother's cheeks, and her father's slow smile of amusement. Amy finished up the last of her cereal certain of one thing-- her parents at least would understand when the time came to explain her feelings for Matt.

As she and Loraine trudged alongside the wagon, Amy knew her chances of seeing Matt during the day were slim. Even though she'd gotten good at guessing his schedule, St. Louis had proven to be a hard man to second-guess. There were so many last minute chores.

Loraine interrupted her speculations. "So why did you come in so late?"

"You were awake?"

"Of course. You didn't want to talk, and it wasn't a safe place anyway."

Amy looked at her and then behind them, deciding Belle was at a safe distance. She didn't want to lie to Loraine. Besides which, she had a desperate need to talk to someone. "I was with Matt."

"Did you two have another fight?"

"No." Amy smiled, looking into the distance at the softly undulating hills, gradually lightening from a soft lavender into their true colors of ochre and brown.

"I knew it," Loraine crowed. "This morning, you had a radiance that glowed. It seemed there could be only one reason. You've made peace, haven't you?"

"More than that."

"More than that?"

"Please don't tell anyone, but we will be married."

"I thought you didn't ever want to marry."

"I didn't until I realized it would be different to be Matt's wife." She gave what she knew was a sheepish smile. "Anyway, for now we have to all keep it secret as he believes the people would turn on me as they do him if they knew."

"Sad as it might seem. He's likely right."

"It's so frustrating. I want to tell everyone. I love him. I've always loved him." Her voice softened, her breath quickened, as she thought again of his kisses, the feeling of his muscular arms around her, the glow of love in his gray eyes.

"You don't have to convince me. I always thought you and Matt belonged together, but I really don't see how you're going to keep this from Mama and Papa. You change all over just at saying his name."

"I'll have to be careful not to be around him when others are near because you're right. With him close, it'd be impossible not to show everything I'm feeling. I suppose that's why Matt thought we shouldn't see each other at all until we got to Oregon."

"Just like a man-- too practical."

"I convinced him of the error of his thinking—at least I think I did. Actually... now that you know, you could help us."

"I don't think I'm going to like this."

"I wouldn't ask you to do anything that would get you into trouble."

"Oh yes, you would. Are you sure you know what you're doing?"

"Of course not. I'm crazy in love."

"I am happy for you. A little jealous, too."

"Don't get ideas," Amy teased. "He's mine and that's that! You just about made me jealous when you started talking about how wonderful looking he is-- that is if I hadn't known how you felt about someone else."

"I said that to stop Mama from asking so many questions," Loraine said. "Not that it wasn't true."

"I appreciated it too. Thank you."

"There are other complications, which will be harder."

"You mean Adam?"

"He's head over heels for you."

Amy shook her head. "Actually, I don't think so." She grinned at Loraine's look of disbelief. "I don't think Adam is that much interested in me. It's more the pursuit. He's a hunter and goes after something once he starts, but loving me… well I don't think so."

"How can you say that?"

"It's easy. He doesn't show any passion. I might not have known it wasn't there, if I hadn't seen how it is with Matt. There is no way Adam could convince me he was in love with me. Something is missing."

"I don't see how you can say that," Loraine retorted. "It looks like everything's there to me and in pretty perfect order."

"I'll tell you what I think," Amy said with a laugh, "the more I haven't wanted Adam Stone, the more convinced he has become that I am the only one." She tugged on the bodice of her dress, lifting it away from her skin to catch what little breeze there was. The sweat ran down between her breasts making her wish women could wear different clothing, something lighter, less constricting. Thank goodness her mother wasn't one of those who thought a corset was a necessary undergarment.

Loraine wiped her own forehead with an already stained handkerchief. "It's not going to be easy."

"I've tried to discourage him."

"He isn't a man who discourages easily."

"We'll have to put our heads together on this."

"Don't think you can use me! I might help you see Matt, but I am not going to stand between you and Adam. He already acts as though I'm as pushy as Bernice."

"Bernice McDowell has been chasing Adam?"

"And every other man on the train."

"That witch," Amy muttered. It was all too easy to remember her sidling up to Matt. The buxom hussy!

Loraine laughed at Amy's glare. "I think Matt will be quite content with you and not even look at another woman."

Amy laughed. "He better be. I understand now why Matt said he wouldn't be around me if I was seeing another man. I can't stand other women around him. It kills me," she finished with a melodramatic flourish of her arms.

"Hardly," Loraine snorted, "more likely in a case like that, you'd kill her, him-- or both."

Standing between boxes and cots in the cramped covered wagon, a pail of tepid water beside her, Amy slipped out of her dress. Washing her hair was out of the question, but she brushed the dust from it as best she could before she twisted it back onto her head.

She tried to shake the dust from her dress. From experience, it was a fruitless effort. Fortunately the dress was already brown. It certainly wouldn't be clean again until they came to a river, deep enough to do laundry, and where there wasn't so much dust in the air that wet clothing was recoated before it could dry.

Dipping a washrag into the clean water, Amy lightly rubbed it over a bar of lavender-scented, homemade soap, and scrubbed her face, shoulders and arms, using as little water as possible. She and Loraine took turns as to who got first use of the water. The practice tended to encourage conservation.

The wagon was hot with the accumulated heat of the day, but with only a thin chemise and light petticoat, Amy's skin soon felt cool. From a trunk, she pulled a neatly folded white blouse and dark blue skirt. The skirt was cut more narrowly than was generally popular. When they had planned the trip their mother had decreed the wide skirts, so in favor, were impractical. She had shortened most of their skirts to barely ankle length to keep them from brushing the ground and narrowed their widths to avoid having them blown into a fire or sucked into a turning wagon wheel.

Then it was her turn to wait outside while Loraine took her turn in the wagon. "Hurry up," she urged her sister.

"Excuse me," Loraine muttered, barely loud enough for Amy to hear. "You took your time."

"I did not. If we don't hurry, Adam'll be here before we can get away," Amy hissed.

When Loraine descended from the wagon, Belle pulled on her sleeve. "I'll come with you. Where are you going?"

"No," Loraine said.

"Why not?"

"Because."

"You never let me go."

"We might-- if you didn't whine," Amy muttered.

"Mama, make them let me go!"

"No," her mother said, "you stay and help me. Your sisters need time to themselves. You'll understand when you get older."

"I won't because I won't get older! Just when I think I am, everybody moves ahead again," Belle protested but to no avail.

Walking into the darkness, Loraine whispered, "I feel like a conspirator. Plots and ploys. It's like a novel or something." She patted her hair. "Do I look all right?"

"You look beautiful," Amy assured her. Loraine had braided her thick brownish red hair into a coronet on top of her head, accenting her high cheekbones and long neck.

"We can't look obvious." Amy smiled thoughtfully. "So, let's stop at the Porter wagon first. I haven't visited Jenny in almost a week."

When they entered her camp, Jenny looked up from diapering Eliza. "You two look as fresh as daisies." She sighed and tucked a lock of sweaty hair behind her ear. "Pretty as pictures."

"Thank you," Loraine said as they knelt on the ground. Jenny fastened the last pin and sat Eliza on the ground with a few homemade toys beside her.

"She's been a handful today." Jenny stood up. "I put some rose hip tea on a bit ago. Would you like some?"

When they nodded, Jenny poured them each a cup. She shook her head looking at her daughter who'd begun to fuss a little. "She's been like this all day. I think she's cutting a tooth."

"When we were teething, Mama said she gave us a teaspoon

of cod liver oil every morning," Amy volunteered, still unable to say the words without wrinkling her nose. Her mother had applied that particular remedy for several things.

"What on earth for?"

"She said it strengthened babies, especially during teething when they might be vulnerable to diseases or such. I thought it was pure sadism," Amy said with a laugh.

"Where's Mr. Porter?" Loraine asked, sipping her tea.

"Off somewhere... I have no idea." Jennie sighed again. "He might be playing cards. He gets impatient when Eliza whimpers."

Eliza began an odd, hitching movement that moved her along the ground at a fair pace. Jennie jumped to retrieve her before she got hold of a thorny bush.

"It appears to be a constant job, taking care of a little one." Amy felt a new interest in babies and their care. "How do you manage?"

"I told you before-- I don't. I just barely get things done. Tonight we had a cold supper. William was not pleased."

"Maybe he could help fix the meal," Loraine suggested.

"Oh my, he'd never do that." Jennie's mouth dropped. "That's woman's work."

"If a man's hungry," Amy retorted, "it's his work too. You've got a baby to take care of. It wouldn't hurt him to help. Washing out her diapers, keeping her clean and fed, why that's a full time job all by itself."

"If I was just more able, I'd get everything done," Jennie lamented. "I'm always doing things wrong."

"Jennie, if you keep thinking that way about yourself, everybody else will too. Remember what we talked about before-- think about the good things you do."

"I try, but it's hard."

"Maybe, but it's the only way you're going to have people think well of you," Loraine added.

. . .

When the sisters were away from the wagon, Loraine told Amy, "It depresses me every time we stop to talk to her. How could a woman make such a mistake on the man she married?"

"She said she got pushed into it."

"I'm not going to let that happen to me. Either I'll find a man who wants me and who I want, or I'll never get married."

Amy nodded with understanding. "I can't think of anything worse than to be married to somebody who treated me the way William does Jenny." She stopped.

Loraine had gone on two paces before she realized Amy was not beside her. She turned and looked back. "What's the matter?"

Amy frowned. "You don't suppose Jenny brings on some of it herself, do you? I like her a lot, but I have to wonder if she likes to be abused, or maybe it's that she thinks people will like her better when they feel sorry for her. Think about it for a minute. We suggest things, we try to help, Mama tries to help, but none of it makes any difference. Every time we go to see Jenny she's saying the same things."

"You think she's a victim because she wants to be?"

"She sounds a lot like a younger Mrs. Collins. Maybe... I mean she might not realize what she's doing. I was thinking of some things she said about her parents. Maybe it's the way she was always treated, and it comforts her in some way."

"You could be right, but then what could we do to help?"

Amy laughed at her. "You're as impossible as I am. Maybe this is one time where we're not helping by helping. Know what I mean?"

"I doubt it."

"If Jenny is feeding off our sympathy, we don't help her by giving it. I'm not sure how you help somebody like her. When Jenny figures out she doesn't want to be mistreated, maybe she'll do something about it."

"So we don't even try to tell her?"

"Frankly, I think she'd see it as one more abuse."

Amy saw that Matt was only aware of them when his father looked up and smiled. Morey's look of surprise quickly turned to what she could only interpret as a leer. Insolently, he raked both women up and down. The sly smile only left his face when Matt rose and began to move toward him. Morey shrugged, smiling again before he strolled off.

"Hello," Amy said to Nathan Kane as she and Loraine came to stand across the small fire.

She knew Matt wanted to look at her, to take a warning glare as a reason to leave. She smiled at his father and ignored Matt's obvious displeasure.

"How's yore family been?" Nathan Kane slurred, as he gestured they should sit on the box he had earlier occupied.

"Everyone is fine," Loraine volunteered, settling her skirts around her as Amy joined her. "We were out for a little evening stroll, and I said-- we haven't seen the Kanes in ever so long. Why don't we stop-- Well, here we are."

Amy dared a glance Matt. He was watching her. That was good. He was scowling. That was not good. She smiled and saw his scowl deepen.

Nathan Kane squatted on the ground, sipping from a coffee cup but offered them nothing. "Good you folks ain't sick. I heard the Clayton wagon had sick children." He shook his head. "Hard thing takin' women and children on a trip like this... Don't figger I'd a ever had the courage."

"I imagine some people thought it was now or never. In a few years all the free land will be gone," Loraine suggested.

"Reckon that's it." Nathan took another swig from his cup. "How's yore ma takin' to the travel? Right good lookin' woman, Martha is. Got to be hard on a woman like her, bringin' three young gals into the wilderness--" His voice dropped off. He seemed carried away at the sadness of families traveling west and facing privations or dangers.

Nathan Kane's comment about their mother's beauty caught Amy off guard. Had he known their mother before? Had he perhaps even courted her? The thought was impossible.

"She didn't really want to come," Loraine admitted. "She came for Papa."

"If my Laura had lived, I'd a never took her. But then-- maybe a lot of things'd have been different... if Laura'd lived." He drained his cup.

Amy half-listened, watching Matt from under her lashes. He was slicing through a piece of leather strap, his sleeves rolled to above the elbows. A thin, light tan shirt allowed her to see the play of his muscles across shoulder and back as he bent to his task. His tension showed with the beat of the muscle in his lean, clean-shaven jaw. He had his hair tied back with the usual leather strap. She wanted it loose, wanted to run her fingers through it. To watch him as he worked, to know that he was hers, was tantalizing. She felt a tight, excited feeling in the pit of her stomach, an ache to feel those muscular arms around her.

Loraine touched her arm, the expression in her eyes clearly saying she'd had all she could stand of Nathan Kane.

"Well, Mr. Kane," Amy said, trying to give Matt what she hoped was an expectant look, "we do have to go. Maybe we'll see you later."

In the darkness beyond the wagon, she sent Loraine on a few feet ahead and waited, hopeful Matt would come to her.

A moment later, he was beside her. "You are not going to do what I say?" His disapproving tone lost any effectiveness as he pulled her into his arms.

"Well, you see, Raine--" Her words were lost as his mouth came down hard and decisively on hers. When she could, she murmured, "She guessed about you and me. I couldn't lie to her. Then, it came to me she could help, and I could come to you because--" Again he silenced her with a kiss that effectively made her forget what she had been about to say.

"Why would she do that?" he asked when he lifted his head.

"For two reasons. One, she thinks you and I are right for each other-- with which I totally agree-- and two, she is interested in Adam." She reached up and caressed his lean cheek. "She is not displeased I am not."

"Adam?"

"In case you haven't been paying attention, for last week or two, everywhere Adam and I went" she said, watching his face and seeing the muscle in his jaw tense. "Raine came."

"All I ever saw was you with him," Matt admitted with a twist to his expressive mouth. "Since that wasn't anything I wanted to see, I turned away as quick as I could."

"You thought I wanted to be with him." She traced his jaw line with her fingertip. "Just as I thought you wanted to be with Bernice."

"Who?" he asked smiling down at her.

"That's what Raine said." Amy snuggled against his broad chest. "See how helpful she can be. She felt his low laugh vibrating through his chest.

"So, if you ever get around to making an honest woman of me, you'll also get a supreme sister in the bargain."

"You are an honest woman," he retorted, dropping his arms to his side as he stepped back.

"I'm not. I'm a woman desperately in love, who wants to be with her man openly-- not just in the darkness."

"It'll come." He pulled her back in his arms. Something about the way he said it made her wonder if he believed it.

CHAPTER 11

When Amy finally rejoined Loraine, her knew her face was rosy, her lips swollen from the passion of Matt's kisses. "Hmmm," Loraine said speculatively, a finger thoughtfully stroking her chin, "I think perhaps we'd best walk this off before we go back to Mama and Papa."

Amy laughed. "Any particular direction?"

"I don't think it matters, so long as it's good and dark by the time we get back. If Mama got a look at you now, you'd never be able to explain your way out of it."

Ahead, Amy saw Adam walking toward them. "Uh oh," she muttered under her breath.

Loraine smiled faintly as Adam stopped in front of them. "I'm a lucky man," he said with a grin. "Two beautiful ladies out for a walk. May I join you?"

"Of course," Amy said, trying to sound friendly. "We were on our way back to our wagon though."

"Then that's where I'll walk you. What have you been up to?"

Amy looked at his face, trying to decide how well he could see hers in the moonlight.

"We spent a little time with Jenny tonight," Loraine said. "You wouldn't know where William Porter spends his time, would you?"

"Why?" Adam asked with what Amy had come to realize was typical male aversion to discussing other men who might have a woman unhappy with them. Loraine was so smart.

"Ah," Loraine said, "the gentlemen's club closes ranks yet again."

Adam smiled dryly. "What does that mean?"

"Just that men tend to protect one another, even when they don't deserve it," Amy said.

"I'm not protecting William Porter. I was just trying to think," Adam countered. "I barely know the man." His tone said he was satisfied to keep it that way. "He could be gambling down by the livestock corral. There has been a bunch down there almost every night."

"Do they gamble for money?" Loraine asked disapproval in her voice.

"I imagine so. I don't join them."

"Ah, we're at our tent," Amy said. "I think you've just been saved by the bell, Mr. Stone."

Adam didn't hide his relief. "I'll take a save anyway I can get it. Good-night ladies."

When he was gone, Amy complimented Loraine. "That was a great diversionary tactic."

Loraine lifted the tent flap. "I really wanted to know," she whispered as they entered the tent, trying not to wake Belle.

"You're still thinking of saving Jenny," Amy accused as they began undressing.

"Not really, but don't you wonder what her husband does when he leaves her every night?"

"And if you knew, what could you do about it?"

"I guess nothing. He not only looks like but acts like a rat," Loraine said, folding her dress neatly. "A beautiful wife and a wonderful baby, and he's never there. Don't you think it's strange?"

"Even so, we can't do anything about it," Amy reminded her, quickly pulling on her nightgown. The night air was surprisingly chilly.

"Marriage can be beautiful, but it can be ugly," Loraine said. "You sure you're ready for it?"

"Yesterday," Amy replied instantly.

"It won't be easy. You do realize that Matt's a complex man."

She more and more did understand that. "I love him. I don't have any choice about the rest of it."

"You think that's how Jenny felt once?" Loraine asked, pulling back her bedding and slipping under the blankets.

"She said she never loved William," Amy said, snuggling down into her cot.

Loraine shook her head. "I don't know why I'm shocked. Very few women have the luxury of marrying for love."

"They should. I can't imagine being married, letting a man-- well you know--if you didn't love him."

"Are you sure you've thought about all it means, I mean marriage and all."

"You're not going to tell me about the birds and the bees, are you?" Amy asked, amused.

Loraine gave a little laugh. "I'm sure Mama already took care of that. No, I was thinking more about all the things you said you wanted. You were going to travel, be a woman of the world, write poems and stories. What happened to all that?"

"Some of that I still want, but I guess nobody gets every-thing. When you love a man, there's nothing else to say. You have to take the whole package."

∼

The quiet of night, stars overhead and only the dying embers of a campfire to keep him company, Matt paced uneasily. He wanted to sleep, knew he needed sleep, but his thoughts wouldn't let him rest. He was flooded with sensual thoughts of Amy, almost immediately accompanied by a painful arousal.

In a thousand ways his body reminded him of her. Her ivory skin had been silk under his finger tips, the scent of her ebony hair filled his nostrils, his chest felt her full, young breasts as though even now they were pressed against him. His lips still felt the pressure of her full lips. A twinge of pain in his shoulder reminded him of fingernails digging into his skin. He wanted

Amy so much the yearning was an ache inside, an ache that would not go down any sooner than his erection. What he needed was a swim in a cold stream. He wouldn't be getting that any more than the other way the ache could be eased.

Kneeling beside the dying campfire, he fed it a few small sticks, stoking its flame back into existence, giving life to the embers. The night air was growing cool, and he began to shake with what he at first believed was cold, then realized was something more. Fear chilled him.

He was clumsy with words, had a quick temper, a family who destroyed instead of built. How can he trust himself to be with a woman like her? He wasn't worthy of her. Condemning voices seemed to come as though from all sides, their cries ones he'd heard before. "You ain't worth nothing!" "No one has ever loved you! You don't deserve to be loved!" "You kill what loves you."

He shrugged out of his shirt and boots and lay on his blanket, too tired to think with any clarity. Staring into the darkness, he sought to put the fear from him.

As a child, he thought he had conquered the mind-numbing grip of fear, learned to put himself beyond its power. He almost laughed, as he suddenly knew why it had seemed easy. He'd had nothing to lose. Not that he hadn't been aware of his own mortality, but what had that meant? Life had held no particular value.

Now he had something, a dream that could be taken away through the actions of others or his own stupidity. What did he know about nursing into life the tender bud of love? He had no experience with male/female relationships, no understanding of love, not much faith of its reality except where it came to his feelings for her.

He thought about taking what she was so clearly offering and letting the devil count the cost. Except it would not be the devil who would. It would be Amy, and the love she offered so innocently. What if a child was conceived on the trail? Who would pay then?

There was another possibility, one he didn't want to believe, but couldn't afford to ignore, that he wouldn't survive to see

Oregon. He wasn't a superstitious man, but a shadowy sense of foreboding had dogged him most of his life. If something did happen to him, Amy must be free to find another love, not in any way be damaged because she'd loved him.

There was an even bigger reason not take her. He had a dream, one he'd carried with him for longer than he could remember, of how it would be when he truly made her his. When Amy lay before him naked, open to his touch and love, he didn't want her afraid or ashamed. Everything had to be perfect. She deserved more than a hurried taking behind a wagon, a quick slaking of his hunger. When he took her, he wanted the world to know he had the right to do so.

Restless, he stood and walked barefoot to the now dead campfire. He took the stick and knelt, poking at the remains, realizing there was no way to rekindle it this time. He pulled on his boots, threw his shirt over his shoulders and decided a walk would work off whatever was eating at him.

At St. Louis's campfire, he saw the older man sitting cross-legged by a barely burning campfire.

"Don't you ever sleep?" Matt drawled.

"No more'n you. What ya doin' up?"

"I get restless sometimes."

The older man studied him. "Ya look like ya had the weight of the world on yore shoulders."

Matt didn't answer but knew his jaw was tight with tension, every muscle in his body taut. St. Louis was too astute at reading people to be fooled. The older man picked up a small stick and began drawing circles on the dirt in front of him. "Earlier tonight, seen Amy, Loraine and Adam."

"Does this have a point?" Matt interrupted.

"I'm gettin' to it. Ya got to give an old man time to tell things his way."

"I might just be getting sleepy."

"You might, but you ain't. Here's my point. I'd hate to see Adam gettin' hurt. He's a good man."

Matt shook his head. He was uncertain how much St. Louis knew and how much he was guessing. "Seems to me," he said after a moment, "that the future's got no guarantees for any man."

"We shiftin' the meat of this here conversation into some phil-o-soph-ical direction?"

"Forget I said anything," Matt retorted, knowing it was too late. St. Louis and his thoughty discussions were like a creek in flood-- no way to turn either. He wished he hadn't come.

"I ain't had much luck talkin' about philo-sophy anyway."

That was too much. "You talk it more than any man I know. You're always going off on some bent or other."

"Wal, if I do, I reckon, this is as good a time as any for it. I'll give ya a little piece of wisdom I picked up along the way." When Matt opened his mouth to cut him off, St. Louis ignored him. "I expect ya'll end up havin' to learn it the hard way too, but old men like me, we always want to tell younguns what we know. Even knowin' they ain't never goin' to pay no mind." He chuckled. "When it comes to loving, man got to take whatever it is the good Lord gives him, not back away from it because he's scared."

Matt almost choked. Had this man been reading his mind? He tried to pierce the darkness, to see beneath St. Louis' hat brim. How could he know about his fears?

"Ya know, Matt, every man's got a destiny. Fate, fortune-- whatever ya want to call it. It's what a man's given to do, the people he's goin' to love, the roads he's goin' to take."

"I don't see where you're goin' with this." Matt shifted restlessly, wishing he had a polite way to shut the older man up.

"Ya got to slow down some, boy. Young folks, no patience atall. Give a man a little time to finish what he's sayin'. Now, where was I?" St. Louis hesitated, but not long enough for Matt to put in another objection. "Oh yeah, I was talkin' about destiny, how there's one out there for every human. It's up to us to figure out what, and claim ours."

"Not so easy."

"It is if ya quit makin' it hard. When I first seen ya on this train, I knew ya was someone I could count on. How'd I know that?"

"No clue."

"I just did.

"And this relates to fate."

The older man chuckled again. "Ya are makin' this more complicated than it needs to be. Ya know, if it wasn't for figurin' there's more to life than the bitty, skeeter irritatin' day-to-day things, knowin' there's a bigger picture, why, life wouldn't be worth livin'. It's that fightin' for what's yores, claimin' it, that's what it's all about. There's a lot a man never shares with nobody-- things that lay deep inside. Like I never told ya about my own family." St. Louis pushed back his hat brim, his gaze meeting Matt's.

"I didn't know you had one."

"I have one but now it's only in my head. I was trapping up in the mountains, the Big Horns. Lots of different tribes was there, a few other trappers. We was all sharin' the same ground, but we got along. None of us takin' more than our share.

"Collectin' pelts one day, my horse got scared by a rattler near underfoot. I wasn't expectin' it and ended up flat out. Hurt. Alone out there, stove-up, I figured I was done for. But the Lakota, who could've as easy killed me. found me and took me in, nursed me like a babe. One mornin', feelin' a mite better, I managed to get down to the creek, set there on the bank, the sun warmin' my bones. Their women and little ones come down to wash. They was all gigglin', laughin', enjoyin' the mornin'. One of the women looked over at me.

"Maybe I'd seen her afore, but it's the first time I really saw her. The sun was shinin' on her hair, hair black as a raven's wing. She was a tiny thing, strong though in every way, and, Lord, she was beautiful. Mornin' Sun's what her name'd mean in English, and she was like the mornin' sun, innocent, pure and full of joy. By the end of that winter, I had married her. Even got myself adopted into the tribe."

He was silent a moment. "Reckon I'll never know or love anything the way I did that woman."

Matt frowned, thought about not asking because he knew things always went wrong, but finally he couldn't resist. "What happened?

"We were together five winters. Some kind of fever swept

through the village. None of the usual herbs or treatments helped. She and our boy both died. Ya ain't so much older than my son would've been today. He was a smart boy, and I was almighty proud of him. When I lost 'em both, I didn't want to live myself for awhile."

"I understand that, but what I don't understand is how you can turn around and say a man should take a chance, not be afraid."

"I won't say it wasn't hard, but her and me had good years. Livin' with the Injuns that way, there ain't no better life, close to nature, doing what is needed and no more, loving her, having a son. Bright Arrow was what we named him although he'd have took his own name when he got to be a man. In the right time, they do it through a vision quest."

"I'm sorry for your loss." It was, however, no more than he'd come to expect.

"She's still in my heart, Matt; so don't say you're sorry for it. Life don't always end like we want, but I tell you this for a reason. What I had, it was mine for a time. Then life went on. It wasn't for me to see the reasons then, nor now. I look back and think how much I learned through lovin' that woman, through our time together. I'll tell ya something, lovin' her brought me more joy than pain."

Matt didn't try to answer that one, not sure if he any longer had a choice, maybe hadn't since the time as a boy when he had first laid eyes on Amy.

"Life's full of trade-offs, son." St. Louis leaned forward. "Ya get the bitter with the sweet. Without one, ya ain't gonna appreciate the other."

"I've said something like that myself," Matt said knowing he'd had considerably less to lose when he'd said it.

"There's lots of regrets in livin', but the biggest one is not livin'. Ya get to be an old man-- ya want to know ya reached out with both fists for the destiny that was yours."

"If a man knows what the right thing to do is."

"I think ya know," St. Louis said with a smile.

. . .

At dawn Matt was up, trying to get the fire started and coffee boiling when Morey wandered into camp. "Saw ya with her," he said slyly, a sardonic twist to his lips.

"What do you mean?" Matt straightened, clenching his fists to resist the temptation to pound Morey into the dust.

"I know the game the two of ya are playin'." Morey laughed. "She comes in here pretending what she come for but it ain't. She come for you."

"What--"

"Never mind. You can pretend too. Pretend I never said nothing."

Matt felt a fist clutch his stomach. "And that's how it better be—that you say nothing more. I don't want to hear her name on your lips."

"Kind of sensitive, ain't ya?"

"Whatever you touch is dirty, Morey. Because you're my brother, I've taken off you what I'd take off no other livin' man, but no more." Matt's voice was low, his eyes narrowed. For Morey, of all people, to have seen him with Amy was like a cold rain, drenching him with its potential for disaster.

Morey looked at him with mingled dislike and fear. "Right now, that suits me, too. If I change my mind, I'll let ya know."

"You won't change your mind." Matt turned his back on his brother and headed down to the livestock corral. He worked to think through the situation with calmness. Morey thinking he knew something only had value if he kept it a secret. He wouldn't give up even that much attempt at domination. For different reasons, he had as much reason to remain silent as Matt did.

Two days passed before Matt was able to find a way to warn Amy about his brother. He had seen a swale, just below the livestock corral, within shouting distance of camp but out of view. With a passing word, he told her he'd be there after supper-- if she could get away.

Because of treating a split hoof on one of the mules, Matt found himself late in getting away from his chores. His mood was not improved by the bite he had received from the stubborn animal. He worried first that Amy would not have been able to wait, then that she had come but Morey had followed her. Before he could think up a new, disastrous scenario, he rounded the swale, and she was in his arms.

His lips against her temple, the perfume of her hair in his nostrils, he murmured, "Lord, I missed you."

"Me too," she sighed. "Every day I don't see you seems like it lasts forever."

"I shouldn't have let you come out here." He felt selfish, but he'd needed to talk to her, even more to hold her. "We're getting close to the Platte River. St. Louis said we might be seeing' buffalo... and where there's buffalo, there might be Sioux."

She pulled back to study his face. She touched his unshaven jaw. Her fingers lingered caressingly, before she pulled his head down to reach his lips with hers.

The moment her lips came against his, Matt felt his control slip. He pulled her more tightly against him as he ran his hands over her body. His tongue probed into her mouth's warmth.

From somewhere, he found the strength to pull back, wondering how much longer he could keep doing it. Swallowing hard, he had to work to remind himself of the need to warn her about Morey without telling her everything.

"Did you have a hard day," she asked before he found the words.

"No more than usual." He smiled, remembering the angry mule.

"You were late."

"Sadie's fault."

"Sadie?" she questioned, her tone cooling slightly.

"Yup, but when she bit me, I figured it was time to get out of there." He lifted his wrist and showed her the reddened marks where the skin had been almost broken.

"Sadie's got a big mouth," she observed, her fingers lightly caressing his wrist as she studied the angry marks.

"Yeah, she's got a kick you wouldn't believe."

"Sadie, huh? Have I met her?" She was smiling now.

"Not if you're lucky. It's Farrington's mule, nastiest disposition I ever saw."

"Why'd she bite you?"

"Likely if somebody took a knife to your foot, you'd bite too."

"Likely," she admitted, laughing. She nestled down into his arms.

"Baby, I need you to watch out for my brother. He saw us together. I don't trust him. You shouldn't either."

"He hates you so much, Matt. Why is that?"

"I don't know. Why'd Cain hate Abel?"

She shuddered, "Don't use that comparison. Cain killed Abel."

Matt gave a short laugh. "I don't think he'd take it that far." Mainly because then his fun would be over. "I just want you to be careful, watch out for him."

"I will."

He drew her back into his arms, and they sat their backs against the side of the embankment, their arms around each other. Overhead the sky darkened slowly as the sun slipped further behind the horizon.

"I remember one time," she mused, "when you came to school with your head hurt and bleeding." She reached up, lightly caressing his temple, a scar no longer visible except in memory. "You didn't say much, but later I heard him bragging about it to his friends, I guess trying to impress them—not that he had many friends."

Matt tightened his arm around her. "I'd half forgotten that. It seemed that rock came from out of nowhere. I was half stunned. I remember looking up, trying to figure out what had happened; then I heard him laugh."

"He was gleeful he'd hurt you," she whispered, remembering the horror she'd felt that day. "He went on about how it knocked you down. I gagged when I heard him laughing. I couldn't understand joy in hurting someone."

He held her lightly, stroking her neck, knowing she would never understand someone like Morey, grateful she wouldn't.

"Morey doesn't come at you in a way you can use your

strength," she went on after a moment. "It's like with the rock--from out of nowhere. Like with the theft. He must have done that because he wanted to see you in pain." She shuddered. "I'm afraid for you."

"I will be careful," he whispered against her neck, "but I want you to watch out, too. Might be he'd think he could hurt me worse through you." His thoughts darkened with the knowledge Morey would be right.

"I wish... I wish there was no one else in the whole world but you and me."

He laughed with the unexpected suddenness of her remark. It was so Amy. "Not very practical."

"Practical or not, we could love each other with no one to care what we did or how long we were together." He brushed her thick hair aside to kiss the nape of her neck. She arched her back, yielding herself to him. "I don't want to be practical," she whispered.

"Got to be some."

"Does that mean we'll have only one romantic in our family?" she asked teasingly, gazing up at him.

"I don't know about this romance stuff." He kissed her, finishing with a nibble on her earlobe. "Don't go looking for me to write poems for you."

"I'm not doing so well with my poems about you. I can't seem to get beyond. I love you. I love you. I love you."

"Now I could write that kind."

"Can you paint word pictures for me? Tell me what it'll be like when we can finally really be together."

"My dreams, you mean?" he asked, thinking he'd have a hard time getting beyond the censored parts.

"Yes. Tell me about when we get married."

He felt a chill, a fear he couldn't define, but he fought off the feeling. Before he could think of an answer, Amy went on, her voice soft and melodic. "I want us to think past these days, past all the things that stand between us to when we are married. I want a picture in my head to make the lonely days and the nights easier, for the times when we can't be together."

"About that life together, I got a few worries here. Maybe we oughta talk about them. I remember you talking about traveling, seeing the world." He settled her into the crook of his arm. "How are you going to take to living on a homestead, not seeing all those glamorous places? You want us to not stay in Oregon?"

"Books will always open those places to me whether I go there. I think I had that dream because I didn't have a real one. I do now. I want to be with you more than anything else in this life. I know I can't do everything. Wherever you are, it'll be enough."

"What about you writing, being another Helen Williams or whoever the hell that woman was who wrote poetry, traveled and gave talks?"

"I can still write. Nothing will stop that. I've been keeping a journal about this trip," Amy said, stroking his arm with a fingertip. "I won't give up writing. Maybe I'll even get published someday, but knowing what love is, how a woman feels about a man, someday having your children. Those things will make me a better writer."

"I don't want you giving up anything because of me. I like that you can do those things."

"But I will give up things and willingly. So will you. That's the way love is," Amy said, moving her hand along the slope of his shoulder, then running it down his chest, mesmerized by the hard muscles beneath the rough cloth. "There might be times I'll regret it more than now." She smiled. "Now I love you so much, it's hard to remember I ever wanted anything else."

Matt said nothing, his eyes closed, his body caught up with the feather-light touch of her hands as they explored his chest.

"Tell me about how things'll be in Oregon," she whispered dreamily.

Matt swallowed and tried to remember his own dream. It was becoming lost in a sensual haze. He cleared his throat. "I got a little money, not much, but it'll get us a start. Not fancy though." He pushed her away, studying her dark eyes as another reality intruded. "We'll file on the land when we get there. Married, we get over 600 acres. We have to work it and then the time will come it'll be ours. First thing we do there will be to build a cabin. I am good at that-- except, the home you had in

Missouri was a fancy place. Were you hoping for one like that in Oregon?" He worked to keep his tone deliberately light, as though her answer didn't matter.

"Any home with you will be wonderful," she whispered. She slid back into his arms, her lips next to his, her breath mingling with his. "If it was just you and me, a tent would be enough."

"It wouldn't, Amy. You don't know what it's like to not have enough-- even for eating."

"You're not helping," she protested. "I want a picture to keep with me, hold near my heart, of a future to look forward to, not dread. I don't want a list of don'ts, but of dos." She slapped his chest lightly. "Close your eyes, Matthew." She smiled as he gave up and obeyed. "All right now the cabin will be over to the west, just one room with a loft, at first. The barn with one milk cow and some chickens is over to the north. South of the house, just above the creek is a garden. Do you see it?

"There'll be flowers mixed in with the vegetables and healing herbs like Mama always has." She ran her fingers over his lips. "Eventually we'll plant fruit trees a little further up the slope and-- well, who knows what else we'll plant." She stopped.

He laughed, as always reading her thoughts with too much accuracy. "I expect we'll think of somethin'-- to plant," he whispered, his lips brushing hers, lightly, teasingly, then with full possession in a kiss that lingered.

"You do want children, don't you, Matthew?" she asked when she could.

His mother had died in childbirth, his birth. Would he lose Amy the same way? Would that be his punishment for having killed his mother? Another fear, more deeply seeded, refused to come to where he could grasp it. It lingered in the shadows. He was not facing something fully, but whatever it was, he couldn't look at it-- not yet.

Delaying the need to find an answer, he nuzzled the soft curve between her neck and shoulder. "Why is it," he murmured, kissing the soft skin, "you always smell so sweet?"

She laughed. "I was just thinking the same thing about you."

He looked up at her in surprise, thinking she was teasing him. He knew what he must smell like. There'd been no time to wash so much as his hands, and he'd spent the day working with animals, greasing wheels, eating dust and riding a horse for eight hours.

"I meant what I said. You smell like hard work and outdoors, like a man ought to smell."

Slowly they walked back, the darkness now cloaking them from interested eyes. Avoiding the small clusters of people, Matt saw her nearly to her own wagon. He stood in the darkness until she was safely with her family.

CHAPTER 12

M att reclined, propped on one elbow at the edge of a circle of half a dozen young men, not a part of their camaraderie but unwilling to be driven away by their unfriendliness. The light of the campfire flickered over their bodies and faces. They talked and laughed, exchanging jokes as they waited for the stories St. Louis had in endless supply-- stories of the trail, of a time they would never see when only trappers ranged across this land.

"Gonna see buffalo soon," St. Louis said. "Ever see one, Matt?"

"Nope," Matt said laconically.

"Figures he wouldn't have seen one," came a snide voice from Brick Webb, the young man Matt had fought at the dance.

"Ya say somethin', Brick?" St. Louis asked, giving him the quelling look that only he could give.

"No-- nothing."

"That's about what I thought. Anyway what was I sayin'? Oh yeah, about the buffalo. They's a sight to see. When they get to runnin', ya can feel the ground quaking for miles on either side, sounds a little like thunder. It's enough to scare any man out of the sense he was born with. Assumin' he had some." He gave Brick a humorous look. "All ya can see is a huge cloud of dust and once in awhile, a buff's body."

"I'd like to see that," Brick said.

"Might be ya will," St. Louis said with a grin. "Might be ya won't like it so much if ya do. Wagon train in the way of a herd like that, it's nothing. When they start runnin', they can go for days. Who knows why, what got 'em started. Maybe it's for the sheer joy of runnin' in a mob, but anythin' in their way gets flattened. Ya ain't never seen power or known what freedom really is 'til ya see a herd runnin' like that."

"What's the Platte River like?" asked a bespectacled man Matt recognized as William Porter. "I have heard it's full of silt."

St. Louis nodded. "Shallow and wide-- some say a foot deep and half a mile wide. Lot of quicksand along it, suck up a man and his horse if he gets careless."

"Think we'll have trouble with Indians when we get there?" Brick asked.

"Never a good idea to go lookin' for trouble when ya don't have to," St. Louis said with a smile, "but never a good idea to under figure the tribes neither. The usual thing is they don't bother ya if ya don't bother them. The real danger's likely just to be the thievin'-- horses, stock we don't keep up tight to the wagons. It's not smart for a body to go wanderin' away from the wagons neither."

"Then you think we might have trouble?" Porter asked anxiously. "You know, I have a wife and baby to worry about."

Matt recognized that speculative look on St. Louis' face. "Nope. Didn't say that. It's just ya never know."

"How often do they attack wagon trains?" Brick asked, his voice cracking.

St. Louis smile showed patience at hearing the same questions repeated time after time. "I only heard of it a few times, mostly on the trails to the south. The man says he can predict the Lakota, Cheyenne, Crow, or Arapaho-- well, that man's a fool. This is a big train though and unlikely to be a target. Injuns ain't stupid."

Adam entered into the circle, poured himself a cup of stout coffee, and squatted beside Matt. "This is their land," he said, "even though they may not have settled it the way we do.

Indians don't believe anybody can own land. To them it is sacred, a gift from god, for all men to use, none to take."

"Doesn't make much sense," Brick said.

Adam smiled. "It did to them for a long time. About now though, that Indian, you're wondering about, he's got to be looking at us, seeing all we're bringing with us, and starting to realize we don't see it the same way. We look to be a greedy people, taking more than we can use. If somebody did that to you, what would you do?"

"Sounds like you're an Injun lover," growled the Carter boy.

"I wouldn't use the word love, but respecter. They have rights, or ought to, just like we do. We're trying to take away what they regard as theirs."

"I can understand that," Matt said, "I'd fight for what was mine too." He looked pointedly at Adam as he said the words.

"You'd fight for just about any reason," snapped Brick. He frowned when the only reaction he got was a smirk.

"Don't go lookin' for trouble," St. Louis interjected smoothly. "Injuns ain't likely to cause us anymore than a notice on this trail. Most of the time they only want to trade a little. Ya want to go worryin', ya can worry about cholera."

"That the way a lot die on the trail?" Porter asked.

"It takes a man quick." St. Louis' eyes reflected the seriousness of his words. "I seen men get up in the morning, lookin' to be just fine. By lunch they got the stomach cramps, by night they're dead." The men listening grimaced, but St. Louis went on as though unaware of their reaction. "Hits some trains hard. Others never get touched by it. Never know why or what causes it."

"They have no idea?" William Porter sat more stiffly if possible.

"If somebody does, it ain't me," St. Louis replied.

"Weak people, maybe?" Brick asked.

"I seen it take a strong man as quick as a weak. Tears a man's guts right out."

Matt listened, saying nothing. Cholera occasionally struck where he had grown up, but no one knew much about it. Even seeing a doctor was little help. No doctors on this trail anyway.

The talk of illness effectively put an end to the evening. Matt thought it a little humorous that the young men didn't mind hearing about buffalo, dangerous rivers or Indians, but a disease, which tore a man insides out, was more than they could bear.

With Matt and Adam left beside the fire, St. Louis shook his head with disgust. "Never can figure some men."

"What do you mean?" Adam asked, swigging the last of his coffee.

"That Porter. He's got him a tiny baby and pretty little wife, but he always is runnin' off somewheres, not takin' care of 'em at all. Don't know what the blazes he's doing either. Makes me think about punchin' him good a time or two," St. Louis said with a faint grin, "knock some sense into that pup."

"I ain't seen where beatin' does much good," Matt drawled.

Adam rose and stretched. "Not that the conversation here isn't stimulating and uplifting, but I think I'll take a walk and see if I can't find somewhere the company is prettier. See you two later."

"I don't understand ya, boy," he said to Matt after Adam had gone.

"About what?" Matt asked, his mind not really on what St. Louis was saying, but filled with disturbing images of Amy and Adam together.

"Why don't ya go on over there with Adam?"

"I wouldn't be welcome."

"They are good folks. Why wouldn't you be?"

"Let's see," Matt began, bitterness underlying his words as he began counting on his fingers. "A thief, ruffian, poor, no education, scum and worse for kin. I mean what more could folks ask for?"

"Yore kin are ain't who ya are."

"Maybe not," Matt said, "but they come with the deal. I should have left 'em in Missouri. That was my mistake, and I'm going to pay for it." He rose and paced over to the edge of the camp.

"Ya did what ya thought was right, didn't ya?"

"It seemed a possibility at the time. Stupid now."

"Yore people ain't who you are. Are you ashamed of that?"

"I've been more favored in my time."

"That waren't no answer."

"No, it wasn't." Matt sat back down, thinking a moment, before he asked abruptly, "Have you got a brother, St. Louis?"

"I got three, all younger."

"Get along with them?"

"When I see 'em. They're more settled than me, but when we was growin' up, we got along."

Matt swallowed, looking away. He'd never said much about his brother to any man. He had not wanted to try and explain what he himself didn't understand, but tonight... with the darkness, like a warm blanket, the small campfire flickering between them, he wanted to talk about Morey. Except where to start? The situation had so many twists and turns.

"With me and Morey, it's--" He stopped and started again. "He's different. Strange in the way he thinks, know what I mean?" He knew St. Louis couldn't, and he doubted his own ability to put into words the truth about the history he and his brother shared. "Littler like I was, I was one he could pick on." That didn't express the sickness in Morey, but Matt wasn't ready to go further. "I reckon I was almost eleven before I finally got enough size to stand up to him."

"Where was yore pa with all this?"

"More'n likely drunk," Matt muttered.

St. Louis pondered a moment; then said, "You're tellin' me Morey likes to hit you around?" Matt nodded but didn't add among other things. St. Louis stared into the fire. "Is that why he set you up for the thefts?"

Matt nodded. "By the time I saw what he'd done, it was too late. He isn't bigger anymore, but I reckon he is some smarter-- at least that time."

"Maybe if you'd tried to explain, that time, maybe we could've stopped him gettin' away with it. Ya can't fight every battle by yoreself, Matt."

"How could I have proved it? It was my bag. I wasn't about to beg," Matt said quietly. "I don't expect you to understand, and maybe it's wrong, but it's damn hard to let go of pride when it's all you've got."

St. Louis shook his head. "Might've been true at one time. Now, it's not all ya have." He rose then and walked to the wagon, coming back with a belt, holster and revolver. "I been forgettin' to give these to you."

Matt rose. "A gun?"

"I know you got the Sharps, but I want you to have this too when we cross the Sioux lands. Wear it when you ride out."

"I can't take this."

"It's part of your job. You dang well can—and will." St. Louis winked.

Needing a place of solitude, Matt left the circle of wagons. Used to moving in the darkness, he found his way easily across the dark, grassy plains. Although he didn't expect trouble, he brought his guns. St. Louis' dry warning about strays was fresh in his memory, but he had a powerful need to remove himself from people-- friend or foe. He wasn't sure the gun belted to his waist made him feel any more secure. He wasn't sure he wanted to be secure.

Finding a small rise, he sat, staring blankly at the land, which seemed to stretch forever with no hills or mountains to break its reign. With a bright moon overhead, the earth was lit with an eerie sense of unreality. In the distance he heard a night hawk as it swooped out of the sky, screaming into the darkness. Prey lost or found?

Peace had been hard to find since he had joined the wagon train. His days were filled with noise--voices, livestock, wagons creaking, chaos, needs. St. Louis had said there'd be precious little privacy. It had proven true.

He needed the vast loneliness around him, the big sky overhead, thousands of stars and the round perfection of the moon. It put his problems in perspective. He could hear nothing from the wagon train. Here it was peaceful, the only interruption a coyote on a distant hill. From farther west, another answered. Their barks and yodels dwindled away when further off yet he heard a wolf. The lone wolf's song stilled all around it.

Was St. Louis right? Should he let everyone know what Amy

meant to him, what he meant to her? Except, wouldn't that allow her to be crucified, dragged down to his level? In his heart, he was sure the path he'd chosen was right, but could he trust his judgment? He was used to only having to think about himself. What would that be like for her?

His thoughts drifted to Morey. Was it possible to change a pattern that had been established so many years before? He didn't want to kill or be killed, but sensed he and his brother were drifting inexorably toward some kind of violent ending. It was another place he had no answer.

When he left the darkness and headed back into the camp, he had no more idea as to what he should do, but he felt a sense of inner peace that he could handle it when the time came.

A day's travel found the wagons settling into their first camp along the Platte River. Looking at it, Matt saw it to be as strange and murky a river as he'd been told. All day they'd traveled with a violent thunderstorm. First had been the darkening sky, then lightning striking on all sides of the column, forcing women and children to ride in the wagons. Canvas covers were no protection as the bolts slashed down-- multiple prongs slamming into the earth and leaving behind burnt sage or blackened earth-- visible reminders of nature's arbitrary and deadly force. When the wind rose, St. Louis ordered a halt. Rain came then in torrents, driving into the wagons and tents, leaving no one safe from its fury nor dry in its aftermath.

Matt struggled against the full force of the storm as he helped one after another of the settlers secure their gear, batten down canvas tops, and settle the livestock, the wind constantly threatening to turn him from his path. At the end of the day, he was soaked to the skin beneath his thin jacket and looking with increased interest at the long coats some men wore.

By the next morning, though the sky drizzled, the wagons proceeded onward, hopeful that afternoon would not bring another storm of such furor. Noon found them pulling into a circle outside Fort Kearney at one end of Grand Island.

Walking toward the fort, hopeful he could purchase a coat

better able to protect him from the rainstorms, Matt saw what they called a fort was an odd collection of sod and adobe buildings-- a store, blacksmith, and a small military headquarters, without many soldiers apparently on duty. No walls or impressive gates surrounded the motley collection of buildings.

Although he had no interest in sending mail, having left no one behind in Missouri, Matt heard others excitedly discussing the possibility they would receive news from home or would be able to let loved ones know they'd reached this point. Some talked of needing to resupply. One man joked he wanted to just be under a roof again after so many weeks of having only canvas as a cover.

Ahead of where he walked, Matt saw Amy, Loraine and Adam. He dawdled to avoid meeting them. He was hungry for the sight of her, had a need to touch and hold her, and doubted his ability to keep the longing from his eyes.

Unfortunately his lingering allowed Bernice to come from seemingly nowhere and attach herself to him. "I'm so glad you waited for me," she said, batting her large eyes and taking a firm grip on his bicep, a grip, he knew from experience, would not be easily broken. "I was afraid I'd have to go to that old fort by myself. Who knows what those soldiers might do to a lone woman. They've been out here, away from women for years maybe. Somebody said there were Indians hanging around the fort. I'm glad I'll have a strong man to protect me."

Matt hadn't forgotten the incident at the river, and Bernice's thinly veiled threats. He also knew Amy was jealous of her. He had tried to explain he'd done nothing to encourage Bernice, but Amy had argued he hadn't done enough to discourage her.

As Bernice chattered on about the dangers for a single woman alone, Matt smiled. "Don't reckon the soldiers would be a problem," he drawled, all too aware of who would be if she went to the fort by herself.

"Oh, but you just never know, and you are so strong." She moved her fingers along his arm, caressing his bicep as she gripped it now with both hands. "You could so easily protect me. Your muscles are so big."

Matt's eyes narrowed. Here he was again, attached to her,

and worse, he looked up and saw Amy, Loraine and Adam had turned around and were walking toward them. He clenched his jaw.

"Well," Adam remarked as the five of them stood in a stiff circle, "here we are."

"Yep." Matt glanced toward Amy and saw the anger building like a thundercloud, starting with frown lines between her brows, flashing dark eyes, and ending with tightly held lips and a stubbornly tilted chin. She can't be thinkin' I want this. He glanced at her again. She does think I want this!

"You all been to the fort already?" he drawled, knowing they couldn't possibly have made it there and back in the little time that had elapsed since he had slowed to avoid them.

"We were on our way," Adam replied, "when Amy took sick." He protectively patted her shoulder.

"Yes," Amy said, her words dripping with venom. "I looked around, and suddenly felt faint!"

Matt allowed his eyes to meet hers and was not surprised to see the anger directed toward him. Polite or no, he knew as Amy's gaze dropped pointedly to Bernice's grip on his bicep, he had to get the blonde detached. He moved a little to one side, but Bernice followed. Giving up for the moment, he thought of a new ploy. "Anything worthwhile over there?"

"Since we never got there, I wouldn't know," Adam said. "Used to be a pretty fair sized store. Hard to say how well it'll be stocked today."

Considering his unappealing options, Matt mentally kissed off purchasing a long coat and prayed no one would read anything into what he was about to say. "Bernice was wanting to see the fort but was afraid to go alone. How about if she goes along with you two? I'll see Amy gets back to her wagon where she can rest."

Bernice smiled up at him, her grip on his arm not lessening. "I thought you wanted to see the fort too."

"Nah, just wanted something to do. I'd be glad to see you go on with Adam." That was an understatement. He firmly peeled her fingers from his arm, giving her an encouraging nudge toward Adam and Loraine.

"Matthew," Loraine said with a smile, "that sounds like a wonderful idea. You just make sure Amy gets back to the wagon and lies down out of the sun. Adam won't mind showing Bernice and me the fort. Will you, Adam?" She smiled brightly from Bernice to Adam, neither of whom showed pleasure at the change in plans.

"I hate to ruin everyone's fun," Amy said through gritted teeth, "but I would appreciate that. I really am not feeling well."

Even at the foot and a half distance she kept between them, Matt could feel Amy's anger. At first, he thought she was so mad that she wouldn't talk to him, which all and all might be best, but after a moment, she hissed, "What were you doing with her?"

"I wasn't with her," he pointed out.

"Wasn't with her! That's funny! I saw you with her. She had a hold on you a buffalo couldn't have broken. I turn my back, and there you are again-- with her!" Her voice rose with her agitation.

"Baby, listen to what I'm sayin' here. I was not with her. She came up behind me before I even saw her. The only reason she caught up with me was because I was trying to avoid you." As soon as the words were out of his mouth, he knew he could have phrased that better.

"Oh! And that's supposed to make it all right," she sputtered, "because... you were trying to avoid me, while totally innocent you were attacked."

He nodded. "Exaggerated some, but basically right."

Walking, while arguing and pretending they didn't know each other, was impossible, even though Matt was reasonably confident anyone passing would only hear isolated snatches of their conversation. When Brick passed them, besides his normally belligerent expression, he had a questioning look. Wagon trains made for boring stretches of time, and a search for interesting gossip was often the only amusement. Matt began to count the moments until he could deliver Amy safely to her wagon.

"I don't want to go back," Amy snapped, shocking him from his train of thought. "We are going to go where we can't be overheard, because right now I want to yell at you!" She turned abruptly to the left and began walking rapidly toward a rise west of the fort.

Clenching his teeth in frustration, he glanced first toward the wagons and then in the direction Amy was striding. He didn't want to go with her, but he couldn't let her go by herself.

Following quickly, his long, angry stride rapidly overtook hers. "This is no way to keep folks from finding out about us"

"Frankly, right now, my dear, I could not care less," she snapped. "Is the real reason you wanted it to be a secret so you could carry on with her?"

"You cannot think that!" He felt his own temper rising.

"Then what were you doing with that woman?"

"Like I said, when she's around, I am not with her."

"A fine distinction," she retorted, a sneer across her wide mouth, the likes of which he'd never seen-- not even when she'd slapped him.

Out of sight of the fort or the other people, Matt looked around uneasily. Here, along the river among the bushes and tall grasses, they would be unseen by their own people, but he had no idea what kind of human predators might be hanging around a fort like Kearney. He wished he'd brought the revolver St. Louis had just given him, on what had started out to be a simple outing to buy a coat.

"Look," he said modulating his voice, trying to be patient and keep his own anger from showing. "What I'm saying is I don't go around looking for her or if I did, it'd be to avoid her."

"You must do something to encourage her."

"I don't have to do anything. Just being polite is too much."

"Then stop being polite. I do not want to turn around again and see her hanging all over you. She was... simpering up at you, holding onto your arm like it was a piece of candy. You won't let me do that in public. Why do you let her?"

"Blast it, baby. I don't let her. I can't get shut of her."

"You'd better figure out how." Amy put her hands on her hips, rising a little in height to give emphasis to her words. "If I see her do it again, I'm going to start tearing that blonde hair out by the roots, and there won't be any way you will be able to pretend you don't know why."

"Hers or mine?" he teased seeing by her not quite hidden smile that this storm was passing.

"Maybe both."

"Is that a threat or a promise?" Thinking, of her attacking him, put a sensual twist to his lips.

"Both."

"Poor Bernice," he said, reaching out and pulling Amy into his arms. "No sympathy for her at all?"

"None." She pushed him away. "I mean it, Matthew. If you don't want a cat fight on your hands, you better keep her hands off your body."

He pulled her back against him, feeling the soft curves of her breasts and hips as they pressed against his own hard length. "And," he whispered, his lips next to hers, "whose hands are supposed to be on my body?" She pushed against him for only a moment before she reached out, wrapping her arms around him, clinging as he kissed her.

Matt bent her backward, hungry for her kiss, his lips slanting first one way then the other across her mouth. Not knowing how, he found them slipping to the ground. The feeling of her hands tangled in his hair, her tongue darting in to meet his, fired his passion. They kissed again and again, seeking to make up for the times they couldn't be together, to heal the hurts their words had caused. He felt her fingers on the buttons of his shirt, pulling it apart and baring his chest to her lips and fingers.

Matt's hand cupped Amy's breast through the soft cotton, caressing and kneading the flesh, feeling her nipple tighten as he knew his own did at her touch. He unbuttoned the top of her blouse, pushing it aside. Bending, he kissed the top of her breast, his lips lingering on the satiny flesh. "You're so beautiful."

Her fingers tangled in his hair. She rolled on top him, her lips covering his face with kisses, her body pressed against his. "I want to be beautiful for you," she whispered, "for only you." It was then that he heard the harsh voice above them.

CHAPTER 13

"Well, what we got here?"

"Ain't that cute, Jeb. A couple a lovers, playin' off by themselves."

Matt looked up, shocked from his sensual haze, to see two roughly garbed men coming down the embankment toward them. Hurriedly he pulled Amy to her feet as he swung to face them.

"What a piece of luck," the taller of the two men chuckled, his eyes raking Amy lasciviously, his eyes settling on the swell of her breast as she hastily rebuttoned her blouse. "I can see why you'd want to keep this sweet thing all to yourself, son. She is a beauty."

"Yeah, look at them breasts, Jeb."

The men were both armed, one tall, the other broad and stocky. Matt cursed himself for not having belted the revolver to his waist. He had a knife in his belt, but it would be no match against two like these. His only hope was to talk them out of trouble. Next choice was fists. Nothing mattered except keeping Amy safe.

Thrusting her behind him, he drawled, "You looking for somethin'?"

"We wasn't," the stocky man answered, "but we shore did find somethin', didn't we, Jack."

The taller man laughed at his friend's crude attempt at humor. Both men were fully bearded, clad in greasy, blood-stained buckskins, reeking with the odor of death that proclaimed them buffalo hunters or trappers.

"It does go to show the advantages of sleeping out beyond the fort," the tall man observed with a sly grin, his cultured voice in glaring contrast to his dress and behavior.

"Yeah. Hey, how about sharin' yore winning's thar, young fella?"

Matt kept his eyes on the men, his lips set in a cold smile. In a voice he hoped would brook no argument, he said, "Amy, start for camp, and I mean now."

"Wait, we don't want the gal leavin'," the short stocky man objected. "We jest got here. The party's jest startin'."

"Amy, run!" Matt yelled, relieved to see that for once, she obeyed.

The tall man lunged forward, trying to run down the slope to cut her off, but Matt dove for his legs, laying him on the ground, winded by the combined force of their momentum when they collided.

Leaping to his feet, Matt was ready when the shorter man reached him, fists flying. Staggered by the first blow, Matt managed to land a right, then a left to the stocky man's stomach. It was softer than he'd expected.

When the tall man rose to his feet and lunged for him, Matt kicked out with his boot, connecting solidly with the man's chin and sending him to back to the ground.

With Amy safely away, Matt was free to concentrate on his own survival, which didn't seem too likely over the long haul. He kept the shorter man busy, but all too soon, the tall one was on his feet. This time there was no trick to drop him.

Enraged, the two came at him. Taking a deep breath, Matt knew he was in for a beating-- if not worse. These weren't men like the boys on the train. He could hold them off for awhile, but he couldn't defeat them both. If Amy found help in time, maybe there'd be a chance, but he wasn't that convinced she would find anyone willing to come to his aid, except maybe St. Louis. He took a hard, rocking blow to his jaw, staggering him back. He might not be able to hang on long enough for it to matter.

""You should have shared her, son," the tall man said as his fists connected with Matt's jaw again, snapping his head back. Landing his fist solidly in the tall man's stomach, Matt heard a satisfying rush of air, just as he was jarred by a crushing blow to his own midsection, the blow landed by the stocky one. Ears ringing, Matt staggered back, a smile on his bloodied lips as he hit the short man with enough power to send him stumbling.

The sounds of fists thudding into flesh, feet stumbling against the ground, loud grunts and curses, and heavy breathing were the only reality. Matt raised his fists again and again, defending and striking out, growing more and more tired, finding it harder to avoid their blows.

With an enraged howl, the tall man came at him from behind, long arms coming around and grabbing Matt in a bear hold, which would end in a broken back if it couldn't break it. Matt's feet left the ground as he was heaved upward. The pressure on his back and lungs increased. He twisted enough to reach back and grab hold of the man's ear, pinching and yanking hard. He heard a satisfying howl of pain and felt the air rush into his lungs, as he was dropped.

Gasping for breath, Matt backed away, but there was nowhere to go. Hunkered low, the two came at him, slightly apart, enough so Matt could not guard against both at the same time. He put his fists up, still unwilling to use his knife if there was any other way, but his choices were dwindling along with his strength.

Matt swung to his left, blocking the first blow from the tall man, hoping to knock him to the ground in time to react to the short one, who was all too close behind him. He landed one solid blow before the stocky one had his arms around him, squeezing, pinning his right arm to his side, seemingly with bands of iron. He kicked out and back, knocking the tall man away as he managed again to break the grip.

Through the haze of his dwindling strength, he heard St. Louis' voice yelling, "Unless ya all want to get blown apart, back off!"

"Mind your... own business, stranger," gasped the tall man, looking up to where St. Louis stood, his shotgun pointed at them. Amy stood behind him, her eyes huge as she held a revolver with both hands.

"He is my business. Get away from him!" St. Louis voice was icy.

"And if we do not?" the tall man asked.

"Wal, I figure yore friend for one is a dead man. Second barrel for you," St. Louis promised, smiling. "Maybe ya better figure out how much this all is worth to ya."

"We wasn't doin' nothin'," the stocky man wheezed, as he backed carefully away, trying to catch his breath. "We didn't hurt him much."

"Shore. Get out of here. Go back to Dobytown. Find the rock ya climbed out from under."

"We were just going to teach the lad a lesson," the tall man panted.

"And it took two of you to do it," St. Louis said caustically. "Toss your guns and knives into the river. Do it now. Ya can come back and get 'em later to clean up. Now get out of here. If I see either of ya again, I'll blow a hole in ya just for the fun of it."

"We'll not be forgetting this," the tall man blustered.

"I'll be shakin' in my boots, worryin' about the likes of you."

Matt stood, heaving for breath. He watched the two back away and head up the river. Then he was aware Amy had run down the bank, her fingers touching his face. "I'm so sorry," she whispered. Her fingers lightly touched what felt like a nasty abrasion on his cheek.

His shirt had been nearly torn from his back, and he looked down at the remnants. "This trip is hard on shirts," he muttered as he headed toward the river to wash off what he could of the blood and dirt.

St. Louis had slid down the slope to stand beside them.

Matt hesitated, then looked down into the wagon master's concerned eyes. "I stumbled across the wrong pair," he said, trying still to keep Amy out of it. "Lucky for me she came by and saw what was happening." He was not fooling St. Louis.

"Uh huh," the older man said. His glance scanned back to Amy and the tears rolling down her cheeks.

"Those two were fixin' to hammer me good."

"Fixin' to, huh? What had they been doin'? Wash up. Maybe Miss Amy can help ya. When ya get back to camp, I'll take a look at that eye."

St. Louis walked back up the embankment, to stand above them giving them the privacy, for which Matt could not ask. He knelt by the river. His fingers were stiff when he reached up to take off what was left of his shirt. Amy gently pushed his hands aside. Her fingers slowly undid the buttons.

Looking up at him, at what he knew was going to be a black eye and the trickle of blood beside his mouth, she said, "I never dreamed it might be dangerous to go away from the others."

"It wasn't your fault," he mumbled, spitting blood into the water, splashing water onto his face and chest.

"I ran for St. Louis. I didn't know who else to get." She dabbed at his face with her handkerchief.

"You did right. Don't reckon there's many in the train'd care if I got my brains beat in." He tried to smile, but it wasn't a successful effort with the cuts and swelling.

"I was afraid we'd be too late. I got us into that mess. I... wanted to shoot them both." She dipped her handkerchief into the water, rinsed out the blood, and came back to wash his chest. Her fingers were a light touch.

"It was just bad luck." He swallowed, all too aware of her touch and his body's quick and heated response—even after a beating.

"But we wouldn't have been there if I'd trusted you."

"That's so," he agreed with a crooked smile. "Just remember that the next time," he teased, trying to lighten her mood.

"I hope there won't ever be a next time. I don't want to see you nearly beaten into the ground again. Not ever."

"Baby, that's not very flatterin'. If there hadn't of been two of 'em, I'd have done all right."

"I saw," She smiled, her eyes dark with her love for him.

He thought of the possible results if he hadn't been able to stop the men from grabbing Amy, and his stomach turned over.

Trying not to think any longer of that scenario, he asked, "How do I look?"

Tears welled up in her eyes as she surveyed the swelling and abrasions on his face and chest. "Like a wagon ran over you," she responded. He appreciated that she was going along with his attempt to lighten the mood.

"Great! Folks'll think I been fightin' again. Which, of course, I have. It's about all they think I'm good for anyway."

"Well," she whispered, swirling her finger across his chest, caressing a flat nipple and causing him to catch his breath, "folks'd be wrong. I happen to know you are definitely good for something else." Her caress became more purposeful as his breath quickened. "Want me to vouch for it," she asked unsteadily, running her finger across his belly.

"You keep doing that and I won't be able to hide anything." He saw her eyes flick down to his groin, where there was an obvious bulge.

"Oh and that would be bad?" she asked with a smile that he recognized for what it was. She was all too good at teasing—getting better at it every time they touched.

He took her hand firmly and put it away, ordering his treacherous body to get control. He reached for his shirt, but before he could shrug into what was left of it, she took it from him. She held it as he slid his arms gingerly into the sleeves. She pushed his hands aside and began slowly to rebutton it, taking her time, allowing her fingers to brush his skin as she worked.

"It looks like this needs some repair. Did I mention that I specialize in replacing buttons and mending tears-- especially when on certain chests." She stopped and smiled more broadly, "I could get enthusiastic about ripping them off too. Come around anytime. That is, of course, unless you'd regard it as more trouble."

He wished St. Louis was a little further away for what he wanted to do. Probably it was good he wasn't. When they walked back up on the bluff, Matt knew from the gleam in the older man's eyes nothing had missed his notice.

"Thanks again for comin'," Matt said. "You kept it from gettin' worse."

"Those two'd a thought nothin' of killin' ya and dumpin' yore body in the river. If they hadn't a wanted to beat ya first, they'd a just knifed you and been done with it."

"I kind of figured that," Matt said, touching his own knife handle.

"You said they came from Dobytown," Amy asked as they walked back to camp. "Is that another town out here?"

"Ya might say. "It's two miles upriver from the fort. It's a place for uh... certain people that uh hang around forts." St. Louis grew red, obviously trying to think of a refined way to describe the sorts of men and women that hung around forts.

"Oh," Amy said in a small voice, blushing.

"We'll pass it when we head west. No place you'd want to visit though."

Back at the wagon, St. Louis said, "Matthew, you come on up to my wagon. I got somethin' that'll take care of thet black eye."

Instead of immediately following St. Louis, Matt turned to Amy. "Thanks again for bringing help," he told her audibly and politely. Mouthing silently, he added, "I love you."

She smiled, her eyes soft. "As a Christian woman, I certainly couldn't watch some poor soul being beaten into the ground, pummeled out of his mind." She grinned at his frown. "And not want to give what assistance I could. I would have done the same deed for any poor man." Under her breath, she whispered, "Who I love more than life itself."

As the wagon train halted at the top of a steep slope, Matt watched, as the men gathered into small groups and stared down the grade. Until now, the land had been mostly flat with gentle grades, but St. Louis had warned them about Ash Hollow. He heard men muttering. "What kind of road's this?"

"Hell, that road's straight up and down!"

Amos Stevens walked up to St. Louis and skeptically asked the question on all their minds. "How do we get wagons down that?"

"Wal, I reckon, we'll do like always and rope 'em down. We shore don't want to ride 'em down." St. Louis chuckled,

Matt remembered St. Louis telling him there would be steeper slopes ahead when they reached the Blue Mountains in Oregon Territory. Then they would look back on this incline as a gentle grade, but then they would also be toughened, more used to dealing with treacherous conditions.

Walking over to where St. Louis stood, Matt asked, "What do you want me doing?"

"Get five men. We'll secure my wagon to the top of the incline, but let the wheels run free."

Unhitching the wagon and securing it took the men only a short time, then St. Louis said, "Wind this here long rope around the hub. Tie the loose end to the first wagon and start lowerin'."

Matt, Adam, Ralph Hall, and Brick Webb held back on the spokes of the turning wheel, letting the rope slowly play out as the animals and wagon worked their way down the road. As long as the rope held, and they checked it frequently, no wagon would go too fast. The process was repeated with each wagon, occasionally trading off on who did the lowering.

When it came time to lower St. Louis' wagon, he tied a team of oxen from another outfit to the rear of his wagon, causing them to balk, to go more slowly than usual. The men attached ropes to the wagon as an additional safeguard, holding back its progress as best they could.

By the time all the wagons were at the bottom, the men were near exhaustion. Matt had fresh blisters on even his heavily calloused hands. Fortunately Ash Hollow provided a rewarding campsite with tall trees, water easy to reach and plenty of grass. The air was heavy with the fragrance of wild roses. It was an oasis after the barren and dry country through which they had come.

Matt knelt by the campfire, sipping a cup of Clem's potent coffee. Everyone was settled in for the night. "So what's next?" he asked when St. Louis joined him.

Adam, accepting a cup of coffee for himself, answered. "Two days and we'll cross the South Platte."

'You'll see a river then," Clem grunted, refilling Matt's coffee cup. "It's a big 'un. Never the same neither."

"All the thunderstorms we've been having, there's a better 'n even chance it'll be in flood," St. Louis said, his own eyes darkened with concern. "Sometimes there's a Mormon ferry running, but we can't count on it."

Adam stared into the darkness. "It's not an easy crossing at best."

"We'll find a way," St. Louis said, rubbing the side of his nose. "Where there's a will, there's a way."

Adam laughed. "That's what you always say."

"And it usually figures to be so."

Amy and Loraine stood looking down at the raging swirls of the river. Mid-morning had brought the train west of where the North and South Plattes came together and to where they would cross the South. Brush and flood debris rushed past in the roiling waters, the river well over its banks.

Amy had been told there would be a ferry, which had sounded like a primitive sort of operation with large canoes used as pontoons to float the wagons across the river. It was disappointing to find no men or canoes at the crossing.

"I don't see how we can get wagons across until that goes down." Loraine shaded her eyes with her hands to stare at the water.

Amy saw a small group of men, Matt among them, congregated on the banks of the raging river, studying the crossing. St. Louis appeared to gesture and talk while the others listened.

"fI suppose we just have to wait," Amy agreed. "It looks too deep for oxen or mules to pull the wagons across."

"Except, I've heard it said that we can't afford to wait if we're to get to Oregon before the snow hits the passes."

"Maybe the ferrymen will be back soon." It hardly seemed possible there was any other solution. Amy couldn't imagine crossing that stretch of water. It would tear the wagons from their traces, drown the animals and probably drag them all to the main body of water in the Platte itself.

Several men left the group and began calking a wagon as if to prepare it for floating across. Amy waited, hoping Matt would be able to break away and find a moment to explain it to her. If they were to camp here, she should start a fire.

She watched, mystified for only a moment, as Matt sat on the bank and began pulling off his boots. Before she had time to realize what he was doing, he had thrown his shirt on the ground and looped the end of a long rope across his shoulder and chest before plunging into the river. As if in a daze, she heard Loraine say, "I can't believe he's doing that."

Matt's arms reached out strongly, pulling his body along through the water as he headed at an angle across the river, fighting through the rapids and eddies and somehow continuing to move steadily toward the opposite bank, somehow escaping being hit by any of the snags on their way downstream.

In Amy's desperate fear, panic gripped her stomach, tying it in knots. Her only solace was the rope Matt had looped around his body. Surely if he was pulled under or struck by a log, so long as he had that rope around him, they could pull him back to safety.

As he cut through the roughest water, his pace slowed but never faltered. Amy had known he was a strong swimmer, but she'd never dreamed he would try it in a torrent like this. Shaking, she felt herself alternating between a rage he would take such a risk and horror he might drown. She couldn't respond to any of Loraine's attempts to reassure her.

It seemed hours, but she knew it had probably only been long moments when she watched him drag himself from the water, staggering a little with exhaustion. Quickly, she thanked God for His mercies as she questioned why she had ever let herself love a man who would do such a stupid thing.

Matt stumbled across the narrow beach still carrying the rope. He secured it to a large cottonwood tree. Walking gingerly on bare feet, he baffled Amy completely when he headed toward the woods. In a moment, however, his purpose became clear as he raised his arm in triumph and began pulling on a canoe bow, hidden unless someone knew where to look.

In watching him so intently, Amy hadn't been aware others had slipped into the water, using the rope to cross, until they were on the bank. They trooped up the beach and helped Matt pull the heavy canoes down to the river.

Soon the canoes had been brought to their side, and the work of ferrying the wagons began. Using the rope as a safety and canoes to float the big wagons, the crossing was relatively safe. It took most of the afternoon before all the wagons were across. The only near disaster was when one of the small boys from the Carter wagon fell into the water but was quickly scooped up by Adam on horseback.

By evening Amy was determined she would talk to Matt about his deliberate courting of death. She'd helped fix the evening meal while the words of a poem began framing themselves in her mind.

Death reaches for my lover, seeking, searching, demanding.

While he embraces it as a brother, risking, challenging daring...

It was more than Amy could understand. What made Matt deliberately court such risk? Was it death he sought? She tried to be calm, but she had alternated between rage and relief so many times, she was no longer certain what she felt.

She walked past his camp, knew he'd seen her and continued on until she came to a place away from the circles of firelight, where in the darkness she could wait, not with love but with a renewed surge of rage. When he was there and tried to hold her, she forced herself to stiffen. She welcomed the anger. It released some of the pent-up anxiety.

When he tried to kiss her, she pushed him away. Totally unprepared for her reaction, Matt stepped back. "What's this?"

"You know."

"I had no time to shave this morning, but you never seemed to mind so much before."

"Don't be ridiculous, Matt. You know why I'm furious."

"You're mad?"

She took a deep breath to keep from screaming. "Every time

someone needs a hero does it have to be you? What are you trying to accomplish?"

He rubbed his bristly jaw thoughtfully, his gray eyes narrowing as he studied her face. "You want to explain what you just said?"

"You need me to define it, spell it all out for you? Fine! Why is it you have to volunteer for every dangerous thing that comes along? Do you think you're invincible? Are you flirting with death for some reason?"

"I guess we are talking about the river today?"

"What else?" she spat. "Why did you do that?"

Frowning, he stepped back from her. "I never expected this from you."

"Is it so surprising I might be sick and tired of having you constantly putting yourself in danger? Always jumping into something without thinking? In Missouri it was the same. I've just had enough of it, that's all. Even you ought to be able to understand that."

"In Missouri? What's Missouri got to do with this?"

"Nothing and everything. It's the way you do things. Then, I felt I couldn't say anything but--"

He interrupted her with a short laugh. "Didn't say anything? That's not the way I remember Missouri."

"Well, maybe sometimes I said a few little things, but not everything I thought. Now, you owe me something. You have to stop taking such risks."

"It's been a hard day. I'm tired. Let's talk about this when you calm down and can talk reasonably."

"Reasonable! What would you know about that word? I didn't know it was even in your vocabulary."

"Baby, cool off. I was doing what I'm being paid to do here and don't deserve having you light into me this way," he said through gritted teeth. She could see his eyes darkening, knew he was growing angry and that upset her even more. How dare he act as though he was the one being wronged!

"How do you think it made me feel? I had to stand on that bank and watch you swim in that river, not knowing if you'd make it across or if you'd be hit in the head by a log. Did you give me a single thought in all of that?"

"I thought about you and everybody else. St. Louis laid out the problem, the choices. Me swimmin' seemed best. You know I'm a strong swimmer. Younger than the others. Horses are skittish around fast water. I didn't much care for the idea of tryin' to ride one across with no rope in place. That could've been more dangerous than the way I did it. I angled across, letting the current carry me. It wasn't as dangerous as you're making it out. I wouldn't have tried it if I had seen it as dangerous."

"Since when have you been a good judge of what is or is not safe? You've done lots of things that were dangerous just because you thought you ought to,"

"Name one," he snapped, clearly exasperated.

"How about when you climbed the tree to rescue that kitten. Remember? You were almost to the top when the branch broke. I thought you'd never stop falling before you caught another limb."

He laughed in half surprise. "I didn't mean for you to go back that far, but since you did, that worked out."

"Worked out! You call the gash you got in your side when you hit the broken limb working out? If you do, no wonder you do not understand a word I'm trying to say here."

"There's a lot about you I don't understand." He was smiling now.

"You went back up, even bleeding and what reward did you get for bringing her down? She scratched your hands and when she was on the ground ran off hissing." she reminded him. Seeing the smile of remembrance on his face, she felt renewed anger. "This isn't funny, Matthew. I've had all of this I can stand!"

The smile faded. "What does that mean?"

"It means you have to stop volunteering for things that are so dangerous. You have to think about me for once, not just your own need for excitement. You have to start thinking that there is an us now... not just a you."

He stared at her for a long moment. "You mean ask permission?"

"Not exactly." She crossed her arms over her chest.

"Then what are you asking?"

"I don't know. I just don't want you taking such risks." She turned away, still irritated, but realizing she wasn't so certain in her position as she had been at the beginning of their argument. Was she asking him to do something unreasonable, something against his nature?

"Look," he said, his voice tired and defeated, "you think on this. If you still feel the same way tomorrow, maybe you'll have to think on whether you want to be with me at all. I'm not going to change, not about this." He turned to walk away.

She gave a little cry and ran after him, blocking his way.

"Amy," he said in a voice not much above a whisper, "it's been a long day. I'm too tired to argue with you tonight."

"I don't want to argue." She put her arms around him.

He stood in her embrace, his arms at his side. "What does this mean?"

"I'm sorry. I was wrong. What more do you want me to say?" Her words tumbled out disjointedly.

He wrapped his arms around her, kissing her hair, the side of her nose and finally her lips, wet with her tears. They moved deeper into the shadows and sat on the ground, their arms entwined around each other.

"Matt," she said against his chest, "I love you so much. I couldn't bear it if anything happened to you."

"Nothing is going to happen," he assured her, caressing her damp cheek with his finger.

"It could though. This whole trip is dangerous. I see it differently now than when we were in Independence. Things happen."

He grinned. "Like I could maybe fall out of a wagon or a buffalo could come along and run over me or I could get tromped by one of the ox."

"This isn't funny."

"Well, if you are bound to have worries, I figured I could hand you a few. I know what you mean, but baby, you can't go worrying about everything. All the same things could happen to you. Nothing is sure in this life." She saw the look of irony on his face even as he said it.

"You could be more careful," she suggested stroking the line of his jaw.

"Are we comin' back to the same argument?"

"Maybe. It would be easy to do. Every time I think about watching you swimming the river..." She hesitated. "But I love you, and maybe the fact that you swim rivers is part of what I love. You have to do what you know is right, but please be careful. There's something in you, a need that frightens me sometimes. Don't you ever think about it?"

"And it is?"

"That you purposely take risks, that you... court death."

For a moment, she thought she saw fear or doubt in his eyes before he managed a smile that took it away. If swimming rivers didn't scare Matt, what did?

CHAPTER 14

In the long, tedious days that followed, Amy felt growing frustration at the difficulty of being alone with Matt. It seemed someone was always around, or she was so tired she wanted only to collapse into her blankets; or if she had the energy, he was busy with somebody else. His protective insistence that they keep their relationship secret irked her. If they'd been open in their love, they could have seen far more of each other. She knew her parents would understand once she explained, and she didn't give a fig about anyone else's opinion.

Wistfully, she watched him from a distance as he worked to repair a broken wagon wheel. He and two men lifted the wagon with a pry bar while others took the wheel off and replaced it with a spare. Even from a distance, she could see how his muscles flexed and bulged with his exertion. His hair was pulled back with the usual leather tie as sweat rolled down his face. A god indeed, she thought with a wry smile.

Afterward, she lingered, hoping he would find an excuse to come to her, but too many people stood in their way. Listlessly she wandered to the Porter wagon.

"I can't get over how Eliza's growing," she told Jenny as she settled the baby onto her lap.

"It seems there's something new every day," Jenny said with a faint smile.

Eliza made guttural sounds, which were beyond Amy's capability to understand. Jenny said, "Sometimes I'm guessing, but I'm sure she says Mama."

William, leaning against the wagon, watched them. Pushing his glasses back on his nose, he finally said, "I need to check the horse." In another moment he was gone.

Amy shook her head. "Are things any better between the two of you?"

"I don't know. I guess so," Jenny said, taking her daughter into her own arms. "He's gone a lot. At least we don't argue like the Calhouns."

Amy laughed. "I guess everybody knows how much the Calhouns fight."

"It's hard to keep any secrets. I suppose people talk about William and me, too."

"I doubt it. You aren't loud." Amy grinned and rose, brushing off her skirts. "I don't think William likes me."

"He's looking for any excuse to escape from me." Jenny sighed, settling Eliza onto a quilt.

Before Amy could think of a suitable reply, Agatha Collins walked up. "Oh," she said, putting her hand to her mouth. "I didn't realize you'd be here."

"And if you'd known, would you have stayed away?" Amy asked, smiling.

"I have nothing against you," Mrs. Collins said, standing stiffly as though uncertain of whether to stay or go. "Even though you do defend the riffraff here on the train."

"Set for a minute, both of you," Jenny said politely to distract from the rancor that Mrs. Collins quickly had aroused. They both ignored her.

"I shouldn't... Just... Actually..." Mrs. Collins looked to be at a loss for words, something that surprised Amy.

"We haven't seen much of you," Amy volunteered.

"I didn't expect I'd be welcome," Mrs. Collins said bluntly, her face creasing in a frown. "After what your ma said to me."

"All Mama said was when you came to our campfire, don't talk against people."

"But..."

Amy shook her head. "Mama doesn't like gossip or people putting down others." She still felt irked at the old woman's words, but she felt sorry for her too. She could see the loneliness in her watery old eyes.

Mrs. Collins considered that a moment. "I'd like to see your ma."

"Mama won't even remember what happened between you," Amy assured her. It was her mother's way to put things aside and not hold grudges.

"I didn't mean to offend Martha that way. Didn't have no idea she'd get so riled."

Jenny looked from one to the other but politely asked no questions. After a moment, she said, "I think I have a little peppermint tea. Would you both like a cup?"

Mrs. Collins nodded. She sat on a stool while Amy settled back on the ground. Waiting for the tea to steep, Mrs. Collins said, "I don't reckon I've changed my mind... I mean about Kane."

Amy narrowed her eyes.

"Not that I feel different, but knowin' how Martha and you all feel, I'd never say nothing to offend."

"Well that's a start."

"I know what the Good Book says about stealing and all, but I wouldn't have said what I did, if I'd knowed how you folks felt about him."

Amy felt a renewed surge of irritation. Did the woman know what the Good Book said about judging, about forgiveness. Biting her tongue, she kept back a sharp retort, which would lead to an argument. Before she could think of something to say that wouldn't cause offense or reveal her anger, she looked up and saw Matt, Adam beside him, riding down the line of wagons. She was not only surprised to see him, but surprised he'd be leaving the wagons at near dark. She wished she could ask where he was going. It was, of course, impossible.

She knew the moment Matt saw her because his eyes grew heavy lidded. As he passed, he said nothing, only nodding, politely tipping his hat to them all, with a small smile as he saw Mrs. Collins deliberately turn her head.

Adam reined in his horse. "How are you ladies this evening?"

"Fine," Amy responded, wanting to turn to watch Matt as he rode on. If she allowed her eyes to show what her heart felt, Mrs. Collins might read the expression for what it was.

"Where you off to?" Mrs. Collins asked.

"With the help of a nearly full moon, a bit of hunting," Adam answered. "We thought fresh meat might be welcomed."

"Shore right about that," the old woman said with a cackle. "I ain't had meat since the venison you brung back weeks ago."

"Well, with any luck, we'll see deer or antelope," Adam said.

"Good luck, then," Amy volunteered.

Adam smiled. "I got to get out of here," he said grinning, gesturing his head toward Matt's disappearing form, "or my partner'll shoot all the game before I get there."

As soon as he'd ridden on, Amy excused herself from the two women. If she stayed another moment, she would be in tears. She wanted to talk to Matt, to drink him in with her eyes, to acknowledge to the world what he meant to her. With a mixture of pleasure and pain, she thought, how graceful he looked on his horse. Riding was something he'd always done well. Loose limbed, like Adam, he seemed one with the animal. She watched until their figures disappeared beyond the curve of the hill. Someday she would be able publicly to declare him hers. She had only to wait, to be patient. Unfortunately patience had never been her long suit.

The sky was darkened, the moon barely visible beyond the horizon as Matt lounged in front of the campfire, half listening to St. Louis and Adam banter over another philo-sophical discussion. Edginess and irritability plagued him when he didn't see Amy, didn't know what she'd been doing or thinking. During the day he'd even barked at Clem, Clem who was finally coming to accept and treat him as a member of the human race.

"Don't see why ya two didn't come back with some meat, St. Louis said. "I was all set for fresh steaks."

"Should've took me," Clem grumbled. "Wouldn't have come back empty-handed if you'd took me with you."

Adam laughed. "You? You talk too much to take hunting."

Clem grunted in protest. "Fix your own supper then," he snapped, glaring at Adam.

"Whoops, maybe I misspoke." Adam quickly apologized.

"Reckon ya did," Clem said with a satisfied smirk, "And maybe it's too late to get your foot back out of yore mouth."

Matt looked up to see Adam watching him. "St. Louis," Adam said, never taking his gaze from Matt, "did I tell you I'm thinking of asking a certain young woman to be my wife?"

"Ready to settle down?" questioned St. Louis skepticism in his voice.

"Man gets himself leg-shackled, that man's a plumb idjit," Clem quipped.

"With the right woman," Adam retorted, "marriage wouldn't be a prison. I have certainly met a young woman who is all a man could want. Shy, sweet, beautiful. Kind, You know, I've never seen her lose her temper or act like any less than the lady she is."

Matt listened but kept his eyes on the campfire. Never lose her temper! Either he's not talkin' about Amy, or he doesn't know her so well as he thinks!

"Ya meanin' Miss Amy?" questioned St. Louis, treading lightly on the subject.

"Who else? You know where I spend what time I have."

Matt glanced up and saw Adam's gaze still on him. He felt chilled, though the air was warm. He edged closer to the fire. "What do you think my chances will be, Matt?" Adam's question was as direct as the expression in his dark blue eyes.

"Why ask me?" Matt drawled, the telltale muscle throbbing in his cheek.

"You and she have been friends a long time. She told me all you once meant to each other back in Missouri. You know her. Do you think she'll say yes?"

Matt worked to bury the angry thoughts roiling to the surface like hungry fish to feed. Was this why it'd been hard to see her? Had she changed her mind? But he had no reason to doubt her love-- that is except for his own inability to believe in love, his own feelings of unworthiness.

Adam repeated his question, carefully watching Matt's face.

"I've never understood Amy, nor knew what she'd think or do." That at least was the truth.

"Yeah, but you must have some idea."

Matt met Adam's gaze, wondering if he could answer honestly and not knowing what honesty was at this moment. "You'll get no answers here. I've loved her, like I said, but I'd never claim to understand her."

"Man claims he knows a woman... don't know much about women—any woman," St. Louis agreed with a chuckle.

Adam laughed. "Guess I'll have to find out for myself one of these nights." He rose. "Maybe tonight."

When he had gone, St. Louis was silent for a moment. "You know he don't intend to ask her to marry him but was tryin' to find out what's goin' on between you and Amy. That's somethin' I wouldn't mind knowin' myself."

Matt stared into space, no more answers for St. Louis than he had for himself.

The wagons rolled on smoothly with little mishap. Each day was a day closer to their goal, closer to homes in Oregon, but for Matt each was an exercise in frustration. He'd heard no more about Adam asking Amy to be his wife, never heard if he did so, never heard any response, but since that night, he'd found it impossible to see her. When he caught her eye, there was always someone interrupting. He refused to take the risk of letting her leave the large encampment, and there were too many busybodies looking for fresh gossip for him to risk going to the Stevens' wagon.

St. Louis began routinely sending Adam and Matt ahead to scout. Although there'd been some Indian sign, there was nothing unusually disturbing or out of line with the expected; yet St. Louis was uneasy. "Ya don't get as old as I am without listenin' to the feelin's in yore bones."

"But what do you think?" Clem questioned, flipping a pancake.

"Don't know what I think, but I got a feelin'. Sometimes a feelin' is all ya get," he replied with a grimace.

Having orders to ride ahead with the scout satisfied Matt. He liked the time on the prairies, with the wind as his companion, the man beside him not a talkative one. The only flaw was spending so much time with the one who was free to spend time with Amy. Worse, with enforced proximity, he found he liked the scout. Working with him, his respect for Adam had grown. He would be a more suitable mate for Amy than he himself ever could.

Several miles from the wagon, looking for a possible campsite, Adam pulled back on his horse and studied the sky. "This doesn't look good."

"Storm coming," Matt agreed. Black masses of clouds, which had been building all afternoon, were now dropping down onto the canyon walls on both sides of them, effectively blocking the horizon in every direction.

"Maybe nothing to be concerned about," Adam said not sounding as though he believed it, "but we'll just keep our eye on it."

The sky darkened ominously as lightning flashed, striking the hills to their left. Thunder rolled, reverberating off the nearby ridge, frightening their horses. Tensely, the two men looked at each other, trying to decide whether to keep looking for a suitable campsite or head back to the wagons. Before they could make a decision, the wind and storm were upon them, the sun blocked out, and blackness surrounded them.

When the sky opened, it was not the heavy rain they had expected, but a bombardment of hailstones—larger than hens' eggs, bouncing and striking them and their horses indiscriminately.

"No shelter out here," Adam yelled to be heard above the storm.

Matt already knew they were in for it. A hailstone struck the side of his head, knocking his hat half off and nearly stunning him. He grabbed at the hat, yanking it back on, even though it was clearly no protection against the force of blows raining on them from the capricious heavens.

Putting his left arm up over his head, Matt kept a firm grip on the reins of the horse with his right. From the corner of his eye, he could see Adam was being brutalized as badly as he. Caught in the full fury of the storm, the animals became almost impossible to control.

"Turn back," Adam yelled, as they wheeled their mounts in the direction of the wagons. "The wagons won't be able to go on in this, even if--" He cursed when a hailstone clipped his head.

By the time they reached the circled wagons, the storm had passed, and the sun was shining. Whiteness on the ground and the unhitched wagons, told them without words that the same storm had hit the train. Men scurried around, trying to secure the livestock. Matt and Adam dismounted to help. Within moments, either the storm returned or a new one struck as wind again buffeted them, followed by hail and a deluge of rain.

With everything as secured as could be, Adam and Matt sought their own shelter. St. Louis was leaning against the protected side of his wagon watching Clem struggle to reattach a tarp to protect his fire. St. Louis saw them, obviously looking badly the worse for wear, and did a double-take. "The two of ya been fightin'?"

"Only the storm," Adam retorted with a half laugh.

St. Louis took off his hat to scratch his bald head. "From the looks of yore faces, ya look like ya had a real set-to out there."

"It was no fun," Matt drawled as he accepted a cup of hot, strong coffee from Clem.

"One of the worst storms I seen," St. Louis agreed.

"How did the rest of the people fare?" questioned Adam.

St. Louis chuckled. "Wal, why don't ya go see for yoreself."

"I will."

As Adam strode off, St. Louis looked at Matt but said nothing. After a few moments, Matt pulled his hat low over his eyes and went off to check on his own wagon.

His pa and Morey were chewing on chunks of jerky when he came up. "What are you doin' here?" Morey growled as a greeting.

"Figured I ought to see if there was any damage."

"Like we need help from the likes of you," Morey said coldly.

Matt stared at him for a moment, before he turned on his heel. Feelings of anger mixed with loneliness surged through him, conjuring up their own storm. He couldn't go to Amy. Adam would be enjoying a meal with the Stevens. At the moment, it was of hollow comfort that all of that was true because of his own choices.

In his black mood, he didn't see Amy and Loraine until he had almost bumped into them. Amy looked into his eyes, scanning his face, taking in the growing bruises and the scowl.

"Howdy," he grunted, knowing that all in this world he ever wanted was to be able to take her into his arms and he was unable even to do that.

She didn't say a word. Taking his arm, she drew him away from the circle of firelight, behind the sheltering cover of an empty wagon. Loraine moved to stand several feet away, concealing them as best she could.

"Are you all right?" Amy asked, her gaze anxiously moving across his face.

He nodded, wanting to say more, but bound by pride and insecurity.

Her hand came up lightly to touch a swelling on his forehead. "Are there more of these?" she asked, her voice little more than a husky whisper.

"A few."

"You got caught in that storm-- with no protection."

"Yeah, me and Adam."

"Couldn't you have found shelter?"

"There was none."

"I've never seen hailstones so big. It was like rocks being thrown from the sky. St. Louis had us circle. We got under the wagon 'til it let up."

He knew they were making small talk, neither able to say

what they wanted. Did she want to tell him she didn't love him anymore? Had Adam's proposal of marriage-- offered now and not at some vague later time-- changed her mind about what she wanted? Whatever she intended to tell him, he was determined not to help her. He clenched his jaw.

"Are you sure you're all right?" she asked again.

"Why do you keep asking?"

"Because of how you're acting. If everything is all right, why haven't you kissed me? Nobody can see us here."

He looked at her, feeling as though he'd just had a smack alongside his head. "I'm wet. I didn't know if you'd want that."

"Since when do I not want that?" The words were barely out of her mouth when he reached out, pulling her against him, giving her all and more than she asked. His lips, wet and cold, clung to hers, feeling the first warmth of the day as he felt his arousal pushing against her body.

When he would have pulled away, she held on, her nails digging into his back, her lips like honey. Her tongue delved into his mouth, mimicking the gestures he'd taught her. He'd never dreamed how sweet it would be to have her entering him, probing his mouth, initiating the kiss and making him wonder what it would be like when they finally made love. She would obviously not just be a politely, submissive wife in bed. That thought caused his erection to grow even harder.

Breathing heavily, her breath against his neck was a heady wine to his blood. "We haven't been together enough."

"You know why," he answered, trying to remember why himself.

"I do not." One hand was on his neck, while the other around his waist held him pressed against her soft curves. It was impossible to be close enough. Her hands stroked down his arm, across his back as he kissed her neck, cupping her buttocks in his large hands and pressing her against his hardness.

"You missed me?" he managed finally. She didn't answer but began unbuttoning his shirt, baring the juncture of neck and shoulder to her lips. Matt swooped her up into his arms, cradling her to him. Amy kissed his shoulder and neck, taking her time, sensuously inching her way to his chin, then his lips.

Pulling his shirt more widely apart, she exposed most of his chest and bent to trace a pattern with her lips across a ridge of muscle, tempting first one hard male nipple, then the other.

Suddenly, pulling him out of his sensual abyss, he heard Loraine hiss. "Break it up! Here comes Adam, and he's heading straight for me."

Matt set her on the ground. Amy pushed her skirt into some semblance of order, smoothing her hair. As for her lips swollen by kisses, the redness around her cheeks, where his bristly jaw had rubbed against her, she could obviously do nothing. They marked her as his, revealing their true relationship to anyone who looked closely. He could only hope Adam would not look closely, would not want to see.

They were standing behind Loraine as Adam walked up. He looked at all three. Abruptly his gaze stopped and rested on Matt. "Ever button your shirt?"

Matt looked down, remembering too late how Amy had pulled his shirt apart, leaving a good part of his chest bare. He had been so concerned that he be in the darkness behind Loraine, hiding his arousal that he'd clean forgotten the shirt. "Uh, I-- Dang button holes just keep poppin' apart." He knew he didn't dare look at Amy as he began buttoning it. One sly smile from her, and he'd have broken out in laughter to match the girls' giggles.

Adam looked from one to the other, obviously trying to figure out what was so funny about a man having mending problems.

Loraine took Amy's arm. "I think we ought to be getting back. We did tell Mama we'd come right back after we took the fresh baked bread to the Carters."

Matt watched the way Amy's skirt swished around her legs as she walked away, the sound, the drape of the fabric over rounded hips enough to enflame his desire all over again. He glanced at Adam and saw his eyes were following the retreat with the same interest.

"I'm starving," Matt said with a shaky grin.

"Let's go see what's left to eat, but I bet it won't be fresh bread." They both laughed. Stale biscuits more likely, but by now anything sounded good.

As Loraine and Amy walked to their wagon, Loraine grinned and shook her head. "You can't keep your hands off that boy."

Amy smiled sheepishly. "And it's getting worse. I am addicted. I get around him, and I just want to touch him-- everywhere."

"Amy!" Loraine gasped. "You better be careful. You know where all of that can lead."

"I hope to marriage," Amy retorted.

"Well, it better happen soon or--" Loraine left her statement unfinished.

"Have you ever felt like that, Raine? Like you just can't get enough of a man. I feel sometimes like I'd like to draw Matt right into myself."

"Amy!" Loraine yelped, reaching out to put her fingers over Amy's lips. "I absolutely have not and it's beginning to depress me, listening to you go on. It's most as bad as standing six feet away from you and Matt while you-- well, it was like you were trying to suck him into yourself!"

"I never thought I'd be one of those women. I mean, only loose women like-- well, you know." She thought of the pale imitations of love she'd read in the novels. Their love stories hadn't begun to prepare her for what it was really about, for what it felt like to touch a man's body, to feel his muscles move under her fingers, his hands and lips touching her, stroking down her skin. She'd been prepared for the emotional connection, but this physical thing overwhelmed all her senses.

Heroines in books allowed the heroes to kiss them chastely on their lips, but that was definitely all, and even that didn't come until the last Chapter. Amy knew now that was not enough, not for her with Matt. She began to wonder if she was one of the fallen women, the ones who the hero wisely rejected for the chaste heroine.

"It's like the storms we've been having. It builds up and

suddenly it's just so heady, so strong you don't know how to keep it under control," she admitted.

"At the rate I'm going, I'll never get a chance to find all that out. I'll die an old maid, still having to listen to you go on about how much you like to kiss Matt!"

Amy laughed. "You'll have your chance."

"If so, it won't be with Adam."

"There'll be someone. I know it."

"Maybe, but not on this wagon train. You have the two most eligible, best looking men chasing after you." Loraine shook her head over the obvious unfairness of such a situation. "I certainly wouldn't set my cap for someone like Brick."

"Well, I have to do more to discourage Adam. The existing situation is causing me some problems too-- with Matt."

"He can't be jealous," Loraine sputtered. "He couldn't believe a woman could think of another man after... well you all but attacked him."

"It does seem unlikely, Raine, but then there is how I feel about Bernice." A feeling of jealousy and insecurity was definitely nothing lightly to dismiss.

They slipped into their tent, hurriedly finding their cotton nightgowns. As Amy shrugged out of her dress, she heard Loraine ask through the rustling, "What do you do anyway that gets them all chasing after you?"

Belle piped up from under a pile of quilts, "It's because she's so beautiful."

"Oh great, you're awake," both older girls sighed in unison.

Belle had her rag doll beside her in the bed, and both faces peeped out from the quilts. "I like to listen to you talk. I learn things. How'm I going to learn things if you always make me leave, or if you be quiet when you think I hear you?" she asked with resentment in her voice.

"The trouble is," Amy whispered to Loraine, "little pitchers have big ears and big mouths."

"I heard that," Belle squeaked, "and I do not have big ears or mouths. I asked Mama and she said I didn't."

"It's just an expression, Arabelle." Amy bent down and gave her sister a quick kiss before she slid under her own quilts.

"Besides," Belle went on, "I already know all about you and Matt, and I haven't said a word to anyone. So there."

"And just how do you know all about something that you're not supposed to be eavesdropping on?" Loraine asked.

"Even if I didn't hear things, I'd know. I see how Amy watches for him, and if Matt's around, she always knows just where he is. And when she sees him, her eyes get all soft and dopey looking."

Amy laughed before she felt dismay. "Pretty smart, but I wonder how many other people see what you see-- or think they do."

"I don't think everybody knows," Belle said, considering the question seriously. "People are too busy. I know, because I wanted you to like Matt. I don't like Adam. Matt's always nice to me. He doesn't treat me like a wart."

"Belle, you won't say anything to Mama or Papa will you?"

"Of course, not," she said indignantly, "what do you think I am anyway?"

Amy snuggled down in the covers, working to suppress a yawn.

"Sometimes it seems love is a big game," Loraine protested. "He wants. She wants, and nobody wants. I don't know if I ever want to fall in love."

"Well, I'm tired of the whole thing. I want Matt with me-- not Adam, but I don't know how to make it happen."

"When you use me as a barrier between you and Adam, he thinks I'm pushing my way in and dislikes me for it."

"What a pickle."

"I could be the barrier, whatever that is," Belle suggested helpfully. "I don't care if he does think I'm a pickle because that's what I think he is too."

Trying to fall asleep, the question kept coming back to Amy. Why wouldn't Matt just let her tell everyone what they meant to each other? What was still standing between them? She wanted answers but suspected something she'd tried to deny. Matt himself didn't have those answers. Whatever was wrong was deeper than the people disliking him. But what could it be?

CHAPTER 15

"It's not possible," Amy moaned as she heard the quiet, morning sounds her mother was making as she stoked the fire to life and began gathering ingredients for breakfast. "It can't be."

Belle was already sitting up and braiding her long blonde hair. "Yes, it is. You can see the sun just starting to light up the east."

"Thank you for the geography lesson," Loraine groaned as she pushed away her covers.

Within a few minutes the sisters had dressed, torn down their tent, folded away their bedding, and were helping their mother with the morning meal. Each day had a monotonous rhythm to it. The same morning ablutions, long days walking behind or beside the wagon over country that looked much the same as the day before and would look the same the next day. Each night they did the same chores, fixed meals from the same ingredients as everyone else and sat around the fire until they were tired enough to go to bed, which was often much earlier than they expected. Sometimes Amos Stevens used what light there was to read to the family from Tennyson's Ulysses or the family Bible. Often they were all too tired to talk or even listen.

The tedium was seldom broken with anything new or different. Although they were traveling through the land of the Sioux and Cheyenne, Amy had yet to see an Indian. Matt had told her the signs of natives were around them, that they were being watched, but Amy wanted to see one. They had been told Indians often traded with travelers as they passed through their land, but not so much as a fur pelt had been offered to them. Amy had read a raft of exciting stories about Sioux warriors, the fierce Plains fighters. She wanted to see one before they left their land.

She and Loraine discussed this problem of no Indians but came up with no better solutions than when they discussed the male problem. No one seemed able to predict when or if Indians would be seen.

"Remember what St. Louis said," Loraine reminded her. "We'll only see them if they want to be seen."

"Hmph." That also sounded a lot like the males in their lives.

Adam rode by their wagon, passing on the word. "Indian camp ahead. Women ride in the wagons. St. Louis' orders."

Amy saw her first Sioux through the flap of the wagon, jostled against her sisters and mother. Roughly counting, she decided there were fifteen tepees made from hides and long poles. The proud, muscular men stood, watching silently as the wagons passed. Their long black hair hung down their backs. Most of the men wore little clothing, a piece of cloth, strategically placed, and sometimes a beaded vest. She saw no weapons, nor were the men painted or acting aggressive.

"Where do you suppose their women are?" questioned Martha, watching with as much interest as her daughters.

"I also don't see any children," Loraine said.

As the last wagon passed the camp, the same question was occurring to St. Louis. "I don't like it," he growled to Adam. "No women. Maybe they're not with them... or they hid 'em."

"Like we did?" Adam quipped.

St. Louis ignored the sarcasm. "An encampment this size should've had women. Mostly would've wanted to trade. Their women must've been hidin'. And I didn't like the look on those bucks' faces. Like we done somethin' to 'em"

"The answers might be at Fort Laramie. We'll be there late tomorrow."

They arrived at the fort just as Adam had predicted. With an afternoon ahead of him, Matt crossed the small stream, heading for the establishment. Nothing, about its plain buildings, was impressive, but he had been told it would have the requisite trading post, a place to mail letters home and to restock-- at the normally exorbitant rates, in supposed proportion to the difficulty of restocking. Indians, wrapped in colorful blankets, lounged in front of the blocky trading post, passively watching the whites come and go.

Matt met Adam and St. Louis on the veranda. St. Louis grinned as he reached out a hand to a tall man, who seemed all black hair, beard and worn buckskins. "John Hunter, I ain't seen ya in a coon's age," St. Louis said, pumping the big man's hand.

Hunter deep voice boomed with laughter as he grabbed St. Louis in a bear-hug that lifted the wagon master from his feet.

"Where you been, old hoss? Last time I saw you it was up in the Yellowstone country." Hunter slapped St. Louis on the shoulder and almost knocked him off his feet.

It was impossible to tell how old Hunter was. Although he had the youthful carriage of a younger man, his beard and hair were long and unkempt, hiding his features.

"I been leadin' that there wagon train camped in yonder meadow." He looked at Adam and Matt. "I want ya to meet Adam Stone and Matt Kane. Boys, this here's John Hunter, best trappin' partner I ever had."

"Then why'd you quit me?" Hunter asked with a broad grin that barely showed through all the hair.

"I got tired of the cold winters," St. Louis said. "Freeze off a man's butt. Get to a certain age, ain't nothin' worth that."

"I wouldn't know. Not that old, I guess. Had a good season last year though."

"And what have ya got to show for it?" asked St. Louis cynically.

Hunter laughed. "You have a point." He pulled out a bottle of whiskey from a pack at his feet. "This," he suggested as he handed it to St. Louis.

St. Louis took a small sip before passing it on to Adam, who took a swig, then handed it back when Matt shook his head.

The men moved to a quieter spot around the corner. "How's the situation west of us?" St. Louis asked as they squatted in a semi-circle.

"Ya mean the Lakota, Arapaho, or Cheyenne?" Hunter asked with a knowing grin, slowly rolling a cigarette.

"We saw Lakota comin' in. They weren't in a good mood. Anythin' I oughta know afore we pull out?"

Hunter's long fingers carefully shaped the cigarette. "No more than the usual. The young braves are riled up, arguing with the older ones." He shrugged broad shoulders. "They not unnaturally don't like all the wagons comin' across their land. They are less and less believing that the white man's telling the truth when he says he's just passing through. With the trappers and traders, people came and went, never stayed more than the winter for trapping. These new folks are carrying all their plunder with them. Looks to be a lot more permanent."

"I understand their concerns," Adam said.

"I do too," Hunter said, striking a sulfur match and lighting his cigarette. "I don't much like what I see either. A way of life's dying and not just for the Indians. I can't stop it anymore than they can. Pretty soon men'll be plowing this land. It's a crying shame, but that's the way it is. I no more know where I'll go next than they do."

St. Louis nodded with understanding. "Why don't ya come on to Oregon with us? I'm gonna file for a homestead there. Ya could do the same."

Hunter laughed. "Maybe it's what I ought to do, but I won't. I'll head north when it gets too tight to breathe around here. There's still country up there that hasn't been touched, places a man can be free. It's going to take them awhile to fill that country up."

"In case ya change yore mind," St. Louis said, "I'll send a letter to the post here for ya, lettin' ya know where I am."

Hunter shook his head, blew out a cloud of smoke, and looked into it as though seeing a future he didn't much like. "Who knows? Maybe I will. I can't see myself pushing a plow though."

St. Louis studied the ground a moment. "So, do ya think we'll run into trouble?"

"I wouldn't look for it with an outfit the size of yours. Seemed like I watched the wagons come in half the morning."

St. Louis stood up. "Ya come on out for supper."

Hunter smiled. "I'll be there."

As they walked away, Matt, unsure of the meaning of Hunter's words, asked for clarification. "So, there won't be trouble?"

"Most likely not," St. Louis said. "I'll talk to the commander anyway. Since he's supposed to be here to serve us, we'll just let him do it."

By the time they left the post, it was almost dark; and they knew all there was to know. There had been several minor skirmishes between soldiers on patrol and Sioux bands. The week before a half-hearted assault had been made on a group of ten wagons northwest of the fort with no serious damage. Earlier in the month, a small outfit, a family traveling alone had been killed in a canyon west of them. The captain was convinced, however, that the size of St. Louis' party would preclude trouble. The only question mark in the figuring was the report that the Cheyenne and Sioux were gathering in the hills northwest of the fort. It was anyone's guess as to why.

"Could just be a seasonal celebration," St. Louis said as they walked back to the wagon encirclement.

"I'm still finding it hard to believe they actually attacked the train ahead of us, small or not," Adam said. Matt knew from the many times of hearing St. Louis reassure others that was not a normal occurrence along the Oregon Trail. To the south, with the Comanche, there had been large-scale attacks, but up here only isolated wagon units had faced danger.

"Just a skirmish," St. Louis reminded him.

"Except to those involved."

When they got back to the wagon, they sat around the campfire and drank some of Clem's murky coffee, while giving him a shortened version of what they'd learned.

"I don't like it, not atall," Clem muttered when they'd finished.

"What would make them attack?" Matt asked, carefully sipping the acrid coffee. No one made coffee quite like Clem, Matt was convinced it would stand on its own if left for a day.

"Could be a lot of reasons," St. Louis said, staring darkly into his own cup. "Maybe somebody took a shot at one of 'em, raped one of their women. Could be they got a new holy man, someone with special power, and he had a dream or a vision. It's like the rest of us. There's days it don't take much to get a body riled."

"They believe in dreams as signs?" Matt asked.

"If it's the right one doin' the dreamin'. When they need to figure out what to do or maybe make a special offering, they go alone into the hills, find a sacred place, and stay, not eatin' or drinkin' 'til the dream comes to 'em. It's powerful medicine."

"I've heard about another thing they do to get medicine," Adam added. "The Sun Dance."

St. Louis nodded, "I've seen it."

"Dance for the sun, in what way?" Matt asked.

"All the people come together for dancin', fastin', prayin'. The medicine man sets up the pole. The men who have decided to participate have a dowel of wood driven through the skin on their chest and back as it's tied by a long rawhide strap that runs to the top of the pole. They dance then, not stoppin', not eatin' as they try to tear the dowel from their skin. It's powerful medicine as they get messages of prophecy, dreams, and experience a trance." He gave Matt a telling look.

Adam gave a laugh. "Deprive a man of sleep and food and have him in a daze with pain, I suppose anyone would get a hallucination."

St. Louis nodded. "The thing is, if the dancer's an important warrior or a medicine man, his vision means something to the others."

"Sounds like religion to me... all of them," Adam said.

"It's big medicine. Some of the Plains tribes meet for it once a year. It's been going on for as long as anybody knows. Nobody forces nobody though. It is a sign of their manhood what they can endure. I seen men with many scars on their chest and back. Lot of folks think it's barbaric, but it's one way they have of tryin' to reach God. They're wantin' to give somethin' more than what's easy. A piece of themselves. They don't mind hurtin' when it serves a bigger purpose. If they crucify the flesh, their spirit grows stronger."

"When you know no matter what happens to your body or what you suffer, it can't touch who you are, it does make you stronger," Matt said as he stared into space, lost for the moment in memories he had no intention of revealing.

"Maybe that's some of the idea," St. Louis said. "You know, the Injuns are a powerful, spiritual people. They look around 'em and see the Creator everywhere, touching everythin'. Wakan Tanka, the Lakota call Him. If somethin' happens, they look to see what the Spirit's tellin' 'em. They look for a message in everything that happens. Too many of our religious folks got God pegged into their services-- or busy off punishin' the sinners, maybe burnin' down the saloons. They leave him out of the pesky little day to day things. Then they call the Indian a savage."

"I never thought you were such a lover of the Indian," Adam said, with a pretend look of amazement.

St. Louis grinned. "I have lived with 'em and see them as folks, but folks being trained a different way than most of us. There's times to admire 'em and times to watch out for 'em. And I'm seein' this as one of the times to watch out."

"What do you want us to do?" Matt asked, breaking free from his own dark memories.

"I wish I knew. If you see tracks, try to figure out how many ponies, whether they got travoises with them. Women and children along, ain't likely lookin' for trouble. If ya see them, and they're painted, get back to me pronto."

"So, you do expect trouble." Adam frowned as he tossed out the remnants of his coffee.

"Ya heard what that commander said, lots of tribes comin' together. The fort's uneasy. That makes me uneasy. Better to worry a little now than take everythin' for granted and make a mistake."

Adam smiled. "Might be the commander's a worrywart."

"Might be I am too when things don't feel right." He went to his wagon and came back with a bottle of whiskey. He handed it first to Adam who took a swig, then it was passed to Clem. Matt shook his head before St. Louis took a swallow.

Matt sat back, recognizing the rush of anticipation, the exhilaration that potential danger always brought him. This business of facing danger, of fighting, was something he understood. Although in his personal experience, the conflicts had not been nearly so noble. Not men protecting their lands or their families but fighting over women, money, or sometimes for the sheer joy of pummeling each other.

If it hadn't been for Amy, he might have welcomed the challenge, something physical to fight, instead of the nervous, emotional tension that had weighted him down these past weeks. When she had accused him of not considering her when danger approached, she was wrong. He'd learned to his chagrin that the love he felt for her could almost paralyze him with the fear she might be hurt or that he'd lose what he seemed so close to attaining.

With the wagon train's usual predisposition of everyone knowing everyone else's business, within two days, the talk of possible Indian problems spread rapidly with no official word. Matt saw the uneasiness in the people. They talked among themselves, sharing horror stories they'd read or heard. Their fear grew as they traveled farther from the fort, making assistance from the soldiers unlikely if they did have trouble.

After saddling his gelding, Matt rode to where St. Louis and

Adam were talking and studying the ground. When he reined in his mount, St. Louis looked up. "I'm just sendin' Adam out today."

"Why?"

"Don't get yore dander up," St. Louis said, correctly reading the jut of his jaw. "Ya'll get yore share of action. I'm not sendin' Adam out all that far either. Yesterday ya saw tracks of a lot of ponies, no travoises. That figures to be Sioux. We'll keep the wagons travelin' in a tight bunch. I want ya on horseback up in the lead with yore Sharps limbered up. You spread the word to the other men. There'll be no firin' at any Injuns unless they're painted and fire on us. Even if ya see them ridin' up, yellin', shootin' in the air, and carryin' on. Only if they fire on us, do you fire back."

"What are you expecting?"

St. Louis smiled. "Challenges maybe. Teases. A lot of times the young bucks like to ride up close to a train like this one, yip a little and make out like they're real he-men. If we don't act scared, likely they'll just ride on. If somebody gets an itchy trigger finger and one gets killed, then we got trouble."

Matt rode past Amy's wagon as he made his circuit, watching from under his brim as she walked with Loraine and Belle, her eyes on the ground. When he'd ridden past, he allowed himself one backward glance. Her gaze met his, the expression unreadable.

The day seemed to go on forever. It was hot and dusty. Sweat trickled down his back, cleaving his shirt to his spine, adhering dust to his face until he gave up and tied his scarf around his lower face bandit style. Around noon, Adam rode in. Matt wheeled his horse to where he could hear what he told St. Louis.

"There's a good sized band of what look like Sioux just over the ridge."

"Any paint?"

"Not that I saw."

"Wal, keep your eyes open and the wagons movin'," St. Louis ordered. He glanced at Matt, "Ya heard what I said earlier. Make sure ya remind the others. Adam you take the rear."

Matt kicked his gelding into a run, heading for the lead wagon, repeating the message as he rode down the line. The drivers didn't like it. Some tried to argue. "We got a right to defend ourselves."

"Take it up with St. Louis."

As the wagons lumbered over the ridge, Matt saw the Indian men, thirty or forty in a bunch, proudly sitting their ponies, waiting. Most of them were naked, except for breechclouts; a few wore leggings or vests. Their horses were adorned with differing marks, streaks of black and red. From what he could see, most of the men carried bows and arrows with a few brandishing rifles. No paint on their faces or bodies. Matt took a deep breath to steady his nerves.

Two young braves kicked their horses into a run, coming straight for the wagons. They were yelling, their arms waving dramatically in the air as they sped forward.

Matt, a little ahead of the lead wagon, reined in Dartan, slowing his gait until he was almost stopped. His rifle cradled in his arm, he watched expressionlessly as the two young braves rode toward him. He waited, wondering when they would stop, then if they would stop, until only ten or fifteen feet separated them from him. He could see their eyes, read the wild excitement on their faces before they spun their horses and raced away.

Only after they'd turned did Matt realize how tightly he'd clenched his jaw. His shoulders were stiff with tension and sweat ran down his spine. Taking a deep breath, he turned and smiled encouragingly to the driver of the first wagon, signaling him to move forward. He saw the same sickly expression on the driver's face he imagined was on his own.

The afternoon progressed with the same pattern. Sometimes an Indian would ride toward them, shout some kind of challenge, but none came as close as the first two, and no shots were exchanged as the settlers obeyed St. Louis' instructions, at least outwardly maintaining their calm.

Finally with a sense of relief, Matt heard St. Louis call a halt to the day's travel."Corral the livestock inside the circle. Keep alert. Adam--" Adam and Matt both rode to him. "Keep an eye out but don't get away from the wagons. A single man alone'd be a prime target."

He gestured to Matt. "Make the rounds of the men again. Tell 'em to stay calm. They done good today, but we ain't out of this yet."

"They're sick of seein' my face," Matt protested, "and don't believe a word I'm sayin'."

St. Louis smiled wolfishly. "Then we'll have a meetin' tonight. I'll make sure they understand."

With dusk, Matt checked on his father and brother.

"Does St. Louis expect more trouble?" his pa asked, as he nursed a mug filled with what was most likely whiskey.

"Today was kind of a game, I guess." Matt looked at Morey and received an ugly glare in response.

"How?" asked his father.

"It's their way. Don't worry. He says we're too big to attack."

Out of the fading light, Amy and Loraine emerged, their faces pale.

"We've been checking on friends," Loraine said, "and thought we'd see how you all were." Amy said nothing, her gaze intent on Matt, where he leaned against a wagon wheel, one boot heel hooked on a spoke.

Morey smiled nastily. "Right neighborly of you." He grinned at Matt. "Nothing to worry about though. Little brother just brought back the report. No trouble he can't handle." He chuckled. "If Matt says it, it must be true." He let his eyes roam over the two young women from head to toe but said nothing Matt could use as an excuse to take action.

Matt pulled his hat brim low over his eyes and studied Amy. Her eyes were big, dark with worry. Although he didn't like having her around Morey and knew she shouldn't have come, he was rapidly reaching a point where he didn't care what should or shouldn't be. He just wanted to be with her.

After a few moments, he stepped back into the shadows, certain Amy would follow, knowing Morey would miss none of it. For this moment he needed to hold her, feel her softness against his body.

As Amy edged into the darkness, Loraine continued talking brightly to Nathan, valiantly trying to include Morey in the conversation. Whatever words Amy might've said, he cut off as he claimed her mouth, plumbing its depths. When he let her breathe, she whispered, "I saw those two Indians riding right at you. I was so scared..." She stopped, clinging to him, her fingers digging into the muscles of his shoulders.

He stroked her soft hair. He hoped she wasn't angry over the risk, that they wouldn't fight when they had so little time. His day had been a long one. The thought of arguing with her when he wanted to hold her was more than he could handle.

With relief, he heard her whispers, soft, caring, not angry. "I hate it when we're not together, when things like this happen. I hate knowing I can't be waiting for you when you come back. And I hate knowing that, if God forbid, something happened to you, no one would even tell me because they wouldn't know it mattered to me."

"I do understand, baby," he murmured, his lips against her hair. He caught his breath as she nuzzled his neck, her breath a sensual whisper against his skin, her fingers driving him crazy with their promise. He wanted her touch; he craved it like a cool drink on a hot day. He wanted to feel her hands on his body, feel them everywhere. He--

"We can't go on like this." He didn't need to hear her words to know his own resolve was weakening. He was beginning to feel like she-- somehow, someway they had to be together. Anything less was tearing them up. "I love you. Don't keep me waiting much longer on this. Do you hear me?" She lightly pounded his chest with her fist.

"I got your message." He grinned, kissing the top of her hair. "We'll work it out. You get back now. I got to go see St Louis, some kind of meeting about tomorrow." He tried to resist the temptation but then yielded. "If later, after supper, you and Loraine were walking by the livestock corral, there's a big tree there."

She frowned, her hand lightly stroking his cheek, her eyes

dark with tension and worry. "All right, but remember what I said. Don't think you can sweet talk me around this. It's complicating things for everybody-- Raine, Adam, you, me. You know there's less resentment of you now than there was. You're running out of excuses, Matthew."

Matt smiled at her vehemence even as he felt a shiver run down his back.

CHAPTER 16

"Matt!" Amos Stevens' voice stopped Matt mid-stride. He turned and saw Amos and Martha walking toward him. He braced himself. They were unlikely to say anything he'd welcome hearing.

"I, that is we, want to say something," Amos began slowly. "I know it's going to seem blunt and maybe sudden to you, but Martha and I have noticed the way Amy seems to be disappearing in the evenings. At first we supposed it was Adam Stone, but it isn't, is it?" He rubbed the back of his neck. "There's no easy way to say this. Is Amy meeting you?"

Matt smiled faintly. Just like Amos, no beating around the bush. He and his daughter had that in common. He studied the couple for a moment, thinking how much he owed them, how many times they'd offered to help him, even if he'd been too proud to take the help. He wouldn't lie to them, but he couldn't bring himself to tell them what he had denied Amy the opportunity to say. "Is there a reason you're askin' me, not her?"

"We do want to talk to her," Martha said, her husky voice a slightly deeper version of Amy's. "Amos and I went for a walk to talk this over. It just happened we saw you first."

"It'd be better you talk to her." He knew those words told them all they needed to know and had not wanted to hear.

"There is a chance," Martha said, swallowing, and then

rushing the words, "that you two might be mistaking friendship for something else. Oh, Lord, I don't know how to say this that won't hurt you." She smiled apologetically.

"Maybe there's no good way to say it," Matt retorted, rocking back on his heels, his arms crossed over his chest.

"It isn't... I mean," she said, "we care what happens to you both. I'm just not sure Amy knows what love is. It would be so easy to mistake compassion for-- something else. You know how she is." Her eyes pleaded with him to understand.

"You mean about takin' in strays?" He kept his voice low, not angry, because even though their words were hurting him, it wasn't from malice.

"You're not a stray," Amos said. "The thing is Amy is head-strong. She rushes into things. Women her age can make wrong judgments. Hopefully they don't have to spend the rest of their lives paying for them."

Matt saw tears in Martha's eyes. "If you care for her, if we're right about what's happening between you, please think about what is best for her. If she had more time, maybe she could decide what she wanted. It would be for your sake as well as hers."

"You mean decide on somebody like Stone?" Matt retorted, trying to keep his tone light. He wasn't surprised by how they saw him or at their reluctance to see their daughter involved with him. They knew too much, and what they didn't know, they likely guessed.

"He's a nice young man, but no I don't mean him," Martha said. "It's a matter of giving her time to think through what she wants. There have been a lot of transitions in her life, things she's had to give up. I'd like to see her be grounded again before she decides something that will impact the rest of her life. Can you understand that?"

"I respect your concerns, ma'am." There was truth in her words, doubts he'd also harbored. Maybe it was all the upheavals with coming west that made Amy want him, want something that she had had. Maybe it was pity. He dismissed her ardent response that had taken even him by surprise. Possibly, it was just newness of sensual touches and not really him.

"We didn't want to hurt you, Matt." Martha put her hand out, taking hold of his arm. "But I can see we have. You'll probably find this hard to believe, but we do care what happens to you also."

Matt clenched his jaw and nodded before he walked away. He couldn't think about it now but maybe, maybe with time, he could put some perspective to it.

The circle of light at St. Louis' wagon was shadowed with the shapes of men. St. Louis looked up as Clem handed Matt a cup of coffee. "I was just gonna send somebody for ya."

"Got held up," Matt said expressionlessly as he squatted by the fire.

"Where you been?" Clem asked nosily. Matt smiled, thinking the old man had become almost as much of a mother hen as St. Louis, watching out for his boys, making sure they had their suppers, worrying if they didn't look well.

"I'm here now."

"All right," St. Louis went on, looking around him at the faces of the men he'd gathered. "I want ya to listen good."

Before he could say anything, Ralph Hall snarled, "We're under attack, and we ain't doing a thing about it. Why didn't you let us shoot them today? We could've killed a half dozen easy." He glared at Matt as though it was his fault.

Matt rose slowly, a smile on his face he knew didn't reach his narrowed eyes. Half the men there would like to pound him into the ground. Let them try. He was in just the mood to meet their combativeness with his own.

St. Louis straightened, moved around the circle to stake out a position, a space back from the others. He raised his arms authoritatively. "We are not under attack. If we had been, there'd be no askin' about it. There are a lot of Injuns in these hills. We saw only a couple of them today, but as of yet, they are not hurting us. We are not going to strike at them unless they do."

"Why are there so many? Why are they following us?" William Porter asked, staring at the hills, shifting his feet uneasily.

Adam, who was leaning against a wagon smiled darkly.

"They might not be following us. After all, this is their land. They've got a right to be where they want. We're the intruders."

"Injun lover!" spat Jacob Carter, the oldest son of the Carter brood.

Adam straightened his shoulders. "And if I am?" he asked suggestively, a hard smile never leaving his face.

There was a moment of pregnant silence. "Nothing," Carter said in a softer tone.

Matt recognized the tension; everyone, including himself, was quick to flare.

"Lay back on this," St. Louis demanded. "Fear is your worst enemy. Half of ya been readin' them stupid little books givin' off with a lot of horror stories, lumpin' all Injuns into one bunch. Most of the time, them stories ain't even written by men who've been out here."

"How about the rest?" Porter asked, looking uneasily out at the growing darkness. "An Indian could be out there, watching us right now."

"Why'd they come at us today?" asked Brick Webb, his voice breaking.

"They didn't." St. Louis' voice was patient. "I told ya. If they'd come after ya, there'd have been no doubt. Today was just a game playin', posturin', testin'. Injuns got a real sense of humor. The worst danger you folks face is yoreselves!"

"Maybe they're just tired of having uninvited guests," Adam suggested belligerently, glaring again at Ralph Hall. The man seemed to swell with his anger.

St. Louis scowled at Adam. "Don't go lookin' for trouble. Not out there nor here. I asked you men to come tonight, so's ya'd go out and talk to the other folks. Calm 'em down. Not get yourselves all stirred up."

He stopped and looked at Adam, "How far ahead's that canyon?"

"If we kept traveling, we'd go through it tomorrow about sunset."

"We don't usually travel at night; so they won't be expecting that if we did. Traveling like usual, that'd put the last wagon through when it's pure dark"

"Are you saying there's a dangerous canyon ahead? The Indians might use for an ambush?" asked William Porter, looking around, his eyes scanning the darkness for enemies.

St. Louis shook his head. "Like I said twenty times now, trouble ain't likely. But... if there was to be, it'd be there."

"Could they then shoot at us from above?" Ralph Hall asked.

"I said I don't figure they will. If I believed that, we'd go at this different. For the most part, Injuns ain't lookin' for the kind of trouble that'd bring the army down on 'em. But to be on the safe side, we'll take a slow day tomorrow and wait to go through in the mornin'." He smiled reassuringly at the stern, anxious faces surrounding him. "Remember what I told ya before. Don't fire unless they fire and it's at you. Be ready when we go through... just in case I'm wrong."

"Is that possible?" asked Brick, his face creasing into a frown.

"That I'm wrong?" St. Louis retorted with pretended thoughtfulness, "it happens now and again-- but not often."

Amos Stevens, who had entered the circle near the end of the discussion, stepped forward "We have a lot riding on you being right."

St. Louis smiled. "I know. Jest remember-- there ain't never been no big trains attacked that I know about. Does that help?"

"I don't know how much. I got three daughters and a wife to think about."

"I understand." St. Louis looked out at the men. "I'll repeat. What a man thinks inside, the way it eats him up, that's what causes trouble. Panic'll cause us to lose more lives than Injuns ever will."

When the questions had finally all been answered, some more than once, the men left. St. Louis turned to Adam and Matt. "I got a couple more things I want to cover with the two of you about tomorrow and where I want you to be as we go through the canyon."

"Can it wait?" Adam asked with a cheerful grin. "I got some-body I want to check on."

St. Louis smiled and nodded. "Before first light."

Frustrated at what he knew would now make impossible

meeting Amy, Matt wandered through the camp, not wanting to return to his own wagon. He spoke to no one. He watched as Jenny Porter bent to pick up her baby, crooning. In another wagon he heard a child crying, a mother reassuring. Everywhere he looked people had someone.

He wondered if Amy's parents were even now confronting her with their suspicions, or would Adam's presence forestall that? His desire for secrecy had put her in a bad spot. Although there was nothing he could do about it now, he felt guilty.

When he returned to his own wagon, his brother and father were asleep. The campfire was dead, the only sounds that of nighthawks out on the plains and a distant coyote-- at least it sounded like a coyote.

Removing his shirt, he slept out beyond the wagon, wrapped in a blanket. He thought he would be unable to sleep, but he must have been wrong. A light touch on his bare shoulder, the lifting of the blanket, and a slim body pressing against his were the first he knew she was there. She cuddled down against his bare chest, the blanket pulled back over them both.

Half thinking this was a dream, he murmured, "You're not here."

"I know," Amy whispered, her lips against his neck. "I'm waiting for you at the tree by the livestock. It's cold and dark. The guard keeps asking what I'm doing there, and you don't come!"

He swallowed, running his fingers through her hair, trying to wake up. "I figured Adam was goin' to make it impossible for you to get away."

"Are you sure that's all?" She reached up and punishingly nipped his earlobe.

"What else could it be?" He thought about mentioning his conversation with her parents and decided against it. If she didn't already, she'd know soon enough. He had no desire to ruin this moment for himself.

"This feels wonderful." She snuggled closer, wrapping one of her arms around his waist, drawing their bodies tightly together. "You're warm," she murmured.

She kissed his smooth chest, her warmth and caresses

arousing his body and making him all too aware of how alone they were, of how easy it would be to take her. But what about tomorrow or the next day? What if he didn't make it? Where would that leave her? He didn't exactly have a premonition of disaster, but something made him uneasy, as though it was waiting for him, something he wouldn't welcome.

Her breath sensual torture against his bare skin, she whispered, "Adam did come by tonight. He and Papa were reassuring about the Indians, but they seemed strange. You were at the meeting. What did St. Louis say?"

"He doesn't expect trouble." He wasn't much interested in hearing about Adam or anyone else. He pushed her hair aside to kiss the nape of her neck as she arched against him.

"It's just I have a feeling," she whispered, kissing his face, the tip of his chin, his nose, everywhere but his lips. "I suppose it's just the tension over the Indians, but something's scaring me." Their breathing was coming more unevenly as the tentative lovemaking began to heat their bodies with desire.

"Worried about Adam?" he asked huskily.

"As a friend."

He laughed. "Think I heard that one before." Before she could protest, his lips, tired of playing games, sought hers out, parted them and received a response that left them both panting, the longing for more growing stronger with each kiss, each unfulfilled caress.

"You know better than that," she whispered when she was able. "You know how I feel."

"Maybe I need reassurance, now and again," he said, greedily taking what she offered for this moment, but aware that at any cost he had to keep control of his desire. This was not the night to take it all, to do what her lips and his hard arousal were begging him to do.

Her fingers caressed his bare back, feeling of his scars. "You have so many scars."

"Is that a problem?"

"I don't like remembering how you got them."

"They're just scars, baby. Old and forgotten."

"I want to stand between you and more."

"Oh and get them on your tender skin," he teased then wondered if her mother had been right. Did Amy feel sorry for him and was confusing that with something else?

"I do want to protect you, take care of you," she murmured, her cheek against the hard muscles of his chest. "It's a strange sort of feeling because you're so big, so strong. It doesn't seem you need protecting from anybody or anything, but somehow I want to." She kissed the spot she had been sensually tormenting; then he felt her tears on his skin.

"What's wrong now?" he asked with a trace of exasperation.

"I'm happy. I never knew how it could be to love somebody like this."

"It makes you cry?" Nothing about this conversation was making him happier. Maybe it was all pity.

"Women cry sometimes when they're happy."

"So, I bring you tears when you are mad, worried, and happy. It doesn't make sense."

"It does if you're a woman," she whispered, smiling through the tears.

"Maybe but--"

Her arms came around him, her hands caressing his back as her lovemaking became more purposefully, almost but not quite breaking his resolve. He sat up. "I reckon a man can only take so much of that, and I reached the limit. We keep on this way, there won't be no holdin' back for the weddin'."

"You think I'd mind," she whispered as she watched him hastily pull on boots and shirt.

"I would. We're goin' to do this right, if it kills me, and it just might," he muttered as he stood to walk her back to her wagon, aware she had heard him only when he heard her soft laugh.

Matt tightened the girth strap on his saddle and patted his horse's rump as he waited for the signal for the wagons to pull out. An unusual fog shrouded the breaking dawn, the mist an eerie cover over people and land. He heard hushed voices but no yelling, laughter, boisterous talk as wagons slowly readied themselves to pull into their places in line. From the tension in the air, obviously St. Louis' reassurances had assuaged few fears.

As they moved out, slowly gaining speed, the terrain changed. Fog altered the landscape into a place where every piece of sagebrush or rock became an enemy. Matt scanned the horizon, looking for something he never saw. It was as though the Indians of the days past were gone, swallowed by the fog.

Adam caught up with him, slowing his own mount to walk beside Matt's. "See anything?" he asked.

Matt shook his head. Dartan skittishly danced sideways. Matt pulled back on the reins, running his hand soothingly down the gelding's neck. His own nerves taut, he felt anything but soothing. "He wants to run," he muttered. "All morning's been like this."

"They sense the edginess." Adam's gaze scanned the rimrock to the north.

"You think the Indians are still around."

"I'd bet on it. You got any money?" Adam's grin was speculative.

"What little I got isn't going into your pockets."

Adam laughed. "When the fog lifted a little, I saw smoke north of us, just over that ridge. From what I could tell, it is a big encampment."

"Which means?"

"Nothing really."

"Folks are scared."

Adam shrugged. "It's to be expected. Likely nothing will happen though." Adam gigged his horse in the side. "Catch up with you later."

Dartan tried to break into a run to follow Adam's horse. Matt reprimanded him, pulling back again on the reins. "I know what you want," he growled as he patted the gelding's neck. "Me, too, but we're both going to follow orders."

By mid-morning, the fog burned off, revealing blue sky. If only the tensions of the people, the feelings of impending doom, could be so easily eased.

Traveling slowly, they arrived at the mouth of the canyon in late afternoon. Night camp was as quietly made as morning had been broken. The only noise and problems came from the complaining livestock, the fear from the people affecting their stock. By the time the families had settled down, the sun had disappeared and darkness claimed the land.

Walking into St. Louis' camp, Matt saw firelight flickering eerily over the faces of St. Louis and Clem who knelt beside the campfire. Adam, sipping a cup of coffee, leaned against the side of the wagon.

Clem glared at Matt. "I expect you want something to eat. Folks get to thinkin' around here all I got to do is cook and put aside food for them as don't come in when it's ready."

Matt lowered himself, hunkering down on his heels, as he poured himself a cup of coffee and tried to look humble. The growl in his stomach went a long ways toward helping. He grinned as Clem lifted the lid from a black pot at the edge of the fire and began ladling out a plate of stew. Gratefully, Matt accepted the heaped tin dish with thanks and began eating hungrily.

"I oughta be out scoutin', 'stead of cookin'," Clem grumbled as he resumed washing tin plates. "I know more'n anybody about sightin' Injuns. Just 'cause Adam's younger don't make him no better at it."

"Maybe so." Matt grinned. "But if anythin' happened to you-- who'd make biscuits? I tasted Adam's. We'd starve. This stew's damned good."

Clem's narrow face lightened with pleasure. He glanced over at St. Louis to make certain he'd heard the compliment. "Ya see," he growled, "somebody appreciates my cookin', even if you don't."

Adam, studying the fire, slid down the side of the wagon to squat, leaning his back against a wheel. He began rolling a cigarette.

"When did ya start smokin'?" St. Louis asked.

Adam shrugged. "Just now and then. You ever smoke, Matt?"

Matt nodded. "I tried it. Didn't do anything for me other than lower my bank account."

Adam looked at him with amazement. "You got a bank account?"

"Until I bought the outfit for going West."

Adam lit his cigarette. "You expecting trouble?" St. Louis asked him.

"It looks to me to be a peaceful group, maybe a summer gathering, but I admit it is a big bunch to be traveling together."

"How many ya figure?" St. Louis gazed intently at his scout as drew on the cigarette.

"If they're coming from all around in the numbers they are from the south, I'd estimate two hundred braves. The smoke from their camp says there could be as many as seventy-five tepees, which means I would expect women and children. It doesn't look like a war party, but it's all guesswork if I'm going to continue staying close to the wagons." Adam gave St. Louis a telling look as he blew out the smoke.

"And you are," St. Louis retorted.

"What if I went out with him?" Matt suggested without much hope. "Two'd be safer than one."

"Depends on what two," Adam said.

"You sayin' I couldn't keep as quiet as you?" Matt bristled.

St. Louis looked from one to the other. "If ya two roosters are fixin' to argue all the time, might just be neither of ya'll go out. Might just be me and Clem'll do it."

Clem grinned as Matt and Adam fell silent. He stirred the fire before he measured out coffee and water for another of his stronger than strong pots of brew.

"Don't like the idea of that many gatherin' together," St. Louis said. "What're they doin'?" Thoughtfully he rubbed the side of his nose. "I don't look for attack though. They'd lose too many of their own. They'd have no gain to hit us as it stands."

Adam shook his head. "I don't know about that, but I do know I wouldn't say anything to the others about the size. They're edgy enough as it is." Adam stared into the crackling fire. "It's possible the gathering is pure coincidence. Could be some kind of religious thing."

St. Louis shook his head, worry furrowing his brow. "Ya boys go on to bed. Full moon night like this, I don't sleep much anyhow. Figure I'll just think on this a mite."

Matt felt a flow of nervous energy through his body, his muscles tight as a drum. This night would hold little sleep for him either. To the south, a coyote yodeled. Another, closer to the wagons, answered. A chorus joined in and as abruptly fell silent.

The four men slouched back to settle themselves round the fire, occasionally adding a stick of wood and poking it to renewed life. Clem dozed fitfully, waking apologetically, soon snoring again. The camp was silent, with the only fire burning their own.

"You know, times like this," St. Louis mused, "I think on the meanin' of it all-- about life. About what's in the good book." He looked over at Adam with a meaningful glance. "There's a lot of wisdom in that book."

Adam snorted. "I don't doubt there is some at least. I know something of the Bible. What do you take me for? A heathen."

Matt grinned at the lean, buckskin-garbed form, sprawled back against a wagon wheel, the cigarette between his lips. "I sure can't see you in Sunday School, Stone."

"If you can't visualize it, it must not have happened," Adam retorted.

"Bible gives me comfort in times like this," St. Louis continued as though nothing had been said. "'But they that wait upon the Lord shall renew their strength, mount up with wings of eagles.' When the night's long, and mornin' seems a long ways off, words like them come back to me. Give comfort I reckon."

"See," Adam grumbled, "that's where you lose me. Do you really believe God hears you? That some god somewhere cares one way or another what happens, whether the Indians hit us or not? Who's to say those Indians aren't also praying that god's going to hear them? Give them wings like eagles. Maybe their god is up there fighting our god." He grinned as he drew again on the cigarette.

Matt stared into his coffee cup, its murky depths almost as black as the night around them. The scream of an owl pierced the sky as it soared high above. He heard the rush of its wings as it plummeted downward for a meal. The sounds fit his own dark feelings, the ominous shadow growing darker each day.

"This'll go on all night. You two arguin'," Clem said, yawning. "Ain't neither of you never goin' to convince the other."

St. Louis ignored the interruption. "I don't know they ain't prayin' to Him and bein' heard-- just like I'm doin'."

Adam laughed. "So what good does it do you?"

Matt looked up, saw Adam's eyes on him. Steadily he met the probing gaze, unsurprised when Adam's next question was directed to him. "So does you believing in a god make you less scared than me?"

"Unlikely," Matt drawled.

"Well then?"

Not particularly eager to argue spiritual philosophies, Matt thought for a moment before he answered. "It hasn't got anything to do with it for me, not protecting me, not killing someone else. It's just I can't explain life at all any other way."

"So do you believe in fluffy clouds and angels?" He watched Matt through the smoke. "Is it that if you get killed tomorrow, you're going up to sit on one? While me on the other hand--" He stopped, chuckled. "Hell, we know what I'd be sitting on."

Matt laughed. "I'm not a religious man as I said. I just see it that there is something out there, bigger than us and maybe there is a plan behind it all even if I can't see it. I can't say I pray though. I don't ask for something. I gave that up many years ago. If you're waiting for me to explain life, you'll be waiting a lot longer than morning. I can't explain what I feel about it anymore than I can explain the fog."

"If I can't see it, taste it or feel it, it's nothing I need." Adam shook his head.

"It helps some, not so much for deliverance as just comforting, giving meaning, and it's not something anybody understands," St. Louis added.

"I don't think I'll ever get it. My mother was a church-going woman," Adam threw the end of the cigarette into the fire, "but she came home ready to beat the hell out of us kids. She was what I suppose most people would call a good woman, but I never saw anything in her narrow-minded, bigoted life that made me think I'd want what she had. She was the most joyless woman I've ever known."

"Bein' a churchgoer don't mean a hill of beans," St. Louis said. "It's how ya live that counts. Talk's cheap."

"This is looking to head into a sermon," Adam said wryly. "And if it is, I might go to sleep after all."

St. Louis chuckled. "I'll put a lid on it-- for now."

They sat quietly, studying the small tongues of flame that licked upward. Nearer at hand the livestock shuffled restlessly, cows bawling, horses nickering. "Sometimes I miss home," Adam said. "Even knowing how my mother was and doubtless still is. Especially when I know I'm never going back and probably won't ever see my family again."

"Ya could go back to Ohio."

"I tried once. It didn't work. Everybody had their life. What they thought was important I didn't think mattered a hill of beans, which incidentally was exactly what they thought was important. All my mother could see was me settling down on a little farm and marrying one of the local dairymaids. She didn't understand the restlessness, the yearning I had to see what was over the hill. She never understood that, and she condemned me for it."

St. Louis nodded. "Women they don't find it easy understandin' a man's got to go after his destiny."

Matt chuckled as he lay back, staring up at the sky. "This is going to turn into a sermon, and I already heard it."

"No appreciation. Ya young whippersnappers think ya know it all. Might be ya could learn a thing or two from us old-timers," St. Louis said.

In the darkness, the stars were more visible, their numbers seeming to fill the ebony sky with glimmering lights. It was a peaceful night, surprisingly so when Matt thought that camped two or three ridges over were Indians, possibly staring up at the same endless sky. They could be plotting mayhem. Or were they engaged in the same meandering kind of thoughts?

"So, are you scared about what we might face tomorrow, Matt?" Adam interrupted his thoughts. "You've never been around Indians before."

"No, my worries are no different than usual. That I won't hold up my end. Doesn't that ever worry you?"

Adam's voice had a smile in it. "Of course, but I've faced things like this before."

"And I'm just a kid," Matt finished for him.

"You can't have seen all that much in your-- what is it-- nineteen years."

Matt leaned up on one elbow, grinning. "Twenty-one," he corrected, ignoring the rest of Adam's challenge. He told himself he had no need to prove himself and then knew it wasn't so. He did have the need, but only to himself. He wasn't afraid—at least not of death. There were worse things than dying. He knew about those.

CHAPTER 16

The morning was still crisp and cold as Amy walked around the end of her family wagon. The column had made it through the dread canyon. The wagons had taken several hours to work their way past the narrow, rock-strewn cliffs and regroup on the other side. They stopped for the men to assemble with St. Louis, with answers to their questions as well as reassurances. Tension still hung heavy in air filled with the bawling of nervous animals.

Her thoughts were muddled, flitting between planning supper, lingering fear of an Indian attack, irritation over the din created by the livestock, worry over her complex romantic situation, and finally, as happened lately with increasing frequency, images of Matt. She would pull up a recent picture of his face-- angry, happy, disgusted, bewildered, or sensual. Her favorites were sensual. She would be pulled from her daydreams by her mother or sisters telling her she'd not heard a word that had been said, which, of course, had been true.

She looked off toward where the men clustered and idly wondered how long they'd continue arguing. Someone had claimed to have seen Indians in the canyon, but her father said most likely they'd seen wind-sculptured rock and edgy nerves had done the rest.

Even at a distance, Matt's head rose above most of the

others. As was so often true, he stood apart. She couldn't believe the ostracism he still endured. She wanted to be with him, to stand at his side, but any arguments on the subject ended the same, with his infuriating smile and stubborn insistence on doing what he believed was right

Absentmindedly, she stared into the distance, aware of children playing around the Hall wagon. Six or seven-year old boys sat on the box, the eldest pretending to flick a whip at the mules, whose ears were already twitching nervously. Amy squinted her eyes, looking for Mrs. Hall. Surely she hadn't left the children alone.

She was never certain afterward when she realized the older boy had gotten the knack of the whip, but at the same moment one of the mules turned to nip the other. The whip cracking over their heads was all the encouragement the animals needed to rear up and break for the open area to the left of where the wagons had halted. By the time the children understood they had done something not only wrong but dangerous, the wagon was racing too fast for them safely to jump. They clung to the wagon seat, the sounds of their wails echoing across the open land, colliding with the screams of the people as they realized what was happening.

The wagon careened crazily, seemingly only moments from turning over on the rough terrain. A tiny head appeared at the back of the wagon. Screaming with fear, a little girl jumped from the rear gate and lay ominously still in the dust.

From everywhere women and men ran after the wagon. Amy's mother stopped at the fallen child, a four-year old Amy remembered watching play several times around their wagon. She watched as her mother ran her hands over the child's limbs.

From the corner of her eye, Amy saw a running horse, and at the same instant knew Matt had to have leaped on his horse urging it to a breakneck speed.

Unable to tear her gaze from him, Amy began running. Matt and his mount gained on the wagon, but she couldn't see what good it would do to catch it. There seemed no way to stop the mules before a wheel broke or the wagon tipped, crushing the two children who still clung in terror to its seat. If Matt reached the wagon as it toppled, he would be crushed with them.

Rough ground, covered with dried prairie grasses, eroded crevasses and rocks threatened to trip her as she ran, but she refused to slow. Heaving for breath, others ran beside her, a running horse passed them, but she had eyes only for Matt as he closed on the wagon.

Terror beyond words or tears filled her chest. As a child, she'd seen the body of a man crushed by a wagon. The children, Matt, they would all look like that, broken and bleeding. At any moment, she expected to hear the crash, the screams of children, but all she heard were her own lungs heaving for breath, feet running, and the wagon careening across the prairie, creaking, the timbers groaning.

With disbelief, she watched as Matt leaned out, his body seemingly in mid-air for an eternity. For a heart-stopping second, she thought he was on the mule, had safely made the transfer and would be able to pull the animal to a halt; then he slipped to the side, disappearing from her sight.

Her lungs heaved so painfully, she knew she couldn't keep running, but she did. The desire to reach him, to be there before he died, to shelter his broken body was so overpowering that she no longer felt tired. Something beyond herself carried her forward.

The wagon slowed. Unbelievably, instead of toppling to one side, it came to a halt, the mules heaving for breath, the children sobbing. The other horseman dismounted, seemingly before his mount had stopped, and grabbed the trailing wagon reins. Only then did she realize it was Adam, his mouth set in a grim line.

She ran down the last slope, her lungs on fire. Adam had disappeared between the mules and with a sick awareness any hope she had vanished. If Matt had been able to stand, she'd have seen him by now.

Ralph Hall, his solid muscular body heaving with sobs and need for oxygen, reached his children and clasped them into his burly arms. Amy could hear him sobbing. "Thank God!" Tears ran down his dirt-streaked face.

St. Louis rode up and pushed his way through the gathering

crowd. Amy followed in his wake, her jaws clenched. She heard Adam's tense voice. "I think the mule must've kicked him as he stopped the rig."

Pressing her hands against her heart as if that could somehow protect her from the pain, Amy got her first glimpse of Matt as they carefully pulled him from between the mules and laid him on the ground. She watched mutely as St. Louis knelt, checked his pulse, then pulled back his eyelids. Matt's leg moved. He was alive. Her heart began to beat again. She felt the blood surge through her veins. If he was alive, she would keep him that way. She would not let him go.

St. Louis glanced at the still gathering crowd. "You folks, go on, get back to yore wagons." He gestured to Adam. "We'll have to make a litter. Tell Clem to get the wagons circled and put out guards."

Amy knelt beside Matt. She took his scraped and bloody hand, needing to hold onto him. Only then did she look at St. Louis's somber face, as he ran his hands down Matt's legs. There was blood on his head and more on his right leg. St. Louis, using his knife, ripped off the tail of his shirt wrapping it tightly around the leg above the wound.

Aware of the bleeding roused Amy to action as she stood to rip the flounce from her petticoat and hand it to St. Louis.

"Likely he was dragged over somethin' afore he could get them stopped," St. Louis mumbled to himself as he crudely bandaged Matt's head wound. "We'll have to get him back to camp to do anything about this."

Amy heard her mother's voice behind her. "I can help. Angie Hall will have a bump on her head but nothing that stopped her wailing; eyes were not dilated."

Adam came up, leading his horse. "I got a quilt and a couple of shovels. It was the quickest way I could think to rig a travois." Within moments, the primitive sling was ready, and they carefully transferred Matt's limp body onto the blanket.

St. Louis looked into Amy's eyes, patted her shoulder reassuringly. "You steady him and we'll get him back up to camp as easy as we can." She nodded unable to speak.

.   .   .

At the wagon, they laid Matt on the ground near the fire Clem had hastily built. Amy knelt at his side, taking his hand in hers, needing to feel the warmth of his skin, the beat of his pulse.

Clem swallowed hard when he looked at the blood staining the bandages. "He ain't dead, is he?"

"He's not dead and not dying, just unconscious from hitting his head," Amy's mother said, running her hands lightly over his hair, checking for a fracture. She gave Amy's shoulder a squeeze. "I'll be back as soon as I get my medicines, herbs and stitching supplies."

Bent over Matt, St. Louis cocked his head to take a suspicious look at Clem's green face. "Don't ya faint or throw up all over me like ya done the last time ya saw blood," he warned. He glanced at the campfire and saw with satisfaction a pan of water had been put on to boil. "See if ya can find my herb pouch."

"Anybody shoot the damned mule?" Matt's husky whisper shocked Amy. She wanted to cry and laugh at the same time as she looked at his bruised and dirty face, the blood running down his cheek.

"You want me to take care of that?" Adam asked with a hollow laugh.

"Bad tempered--" Matt's voice tapered off. His blue-gray eyes slowly opened, unfocused, the pupils dilated. "The... children all right?"

"You stopped the wagon. Playing hero again," Adam complained.

St. Louis untied the crude bandage around Matt's forehead, revealing a nasty gash several inches long. "Couldn't of ducked, could ya?" he asked, frowning at the injury.

Matt grunted, "Don't reckon I'm goin' to get any tender lovin' care from either of you."

"Wal, me and Adam, we know ya oughter had better sense than to get yoreself bunged up." St. Louis put his hand in front of Matt's face. "What's this?"

Grimacing with pain, Matt managed a smile. "It's either your ugly hand or another of those trick... philo-sophical questions."

"Anyplace besides yore head hurt?" St. Louis asked.

"You mean besides every muscle in my body?" Matt asked, his eyes closing again.

"Yeah, besides that.

"I must have... wrenched my right shoulder. My leg."

"Ya gashed it open. Plumb ugly lookin'. It's bleeding some, not gonna be no fun cleaning it up, but ya didn't rip an artery. Right now I'm most worried about the head. Your pupils look a mite dilated, like a concussion." St. Louis looked across Matt's chest at Amy. "And if ya lookin' for sympathy here, Miss Amy's yore best bet."

Matt, seeming to realize for the first time she was beside him, turned his head slightly to see her kneeling at his side. She could see him struggle to find the words to reassure her. His smile turned into another grimace.

Amy tightened her grip on his hand. "I'm not sure you've much hope for sympathy here either. You were definitely being the hero again." She had to work for a smile and to keep her tone light.

St. Louis sat back on his haunches. "Goin' to have to put in some stitches to stop the bleedin'."

Matt swore as St. Louis rummaged in the medicine bag Clem had handed him.

Adam grimaced. "Oh Lordy, not the salve."

"Make fun of it all ya want," St. Louis said with a smile of confidence, "but if ya end up hurt, ya'll be talkin' out of the other side of yore mouth."

"If I get hurt," Adam retorted, "I'll make sure it's miles away from that stinking stuff."

Matt looked back at Amy. "I'm goin' to be fine. You can get on back to your wagon. I..." He got no further before her fingers were over his lips.

"Nothing," she said in a firm voice, "not you, nor anybody can make me leave you, Matthew Kane." She bent and kissed his lips to emphasize her point.

He gave up gritting his teeth against a fresh onslaught of pain as he shifted his weight, trying to pull himself up. The pain shot through him, and he realized to his chagrin that his injuries were more than he'd hoped. He remembered falling between the mules, digging in his boots as he slowed their run, then something hit his leg and knocked it out from under him. Last thing he remembered was the slowing of the wagon. When he had thought it was over, the side kick of a mule's hoof, which he had been unable to avoid, brought blackness.

St. Louis knelt at his side, his fingers probing Matt's chest for other injuries, hidden ones, the kind that would take his life and that they could do nothing about. When he had decided the only wounds were head and leg, he brought out a whiskey bottle. "You know what I need to do."

"Then do it."

"Brace yoreself, boy." St. Louis tilted Matt's head back and poured whiskey onto the laceration. Suppressing a yelp of pain, Matt wheezed, "God."

St. Louis smiled faintly. "Wal, I got a little somethin' that will feel better." He studied the wound for a moment, walked to the campfire, and poured hot water into one of two small tin cups. He talked as he worked, his words a soft, rhythmic cadence, soothing and reassuring. He stirred the contents. "A little of this, a little of that, but the main one's yarrow. Lakota call it taopi tawote, wound medicine."

Cup in hand, he knelt at Matt's side. "Even old Adam over there." He cast a disparaging look over his shoulder. "He'll have to admit yarrow speeds up healin'." He checked the temperature of the mixture against his own wrist. "Later we'll use my salve, despite what some here folks think about it, but for now, hot poultice, that's the thing to ease the pain, fight infection." Gently he patted the still warm mixture on the wound.

"Injuns lived on this land a long time. They know the plants. Know what they can do. Might be we could learn plenty from them." He shot Adam another quelling look, then sat back on his haunches, letting the herbs soak in. "This is gonna need stitches though."

Matt let his shoulders relax as the agony released him enough to talk again. "Just do it." He fixed is eyes on the blue sky overhead.

"Actually," St. Louis said, looking up at Amy, then beyond her to where her mother was approaching. "I was waitin' for my assistant." He smiled as Amy's mother knelt beside them. "Ya did say you could do this," he said, his voice reflecting relief.

Martha Stevens bent over Matt, her hand cool against his forehead. "It won't be the first time I've stitched up this one." A frown line formed between her finely arched brows as she studied the gash. She put the poultice of herbs back in the tin cup. "This will hurt," she said. He tightened his mouth against the pain of the alcohol rinsing the wound before she began to stitch it with a needle and thread she had soaked in alcohol.

"Don't--" Matt gasped, "worry about bein' neat." She smiled and kept on with the small even stitches. When she finished, St. Louis renewed the poultice, then wrapped a bandage lightly around Matt's head.

Rubbing his finger thoughtfully along his nose, he then turned to the leg wound. After a moment he looked up at Amy. "Reckon ya'll have to leave us be for a little, Miss Amy."

"Why?" she asked indignantly, "I've seen everything else."

"Wal, ya ain't seen this," St. Louis said with a wicked chuckle. "And if ya have, with yore ma and pa right here, ya better not admit it. We got to take this man's pants off."

"Oh." Amy yielded her position at Matt's side to allow the men to remove his clothing. When they had stripped him and covered his private parts with a blanket, she returned to pillow his head in her lap and stroke his hair back from his forehead.

Pulling the quilt away from Matt's injured leg, St. Louis shook his head. "Looks like ya got drug across a dead branch. It ripped ya good but…" He studied it a bit. "Didn't break the bone. I don't see that it ripped the muscle loose and not bleeding a lot."

"In other words," Matt managed, "you don't plan to cut off my leg--yet."

Frowning with concentration, St. Louis looked up at his face. His gaze met Matt's. "We got to clean out the wood and dirt. If we close it up without--" He didn't need to finish his sentence. Matt nodded. He'd seen men working in the woods, with seemingly insignificant wounds, who were suddenly overcome by some sort of poisoning. It took them fast.

St. Louis went back to the fire and fished a long, thin knife from a sluggishly boiling pot of water. When the older man again knelt, he put a chunk of wood between Matt's teeth. "Bite down hard, keep ya from biting yore tongue." He looked toward Amos who had just arrived and Adam standing at his side. "Hold him as quiet as ya can." They each knelt, applying pressure on one of Matt's legs. Amy and her mother bent over his shoulders.

St. Louis took a deep breath, looked toward the sky for a second and then bent to begin probing the wound, cleansing it, removing anything foreign. Matt bit down on the wood. His jaws clenched as the probing delved deeper into the wound.

Amy gritted her own teeth as she saw the muscles in Matt's chest and arms tighten with his effort to remain still under St. Louis' knife. Then, letting out a strangled gasp, his eyes rolled back in his head, and he fell back limp.

Kneeling beside Matt where he lay on a cot in St. Louis' wagon, Amy watched as he slept restlessly. She wanted to take him in her arms, cradle him to her, but she dared do nothing that might reopen the wounds. As she watched him twist restlessly against the pain, his lashes dark against his cheeks, a bruise forming along one side of his face, her thoughts turned darkly to her own ingenuous expectations for the Oregon Trail. What a romantic fool she'd been.

"You don't seem at all excited," her words rose to taunt her. His feelings had been the mature ones, the ones that knew to count the cost. She'd been blind, never thinking excitement meant danger, danger meant possible injury or death.

Over the last weeks, the word adventure had taken on a reality that made it less enthralling, less romantic. First there'd been the tedium of long days, the endless dust or deep mud, the monotony of travel where the scenery never changed, the growing tensions among the people, the sometimes perilous crossings of rivers, the crosses alongside the trail telling of earlier lives lost, and now this. A simple thing like mules and wagon, the very things that carried their belongings and made the trek possible, had nearly cost Matt and three children their lives. Nothing was what she'd dreamed.

Danger had been an abstract, an unknown, something poetic almost. On this trip it had become a frightening reality, the consequences of which lay before her. Matt could have been killed and still might be crippled.

Interrupting her painful introspections, St. Louis leaned his head in the end of the wagon. "How is he?"

"Still unconscious."

"Just as well. We'll lay over the rest of the day. If ya need anything, holler. We'll be outside."

Amy nodded but didn't take her eyes off Matt, not through the afternoon as she watched him sleep, not when she drank the coffee her mother brought her or nibbled unenthusiastically at the food she was given.

Restlessly, he groaned, moved his legs, twisting in the blankets, while she smoothed back his hair, disentangled his limbs and wiped his chest and arms with a cool cloth, trying to bring him what comfort she could. Now and then she felt of his forehead, trying to decide if his fever was rising to dangerous levels.

It was almost dark when he opened his eyes. The campfire dimly lit the interior of the wagon, allowing her to watch his face as he grimaced, orienting himself. Amy said nothing. For the moment it was enough to see his clear gray eyes open. When he looked toward her, he seemed unfocused as though uncertain of all that had transpired.

"Welcome back," she whispered, filling a dipper with water and putting it to his cracked lips, gently lifting his head for him to drink. When he had taken all he would, she laid him back down. "How are you feeling? Or is that a silly question?"

"Like I was in a fight and lost." He tried to shift his weight. Grimacing, he looked down at his body with disgust.

Recognizing his impatience, Amy assumed what she hoped was an air of authority. She counted on her fingers. "Your arm is strapped to your side until it heals. Your head and leg wounds are stitched and poulticed. The dressings will be changed again in an hour or so. You are to lie on this cot, not to move so much as a muscle if it isn't necessary. Anything you need, I'll get."

"Anything?" he drawled.

"Almost anything." She bent and kissed his forehead.

"There are better places to kiss."

She lightly touched her lips to his.

"Not much of a kiss," he complained when she pulled away.

"You have to get better before you get anything more demanding of your energy." She took his hand into hers, bringing it close to her lips.

"I remember hearing the Hall children were all right."

"Yes. Monsters though they are, they're fine, up and bouncing around, probably determined to cause another runaway for the sheer excitement of it all. Mama came in an hour or so ago and said Mr. and Mrs. Hall are in near apoplexy over it, but the children are babbling about what an adventure they had."

He tried to shift his weight again and grimaced when it proved not only painful, but nigh impossible.

"Let me help." Amy lifted him and smoothed his pillow, adjusting the blankets under him until everything was smooth. "Don't try to move or get up for now."

"Sure," he whispered too quickly for her to believe him.

She smiled brightly, tears in her eyes. "Your good intentions will last about a day before you get restless and are complaining." She scrunched up her face. "Remember how sick you were when you had the whooping cough?"

Reluctantly, he nodded, aware of where this conversation was heading.

She raised her eyebrows. "So, did you stay in bed like Mama and the doctor ordered?" She left no space for a response. "No, you rushed outside, ended up with lung fever."

"Anybody can make a mistake once."

"Once? Did you say once? How about the time you broke your arm? Just had to go climbing that cliff before it had healed all the way? Do you remember the result that time?"

"Beginning to sound like I'm accident-prone," he grunted.

"You rebroke the arm," she retorted, not about to be diverted. "Did you learn anything that time?"

"Baby, don't make me laugh. It hurts," he complained,

trying for a distraction and maybe a little sympathy if he got lucky.

"Maybe that will remind you to be careful. Maybe..."

"You got too long a memory," he groaned.

"You can believe that." She bent, kissing his cheek, resting her head beside his on the pillow. "Sometimes that works to your advantage. I remember how you brought me the first wild-flowers in the spring. I don't know how you found them, but you always did."

"Climbing that damn cliff."

"I remember your touch, the feel of your lips on mine. No, lie still. I love you, Matthew, and you will take care of yourself."

"I will," he reassured her again, grimacing at the dizziness. At least for now he'd have no choice. "I'll be fine now. You go on back to your own wagon. You can't hang around here, or folks'll get to talkin' about what's going on here."

She sat up and looked down her nose at him with a deter-mined smile. "Whatever could they say? Perhaps that Amelia Stevens is madly in love with Matthew Kane! She can't keep her hands off him. Whenever you see him, you see her. He's all she wants to talk about. The poor girl is clearly besotted. Is that what you're afraid they'll say?"

"You think this is funny?"

"Funny or not, it's too late for you to worry about all this. Our days of hiding are finished. For all intents and purposes, you can consider yourself betrothed, and if you don't, you've got some tall explaining to do to Papa." She glared down at him, hands on her hips. "I've seen that mulish expression on your face before," she said, "and you ought to know I can be just as stub-born. Consider this issue settled."

Matt tried to summon an argument that would send her away from his side and the danger lurking there; but he was just weak enough to want her with him. He hurt in so many places he wanted her there when he awoke, her hand stroking his brow, easing the pain as only she could.

"Matt, when I go back to my wagon, it'll be to get some extra blankets. St. Louis prepared a pallet here for me. I'll explain the situation in more detail to Mama and Papa-- if necessary-- but this last little accident of yours ended any pretense." She placed her fingers over his lips, stilling any protest. "Your days of ordering me around have come to an abrupt end. You will be laid up for awhile. I will be here with you as much as I can." She kissed his cracked lips, then stood up. "I'm going but count on it-- I'll be back."

As she slipped out through the wagon flap, he watched with a mixture of love and fear. She'd made up her mind; at this point, he wasn't likely to change it. He could only hope she was right. He was in no shape to make her do anything, but neither was he in shape to protect her if she was wrong.

CHAPTER 17

Returning to St. Louis' wagon, quilts in her arms, Amy saw Adam leaning against the wagon wheel. Stopping, she looked up into his dark face.

"You're spending the night with him," he observed with a less than pleased look.

"To nurse him, yes."

"I hope you're not going to lie to me. I watched you while they were working over him."

She deserved the reproof in his eyes. "I haven't been fair." He waited, not giving an inch, his expression cold. It was to be expected. "I wanted to tell you." She looked up into those intense, blue eyes and knew only truth would do now. "Matt didn't want anyone to know we were in love. He thought it would endanger me and my reputation. I let him have his way, but it was unfair to you."

"I certainly played the fool, ignoring the signs," he said with irritation. "I built a pipe dream around something that was never there."

"It seems all I do is burst into tears," she complained as the tears again came to her eyes, "but I feel bad about this. You're a good man, Adam, and you deserve to have somebody really love you. I just wasn't the one."

"That hard to do huh?"

"When I met you, I was already in love."

He sighed, staring up at the sky. "Now I think back, I can't say there weren't signs. I just didn't want to see them. Too caught up in having it my way." He smiled wryly. "If it doesn't work out with him, if you ever need me, I'll be there."

"Don't." She took his arm. "You deserve to have a woman who thinks of you first. When you find her, you'll know the truth of what I'm saying. In fact, you'll probably realize you never cared that much for me." She smiled at his expression of disbelief.

When she entered Matt's wagon, his eyes were open, his expression dark. Canvas walls did not keep out much if any sound. "You heard," she said, wanting them to talk about it. She brought a dipper of water to him, gently lifting his head and shoulders, helping him to drink. "Are you hungry?" she asked.

"No."

"Tell me what you're thinking," she asked, as she eased him back down.

"I don't know." He closed his eyes. The telltale muscle in his jaw throbbed.

"Are you angry?" In her exhaustion and the emotional stress of the last days, she felt near tears again.

"Don't cry. You know how that makes me feel."

"No one would believe my feelings for you are just friendship, not even someone who wanted to believe it."

"I suppose you talked to your folks, too."

"They told me what they said to you. They feel terrible for it."

He felt incapable of arguing with her anymore. It was hard to think beyond the pain. He heard Amy's voice as though through a fog. "You've always been part of the family. I know there was a time when Mama and Papa didn't want us to fall in love, hoped we wouldn't, but it's happened, and they accept it. They have always loved you, Matt." Her fingers stroked his jaw. "There've been promises made between you and me. I told them that too. You better make good, or you'll be facing Papa's shotgun. Maybe with Mama holding it, which is far more dangerous."

Matt laughed, choking on a groan as a muscle in his leg spasmed. "Lord, don't make me laugh." When he could manage his voice, he asked, "What about the others? How are they treating you?"

"Brace yourself," she warned. "You won't like this much either. People are talking about you, all right. They're saying no sneak thief would turn around and nearly die to save children he barely knew. They can't quit talking about what an amazing thing you did when you leaped from your horse. You're a hero."

"Hardly." He wanted to keep his eyes open but felt pulled back into a sleep he didn't want because delusion and nightmares kept pulling him toward what felt like a pit.

"It looks to me as though you have a new problem on your hands."

His eyes snapped open at that. "What?"

"Hero worship. There are going to be little boys following you around, asking how you did it." She smiled ignoring what he knew was his grimace of disgust. He knew he had been no hero, only done what he believed he could when faced with an emergency. He hadn't expected to end up laid up from it; but if the situation arose again, he likely would do the same thing. He was no hero but maybe he was a fool.

Her hand stroked his forehead. "No fever, or not much of one," she whispered against his temple. "Rest, love. Don't worry about tomorrow. Tomorrow will take care of itself."

The jolting of the wagon as it tilted from side to side, rode over bumps and lurched ponderously ahead, added to the fever and pain from Matt's wounds. Only Amy could distract him from it and that for only brief spells of time.

Throughout the day, St. Louis put on the evil-smelling salve and checked the wounds. Except at night, the leg was left uncovered by even a blanket.

"Looks good," seemed to be St. Louis' standard comment each time he examined him or came to help Matt tend to his bodily needs.

The nightmares continued whenever he slept-- dreams of

tragedy and disaster. Something felt evil and cold. When he woke, he couldn't remember what it was. Waking, his legs would be tangled in the quilts, his body bathed in sweat, and sometimes twisting against Amy's restraining hands. Whatever pursued him, he couldn't escape it.

"You're safe. We're all safe." She held his shivering body against hers, reassuring him the danger was past. After a time, he slept again, only to be dragged back into the dream.

No matter how much Amy's presence soothed him, he could see what it was doing to her, being with him night and day, the thinness of her face, the pallor of her skin. She had to get some rest, or she would be the sick one.

"I'm better, and you're wearin' yourself thin."

"But--"

"I mean it, baby. I don't want you tryin' to sleep here again tonight. You get to your own bed." He edged down the quilt a little and narrowed his eyes threateningly. "If you don't, I'll have to get out of this wagon and make you."

"You're stubborn enough to do it," she retorted, hands on her hips.

"So then get out of here.

Reluctantly, she smoothed back his hair, which now lay down around his shoulders with the thong gone. She sighed, but kissed him and left.

When he next awoke, the night was dark, a dim light from a flickering fire outside barely lit the wagon. For a moment, he thought Amy had come back. Instead, it was Martha Stevens who sat by his cot. He looked at her blankly, his mind a confusing jumble of dreams and reality.

Wordlessly, she put a cup to his lips, gently lifting his head, helping him to drink. "I don't suppose I have to ask how you're feeling," she said as she laid him back down, smoothing his quilt.

"Not too bad," he lied. He hurt. Parts of his body he hadn't even known he had hurt. Where there were no injuries, the muscles were spasming in protest. He started to ask why she had come to sit with him, then stopped, shutting his mouth on the words because he could think of no way to phrase the question that wouldn't sound rude.

"I made some broth. Do you think you could drink some?"

When he didn't answer, she took a damp cloth and washed the sweat beads from his forehead. The cloth was soothing and cool, her touch so much like her daughter's that when he closed his eyes he could almost forget who it was. When he looked up, she was gazing into his eyes, the expression on her face resolute.

"I said some harsh things to you before this, and I was wrong, Matt. Will you forgive me?"

He swallowed, his emotions too near the surface to hide. "I understood. It was your love for Amy."

She smiled and shook her head. "For years Amos and I saw the devotion between you two. I won't deny we were worried for a number of reasons. Foremost was the fear that it wasn't the kind of love a man and woman ought to have. Sometimes friends mistake friendship for love."

He had no answer to that and shifted his gaze to the blackness beyond the wagon opening.

Her cool fingers were against his forehead. "But now, I've seen how it is with Amy. How she feels. Our doubts were misplaced." She stroked back his damp hair. "Before you sleep can I get you to take some of that broth? It will help you get stronger if you can eat."

He wanted nothing except to sleep, but as it was with her daughter, he could deny her nothing under his power, and so he nodded.

When he awoke again, the wagon was moving, Amy sitting beside him, her eyes closed, her head leaning back at what had to be an uncomfortable angle. She looked so beautiful, long black hair pulled away from her face, dark thick eyelashes against smooth, silky skin. But, there was something else. He struggled to think what it was, to define it and realized that for him to see her brought a sense of serenity and peace, of coming home. Even when she fought with him, she made him feel he belonged, gave him a feeling of tranquility he knew from no one but her. Why then did he feel a mixture of fear and desire when he thought of marrying her?

The wagon rocked, knocking her head back against the crate and waking her. Her dark eyes opened, then turned to look at him. When she saw he was watching her, she smiled, and bent to kiss his lips. "Do you want water or more of the broth Mama made?" she asked, stroking his cheek.

"Then your mother was here."

"Last night." Amy put the water ladle to his lips.

"Dreams seem so real sometimes. When I'm awake, everything is slippery. It's hard to keep straight what happened, what didn't." Lord, how he hated being weak.

Amy stroked his hair. "St. Louis said a lot of that is the head injury, but you're looking better everyday. Things will be clearer soon." She kissed his bare shoulder, then his bicep, working her way to his fingertips. She lifted his hand, holding it against her cheek. "Everything will look different to you then."

He wondered, but was incapable of thinking it through, not when lying there feeling like a limp rag, good for nothing. A thought drifted into his head, something he needed to tell her, but it seemed he couldn't hang onto it. Could he marry Amy? Her parents no longer objected. Did the people no longer see him as a bad? Was there nothing left standing between them? But if that was true-- why was he afraid?

St. Louis removed the dressing from his leg, looked at the wound, and nodded with satisfaction. He had brought more of the taopi tawote with him, applying it to Matt's head and leg, leaving the wounds open to the healing air. "This is lookin' good. Ya still got a little fever but nothin' more than I'd expect." He readjusted Matt's thin blanket, then sat back to ask what seemed to be everyone's favorite question. "How ya feelin'?"

"Like hell. It's the weakness that's worst. I've been hurt a few times but nothing like this."

"Ya bruised yore body up good."

"You think I'll-- that is will my leg be all right?

"Ya mean will ya limp?"

Matt nodded not wanting to think of being a cripple, of not

having the strength he'd had before his injury, but he'd seen enough men with stiff legs to know what could happen.

"Knowing you, I'd say not. I seen men with less of a leg tear, and they ended crippled but because they coddled it, laid around too much. When you start moving, you got to make it work for you." He stopped, beetling his brows into a frown. "I seen that stubborn look on yore face afore. Ya just wait 'til I tell ya. Don't want ya breakin' the wound open afore it's had a chance to heal."

"I don't like lyin' here," Matt said, "but there's not much chance I'll overdo with Amy watchin' like a hawk."

"Ya feel up to talkin' to Ralph Hall?" St. Louis asked.

"What for?"

"He's been waitin' outside. I didn't ask him what fer."

Matt looked at him dubiously. "I guess there's no reason not to. So long as he isn't tryin' to thank me or something."

"Now why'd he want to do a thing like that?" St. Louis' eyes narrowed. "If that is what he wants, ya let him go to it! A little humblin' won't hurt that man a bit and might do some good!"

In a moment, Ralph Hall's blocky body filled the entrance to the wagon. He took off his hat, his normally truculent frown was gone, replaced by an expression of abject penance. "I-- I don't know how to thank a man that saved not only my kids but my outfit," Hall said.

"No need."

"It is and even more after the way I treated you. I feel like a fool, and you turned around and-- I don't know what to say."

"Any man would've done the same." Obviously Hall hadn't expected him to act like a man.

"I don't see it that way. I just..." He hesitated. "I wonder if you'd mind talking about it, about what happened. I need to know how... I'm a strong man, and I still don't understand how you stopped that team."

"I don't mind, but I don't expect it to impress you all that much. Actually when I started after the wagon, I didn't know how I'd stop it. When I caught up, I figured to slide onto the back of the lead mule. Trouble was I couldn't stop myself, slid right on between them.

"I held onto the traces with my right hand but got pressed against the singletree. At that point, I reckoned it was over if I didn't get hold of the other mule's harness. I don't honest-to-God know how I did it. They were draggin' me across the ground. That's when my leg got hit, near to knock the straps out of my hands, but I dug in my heels and slowed them. I wasn't goin' to end up under a marker that read-- Killed by a Wagon."

Hall managed a laugh.

"It would've been over then except," Matt growled with irritation, "for that jack of yours. After I'd stopped the team, he spooked, kicked out and knocked me cold."

"Ya were lucky at that," St. Louis said.

Matt shot him an expression of disbelief.

"He likely only hit ya with the side of his hoof, grazed ya hard enough to knock ya out but not crack your skull open."

Hall shook his head. "No man could repay you for what you done, but--" He put out his right hand before he realized Matt's arm was still strapped to his side. He switched hands and firmly grasped Matt's left. "If you ever need anything, anything at all, I'm your man. I owe you, and Ralph Hall never forgets a debt."

"Thanks are plenty." Matt thought a moment, then added, "Just don't go tellin' folks I fell off a mule."

St. Louis removed the strapping that held Matt's right arm to his side. Testing it, Matt found that, although the shoulder hurt, he had full mobility. "I'm still a little dizzy," Matt grumbled. It had been too many days since the accident. He had expected to be back on his horse and not still in bed.

"To be expected. We'll be headin' out in an hour. Need anything?"

Matt rubbed his hand over his bristly jaw. "I need to shave."

"Ya need help?" St. Louis grinned at Matt's scowl.

"Just water, soap and a razor." If he cut his own throat, he was bound he would shave himself.

While he lay waiting for the warm water and razor, Matt knew he'd been behaving badly, but how could St. Louis understand how he felt? His body had betrayed him. That which had been strong all his life had turned weak and left him needing help for even the most basic needs. When they had passed Independence Rock, and he had been barely able to look at it from the opening of the wagon, it seemed apropos of his whole situation.

St. Louis brought the shaving materials, setting them beside the bed. "Ya sure ya don't need help?" At Matt's scowl, he grinned. "I'll be around if ya change yore mind."

Still glowering, Matt bent to pick up the soap. When he took the razor in his hand, he knew his right arm was too shaky, too unsteady. It wasn't a question of whether he would cut his throat, but when. He used the cloth to wash his face, panting when he was finished, infuriated at yet another betrayal of his body.

Amy peeped through the wagon opening, obviously the only one with the courage to face his curses or perhaps the one sent to face them. "Do you need help?" she asked in a sweet voice.

"No," he muttered through clenched teeth, "I changed my mind. I'm going to grow a beard."

"Getting a little peevish, are we?" She stepped into the wagon.

"I'm not in a bad mood," he muttered, closing his eyes to block out the sight of her cheerful smile. The rustle of her skirts and splash of water in the basin brought his eyes wide open. "You're not goin' to wash me."

"I'm not?" The soapy cloth came into contact with his skin.

"No," he gritted as she took the rag to his face, rewashing what he felt had been adequately done already. Not wanting to watch, he closed his eyes again, clenching his teeth against the feelings that began warring within his body. As she began washing his chest, he thought, At least I'm not dead yet. The sensuality of her hands on his skin quickly led to a heated arousal. As she washed further down his chest across his flat belly, he had to move his good leg up to hide the impact she was having on him. He found his breathing hard to control. How far would she go? Tension replaced physical pain at least for the moment.

Taking her time, humming a little, Amy washed each of his

RAIN TRUEAX

arms, then with a pail of fresh water, rinsed and toweled dry his skin. The blanket remained covering the lower half of his anatomy; the bent knee served to cover what it didn't.

When he saw she'd finished, he opened his eyes. "Thank you."

"Oh, but we're not done." She laughed, obviously amused at the consternation he couldn't hide. "Now for the shave. You don't think I'm going to put up with this." She ran her fingers over the bristle. "Not when I'm the one getting the rough end of it."

"You ever done this before?" he asked with concern, as she sharpened the razor on the strope.

"I've seen it done." She gave, what seemed to him, a mean laugh. When she disappeared, he hoped it meant she had been teasing, but soon she was back with a fresh pan of warm water. "Trust me," she murmured, her eyes alight.

He had no choice. Besides, it couldn't be as bad as having her washing his body. Not even if she cuts my throat.

Taking her time, she lathered his face. Placing the razor against his cheek, smoothly she stroked away lather and beard. Each step was equally smooth and within moments she was finished, without a nick or scratch. Taking a damp towel, she rinsed away the few remaining flakes of lather. "Now was that so bad!"

"No," he admitted with a crooked grin. Now that it was over, it wasn't so bad. She'd been right; his strength had not up to doing it, and it had needed doing. If he had to rely on someone, it wasn't so bad it was her.

"It'll be easier next time," she said with a wicked grin.

His eyes narrowed. "No next time. I'll be doing this myself," he told her, the telltale muscle beating in his jaw.

"Well, we'll see about that," she teased, lightly testing the quality of her shave.

When the wagons rolled out the next morning, Amy sat on the palette beside Matt. He knew she was doing it to amuse him, ease his discomfort, help him, but he felt too irritated to appreciate help. The inactivity was near to driving him crazy. Between the rocking of the wagon and the pain of his leg, he'd heard all the sympathetic words he wanted and more.

"You look like you're in pain. Can I get you something?" she asked for the third or fourth time.

"Blast it, baby, leave me be!" he finally exploded.

She rose from her seat as though from a hot coal, outrage in her dark eyes. "Well, if that's what you want. At least I know how to do that right." She rushed to the back of the wagon and dropped to the ground before he could react.

The moment the words were out of his mouth, Matt regretted them. She had been tender, caring. He didn't deserve her, and she didn't deserve his frustration turned against her. Swaying to his feet, he tried to keep his balance, fighting the feeling of lightheadedness.

Naked. He couldn't go after her without at least pants. He bent to look for his clothes and instantly knew it had been a mistake to get up so quickly, a bigger one to look down. He tried to turn, to get back to his cot, but it was too late. Everything went black.

The faint only lasted a few seconds. Dazed from the fall, he tried to collect himself enough to crawl back on his cot. A flurry of skirts enveloped him. "Matt," Amy cried, "you fool, you could have hurt yourself. Why did you try to get up by yourself?" As she chided him, she pulled on his good shoulder to drag him back to his bed.

"No," he growled, "I can do it." He felt a renewed flood of humiliation that she would find him like this, helpless and naked as a baby.

"You make me so mad. Damn it, Matt, let me help!"

Defeated by his weakness, he realized if he wasn't going to lie in the middle of the wagon buck naked, he needed her help. Between them, half crawling, half dragging, he climbed back onto the bunk. Amy threw the blanket over him. She sat back, glaring at him with large accusing eyes.

He closed his eyes, waiting for either his pain or her anger to abate-- preferably both-- before he attempted to explain himself.

"I can't believe it," she snapped. "I really can't, but I ought to. You could have hurt yourself!" Angrily, she pushed the blanket aside to check the dressing on his leg. "Did you start the wound bleeding?"

He lay quietly through her examination. "I just wanted to tell you I was sorry."

"Matt," she whispered, her voice softened, "you have to be good." She bent, resting her head beside his on the pillow, kissing his neck, then his bare chest, one hand stroked his arm.

"I'm a fool. Forgive me?"

"I'll think about it, if you promise not to do anything like this again. I came back because I understood how you must feel, how hard this is on you, but you just have to follow orders." Her fingers caressed his cheek, then his neck.

"I will," he murmured, desire for her stirring to life. It seemed nothing, no pain, no weakness, was strong enough to stop that.

As her lips tenderly sought his, he put his arms around her, drawing her down onto his good shoulder, to lie against him. Their lips met with a gentle tasting, then with more purpose as they clung together. She reached down and began kissing his bare chest. Her hand slipped to his waist as her lips moved across his chest.

Swallowing hard, aroused from the first touch of her lips, Matt managed to push away. "Amy," he muttered, trying to control his breathing. "I got to tell you somethin' you might not like hearin'." Instantly defensive, she pulled away to sit on the edge of the bunk. "You're killing me."

"What?"

"We kiss and touch like this; it's like a fever's in my blood. I want you so bad, it'd be easy to give in."

"Would that be so terrible?" she asked with a smile.

"I don't think you understand what I'm sayin'."

"Don't I?" Her dark eyes filled with a longing he finally recognized for what it was. "Do you think men are the only ones who can feel desire? How do you think it is for me? When I saw you, just now, it stirred all sorts of feelings, beyond being mad that you'd gotten out of bed. I had no idea how beautiful a man's body could be until I saw all of yours." Her husky voice, little more than a whisper, the soft promise of her words, aroused him further. He no longer attempted to hide the physical evidence.

Amy smiled shyly. "I know a lady isn't supposed to-- uhm say things like this, but we're going to be married, would it matter so much if we didn't wait? I know you're hurt now, but I could help, I think, and..."

"No." He stopped, wondering how to put a dream into words. "When I take you to our bed, I want us married and with every right to each other, with our people knowing. I don't want you hiding or being ashamed or having to worry about a baby."

"Then, Matthew, I think we should get married as soon as you are healed."

"I don't see how we can. Where would we live, where would we sleep?"

He shared those doubts but not the deeper ones. He wasn't ready to share those or even probe them for himself. Someday he would have to-- when he was stronger.

CHAPTER 18

A s she walked back to her family wagon, Amy considered the problem she faced. She respected Matt for his idyllic dream, even understood some of what he was saying. At the same time, she resented his ongoing need to protect her from everything that might hurt her—by his definition. Would he ever stop trying to wrap her in cotton?

The warring feelings did nothing to ease the frustration of her body, and she knew Matt was in no better shape. He hadn't lied when he said he wanted her. His body told her how much. No longer a sexual innocent, many times she'd felt Matt's hard arousal. She knew what it meant.

Seeing him naked had only exacerbated the problem for her. She'd imagined, but she'd never dreamed a man could be so beautiful. Tight buttocks, long legs, muscular back. His chest was hard, the muscles defined, and his... God, she had to stop thinking of that or she'd be the one raping him!

She had grown up with a simple understanding of what a good woman was, and such a woman certainly wasn't supposed to lust after a man. Her mother had told her the basic facts of the marital bed but hadn't gone into much detail about how it was supposed to come about. She had been much more emphatic about how it was not supposed to come about.

The information in romance books gave even less information. They stopped with chaste kisses, rapidly beating hearts, and quick clasps to the bosom. There was nothing in them about a body on fire with desire. On their pages, a lady behaved in a certain way, permitting only certain liberties. What about a woman who wanted to take liberties with the hero's body? She shook her head. She'd never dreamt she'd be the one doing the tempting, ready to beg him to take her. Please seduce me? She laughed and admitted, No, that's not right. I'm the one out to seduce.

If Matt was to have his dream, and if it was within her power, she wanted him to have every dream he'd ever had, there was only one way. She would have to be careful how and when she touched him, especially when they were alone. Constantly touching, caressing, had come so easily, so much a part of what she felt for him, but she hadn't been considering its impact on him.

She just had to keep her hands off him. That was all. She sighed with regret, already missing what she had only just decided to deny herself. It wasn't going to be easy.

The freedom, the feeling of the soft, almost caressing breeze on Matt's face, as he was able to sit outside in the evening, was a gift, a blessing he had almost forgotten existed. Amy fluttered around the campsite, fretting over him, asking if he was chilled, tired, or hungry: but being outside improved his mood sufficiently to endure her worrying with relative good grace

When Matt saw Adam walking back from the corrals, he recognized the tight lips, the tension in the scout's shoulders for what they meant. Adam said nothing as he walked into the campsite.

"Amy," Matt said, giving her a loving pat, "how about you leave us to talk."

She looked from one to the other; then nodded, kissing Matt before she left.

"I'm not much for talking," Matt said after she was gone, "but this needs airing."

Adam leveled cold blue eyes on him as he rolled a cigarette. "I suppose you're right although we're not likely to be friends no matter what we say now."

"Maybe not."

"Would you have wanted to be friends-- if it'd gone the other way?"

Matt smiled. "I didn't like you at all-- when I thought it was going the other way."

Adam watched as Matt tried to shift his weight, easing the pressure on his leg. "Can I get you anything?"

"No, it just aches a little." Understatement of the year.

"Was there a reason you didn't tell me which way the wind was blowing where it came to her?" Adam asked, lighting the cigarette.

"I was trying to protect her. Maybe I was wrong. She said I was often enough. For what it's worth, she wanted to tell you."

"It would have been kinder."

"So what's really riling you?"

"Among other things, being made to feel like a fool. When I think of the things you let me say. You knowing all the time, laughing."

Matt snorted. "I was jealous of you every time you went around her. You being with her never seemed funny to me. I kept thinking she'd change her mind."

"Jealous?" Surprise tinged Adam's words as he lowered himself to the ground smoking the cigarette.

"Pretty damn near drove me crazy."

"But she loves you. I don't get it."

"I figured she should've loved you. It would've made more sense."

"I can agree with that at least." Adam's grin was sardonic as he blew out a puff of smoke.

Matt laughed, shaking his head. "I don't reckon we'll ever figure out the mind of a woman."

"Did she tell her I told her I'd wait around, hoping it didn't work out between you?"

"She didn't have to. I heard you."

"What did you think of that?" Adam asked, pouring Matt

and himself a cup of coffee, which had been simmering on the edge of the campfire.

"It's about what I'd of done, if it'd gone the other way— hoped you'd blow it." Matt stretched out his leg and smiled genially as he sipped the coffee. Maybe they wouldn't end up friends, but they wouldn't be enemies either.

Matt spent his days trying to rebuild the strength the injuries had cost him. His nights suffered the results of those efforts. He walked alongside the wagon until his strength gave out and panting pulled himself into it. As the days passed, with the pain lessening, he was able to begin riding a few hours a day.

More himself, he became aware in a change in Amy. Now when they could be openly together, she pulled away from his embrace, giving him only quick kisses. When she came to see him in the evenings, she had Loraine or Belle in tow. That was the pattern she had followed with Adam-- when she didn't want his attentions.

Was she having second thoughts about them? Was Adam making more in-roads than he thought? At first he felt relief that she wasn't bringing up the subject of marriage-- until he began to wonder why. Was she having second thoughts? Perhaps in the rush of their new feelings, she'd lost track of those dreams she had wanted. Maybe now she wanted them more than him. He couldn't allow himself to think of bringing this to a head by the one thing to solidify their relationship—marrying her. Every time the thought came into his mind, it was accompanied by a strange, paralyzing fear.

Darkly considering the situation, he lounged in front of the fire. St. Louis was off taking care of a problem at the livestock corral; Clem had gone to the Collins to play checkers with the old man, and just exactly where was Adam? He got his answer a few moments later when he heard Amy's laughter and saw Adam walking at her side, his tall height dominating as they made their way down the line of wagons.

When they reached Matt, Amy kissed his cheek, then sat a

safe distance from him, smoothing a faded blue skirt over her knees. Adam settled across the fire from them.

"Where you been?" Matt asked determined to keep his voice casual.

"My folks," Amy said. "I'm sorry I couldn't come sooner, but Adam stopped in. Everyone got to talking, and I lost track of the time. How are you feeling this evening?"

"Fine," he answered his tone as coolly polite as hers. "Nice night."

Adam smiled. "Cool at night, makes the daytime heat almost bearable." He swatted at a mosquito. "Pesky things. Always get them along the Sweetwater. Beautiful place, fresh water, lots of grass, but I sure wouldn't want to settle near all these mosquitoes."

"How soon before we reach the pass?" Matt was determined to be sociable even when he felt more like slamming his fist into Adam's handsome face.

"Couple of days. It's an easy grade from here to the top of the Rockies. You'll hardly know when you go over South Pass, except the creeks and rivers start running toward the Pacific." Adam was in an affable mood, which was more than Matt could say for himself.

"Wish I could help more," Matt grumbled.

"You'll do your share when we need it. Just take it easy for now. We're managing."

In other words stay out of sight and give him free rein with Amy. Grimly, Matt rubbed his leg, trying to ease the ache in the muscle. "Reckon I'm tireder than I thought," he said after several moments of uncomfortable silence. "See you both tomorrow." With an effort of which he hadn't known he was capable, he managed a weak smile before pulling himself into the wagon. He would give Amy her freedom, whatever it cost him. Dropping onto the bunk, he threw his arm over his eyes, not letting himself think or feel.

It took him a moment to realize she had followed him and was sitting on the edge of his bunk. "What's wrong?" she asked, reaching out to check his forehead. "Are you feverish?"

He shook his head.

"Then what is it?" She frowned. "Something's definitely wrong. Is it something to do with your father or brother?"

He watched her through narrowed eyes. "Nothing."

"I can see that-- not."

"If you changed your mind, why didn't you come to me and tell me yourself?"

"Changed my mind about what?"

"About us-- about me and you."

"You must be delirious—fever or not. What makes you think I've changed my mind about me and you?" she asked, mimicking his drawl as she had a wont to do when she was teasing him.

"You think I can't tell you don't feel the same anymore. I understand, Honest-to-God, I just wish you'd told me yourself."

She dramatically placed her hand back on his forehead, allowing it to linger. "Cool or not, it has to be a fever. You're ranting like a man in delirium."

"This is not funny." He brushed her hand aside.

"Wait a minute! This isn't... you aren't having a jealousy attack, are you?" Her eyes sparkled with amusement.

He was trying to be magnanimous, and she was making fun of him. "I've got no right to be jealous," he said trying to keep his tone even.

"Oh, I don't know about that, you might have some tiny right, if there was a reason, but Matthew, surely not now?"

"I'm tired," he said, throwing his arm back over his eyes. He knew during his recovery, he hadn't had much control over his emotions, and he was past being reasonable when it came to Amy with any other man.

"Maybe this is part of the healing process St. Louis forgot to mention." She pulled his arm away, forcing him to face her. "Adam only walked me here because he was headed back anyway."

"Sure," he muttered. "If that's true, why've you been so different, almost cold?"

"Cold?" she repeated, then laughed again, filling him with renewed resentment. "I think I finally understand. We're at cross purposes again. Think back, Matthew... Who told me not to touch him so much? Who said we couldn't be married right away?"

She reached out, caressing his cheek. Her fingers moved down his jaw line to his neck. She brought her lips tantalizingly close to his. "You see," she whispered, her fingers now under his collar, "if I let myself do what I want. If I--" She reached down and slowly unbuttoned his shirt her fingers brushing his skin with the lightest touch. "If I do everything I want."

His breath came unevenly as his hands tangled into her hair, stopping her words as he parted her lips with his own. In his hunger and need, his kiss was hard and demanding. Nothing existed outside the wagon as his lips searched hers. His tongue delved into her mouth as he moved purposely down her back, his fingers cupping her buttocks, pulling her hard against his length.

As he unbuttoned her blouse, he felt her pull his shirt from his pants, her hands now against the naked flesh of his back. Impatiently without thinking, he rolled her over onto him. The sudden action twisted his leg, sending a searing stab of pain through it and into his hip. Sucking in a harsh breath, he doubled up with the unexpected agony.

Amy held him in her arms, her hands stroking his hair, until he could again master himself. For awhile, they lay, close together, trying to quiet their breathing.

"Lord," he groaned when he could finally speak.

"Your leg?"

"No." He took a deep breath and shook his head. "I love you, baby-- too much."

"There can't be too much between us," she whispered, her hand caressing the side of his face.

"Reckon I made a fool out of myself tonight." He thought of how he'd behaved, of the wrong interpretation he'd put on everything.

"Reckon so," she mimicked, "but I expect Adam thought it was funny."

"I thought--"

"The trouble with you, Matthew Kane, is you're too quick to think me out of your life. I thought when I told Adam how much I love you you'd stop seeing him as a rival, but I can see the trouble is you don't believe enough in yourself or in my love."

"I want to."

"Listen to me then. When it comes to you, I don't know how to say no. I want you so much. Tonight only proved that again. I've been trying to do what you said you wanted. I even read the Bible, trying to cool myself down. I thought if I was less physical, it would be easier for both of us. I guess I should have talked it over with you instead of just doing it."

Matt shook his head, feeling every bit the fool he'd just acted. She smiled, running her finger along the edge of his jaw. "Maybe we need a new approach. Being alone like this isn't going to work, because if we do this very much, your dream is not going to happen."

Without the agonizing pain in his leg, Matt knew she was right; he wouldn't have pulled back this time. He had wanted her too much, needed the ultimate reassurance of her being his woman.

"You know, Matthew," she whispered, letting her breath brush his neck, "the Bible does have some words for our situation."

"It does?" he asked with a wry smile. "Like damnation and hellfire?"

"I was thinking before the fact," she teased. "It says if they cannot contain, let them marry, for it is better to marry than to burn."

She watched as a slow smile spread over his face. "I think it's referring there to a different kind of burning."

"Oh you think so," she teased. "We thought it was rather apropos for our situation."

"We?" Just exactly with whom was Amy talking about their private life, and it had better not be Adam.

"Actually, it was my mother and me." She smiled as his mouth dropped open.

"Your mother! You talked this over with your mother?"

"She and I have been talking about things. Well, mostly she's been talking, but I did admit to her a little of what I'd been feeling."

"God," he groaned, "I can't believe you'd tell her something like that. She's going to get that gun of your pa's for sure now."

Amy laughed. "She understood. She really did."

He lay there for a moment, trying to absorb what she was telling him.

Amy looked into his eyes, reading his skeptical thoughts without much difficulty. It would have been even harder for him to accept knowing she and her mother had giggled over the verse. Their relationship was changing. Her mother was accepting her not just as daughter, but as a woman, a friend even. It had made possible the discussion they'd had.

Matt shook his head. "I will never understand women."

Amy laughed, stroking his arm. "Well, I wouldn't want you getting cocky on the subject anyway." Then she laughed louder at her choice of words.

"Then you think your folks won't object to us marrying?"

"I think," she said, rising to sit above him as she rebuttoned her blouse and then his shirt, "they understand what it's like to be young and in love. They might even be relieved at a wedding."

When she saw his look of disbelief, she frowned. "Matt, you have to start seeing yourself as you are, and not as you think others see you. You have a lot of qualities that should make them want you for a son-in-law."

She bent and kissed him, stilling any protests. When he tried again, she repeated the kiss with a little more feeling, more testing of what a kiss could be. She ran her tongue along his lip, loving his sharp intake of breath and her own knowledge of the power she was learning to exercise. After a moment, she whispered, "This is a good way to stop quibbling over things that don't matter when we both know what does."

"We do?" he asked, a slow smile coming over his face.

"We're what matter-- us. Having a cabin like we talked about. Us being together whenever we want, however we want. Knowing there's a whole string of tomorrows for us."

"You sure you won't miss being a bluestocking in like San Francisco?" he asked facing his other fear head on.

"I might sometimes, but I visualize a different life now. One where I am Matthew Kane's woman, where I have a baby in my arms and maybe a toddler hanging onto my skirt. Dreams change, Matt. Mine have."

He smiled, caught up in the word picture she'd created. "You know, that medicine St. Louis used, that taopi tawote, that's what you are for me, baby. You're my wound medicine."

"I love you. I want to be everything for you," she whispered, her arms entwined around his neck. "We just have to keep believing in us, then what could stand between us?"

"Nothing. Not when you say it like that."

But there was something, a fear deep within him. From where was it coming? What caused it? He had no answers, just a sick feeling of dread that he could push away when Amy was there but that returned in his dreams and when he was alone.

"You've done enough for me," Matt told St. Louis as they finished their evening meal. "I'm crowding you, can't work yet. It's better I go back to my own wagon." He clenched his jaw and didn't let himself think about the depressing conditions he would find there. Neither his father nor brother had inquired about his recuperation, not once in the ten days since he'd been injured.

"It ain't necessary for you to go," St. Louis said, his gaze meeting Matt's over the rim of a coffee cup.

"Ain't crowdin' us," Clem chimed in to Matt's surprise. "Stay on, long as you want."

Matt smiled. "I appreciate everything you all have done for me, puttin' up with my foul temper, takin' care of me, but there's no reason for me not to go back."

"Wal, if it don't work out, come on back," St. Louis said. "Like Clem said, there's room, and I'm expectin' ya back to work soon as ya feel up to it."

· · ·

By the time Matt got to his wagon, his father was asleep. Morey sat by the back of the wagon, staring moodily at the ground.

"I'll be sleeping here," Matt said, as he threw his blanket to the ground.

"Why?"

"It bother you, Morey, having me back?"

"You ain't never been my favorite person."

"I noticed."

"So what lets you be the one doin' the decidin'?"

Matt yawned. "Let's see, maybe because I own the wagon, the team, the supplies."

Matt ignored his brother's sullen glare and shrugged out of his shirt. Dropping down onto his blanket, he rolled himself into it, turning his back on Morey.

"Think you're smart," Morey griped, grabbing his own blanket as he muttered darkly. "Somebody oughta take you down a notch or two."

Already half asleep, Matt ignored the threats. Arguing with his brother was a waste of what energy he had.

In the early dawn light, Amy caught up with Matt as he headed toward the corral for the oxen. "St. Louis told me what you're doing. I don't like it."

He didn't have to ask what she meant. Her worried eyes told him. "It's my wagon; it's where I belong at least for now."

"But--"

Matt grinned. "I need to be doing something. This seems about the extent of what's possible."

She looked up into his gray-blue eyes, aware he wasn't going to be giving in to her on this. Taking a deep breath, she asked, "May I help?"

He laughed. "You pull many oxen around in your day?"

She shook her head. "I could though," she argued.

"You're not planning on mothering me, I hope?" he asked with the expression that warned her of the results of such action.

"Of course not... You are going to be careful though. I mean with the oxen." She gave him a weak smile.

Matt laughed again. "You watching over me, what's my choice?"

Amy watched with a mixture of pleasure and worry as he moved into the enclosure, found his team and roped the big beasts. When he brought them up to her, she asked, "The work isn't hurting your arm, is it?"

He raised his brows at her concern. "You want to take them?" He grinned as he held out the ropes and watched her step back.

"They're awfully big," she said uneasily but ready to try.

He laughed and pulled the team behind him as they started back to the wagons.

As they walked, Amy was pleased the way the men responded to Matt. It wasn't so much that they said anything important, but more that they talked to him at all. A friendly wave or hello made it clear he was at last accepted. Matt seemed amused at the change but even more so at Mrs. Collins who walked by with her nose in the air. Her dislike of him had obviously not abated in the least.

"I can't believe that woman," Amy muttered when she'd passed.

"Well, at least you can count on her."

At night, Amy brought Matt a plate of food. Left to his own devices, she knew he would eat anything or too often forget he hadn't eaten at all. She was determined to watch over him, even if it occasionally made him mad.

Putting aside the emptied plate, Matt looked down to where Amy sat curled up at his feet. "That was good," he said, adding, "Thank you for bringing it."

"You don't mean that," she retorted, running her hand lightly over his knee.

"I mean it. It's just I don't want you thinking you got to take care of me."

She laughed. "But it's all right if you take care of me?"

"You know I don't mean that."

Amy felt him flinch and looked up to see Bernice walking into the circle of firelight. "Oh great," she muttered.

At first, Bernice seemed to have eyes only for Matt. When she became aware of Amy, her eyes narrowed, but she continued her path and sat across from them. "How are you both?" she asked, her smile large and as usual not very authentic.

Nathan Kane leaned out of the wagon. "Heard somebody." His wandering gaze settled on Bernice. "Don't reckon I've met this young lady," he slurred.

"Mr. Kane, this is Bernice McDowell," Amy said. "But I can't imagine why you don't know her. She's friends with most everybody on the wagon train." At least the male population.

Bernice smiled coyly. "I do try."

Amy met her smile with one of her own. "Perhaps you shouldn't try so hard, Bernice, dear."

"Isn't it what the Good Book says? That we're supposed to be good people and do nice things for others." Bernice batted her eyes at Matt, making it obvious who she'd most like to do nice things for.

Amy raised her brows. "And you read the Good Book?" she asked with mock amazement. "I didn't realize you read any books?"

"I do sometimes."

Matt looked from Bernice to Amy, his eyes reflecting amusement. He raised his brows a little as he met Amy's gaze. She looked back innocently. It wasn't nice to be catty, but Bernice never brought out the best in her.

"I'll leave you young folks to talk," Nathan Kane said as he disappeared back into the wagon.

"You look as though you're in pain, Matt," Bernice said, misreading his expression of irritation. "How are you feeling?"

"Fine."

"He's stronger everyday," Amy said. She leaned back against Matt's good leg, taking his large hand in hers, possessively stroking it.

"I can see he's doing well." Bernice glared at Amy before she looked back at Matt. "Could this be the someone you spoke about one day? The someone it could never work out with?"

"Turned out it could."

"Why didn't you tell me who it was?" Her smile held no warmth.

"At the time it didn't seem to matter. I figured she loved somebody else."

"But, of course, he was wrong," Amy said.

"I can see that for myself," Bernice retorted. "Are you two engaged?"

Drawing Matt's hand to her mouth, Amy kissed his long fingers before she said, "You are the nosiest girl, Bernice. Whatever possesses you to ask such personal questions?"

Bernice shrugged, thrusting her breasts out less than subtly. "It seems a good way to find out things."

"But," Amy countered, "some things are none of your business." She tilted her head to one side. "Of course, in those cases, if you just have to find out, you could listen to the gossips, people who love to snoop into the business of others because they don't have enough things of their own to do."

"Well, I never!"

"I sincerely doubt that."

"You are being frightfully insulting tonight, Amy," Bernice retorted, retaining with an obvious effort her strained smile.

"Perhaps it's because I can be rude when something I love is threatened."

"And is something you love being threatened?" Bernice asked with a provocative glance toward Matt. "You seem more than a trifle insecure." She tossed her blonde hair behind her shoulder.

Matt stretched out his bad leg, wincing as the muscle cramped. "If we're talking about me-- and I'm never just sure what you gals are talking about," Matt drawled. "I've loved Amy as long as I can remember. She'd have no reason to be insecure, not ever."

"How sweet," Bernice said, looking from one to the other. "I hope someday I have a man say that about me."

"I'm sure you will, dear," Amy said, adding pointedly, "that is if you relax and quit trying so hard to get a man. Tends to scare them off."

"Relax?" Bernice repeated, at first not understanding, then her smile became frozen in place as she excused herself and left.

When she had gone, Amy took Matt's hand again, brought it to her cheek. "Were you disappointed in me?" she asked without looking at him.

"For what?"

"Acting like a cat."

"Staking out your territory?" he teased, as he rubbed his thigh.

"Flexing my claws." Pushing his hand aside, she began kneading and massaging the large muscle in his thigh, avoiding the injured area. "I wasn't very nice." She looked up into his clear, gray eyes. "I told Loraine once I'd die if you flirted with another woman. She said more likely I'd kill her, you, or both."

Matt chuckled before he leaned back, closing his eyes. "I'll take that as a warning, but it's one you don't need. Bernice holds no attraction for me."

Morey smirked as he walked into the circle. "Well, now, what am I interruptin' here?"

"How long you been there?" Matt asked through clenched teeth.

"Long enough to see what there was to see." Morey laughed. "She's real familiar with your-- uh, leg, ain't she?"

"Mind your own business." Matt rose to face Morey.

"Matthew," Amy whispered, clinging to his arm, "please ignore him."

Morey laughed. "Yeah Matthew," he said mocking Amy's solicitous tones, "got to be careful now. Don't do nothin' to hurt yoreself."

"I've taken all I will from you," Matt snapped. Amy, feeling the tensing of his muscles, took a tighter grip on his arm.

"For now, maybe that's all I got to say-- for now. When I got more, I'll let you know," Morey said as he sauntered back into the darkness.

Amy put her arms around Matt's waist, drawing him against

her. "Forget him." She could feel the rapid beating of his heart against her cheek.

"You're asking too much."

"He just wants to upset you. Don't let him know he's doing it."

She heard the chuckle, felt his muscles relax. His arms came around her, his hands played across her back. "I can't believe I'm hearing this from you. Isn't this something like the pot calling the kettle black?"

"Maybe I do preach better than I practice," she admitted, running her hands down the muscles of his back, "but Bernice isn't really dangerous." Amy ignored Matt's snort of disbelief. "Morey is. Even if I didn't know what he'd already done to you, I'd know by his eyes that he wants to hurt you. He won't just go away if you ignore him, but maybe he won't find it so much fun to bait you-- if you don't play bear."

Matt laughed. He leaned away from her, taking a tress of her long hair between his fingers. "Play bear huh? First it was sheep-- now it's bear. Am I comin' up in the world—or going down?"

CHAPTER 19

G oing over South Pass was as easy as Adam had said it
would be, a gradual ascent, an easy road. Although in the
distance they could see snow covered mountains, their own way
was free of ice or snow. When the wagons reached the top, the
emigrants stopped long enough to savor the moment. Matt
stood with his arm around Amy, as she talked about her excitement that the land they would claim for their own waited for
them in Oregon.

The night's camp was Pacific Springs, an oasis of rich grass
amidst a dry land. St. Louis told Matt the water from this spring
flowed-- unlike all the rivers he had crossed, all the rivers he had
known-- into the Pacific Ocean. "First to the Big Sandy, south to
the Green, the Colorado, Gulf of California and finally to the
Pacific Ocean."

Matt had knelt dabbling his fingers in its cold water. His
thoughts had turned dark. These waters would reach their destination, would he?

That night he lounged against a wagon wheel, Adam on his
haunches beside him as the elected council and assorted other
men gathered around St. Louis to hear a choice they were to
make.

"Used to be all wagons went down this way." As he talked,
St. Louis drew a crude map in the dirt. "Followed the Big Sandy

River, then stopped at Fort Bridger for supplies and wound up along Muddy Creek before they cut back across to Bear Creek.

"The advantages were water, plenty of feed for livestock and at one time-- old Fort Bridger itself. In those days, it was well stocked, but now with Jim not there much, it's been goin' to seed. Then a mountain man called Greenwood found a cut-off." Again he drew in the dust. The straight line made a backward D out of his earlier map. "Some folks call this Greenwood's cut-off and others Sublette's. Whatever ya call it, it lops off about a hundred miles."

"Sounds like a great idea good to me," said William Porter, nudging his glasses back on his nose. "I'm sick of traveling. Don't want to go one mile farther than we must."

"Any shortcut's got to be a good one," Ralph Hall agreed.

"Usually so, but from the Big Sandy to the Green River, near fifty miles it's straight across a desert-- no water, no grass, no shade, no stops."

"You can't mean we'd do that many miles all at once," Amos voiced what Matt could see was the question on everyone's mind.

"How it has to be. Start at three or four in the afternoon and go straight through."

"You mean morning," Hall corrected.

St. Louis smiled. "I meant what I said. Ya rest in the mornin'. About the time the sun's edgin' down a little in the sky, ya start out, carryin' water for folks and stock. Goin' that way, what ya bring with ya is what ya got. Ya walk straight through the night and the next day. No stoppin' 'til we hit the river."

"No breaks?" Hall said with disbelief.

"A short one about halfway."

"Can it really be done?" Amos stared at the map in the dust.

"I've done it. Our stock is in good condition as are we. I won't lie though. It's not easy. Women, kids and sick folks would ride most of the way in the wagons. But every able body would walk to make it easier on the stock. It can be done in little over twenty-four hours."

"You really think we can do it?" questioned Jacob Collins.

"If I didn't, I wouldn't have told ya about it."

"I like the idea of shortening the trip-- if it's safe," Amos said.

"I vote to do it," Hall stated, and the rest of the men followed suit.

"All right then," St. Louis said, "don't forget what I told ya. We'll be headin' through some of the most barren, seemingly God-forsaken country ya ever seen. Besides no water, there's no animal feed neither. Ya'll have to give the stock flour mixed in their water... or even bread when ya take yore break."

He looked from man to man. "I know ya never traveled even half this distance in a day afore, but ya ain't the same folks as left Independence."

As the other men left to explain the situation to their families, Adam straightened to stand beside Matt. "Think you can make it?" he asked.

Matt grinned. "Think you can?"

"I didn't rip holy hell out of my leg."

"No foolishness, Matt," St. Louis ordered. "You ride in the wagon. Ya don't want to stretch yore luck."

Matt said nothing as he met St. Louis' gaze. He knew he wasn't well yet, nor by any stretch of the imagination back to the strength he had earlier enjoyed, but he also knew he needed to do this. He would not be the cripple St. Louis had described. He would demand from his body what it had once delivered, and it would again.

Through shimmering waves of heat, Matt could see the distant hills ahead, appearing to move before his eyes as a mirage. There was little talk as the train hesitated, the people staring out at the barren valley.

When they reached the valley floor, Matt realized what had looked in the distance to be flat and level was instead a series of beds and eroded gullies, none so deep as to make crossing impossible, but rough enough to make it unpleasant. To the south a lone butte stood tall and aloof, on the other side, alkali beds. From what he could see, no living thing moved alongside the road, no plants grew-- only rock and sand. Walking into the vast, seemingly lifeless valley was one of the eeriest experiences Matt could remember.

By starting in the afternoon, there were only a few hours of heat with which to contend before the air cooled. When the sun set, the wagons continued, the walkers plodding beside them as they followed the winding road that snaked its way through one sandy depression after another.

Time after time, Matt felt his strength gone. He thought he could not walk another step; but from some unknown source, he was able to keep going. He began to count steps, anything to take his mind off the ache in his leg.

He looked down, watching his boots as he walked beside the oxen, nothing to look at, nothing to think about except to place one foot in front of the other. The air was now cold, rapidly becoming bitingly cold. Matt began to shiver despite his exertion. In his increasing misery, he was grateful he had insisted Amy stay with her family for this trek. If she'd been with him, she'd have pushed him to lie down, to give up. Giving up some of his pride, he did pull a cane St. Louis had made for him from the wagon and used it to support more and more of his weight as the night wore on.

Seeing the sky lighten in the east came none too soon. The mind was willing; the body at its limit. With an hour to water the stock and rest, he hoped to recoup his strength.

Lying flat on the ground, limbs sprawled, Matt didn't bother to look up when he heard footsteps. He knew who it was. "Don't you get tired?" he asked as he squinted up to look at her beautiful face.

"I needed to be sure you were all right." She knelt, putting her cool hands on his forehead. He could see the circles under her eyes, the paleness of her skin, even under its coating of dust.

"And you don't need a rest right now? You worry about me too much." He raised her hand to his lips and kissed it.

"I wouldn't have to, if you showed better judgment. How is your leg?"

He thought about lying but the truth was too much work to conceal. "It hurts as expected but is holding up."

She shifted and began kneading and massaging the large

263

thigh muscle avoiding where the wound was healing. "Amy," he protested, aware Morey was not far away, his eyes watching with a disturbing intentness.

"Yes?"

"You can't do that where folks can see."

"I can't?" She didn't stop.

"It doesn't look right." It did feel right.

"When are you going to learn I don't give a damn what looks right."

He gaped at her. "Since when did you start swearing?"

"It's become more essential since I started hanging around a certain stubborn male." The motion of her strong hands ended the cramping in his leg, easing the pain at least temporarily. "Is it helping?"

"Yes."

"Good." Finally, she sat back. Cocking her head to one side, she studied his face.

"So, what do you see?" he asked.

"I see a man who looks much too tired."

"You too, but at least I add-- you look beautiful tired." She gave him a look but left after kissing him. All too soon, they had to move on.

The morning turned blistering hot with a baking heat to make the walk of the night before seem like a gentle stroll. The dust rose around Matt, choking, coating man and beast. He had to concentrate-- one step, then another, keep moving.

With the afternoon came a breeze, which at first was welcome, cooling as it evaporated the sweat from his body. Soon the breeze became a wind of seemingly near gale proportions. Stinging particles of rock and dirt drove into his face and unprotected skin. Tying a kerchief over his mouth and nose helped only a little.

He had wanted to walk the whole way, as a test of his rebuilding strength, but as the afternoon wore on, he gave up in defeat, flopping into the back of the wagon to take breaks enough to get him moving again. His father and Morey took turns driving the team. He was forced to stop, rubbing another cramp from his leg. Eventually, the three of them took turns riding in the wagon, if nothing else, it got them out of the driving dust.

They had been warned, as they approached Green River, they would have to keep a strong arm on their teams. At the smell of water, they might stampede. Matt watched as he saw the animals' heads rise up, a growing excitement in the way they walked. They were beginning the descent to the river. They had crossed the barrens in twenty-five hours.

At the bank of the river, the animals were allowed to drink, slowly at first, then freed to cool their bodies in the cold water. When Matt finished caring for the stock, he lay on the muddy bank, spent by the effort he had put out, but exultant. His leg was growing in strength and mobility despite what he'd just put it through. He would not be walking with a limp the rest of his life.

～

Traveling over a low mountain range, the wagons dropped into Bear Valley, Amy would have thought it a paradise, after the rugged terrain through which they'd just passed, if it had not been for the abundance of mosquitoes.

At Soda Springs, the wagons halted for half a day's rest. Matt joined Amy to walk the mile and a half to see the hot springs themselves. Some were four feet in diameter and looked to be over a man's head. The water was in continual boiling motion. While some of the springs were so hot they would have burned the flesh, others were warm or even cold. Matt cupped his hands and drew water from one of the springs, bringing it to Amy's lips. Its taste was salty and carbonated.

"Too bad we're not little or already married." Amy looked at the pools, then cast her gaze toward Matt.

"What are you suggesting?" The soft expression in his eyes told her he knew full well.

"Remember when we were children and went swimming-- without our clothing? She smiled up into his cool gray eyes.

"How could I forget?" He grinned. "The beating was enough-- if nothin' else-- to remind me."

She took his arm, leaning against him, stroking the sinewy bicep through the thin layer of cotton. "It would be fun though to do it now. Wouldn't it?"

His eyes were heavy-lidded with his thoughts, his breathing coming a little faster as she pressed against him. "Are you tryin' to tempt me?"

"Could I?"

"Where it comes to you, it's been known to happen."

"Maybe then, just a little. But it would be fun, if we were married, I mean. Wouldn't it?"

He turned and put his arm around her waist, drawing her more firmly against his hard length. "You know the answer to that."

"Maybe, we can come back here someday," she murmured, wistfully thinking how good the cooler of the pools would feel, how relaxing to her muscles to soak in the warm water. Smiling she let herself consider the excitement of sharing that with Matthew, their clothing thrown on the bank. She could visualize how he would look, wading out of the water, broad shoulders and narrow hips, the sun glistening off his wet skin, his hair loose and hanging down his back. She shivered as she realized how much she wanted him holding her that way, his naked skin against hers.

Matt's voice interrupted her pagan thoughts. "Maybe there will be springs like these a little closer to where home'll be. Then we'll just have to see-- if you're as game as you talk." He lifted her chin for his kiss.

As they walked back to the wagons, hand in hand, Matt said, "I learned something today."

"What?"

He had a faint smile on his lips. When he looked down at her, his gray eyes were smoky with emotion. "I don't expect it's a big thing to you or something you didn't already know, but I never really what it meant when people talked about belonging. It's not the big things at all. It's the little ones-- having somebody to walk with, to see things with, that's what it's all about."

Dropping his hand, she put her arm around his waist, felt his come around her, his hand resting on the rise of her hip. "I love you so much," she said, looking straight ahead, unable to meet his gaze because she knew she'd cry.

"I believe that," he said. "It's hard for me to know why. How it happened something so good like this came into my hands, but I won't let loose of it."

She squeezed him. "I'd like to share something more with you. Would you come meet some friends of mine?"

He laughed. "After what I just said, how could I say no?"

Walking into the Porter circle, Amy was glad to see William for once was beside the campfire. She made hasty introductions. After they'd been invited to sit on a combination of plain stools and boxes, she said, "Someone's missing."

"She's supposed to be taking a nap," Jennie said, "but I just heard her start to complain. She's been fussy, cutting another tooth, I think. I don't know how she'll take to a stranger." She smiled apologetically at Matt. "Eliza doesn't usually like men until she's knows them."

"That's all right," said Matt, stretching out his leg. "I won't take it personal. Sometimes it takes the ladies a spell to get onto me." He looked over at Amy, grinning.

Jennie went to retrieve the now crying baby.

William, more congenial than Amy had ever seen, said, "I hear we're going to be coming to the Snake River soon. Do you know much about that country. Think we'll have any Indian trouble there?"

"St. Louis says no. The Shoshoni haven't fought in big bands. He said they'd maybe take a stray wagon if it was easy, but so long so we keep our stock up close to the wagons, we likely won't even see them."

"Well, here she is." Jennie walked into the circle, carrying the still sleepy baby. "She has a little runny nose. I hope she's not coming down with another cold. She just got over one."

She set Eliza down safely away from the cook fire. The baby's eyes widened when she saw Matt. Using a crab-like, hitch-along walk, she sidled toward the adults. Matt smiled when she reached his leg. He made no attempt to touch her.

"I think she's put on a couple of pounds since I last saw her," Amy observed.

Using Matt's good leg as a support, Eliza pulled herself up. She stood teetering, holding onto his pants with one hand while she sucked on her chubby fingers with the other. She said something in words and sounds Amy didn't recognize.

"And what's your name?" Matt asked.

Eliza clapped both hands over her mouth, nearly falling except for Matt's big hand reaching out and steadying her. Reaching up expectantly, she cooed.

"That means Eliza wants you to pick her up," Jennie said amazement in her voice.

Matt reached down, helping the baby to crawl into his lap, grimacing as he bent his bum leg.

"I guess," Amy said with a grin, "I'm not the only woman taken with your charms," and added nearly under her breath, "as if I didn't know that already."

Eliza began an exploration of his pockets, finally stopping to study his large hand. "Bigger than you're used to, huh?" Matt murmured.

"She does seem to like you," said William, smiling himself, a sight Amy had never seen and had never expected to see.

"It's the bane of my life," Amy quipped, "the women are all drawn to him." As she watched him, Amy imagined what it might be like when she put his own son or daughter into his arms. He looked so at ease, so right with the baby. He had so much love to give. She was certain he'd make a wonderful father.

"Do you have little brothers or sisters, Mr. Kane?" asked Jennie.

"No, Ma'am, and call me Matt. Mr. Kane sounds too much like my pa."

"All right, Matt, but then you must call me Jennie. I'm just surprised you're so good with babies. Eliza is quite taken with you.

Looking at Amy, his smile softening, he said, "Might come in handy someday."

Eliza began to tire of her search through his pockets and indicated she wanted down to explore other worlds. William took advantage of the opportunity to ask Matt about a problem he'd been having with one of his mule's hooves. After a moment of questioning, the two men went off to look at the animal, leaving Amy and Jennie to talk over a cup of tea.

Jennie said, "He is the man, the one who was a friend and you were upset with when we talked that time, isn't he?"

"Yes, he is."

"He's very handsome."

"Bernice would agree with that." Amy watched to see if Jennie had any misgivings about Amy being the one he had chosen.

Jennie laughed. "But that would be all my cousin would see in him. She wouldn't notice the kind eyes or the soft smile. So it wasn't just friendship?"

"No, it wasn't."

"The difference between you and Bernice is you don't just love him because he's handsome, do you?"

Amy shook her head. "Although I can't deny I do appreciate what he looks like."

"As any woman would," Jennie said. "The trouble with Bernice is she never sees beneath the surface of anything. She's got an itch for what she can't have. I expect that has made Matt even more desirable, the fact he never wanted her."

"I wasn't very nice to her the last time we spoke." Amy wondered if Bernice had told her cousin about her less than friendly manner.

"Most of what you said probably went right over her head."

"I've been jealous of her."

"I can't imagine why. It's obvious the man is besotted with you."

"I think the jealousy comes," Amy said with a laugh, "because I'm so completely besotted with him."

They sipped their tea in a companionable silence, watching the two men examining the hooves of a mule. After a few moments, Matt took his knife from its sheath and knelt, grasping one hoof, as he said something to William and began cutting.

Jennie's gaze met Amy's over the rim of the tea cup, "He's nothing like I thought. His name's been on everyone's lips practically since the train pulled out of St. Louis. First it was Bernice going on about how beautiful he was. Then there was the theft. Some talking about what a bad man he was. Others how bravely he'd withstood the whipping. There were his fights." Jennie lifted her finely arched brows and smiled. "He's been half the gossip on this train, kept people talking when there wasn't anything else. Hearing about him, but only seeing him at a distant, he seemed bigger than life."

"I hadn't thought of him that way but can see how it might be."

Jennie smiled sheepishly. "I wouldn't doubt he's had a lot of women wondering about him. I'd see him on a horse or stalking past the wagons-- eyes straight ahead-- and he was like a character out of a novel. It would be easy to imagine him on the cover of one of those paperbacks floating around, holding a knife and slaying an Indian." She giggled. "But now up close, here, holding Eliza, he seemed like-- well, like a big, easy going Missouri farm boy."

Amy laughed. "Well, he's all those things."

"You're a fortunate woman, Amy, and I'm happy for you. Do you--" She was interrupted by Eliza's pursuit of a large ant. With her daughter safely in her arms, she asked, "Do you have wedding plans?"

"No date, but we will be married. I don't want us to wait 'til we get to Oregon. I wasted so much time not being sure what I wanted. Now I just want to be his wife as soon as possible." Her thoughts grew dreamy as she contemplated the passion she felt, the way her hands yearned constantly to touch him.

"I envy you," Jennie said, reminding Amy of the things she had said about her own marriage not being blessed by passion or love.

"Are things no different? I mean between you and William. I thought maybe since he was here, with you and Eliza, it meant things were better."

"Well, I have learned to cook over the fire, but no, they aren't better. I have to remember to count my blessings. I have Eliza. William and I do have that in common. He adores her. He's proud of how pretty she's getting to be."

"Then maybe the situation in the other areas will get better."

Jennie pinched her lips together. "I think I just have to settle for what can be, not dream about something more. It's just... I don't have what I saw in your face when you watched your man." Her voice softened. "I guess I do wish William and I had that or even something like it. Maybe it's simply not supposed to be that way for everyone."

"There are quieter types of loves. Sometimes those ways of caring are just as strong as the others." Amy knew that at this moment, with her love so fresh and passionate, her heart believed nothing of what she was saying, but her head told her it was so.

"Eliza makes it worthwhile," Jennie said, watching as her daughter played with a carved wooden animal of uncertain species.

"Maybe things will change with time."

Jennie smiled, looking again toward the two men. "To be honest, where it's William, it's hard for me to really enjoy his attentions-- that way-- when he's just been telling me what an idiot I am." She shook her head. "Besides, I don't think he'd want more uh... physical affection between us. When we... er did do it, it was just getting it over, you know."

Amy watched Matt as he worked with the Porter mule. Even from this distance, he seemed to feel her eyes on him. He looked up, smiling at her before turning back to his work on the hoof. She looked back at Jennie who was washing Eliza's fingers. "Perhaps William needs encouragement."

"I don't think I could do such a thing. I've seen how your family is. You're used to hugging and such, but I've always been shy about that. I'd be so embarrassed if William pushed me away."

"Matt pushed me away," Amy said, but she knew it was different. In her heart she'd known Matt loved her. Jennie had no such assurance.

"You find it easy to show love to Eliza," Amy said, watching as Jennie kissed her baby's fingertips.

"That's different. I don't have to worry she'll reject me."

"There is a risk with a man," Amy admitted, "but when I think back on the problems Matthew and I have had, mostly they've come because we misread each other. Could that be what's happening with you and William?"

"I don't think so." She shook her head. "I suppose it's possible, but you know, sometimes it seems life's like a dress. You find a pattern that fits; you put it together, and wear it. If you try a new pattern, it might not fit so well." She frowned then and put her fingers on Eliza's forehead. "You know, Amy, I think she's got a fever."

Amy felt of the tiny forehead, then the back of her neck, bending to listen to her chest. "She does feel hot. I think I hear a little congestion too."

"She was just sick," Jennie said, her face paling.

"Why don't we take her over and let Mama look at her. She might have an herbal tonic or chest plaster that would help."

William and Matt were walking back, talking about the mule when Jennie stopped them. "Eliza has a fever. We're taking her to Mrs. Stevens."

William, looking even more slightly built than usual next to Matt's towering height, frowned. "You don't think it's something serious do you?"

"Probably just a cold," Amy said.

"Mrs. Stevens knows about herbal remedies," Jennie said, her eyes on the baby. "She gave us a tonic when Eliza was teething, remember."

William didn't seem reassured. Amy felt grateful when Matt put his arm around her waist. "Reckon we'll walk along to see the baby's all right."

When the four of them reached the Stevens' wagon, Eliza had coughed several times, and her nose was running. She fussed as Amy's mother opened her mouth to look down her throat, sniffed her breath, felt of her forehead and listened to her chest.

"You've had enough of this, haven't you?" Amy's mother crooned to the irritable baby. "It does sound as though she has a cold again." She studied the baby a moment, a frown line between her brows. "Since it appears to be in her chest, I think wild cherry bark would be best. Put the amount I give you in a quart of boiling water but don't let it boil or it'll take the value from the bark. Then add a little honey and give her half a cup if she'll take it every hour or so. A mustard plaster for her chest wouldn't hurt either. Do you know how to apply one?" Jennie nodded.

"Another thing that has helped when mine had the croup was a tent with steam. You get some water boiling and with a quilt over you and Eliza, let her breathe in the steam. I just wish I had more herbs with me. I don't know the ones that grow in this country. I think we should ask St. Louis if he's seen anything along the way that might help."

"St. Louis," William asked, "what does he know about babies?"

"He knows Indian medicine," Matt said.

"A bunch of heathen savages, what could they know about doctoring?" William scoffed as he nervously felt of Eliza's forehead.

Matt's voice grew cold. "Those medicines worked for me more than once."

William shook his head. "I don't want pagan tricks used on my daughter. They might poison her."

"William maybe we should--" Jennie began meekly before he cut her off. "That's enough, Jennette. I know what's best."

"You do as you will, Mr. Porter," Amy's mother said. "She is your daughter, but Indian herbal medicines are no different than the ones my mother and grandmother taught me to use. It's amazing the things those so-called savages have successfully treated. It's ridiculous to imply there is something spiritually wrong with using any plant growing in the earth-- put there by God-- simply because an Indian learned of it first."

"Nevertheless," he repeated. "We'll stick to what we know. And that's final. I don't believe God would approve us using anything a heathen used."

Amy's mother sighed with exasperation but didn't argue further. She gave Jennie the bark and ingredients for the mustard plaster and suggested ample fluids, especially broths, going light on nursing until the baby seemed better. She shook her head as they left. "Stubborn, foolish man," she muttered to Amy and Matt. "I hope he doesn't live to regret it."

CHAPTER 20

M att and Adam rode ahead of the wagons to find a camping site. Matt was still depressed over the wagon train's disappointing stop at Fort Hall. The scantily supplied fort had neither doctor nor medicine for Eliza, who was now seriously ill, unable to keep anything on her stomach with her temperature risen to a dangerous level. An unseasonable cold spell contributed to the worry as other children came down with the croup-like cough.

In the distance, there was a dull roar as Matt and Adam reined in their horses on a bluff high above the Snake River. "American Falls," Adam explained. "And we're several miles from it."

Matt had little interest in hearing or seeing the falls. He crooked his good leg over the pommel of his saddle and stared at the turbulent water of the Snake below.

"Over there might work for a camp." Adam gestured without much enthusiasm to a spot several miles farther ahead.

"Good enough," Matt agreed.

"You know, it's funny," Adam said, shaking his head and addressing what Matt had no stomach to talk about. "I've seen a lot of people die. Going back and forth as many times as I have, you'd think I'd be used to it, but when it's a baby. Never."

"She isn't going to die." Matt wished he believed the words.

"How'd she look to you last night when we stopped?" Adam asked.

Matt shook his head. He didn't want to say how she'd looked.

Camped at Register Rock, where Matt had already carved their initials and the date in the rock, Amy sat on a large rock, watching, while he struggled to repair a damaged wagon wheel. The owner spent his time complaining-- this should never have happened because he'd greased the wheel just like Mr. Jones had said-- then watched over Matt's shoulder to assure himself the work was progressing satisfactorily as he asked repetitive questions. He finally helped the most when he left for a card game.

Amy could see Matt was tired, hot and sweaty. As the evening wore on, she added cranky to the list. He tied and retied his hair back several times accompanied by a curse under his breath before he would bend again to his task. She wished she had some way to help him. At such times, it was best to say nothing. In the mood he was in, a fight would be all too easy to arrange. Any offer of help would not only be rejected but scoffed at; so she sat on the large rock, her knees tucked up, her arms around them.

When he had at last finished, he flopped down beside her. "I'd like you to cut my hair." He pulled off the thong that had held it back.

"I love your hair. Why would you cut it?" she asked, certain she must have misunderstood him.

"It's in my way and it's hot. Just chop it off."

"I've never cut a man's hair." She looked at his thick mane of blond hair. "How short did you mean?"

He shrugged. "I suppose I could hack it off with a knife."

She climbed off her rock to walk around him, considering his head from several angles. It did hang way down his back. If she just took off a few inches would it be less bothersome to him? "Suppose I make a botch of it? You might decide not to marry me when you find out how awful I am at cutting hair." She teased as she considered the task ahead.

He laughed, reached out, and took hold of her hand, kissing her fingers. "I think there might be a few things more important than whether you can cut hair. Don't worry. If you ruin it, it'll grow back."

"What about your ear?"

"You shaved me without cutting my throat or rearranging any outstanding features. I want it cut. Come on." He stood up, waiting for her to get the scissors. "Unless you want to use my knife," he teased, reaching for his belt.

"I might be tempted," she grumped, going to her wagon to gather her mother's scissors, a towel and comb.

When she came back, Matt had stripped to the waist and was sitting on her large rock. "I'm not very excited about this," she muttered, tucking the towel around his neck. "Hold this tight." Uneasily, she ran the comb through the thick hair, pulling it out from his back. Standing back for a moment, she considered, comb against her chin, before she caught a length of hair in the teeth of the comb, held it out and snipped off four inches before she lost her nerve.

Playfully she discovered a new game as she allowed her fingers to glide down, touching his bare shoulder, as if by accident. "You know," she said, as she stepped back to survey her handiwork, "I might consider doing this for extra money." She smiled at the picture he made-- bare-chested in the fading sunlight, the towel draped loosely around his neck. "Think any of the other men on the train might like the same treatment?" She ran her finger provocatively down his chest, circling around a flat male nipple, seeing it tighten, before she moved back up with her teasing finger.

He exhaled a deep breath. "They better not. You're my woman and don't you forget it." The towel fell to the ground as he grabbed her wrist and pulled her tight against him, broad daylight or not.

"Jealous?" she asked, her arms coming around his neck. If he didn't care about watching eyes, she certainly didn't.

"Possessive of what's mine."

"There's a difference?"

"One I'll admit to--the other I won't." Taking his leather thong, he retied his hair tight against the back of his neck.

"I see we're discussing an issue of semantics."

"Whatever that is."

"The way words mean. The uh... the exact meaning of words." She stumbled around trying to find other words that would explain semantics.

"I like the big words you use," he drawled, kissing her hand, "but don't go using them against me. I like to know when you're insulting me."

"When I insult you, I'll keep the words very clear."

Amy looked up from the potatoes from which she'd been peeling as William Porter, a bleak expression on his narrow face, walked into the Stevens circle. He faced none of them but stood by the fire, staring into the flames. Amy's mother dusted flour from her hands.

"Eliza's not better." His voice was toneless, his shoulders more shrunken than slumped.

Amy flinched. She'd come to dread hearing from anyone who'd been to see the baby. Her own visits with Jennie were filled with pain at hearing the tiny body cough and choke. Nothing stopped the onslaught of the disease stealing Eliza's life energy.

"We need to do something. I need to do something. Anything," William said, his face scrunching together. "If we don't--" He stopped, unable to go on.

Amy's mother shook her head, tears in her eyes. "I don't know anything you haven't already tried."

William groaned. "I can't go back to Jennie and..." He took a deep breath. "I was wrong not to go to St. Louis. Maybe... maybe he does know something different." He looked from one face to the other, then turned and stumbled from their camp.

Watching him go, Amy's mother wiped the tears from her eyes. "I didn't have the heart to stop him, but I've already asked St. Louis."

"Then you don't think--" Amy couldn't bring herself to finish the question.

"A miracle," her mother answered bleakly.

Matt was sitting beside the campfire when he saw William Porter approach St. Louis. He rose as he heard the man's desperate appeal.

St. Louis shook his head. "I don't have nothin'. If I had, I'd a come to ya a long time back, made ya take it. Ya don't think I'd of held back somethin' that would've helped? When my wife and son died, it was somethin' like this. We tried a lot of things, like Martha done-- horsemint, ferns, sage. Nothin' stopped it."

William's face fell. "You were... my last hope." His voice broke on the words, as tears streaked his cheeks. "It's my fault. All my fault." Like a blind man, he turned away, stumbling back to his own wagon.

Adam, who heard only the end of the conversation when he arrived late, stared at Matt. "Ever ride out at night? Full moon, it's easy to scout ahead. Night like this, it's practically as bright as day."

"Anything'd be better than staying here," Matt said, rising to go find their horses.

Matt and Adam rode back into the circle of wagons at dawn. When Matt saw the cluster of people standing around the Porter wagon, staring sorrowfully into the campfire, he knew.

As he swung down, Amy came to him in tears. "Eliza's dead." He folded her into his arms. He had no words, no way to express the stabbing ache the news brought him. Until now he'd believed he'd felt it all. "I can't believe it. She was so precious, so full of life," Amy cried. "I kept hoping for a miracle, but it didn't come."

Adam stood back, his face stony, holding both horses as Amy sobbed out the tears that Matt knew both he and Adam longed to cry but couldn't release.

"Why did God let this happen?" Amy asked, wiping her eyes and pulling back from Matt's arms. "Why didn't He heal her?"

Matt shook his head, wishing he had an answer. Jennie walked slowly to them. Her eyes were dazed and tears streaked her thin cheeks. "We... Well, you know, we have to do something about... burying her."

"Adam and I'll take care of it," Matt said. He couldn't bring himself to say the word grave.

"We'd appreciate that." Jennie's voice was little more than a whisper. "We have another favor to ask of you."

William had risen and come to stand with them, guilt and grief written in equal measure on his face. "We-- that is Jennie and I would like you to say the words over her."

Before Matt could respond, Jennie said, "We have no minister with us, but even if we did, we'd want the words said by somebody who knew her, somebody she liked." Her voice broke as fresh tears ran down her cheeks. "Please."

Matt swallowed, trying to control his voice. "All right, if you want, I'll do it." He wheeled to tend to his horse, not wanting anyone to see the tears in his own eyes.

He and Adam walked, shovels on their shoulders, through the sage and dry grass until they came to a high point. They sought a place above flood, where the grave would oversee the river. Their shovels dug into the rocky soil. They took wordless turns, working their way deep into the earth.

When Matt climbed out of the finished hole, Adam said, "I don't understand any of this. It's what's always kept me from wanting to believe, from expecting anything from a god."

"Tragedy?" questioned Matt, feeling a bleakness to match that he saw in Adam's eyes.

"What kind of god would let something like this happen?"

Matt stared out toward the river. "From what I have seen, life is just what it is. It doesn't have a thing to do with whether there's a god or not."

Adam rubbed his hand over his unshaven jaw. "Why pray then? Why believe in some pie-in-the-sky god?"

Matt shrugged. "Prayin' is what folks do to get comfort for themselves." He stared at the river, his thoughts going beyond what had happened to Eliza, even what might happen to him. "Dying's part of living, like rain's part of sunshine. Tragedy goes with happiness." He shook his head. "Maybe I'm not makin' much sense, but the way I see it a man's life rolls out like that river."

"With no more meaning?"

"That river has meaning. Except, it don't know it." He dropped to the ground, leaning back on his elbows, facing the river. Adam settled onto his haunches beside him. "There's a current in it like life. It carries a person along through the years. We can't make our river flow backward just by demanding. We don't control all of what happens."

"Fate?"

"Maybe that's a name for it."

"Well, whatever it is, it's not fair." Adam took a little of the dirt into his hand, allowing it to sift through his fingers. "Eliza had her whole life ahead of her. She should have had that."

Matt smiled grimly, his thoughts turning inward to his own childhood. "Who's to know what kind of life that would've been. Sometimes death might be easier."

"Would you have chosen not to live?" Adam asked, obviously reading all too accurately between the lines from what had been said to that, which had been left unsaid.

"That's the beauty of it. I didn't have to choose. Neither did Eliza. Who knows, if we knew what was comin', how we'd choose. It isn't for us to know. So we make the most of what we can know."

"I don't like it," Adam grumbled as they rose to make their way back to the encampment.

"Me neither," Matt agreed. "But what we don't like, we just got to live with."

Adam smiled thinly. "I think I've recently had a brush with that one too."

. . .

Gray, rainless clouds passed overhead, a darkness on the land to match the black mood of those gathered around the small grave marked only by a simple wooden cross with Eliza's name carved on it. Matt heard women sobbing while the men stood by stoically. Although they'd seen the trail lined with graves of children and lost loved ones, it didn't make this lonely little cross any easier to bear.

He spoke words he thought might bring comfort and then read a Psalm. Did any of it help? Maybe or maybe not. When he was finished, they laid the baby's body into the hole. Adam stayed behind with him to fill in the grave as the others made their way back to their wagons.

For a time Matt thought they were alone, then realized William Porter had stayed with them. "It's my fault," William moaned when they had filled in the grave.

Adam shook his head. "Something like this is no man's fault."

"It's mine." He took off his glasses and rubbed watery, blood-shot eyes.

"St. Louis told you it wouldn't have made a difference," Matt said.

William sank to the ground, staring at the pile of fresh dirt. "I wasn't there for her. Didn't spend time. When she cried, I was impatient. And now, this cross is mine to bear."

Hell, Matt thought, looking toward Adam and seeing the same expression of dismay on his face. Matt had no idea what to say. Worse, there was some truth in what William was saying. He had neglected his family, but he hadn't caused Eliza to get sick.

"Guilt doesn't do any good," Matt said knowing he was the last one to be dispensing such advice when guilt had a way of eating into him all too regularly.

"Kane's right. You can't change what's past." Adam glanced at Matt gamely holding up his end of a conversation neither of them wanted.

"I can't live with it either," William said, taking a gun from his pocket. "I can't go back and face my wife, knowing how every time she looks at me, she blames me, and she's right."

"Man," Adam said, "you can't kill yourself. What would that do to Jennie?"

"She'd be free then to find a better man." William slumped to the ground, his arm loosely draped over his bent knees, the gun hanging from his hand.

"You'd leave her out here to get that wagon onto Oregon?" Matt edged closer to the grief-stricken man. "You think about this tomorrow, and you'll know you can't take the coward's way out."

"I can't go through another night," William cried. "I can't sleep. If I do, I dream Eliza's condemning me, asking why I never loved her." He shook his head. His eyes scrunched closed. "I can't live like this."

"So you'd leave Jennie alone to deal with her grief, feel her own guilt?" Matt asked aware Adam had edged a few feet closer, approaching William from the other side.

William glared at Matt, then at Adam. "Don't you try to stop me," he snarled, pointing the gun at first one, then the other. "I don't want to hurt either of you, but I will if you try to stop me."

"How would that make it better?" Adam asked. "You kill us, then you have more to feel guilty for."

"I don't want to do that." Tears ran down William's cheeks. "I didn't want Eliza to die either, but it was my fault."

"Damn it, man," Matt growled. "It wasn't anybody's fault. It was just life."

"She was a baby. I should have never taken her west."

"You can't second guess life," Matt said, taking another step, the muzzle of the gun now pointing at his chest.

"I don't know what to do," William cried. The barrel of the gun wavered.

"Put down the gun to start," Adam said, taking a step closer.

William looked at Adam for a second, and in that instant, Matt leaped, grabbing the gun and forcing William's hand toward the sky. The gun exploded, then Adam had him, wrestling the gun from his hand.

William collapsed onto the ground. "I can't even do this right," he sobbed.

"Then be a man about it," Matt snarled. "If you failed your wife and daughter, there's no saying you have to keep doing it."

"I can't change what's past." He sobbed harder.

"You can damn well change the future," Adam retorted.

William looked from one stern face to the other. "I don't know how."

"You take it one day at a time," Matt said. "You start by going there and taking your wife in your arms and telling her you love her! She needs you now."

William looked at him as though he was the daft one. "I can't do that."

"Why not? Even if it isn't true, you can do it. If you say it often enough, maybe you'll believe it yourself."

"I do care for, Jennie," William said his tone defensive. "In my own way, I do."

"I got no time for cowards," Adam retorted. "You help your wife right now, or I'm going to give you the beating of your life. When it's over, you'll just wish I'd killed you."

William gaped. "You wouldn't do that. I just lost my daughter."

Adam's laugh was harsh. "That's exactly why I'd do it. Now you make up your mind what you're going to do."

"I..." William stopped and stared at the ground again before he looked back at the two men. Adam still held his gun. "I... I could try."

Matt slapped him on the shoulder with enough force to push him two steps forward. "That's the idea. All you can do is try. That's all any man can do."

William looked at him with a tiny spark of hope. "You think I could?"

Adam nodded. "Remember what happens if you don't."

"I don't believe you'd do such a thing, but I guess I could try. Maybe..." He looked back toward the wagons where they could see faces anxiously watching them. "I suppose," he said, "they heard the gun go off."

"If they ask, tell them it was a salute for Eliza," Adam said. "Matt and I'll never say different."

"Can I have my gun back?" William put out his hand.

"That depends. Why?" Adam asked.

"So they'll believe me. I won't try this again. You're right. You're both right. It would have been the coward's way. I've been a coward all my life." He straightened his shoulders. "It's time I stopped."

Adam handed him the gun. "Don't load it 'til tomorrow."

When he'd gone, Adam slumped onto the ground.

"God... I didn't know for a minute," Matt said shakily.

Adam held out his own hands to show their trembling. "I was afraid we'd have to dig another hole."

"Or two." Matt lowered himself to sit beside Adam.

"Couldn't be two," Adam disagreed with a crooked grin. "His gun was a single shot."

The barren land seemed apropos for the bleakness of Amy's spirits in the long days that followed the leaving of Eliza's grave. The death had been an ugly reminder of the frailty of life, of the insecurity of bringing children into this world, of loving anything. She felt afraid and at the same time knew there was no escape for her. She already loved Matt too deeply to turn away; even if the eventual cost was the kind of pain she saw daily on Jennie's face.

At night with only an oil lamp to illuminate the pages, she found the energy to write in her journal, something she had ignored since Eliza had taken ill. She felt an obligation to provide a record of their family's westward movement, but words seemed so inadequate, could not possibly explain the hard days they endured.

She stared into space, thinking about her personal situation, about the words she could not bring herself to write. Matt was driving himself at an impossible pace. No matter how she tried to see that he ate, his body had become little more than sinew and muscle, devastatingly handsome, but worrisome, especially when there were two cases of cholera—both fatal. Her requests that he rest, take it easier, give himself time to recuperate were met by a maddening smile, and the total ignoring of any admonitions. If possible, it was even more frustrating that he had avoided all talk about their future. Was it purposeful?

She dipped her pen in the inkwell as she tried to remember what had occurred in the days since she'd last written.

'After many days of traveling high above the Snake River, enduring dry camps because of the near impossibility of traversing the steep cliffs, we stopped overnight at Fort Boise, where we had the opportunity to resupply at the exorbitant prices we've come to expect at such establishments.

'My sisters and I visited the store and were able to find licorice sticks, which we then gave to Jennie, hoping it would cheer her. There is so little we can do. Beyond the fort, the Snake River was high. Canoes were hired to float the wagons across-- this time with no accidents. Hardly had we put the Snake River behind than crossing the Malheur River loomed in front. There seems no end to rivers in this country.

'We camped and did our laundry along the banks of the Malheur, a safe distance from an array of hot springs. The water in some of these pools was hot enough to boil whatever might hazard to fall into it. The children had to be watched carefully. It begins to seem with everything of beauty there is something ugly, with joy comes pain, with love--loss.'

She closed her journal and stared into space, wishing she could see into the future, know what the next weeks would bring. Then she thought of Eliza and knew it was better this way-- better not to know.

CHAPTER 21

Amy felt her legs, conditioned though they had been to walking, ached with new pains each night as the wagons crossed over some of the harshest terrain they'd yet seen. The hills were steep, the canyons rugged. Each day seemed more arduous than the one before. She wondered how the livestock kept moving, how the men managed to keep the wagons rolling. The graves, weathered bones of mules, oxen and remains of wagons along the roadside told her they didn't always.

With a sigh of relief, she looked out over the Powder River valley. After the steep descent, the fertile valley, richly watered with tall grass, the river edged with willow and cottonwood trees, the hills with pines, was a paradise. On the surrounding hills she had seen antelope. Earlier Matt had shot a large, antlered buck deer. One of the men told her father wild turkey had been heard. Fresh meat was a godsend.

St. Louis sent a message down the line to halt while the council convened. Amy sat beside their wagon with her sisters and mother, enjoying any respite from travel. When her father returned, he had good news.

"We've reached here ahead of schedule. St. Louis suggested even though it's early today that we set up camp. A rest will make crossing the Blue Mountains easier. It'll be good for the stock. We can use the time to grease and repair the wagons.

"He also said you ladies need time to yourselves. You get no rest, from morning to night--cooking, washing up, walking all day, trying to keep everybody healthy; he's set aside one section of the river for female... well, whatever it is females wish to do."

Before Amy headed to the river, a basket of laundry balanced on one hip, she went by Matt's wagon. He was sitting on the tailgate, sewing a piece of strap to a worn harness, a job she had watched him do so many times it seemed second nature for him to be so engaged. He looked up, his eyes smoky as he watched her walk toward him.

She smiled. If she was any judge of masculine desire--and she was beginning to become one--her subtle and not so subtle, sensual ploys were having the desired effects. She was no longer arguing for marriage, but was using little touches to remind him what he wanted or should want and how he could get it. So far as she was concerned, if he had pulled her into the woods, she'd have not cared; but it wasn't what Matt wanted. She was determined he would have his dream.

She put down the laundry basket and moved onto the next phase of maneuvering. "I'm on my way to the river and thought I'd wash anything of yours that might need it."

He grinned. "I can see to it later."

"You're busy and helping others. I'd like to do it for you."

He laughed, eyes glinting with amusement and something more. "Like washing my shirts, and uh any other unmentionables?"

"Well it is in self-protection." She stuck her nose in the air, sniffing pointedly.

"Didn't notice you complaining last night."

"It wouldn't be ladylike to mention such a thing at such a moment."

"You'd think though you might've pulled away just a little," he suggested with a grin, reminding her without words how she'd clung to him and how sweet the kisses had been. "The way you were carrying on, a body'd never get a clue there was something about me you didn't like."

"I didn't say I didn't like it, and you're not being very gentle-manly to be mentioning any of this," she retorted, chin up and one hand on her hip, repressing her own smile.

"Now you knew I wasn't a gentleman," he drawled, "but I might let you wash a shirt."

"Might?"

He gracefully jumped up into the back of the wagon and was back in a moment with two threadbare shirts. "Not much to look at but here they are. Except, of course, the one on my back. Don't reckon you'd want that." He raised his brows.

She tried to keep a somber expression as she studied him, the lean muscle and sinew barely covered by the thin pale blue cloth. Sensual images came temptingly to mind, and with them, her body's reaction. The thought of him naked, made her breasts feel fuller, her cheeks flush and her lips feel moist and swollen.

"I am thinking about that," she managed finally, yielding to the temptation if only verbally, "it might be my duty to wash everything."

He laughed. "And have old Mrs. Collins decide she was right. There he be," he mimicked, almost perfectly imitating her nasal tones, "actin' like a heathen--bare chested and all--that pagan! You expect me to go offending her ladylike sensibilities?" He shook his head in horror at the very thought of it.

"It might be worth it," she said with a smile, "except, of course, the merit, of seeing you like that and watching poor Mrs. Collins' face when she saw you, would be counterbalanced by Bernice seeing the same thing. It's hard enough keeping her away as it is."

"You know I only want one woman." He put his arms around her, drawing her against him. She pulled his head down, their lips almost touching, almost but not quite kissing, almost but not quite driving her crazy with the tender promise. "And," he added, "you keep teasing me that way and…"

"Ah is that a dare?" She tried for a provocative smile, which earned her an appreciative masculine chuckle.

Laughing, he pushed her lightly from him. "If you're going with the rest of the ladies, baby, you better get."

She sighed, wishing she had an alternative, but she didn't. Men and women congregated at different places. Certainly Matt couldn't join her at the river, even if he had wanted.

Women and children spread all along the grassy riverbank. The older women were content to sit on the banks, talking and tending to their family laundry while their children splashed and waded. Upstream Amy saw several of the younger women and older girls gathered on rocks around what looked to be a pool wide enough for swimming if one was so inclined.

Amy scanned the bank until she saw her mother, then went to help her wash the family laundry--sudsing, scrubbing and rinsing until things were as clean as soap and sand could make them.

When Amy washed Matt's shirts, her mother said nothing until they were hanging the wet laundry on bushes. "Matt could use a new shirt."

"He might think it was--"

Her mother smiled and finished for her, "A wedding shirt? He might at that." She laughed." Might be it will be. I've always thought old traditions were worthwhile. I think we might even have a length of linen." She quoted the old lines. "You'll have for to make me a cambric shirt, and every stitch must be finical work."

Amy smiled. "I know he wants to marry me, but he's not talking about it at all. A promise shirt might scare him off."

"You know, men have a way of changing their minds about such very suddenly. I think you ought to start on the shirt tonight—just in case that happens with Matt. These shirts will let us be sure it's the right size." She measured one with her hand's length to judge the required width and length.

"If he doesn't promise to marry me, I might just give it to somebody else," Amy retorted.

"I'll believe that when I see it. Now, why don't you go find Loraine and Belle? I think they went upstream. I'll sit here on the bank and enjoy the shade." She leaned back against a tree, her eyes closing almost immediately.

Wandering along the bank, Amy gazed longingly at the water. It looked heavenly, sunlight dappling it, moving as the breezes moved the leaves overhead. It was as though she'd stepped into paradise itself. Paradise with a serpent, she thought, when she saw Bernice, then did a double take to realize the brazen hussy was swimming without a stitch of clothing between her and the water. Obviously there were no men to see, but still, it seemed indecent.

Amy found Loraine sitting on a rock, a bar of soap beside her. Belle was playing with the other children along the bank. Removing stockings and shoes, Amy dabbled her toes in the water in no hurry to shampoo her hair. They both watched as Bernice splashed happily through the water, their expressions a mixture of shock and envy.

"I couldn't believe it either," Loraine said, grinning.

"She's got no shame," Amy grumbled, unfastening her hair and letting it fall heavily down her back. She felt bound by her own dress, chemise, and petticoats.

"We could swim in our chemises," Loraine said with a smile. "What do you think?"

"It also seems sort of decadent." Amy laughed.

"Doesn't it just?" Soon the two sisters had unbuttoned and unhooked all they could and were wading in their thin cotton shifts. As the water hit them, the fabric seemed to disappear, but Amy still felt more comfortable knowing it was there, whether it covered anything strategic beside the point. Taking a quick dive, she began stroking across the pool. Although not the strong swimmer Matt was, she moved easily through the water.

Her peace was broken by Bernice. "Isn't this just the loveliest place?"

Amy nodded, trying not to look at the voluptuous body now treading water just beyond her.

Loraine who had paddled to them, said, "I wonder if the Willamette Valley will be anything like this. The water's so cool and clean here."

"So, why didn't you two take your clothing off? It's a lot more fun this way," Bernice said, smiling, the water lapping her chin.

For Amy, the idea of swimming nude was alluring but impossible. "I'm positively certain to do such is wicked," she said trying for a righteous tone.

Bernice laughed. "Of course. That's the appeal. It's too bad certain men can't enjoy the river with us."

"That wouldn't be proper, and you know it," Loraine retorted.

"Who cares?" the blonde said with a grin. "I've seen men do it." She gave Amy a telling look.

Having reached a shallow enough place where she could stand, Amy turned to scowl at her. "What are you talking about?"

"Amy, you're so naive. You don't think Matt's such a prude that it would bother him to swim in the raw with a woman!" Bernice laughed at the very idea.

Feeling the anger rise up, heating her blood despite the cool water, Amy snapped, "I think you're a lot of talk."

Bernice smiled. "Am I? Ask him?"

"Just you stay away from him if you want any of that hair left on top of your head." She waded to the bank and grabbed a bar of soap.

Loraine paddled to her side. "Don't pay any attention to her," she said, pulling herself out of the water.

Amy scrubbed her skin almost violently, then ducked under the water to rinse. "She makes me so mad. Do you think Matt swam with her?"

"I think she was just talking." Amy stared toward where Bernice had left the water and was pulling on her chemise and slips.

"I'm not so sure. She sounded as though--as though she's seen him naked."

"That's what she wanted you to think," Loraine hissed. "Don't let her win. You know Matt can barely stand her. Why would he do such a thing?"

"Maybe it was before he and I worked things out, before he realized what she was, I don't know." Amy waded out of the water. "But I intend to find out."

"You'll just cause yourself and Matt trouble," Loraine

warned, "which is exactly what Bernice wants. And if you don't keep your voice down, others will hear, and the rumors will fly."

Amy knew all that, but it didn't matter. She couldn't let it alone. She walked over to where the blonde was sitting, toweling her hair dry. "What were you suggesting?" she asked, hands on her hips.

Bernice looked innocently up at her, then beyond at several other young women who Amy realized were watching with curiosity. "Whatever do you mean?" Bernice asked.

"You know exactly what I mean!" Amy said, trying to keep her voice down, continuing to glare at Bernice.

Smiling, the blonde lowered her voice just enough so only Amy could hear her. "Oh, you mean about seeing Matt naked. Well, so what? So have you by now. He's a magnificently made man, isn't he?" Her smile was purposely lustful.

Amy inhaled a deep breath in an attempt to keep from letting fly with a fist. She could hear Loraine, standing behind her, giving her a warning hiss.

"I'm sure he told you all about it anyway, didn't he?"

"There was nothing for Matt to tell," Amy hissed.

Bernice smiled again. "Are you sure about that?"

"Of course."

"Well, if I haven't seen anything, how do I know about the scar across one side of his abdomen that reaches almost to his thigh?"

Amy felt a shock that went through the center of her body; that was the scar Matt had gotten when he'd fallen out of the tree. Bernice couldn't have known about it unless she'd seen it. She gritted her teeth as she debated whether to drown Bernice on the spot or wait and kill Matt with her.

"The only way you saw anything," Loraine said, "was if you were spying."

Bernice flushed, and Amy saw the truth of Loraine's accusation. "So that's it; you spied on him," she muttered, so mad she could spit, but at least now sure where her anger should be directed.

"I came on him by accident," Bernice said defensively, obviously reading murder on Amy's face.

"But stayed long enough and looked hard enough to see his scar," Amy snapped. "How dare you! You're lucky I'm a lady, or more or less a lady. If I wasn't, I'd pull every hair out of your head."

"Amy!" Bernice inched away uneasily. "For heaven sakes, what did it hurt anyway?"

"Watching people in private moments is rude and immoral, Bernice," Amy hissed.

"As if you're worried about morality," Bernice countered. "I've seen how you hang all over him. I don't imagine your own life could take much inspection these days."

Amy didn't respond, not because her anger was abated, but because the thought came to her that her chastity was due more to Matthew's self-control than her own. Still what they did was between them and their own consciences; it involved two willing partners who would be married. Spying was sneaky.

Bernice put up her hands protectively, smiling coldly. "Please, spare me the denials or lectures," she said, "I don't care what you do with Matt." She stopped and laughed. "Actually, I do care, but there's not much I can do about it. He's yours, and that's that. I'm a good loser."

"Sure," Loraine retorted, "when you have no choice. Say, if you're so eager to get a Kane, there's always his brother."

"Ugh," Bernice yelped, "I'd sooner be without a man forever." She wrinkled her nose with distaste before she stood up and slid her dress over her head. "You don't like me much, do you?" she asked Amy as she buttoned her bodice.

"I hardly have a reason to."

"I don't know why we can't be friends. You have no reason to be jealous."

Amy exhaled loudly. "You have to be jesting. You just told me you snuck up on the man I love to watch him naked. Now you turn around and suggest we could be friends. You must be as crazy as Morey."

Bernice narrowed her eyes. "Now, that I do take as an insult."

"I meant it as one. As for you and Matt, you're right, I have no worries--not because you wouldn't--but because you couldn't."

Bernice raised her eyebrows and shrugged. "There's that too," she admitted, then eyes glittering, added, "I do understand how you feel, why you'd be jealous of him. Those gray eyes of his get that look in them, the lids drop down, and you know what he's thinking and what he wants to do next."

Amy clenched her jaw against a sharp retort. He had never had that look for Bernice. She was sure of that, but how did Bernice know? She had an almost overwhelming urge to throw her back in the river. Somehow she restrained herself and smiled. "Bernice, you're a slut!"

"I wouldn't go calling names, if I were you, Miss Purity. I have seen that bedroom look on his face, but it's been when he's watching you. There must be a reason." She smiled raising her brows suggestively.

Amy's breath hissed out.

"I do have hopes though," Bernice added before Amy managed a suitable retort. "I mean with Adam, not Matt. Have you seen how that man looks in his buckskins. They certainly don't leave much to the imagination." She smiled at the outrage on both Loraine and Amy's faces. "Well now, I've managed to offend you both." She smiled more broadly. "However do you suppose I did that?" She looked at them for a moment, her blue eyes cold, then turned and walked away, hips undulating.

Loraine watched her. "How do you suppose she manages that walk without disjointing her spine?"

Amy laughed. "She might throw out a hip—such a shame that would be."

Loraine picked up the large comb and began untangling her wet hair, yanking out knots as she worked. "I detest her."

"From what she said," Amy mused, "I'd say, the feelings are mutual. She's got a lot of anger in her for a woman who's supposedly looking for love. Come on, let's not let her ruin the rest of our day."

They lay back on the bank, letting the sunshine dry their hair and talking idly about poetry, men, clothing, food, Jennie-- anything but Bernice.

. . .

Matt stood by the wagon staring into space, his mind a thousand miles from the harness he had just repaired, the wheel he had yet to work on. The hand on his shoulder caught him off guard.

"How about you and me going fishing?" Adam suggested.

"Fishing?" Matt repeated, unable to believe he'd heard right.

"I believe this stream ought to have some good rainbows if we go upstream from where the ladies have been muddying up the water."

"You... uh want me to go fishing with you?"

"That's such a shocking idea?"

"No. Just I--" He stopped and laughed. "I never figured you for a fisherman."

"Which shows how little you know--about a lot of things," Adam jibed. "I not only am a fisherman. I'm a fly fisherman."

"Fly fisherman?"

"You got a hearing problem, Kane?"

"What the hell is a fly fisherman?"

Adam shook his head with a smile of superiority. "Callow youths. The things you have to teach them. I still don't understand why Amy preferred a man of such limited perspective."

"I thought we'd already hashed that one out."

"A fly fisherman is a man who fishes with a special, lightweight, flexible pole. In my case, bamboo of the finest quality." For the first time, Matt noticed the pieces of long, thin wood in Adam's hand. Adam demonstrated how they connected together to form one, long pole.

"What's so special about the pole?"

"With it you can fly fish, the finest sport known to civilized man." He produced a small box from his shirt pocket and opened it to show Matt several feathery looking, insect-like objects, to which Matt saw hooks were attached. "You see before you, a fly. Tie it onto this fine line, cast it out. Voila! A succulent trout."

Matt stared at the small, artificial bugs. "Fish fall for them?"

Adam glared at him with outrage. "Fish of good taste anyway." He smiled again. "That's all we want anyway."

295

"Why don't you just use bait--like worms or a grasshopper?" Matt drawled grinning at the eagerness in the eyes of the normally cool Adam Stone.

Adam shook his head at the hopelessness of the question. "My poor lad, all you have to do is try this once, and you'll see the superiority of fishing with flies. It is the sport of kings."

Matt snorted. "I'm no king, and I'll take bait fishing any day. All you need is a line, any long stick and worms. It doesn't take a genius to see that it's more sure fire than those ugly little things you got there."

"You care to make a wager?" Adam asked smiling broadly.

"On what?"

"Who gets the first fish. Loser cleans and cooks the fish--the whole mess."

"Confident there'll be a lot, aren't you?" Matt laughed, looking a little more carefully at the so-called flies. "It'll be like taking candy from a baby."

"Well then?"

Jumping up into his wagon, Matt returned in a moment with a line, hooks and shovel. "I got to get my bait first. That's only fair considering you already have yours."

"Fine with me," Adam agreed congenially.

Amy and Loraine dressed slowly, then walked back to where their mother and Belle were folding the dry clothing.

"Did you two have a nice afternoon?" their mother asked before she looked up. When she did, she smiled faintly. "I guess you didn't. What on earth happened?"

"Never mind," Loraine said.

Amy picked up a shirt, folded it methodically and put it in the basket.

Loraine looked toward the water, then back at her mother. "Mama, how did you know Papa was the one?"

"The one?" her mother asked with a smile.

"You know. How'd you know you loved him?"

"Why are you asking?"

"I guess because of Bernice. She's so desperate to find a man she doesn't care how or maybe even who. Amy tells me you find one without thinking about it. I wondered how it was for you and Papa."

"There were a lot of things," her mother said, a reminiscent smile on her lips. "There was nothing in this world I wanted that he couldn't give me. Nothing I didn't want to do for him. When he was with me, I was whole. It was as if some part of me left whenever he walked away."

"Was that how it was with him?" Loraine asked.

Her mother smiled. "Not in the beginning."

"Then?"

"Are you asking how he came to believe I was the one?"

Loraine nodded, smiling wistfully.

"I never discussed this because it didn't really matter but your Grandmother Stevens did not like me one bit."

"Why?" Amy knew she looked as shocked as Loraine.

"My mother and grandmother were regarded as... well witches." She gave a little laugh. "Not that people minded coming for help when sick, but such knowledge can be regarded as dangerous. Grandma Stevens looked at it that way. Besides, they had three stores, the money. My family was nothing special. Amos, being her only son, could do better in her mind."

"He didn't appear to feel that way."

Their mother smiled. "An accident turned the situation. He had been shot and ended up my mother tending the wound. My father standing around with a shotgun." She giggled

"That's right. Papa tried to stop a fight, didn't he?"

"More or less." She smiled again.

"And you nursed him afterward."

"I helped. I had my own reservations to be honest. Oh, I was much taken with him, but that man was quite the hell raiser at that age. Moreover, he was such a handsome devil that I didn't think he'd ever notice me with all the other women chasing after him, spoiling him. It took him being laid up to turn his eyes toward me."

"So then, I just have to shoot one," Loraine mused, "get you to patch him up and Papa to stand around looking mean."

Her mother chuckled. "If you'll recall, I wasn't the one who shot your father. Unless you're an excellent shot, you might kill or permanently disable your man."

"I suppose it isn't a good idea," Loraine said with a laugh, "but it is tempting. Bernice is chasing after him. I'm sure she wouldn't mind shooting a man to land him."

"I came close to punching her today," Amy said with vehemence. "One more stunt like that last one and--bamm!"

"That's not at all the right way to behave, Amy," her mother admonished, then with curiosity asked, "What did she do that was so terrible?"

"She spied on Matt when he was nude, washing up in a river —at least it's what she claims. Matt hasn't ever bothered to tell me about it."

Her mother narrowed her eyes. "It probably embarrassed him. Maybe hitting her wouldn't be such a bad idea." She slammed the last of the clothing into the basket.

"If Matt would just marry me, then I wouldn't worry about her. He's putting me off, and I don't know why."

"Amy, you have to deal with this jealousy of yours. It won't go away when married. Learn to trust him now, or it'll dog you the rest of your life. And don't go pushing him one way or the other. When he makes up his mind, then you'll know it's what he wants. It's not worth having any other way."

"But--"

"I mean it. Men have a way of coming around to things in their own time if you don't nag at them." Thoughtfully, she stared toward the river. "However, it might be Amos would be willing to talk to him, just to make sure he understood we didn't object."

"Could he carry his shotgun when he did it?" Amy asked, raising her eyebrows hopefully.

Walking back from the river, Matt, cold and wet, could hear Clem and St. Louis talking before he and Adam reached the camp. Clem's face was lit by firelight as he stirred a pot of stew, now and then gazing toward the river. With the glare of the campfire, it had to be too dark to see much of anything.

"Ya worried about them boys of ours?" St. Louis asked.

"Nah. Just wondered when they'd be getting back," Clem answered and then looked up as Matt and Adam walked into the circle and headed straight for the fire, dripping water, their boots squeaking.

Clem watched them for a moment. "Where's the fish?" he asked when he could obviously stand waiting for the answer no longer.

"In the river," Adam said tersely. He knelt by the fire, holding his hands up to the warmth.

Matt eased himself to the ground, stretching out his leg in an attempt to find a comfortable position.

"All of 'em?" asked Clem finally.

"You see any fish on us?" Matt retorted, edging a little closer to the fire.

Clem chorted. "You two got skunked!"

Adam grimaced with distaste. "Can't you think of a better word for it? Besides it wasn't my fault."

"It wasn't?" challenged Matt.

"I had it hooked!"

Matt snorted. "Ah yes, hooked. That's the trouble with that funny lookin' pole of yours. It doesn't do you any good to hook them if you can't bring them to shore." He spoke slowly, as though to a slow-witted man.

"How'd you two get wet?" Clem asked, looking from one soaked figure to the other.

"He thought it was one way to land the fish," Matt quipped when he saw Adam wasn't going to answer.

"I did not."

Clem handed them each a cup of coffee.

Matt took a restoring sip of the hot brew. "You saw that fish slipping off, and you lunged for it." Matt shook his head as he added, "Thanks to my bum leg, he knocked me in at the same time."

"You damned near broke my pole," Adam accused, his eyes flashing.

299

"And you damned near drowned me." Matt shook his head with disbelief as he looked at Clem and St. Louis. "Got me tangled up in that funny line of his, thought I'd never get back to shore."

"If I'd have gotten my hands around your neck, you wouldn't have," Adam muttered almost under his breath.

Matt smiled. "If I hadn't broken his line, I'd be in the bottom of the pool."

"I thought you did that on purpose. Do you have any idea how expensive good fly line is," Adam grumbled, staring moodily into the fire. He glared accusingly at Matt. "Why were you so close when I hooked him anyway?"

"I wasn't. You got buck fever, ran up the bank like a kid seeing a fish for the first time." Matt laughed at Adam's expression of suppressed outrage.

"I do not get buck fever," Adam snapped. He looked to St. Louis for confirmation. "Have you ever seen me get buck fever?"

"Nope, but then I ain't never seen ya go fishing neither." He stared into the campfire. "I seen a lot of good men lose their heads over trout. Craziest thing I ever seen the way men go nuts for fishin'. Good men just can't think of nothin' but catchin' a little bitty fish on a hook."

Matt and Adam glared at him with indignant faces. "Little bitty!" they growled, almost in unison, "you should've seen it!"

CHAPTER 22

"How do you think Jennie and William are really doing?" Amy asked Matt as, arms around each other, they walked away from the Porter wagon, darkness all around, the last cook fires banked to slumbering coals. The wagons were camped at the west end of the Grand Ronde Valley. Matt had suggested the visit with the still grieving couple, telling her that in a few days they would be in the heart of the Blue Mountains when his energy for anything beyond work would be limited.

"What do you mean?" he asked.

"I mean how do you think they're coping with the loss of Eliza?"

"That's hard to say."

"What do you think about the way William treats Jennie?"

This had all the earmarks of a question designed to cause him personal problems. Matt glanced at Amy's face, saw the serious set of her lips and the darkness in those wide, beautiful eyes. He saw they wouldn't just be talking about Jennie and William. He considered his words. "He's highhanded with her."

"Do you think he treats her right?"

"No, he puts her down too much."

"He's gone a lot too," Amy said. "Do you think men should stick with men and women with women?"

He laughed. There were no more doubts about where this was heading. "So," he said, "we're not just talking about the Porters."

She smiled, tightening her grip on his arm. "Well, I do notice the way a lot of men treat their wives, not Papa, but others, as if they were pieces of property. It was one of the reasons I wasn't sure I ever wanted to be married. If a man beats a woman, that seems to be all right with the other men. Men go off and discuss the important decisions, things like which trail to take, whether to rest, and women have no vote at all." She stopped and looked up, waiting for his response.

"I haven't been around that many marriages," he said, hoping to avoid this becoming about them. "But what I have seen says a lot of men do it wrong. They force their will by the might of their fist or loud voices. I wouldn't ever want to do that." He wished Amy would be satisfied with that. He had little hope she would.

"I never thought you'd hit me," she said, stopping and looking at him somberly, "but will you talk to me about decisions that are to be made? Will you do what other men think you ought to or talk to me first?"

"You mean," he said, "will I be tied to your apron strings?"

"I wouldn't want that either."

He reached out and took hold of her shoulders. "I respect your mind. I know you, and you know me better than anybody in this world. If I had a decision to make, I'd be a fool to not talk to you about it." Then he thought of a caveat. "If I had time."

Amy smiled, putting her arms around his waist. "I think I knew that. I just needed to hear it. Sometimes, seeing how the men all congregate one place and the women another, how the council is made up of all men--well, it kind of makes me think how unfair it all is."

"It's the way it's always been, but I wouldn't want it that way with us either."

She reached up to caress his cheek. "Even if people did think you were tied to my apron string?"

He laughed, took hold of her hand, and kissed her fingers.

"I don't care what people think of me, just what you think." He reached down and kissed her nose, then slanted his mouth across hers, his tongue teasing her lips apart for fuller access as he delved into the sweetness within.

At the sound of footsteps, they broke apart as Mrs. Collins walked past. "How you folks be?" the old woman asked surprising Matt with a small smile that included him.

"Fine," Amy said huskily.

The old woman walked on, heading toward the Stevens wagon.

"I suppose she'll report back," Matt guessed.

"It won't matter." Amy took his hand and raised it to her lips. She smiled as she turned his palm over, running her finger down his lifeline, which was satisfyingly long. "I thought it would be all right between us because you've never ridiculed any of my thoughts. Teased me a little, but you've always listened to me. But then on this trip, you've done things that seemed reckless, and you haven't talked to me about them first."

"I did mention if I had time. There are some things you just have to trust me about. It works two ways, doesn't it?" He took a deep breath to get a handle on the feelings she was inducing through her sensual exploration of his palm.

"You've got a new blister," she said.

"You'd think by now that wouldn't happen, but it still does sometimes."

"Mama has some salve for it."

"It'd just break open again."

She brought his hand to her lips and kissed the fingers one by one. "Do you suppose you could talk to William about things?"

"Things?" he asked warily.

"Like how he treats Jennie."

Matt pulled his hand away. "I did say something to him the day we buried Eliza. He wasn't listening."

"It wouldn't hurt to try again. I know William likes you, respects your advice."

Matt snorted disbelievingly. He still held out a tiny hope of remaining uninvolved, but the hope was fading fast. "Damn it, Amy, you get the dangedest ideas. I can't go interfering between a man and his wife." He stopped as he realized what he'd said. It was true men were taught to let another man beat his wife or children if that's what he chose to do. As an unspoken rule, it wasn't right. He shook his head ruefully and tried one more time to dissuade her even though he had about determined the cause was lost. "If he didn't listen to me the first time, he won't now."

Amy stared at Matt's hand, her fingers rubbing absently over the calluses. "Bad things can bring people together or..."

"What's going through your head?" Matt asked, uneasy at the introspection he sensed going on. He didn't want to interfere in other people's lives. He didn't like even considering the motives behind what they did, but he had learned, as his relationship with Amy deepened, that she very much liked to do all of that.

"Do you think there is a chance that their marriage will ever be happy?" The tone of her voice shifted slightly.

A loud warning bell went off in his head, but he was still mulling over in his head his doubts that interference in another's private life would gain anything, the disturbing idea of breaking a code of letting others be, and he couldn't think of a suitable answer fast enough to avert the coming storm. He tried what he thought would be an innocuous reply. "It's possible."

"Are you seriously considering anything I'm saying?" she asked impatience in her voice.

Obviously, one too many innocuous replies. "I'm thinking. You know I don't do it as quick as you."

Her hesitation was brief. "If you don't want to talk about William and Jennie, how about Bernice?"

He stopped walking, sure now that he had lost control of the conversation. "Why would I want to talk about Bernice?"

She turned to face him. "For instance, is there something you haven't told me about her?"

"Oh Lord," he groaned, "we're going to do it again."
"What?"
"Fight over something I don't even know's comin'."

"If you don't know it's coming, how can you know we're going to fight?"

"Just let's hear it." He folded his arms over his chest.

"There might be nothing."

"No games, baby." She stared beyond him at the dark hills in the distance. He could see the wheels going around and waited.

"Well, there's this. Did you go swimming with Bernice— alone just the two of you?"

He shook his head and laughed. The workings of a woman's mind were indeed mysterious things. "Did she tell you that?" he asked. "If she did, it's a lie. There was a time though... I had not been swimming so much as trying to take a private bath. She followed me uninvited and unwanted."

"Why didn't you tell me about it?"

"First of all, it happened when we weren't talkin' to each other. You don't think I wanted her to catch me naked, do you?"

"I don't know." She frowned. "No, that's not true. I didn't believe her. I just wished you'd told me first."

"It was embarrassing," he said. "It could have turned even worse."

"What do you mean?"

"She threatened to say I'd raped her if I didn't do what she wanted." Amy whitened. "All she'd have had to do is rip open her top and back then, folks would've believed her. I told you she's dangerous and that's why."

She felt furious. "No scruples."

"Whatever that means, yes, she has none of those. That day I felt like she was capable of anything. I managed to convince her to let loose and from then on stayed as far from her as I could. She made me feel like a fool."

Amy moved closer to him, putting her arms around his lean waist. "When she described your scar. I wanted to tear her hair out by the roots." She leaned her head against his chest.

Matt kissed her silky hair. "She's her own worse enemy."

"What did she want from you?"

"Beyond seeing me naked you mean... She wanted what you would guess and she thought I would want it too."

Amy looked up at him with shock. "You're not serious."

"It's not the sort of thing I'd be apt to joke about." His mouth twisted bitterly. "She could have had me hung. I don't doubt that."

"How did you convince her?" she asked, reaching up and caressing his lean cheek. The muscle was throbbing with tension.

"Basically that hanging or not, she wasn't getting what she wanted. Actually I told her I was in love with someone else, wasn't ready for something new, not mentioning your name, of course."

"I can't believe. Well I do believe that she'd do that."

He shrugged, the memory not one he liked recalling. "Whatever, she backed off."

Amy kissed his chest, running her hands down his back. "I should have punched her when she told me. Maybe I still will." She smiled then.

"And the smile means?" he asked.

"If even a threat like that didn't make you do what she wanted, I should quit being jealous of her, shouldn't I?" She giggled.

"You never had a reason to be jealous of her." His arms went around her. "And I could talk to him."

"To William?" she asked, surprised because she'd almost forgotten the first part of their conversation.

"Yeah, damn it. I don't think it'll do any good though. People pick their own path."

Amy smiled. "No, I think you were right. It wouldn't do any good."

He pulled back a little, looking down at her. "I never can figure you out. You sure about this?"

"Yes. I've tried to talk to Jennie. You said you had with William. They've made their own choices. I wish it was different, but unless they want it to be, nothing will change." She smiled up. "I'm just glad it's the way it is between us. That we can talk like this."

Matt shook his head and grinned down at her. He bent and slanted his lips across hers, for a time forgetting about the

Porters, his own family, or the nameless fears that seemed always to lurk in the back of his mind.

Two nights later, exhausted from a hard day of one problem after another, dirty, hungry, and his leg aching, Matt walked into his camp.

"Well, if it ain't the big shot," Morey sneered.

Matt met his brother's hate-filled eyes, keeping his own gaze level. He'd had a bellyful of the smirks, sneers, and ribald comments. Since they'd left Independence, the problem had grown worse by the mile.

"All right," he said finally, washing up as well as he could using tepid water from the nearly empty barrel. "What is it this time?"

"What do you mean?" Morey asked, his habitual smirk widening.

"You've got something against me when it ought to be me against you," Matt said. "I thought when you said you wanted to go to Oregon, that it would be a new chance for you, that you meant it. I was wrong. So what is it you want?"

"You don't know?" Morey again laughed. "Is it possible there's something little brother doesn't know?"

Matt leaned against the wagon, trying to read beneath the sneer and angry eyes. He had no idea what his brother was getting at, and he'd already spent too much time trying to figure it out. He took a deep breath and looked over to where his father was nursing a coffee mug and watching the argument without a word. For the first time he thought how much his father and Morey looked alike—only years separating them from seeming to be twins.

Morey chuckled. "You been romancin' that woman again? Is that why you look so tired? Spendin' all your time makin' up to her. You know it's not going to do you any good. In the end, she'll figure you out for what you are and find somebody else, somebody who ain't a weakling."

"Are we ever going to get along?"

"Me and you? Why would I want to? I've got no use for you."

"Then why," Matt asked, exasperated, "did you come with me?"

Morey's smile was ugly. "Because you'd have gotten away if I hadn't. You think I wanted you to get to Oregon, get a new start. You think I wanted you to escape what was coming to you. All I had to do was pretend I wanted it to be different, and you were so stupid that you believed me."

By sheer effort, Matt kept his face expressionless. He could only think he should have known. "And what did you think you could do about it?"

Morey smirked. "You don't know? You're dumber than even I figured. Didn't the whippin' teach you anything?"

"What was it supposed to teach me?"

"Who the smart one is. All it took were brains, something you don't have. I trapped you like a skunk caught in a steel trap. You could squeal but couldn't pull out."

Matt pushed away from the wagon and walked toward Morey, stopping when they were only a foot apart. "And what did you get out of it?"

"Satisfaction. I wanted you punished and I did it. I watched the look on your face that day when you knew what I'd done. It was even sweeter that you knew but couldn't do anything about it. You were in a snare and knew it was me who had put you there."

Matt stared down at him, sickened as much by the avid expression on his brother's face as by his words. Equally bad was to realize his father, who sat only a few feet from them, heard and didn't care. Morey wasn't right in the head, something was wrong with a man who enjoyed inflicting pain on others, but what about a father who allowed it or was it just allowed it? He looked again at his father trying to read his blank expression.

"I've always hated you," Morey snarled. "You've had it all."

"What?" Matt shook his head with disbelief. "What did I have?"

"Good looks, tall. Your brother's so cute. Your brother's so strong." His voice was high pitched as he mimicked others in their praise of Matt. "How do you think that made me feel? All the time knowin' you were the one killed my ma."

Matt turned away unable to meet his brother's condemning eyes, overwhelmed by feelings of guilt, which he knew was unreasonable, made no sense; nevertheless the feelings swamped him at any reminder of how their mother had died.

"If you'd never been born, she'd still be alive. Is it any wonder I hate you? I hated you the day you was born and every day since."

Matt could say nothing. It was a lie. A baby didn't ask to be born nor have control over his birth. None of it changed the feelings. The accusation struck home.

"People go on about what a hero you are! What a good man!" Morey shook his head. "You're no hero. I've seen you scared; I've made you cry."

"I know I'm no hero, but what does that mean to you, Morey?" It was no use arguing with him. Shaking his head, he started to walk away, sick of hearing the garbage that spewed from Morey's warped mind, sick of trying to deal with the unreasoning hatred.

"I'll show that Amy Stevens too someday," Morey went on, his voice low and snide. "Right now she's followin' after you, leanin' against you, can't keep her hands off you, but that will change."

Matt turned slowly to face Morey, his eyes narrowed and hands in tight fists. "Keep her out of this."

"Why should I? Are you going to beg me like you used to?" Morey laughed as he walked away with a tuneless whistle.

Short of killing Morey, there was no way to stop him. Matt had no fear for himself, but what about Amy. The thought of Morey's warped mind and behavior touching or hurting her in any way, even with his crude words, left Matt shaking. He tried to think through exactly what Morey had said. Was Amy at risk?

At the edge of the Stevens camp, Matt hesitated. He didn't feel easy stepping uninvited into their family circle. At the fire he could see Amos. Amy's mother sat a little behind him, some kind of mending in her lap. Amy and Belle were clearing up the last of the dishes. He heard the gentle exchanges of laughter and bantering discussion, a peaceful, almost idyllic scene. He hated to interrupt it, to bring into it the darkness that traveled with him, but he had no choice.

Striding into the flickering light, he saw Amos rise. "Ah, Matt, good to see you. "I'm overrun by women here. Come on, sit with us."

Amy wiped her hands and came to him, lifting her head for his kiss.

He needed to talk to her, to tell her about Morey, but he didn't know how to begin. "Where's Loraine?" he asked instead.

Amy laughed. "Wherever Adam is."

"Would you like a cup of coffee, Mathew," Martha Stevens asked, rising to get a cup before he nodded. In moments over his protests, he was seated on one of their stools. Amy knelt at his feet, her arm resting possessively on his knee. Her parents settled companionably across from them. He waited to see their reaction to Amy's casual affection, but there was none.

"Papa says we're likely to get lightning tonight," Belle said. "What do you think, Matt?"

"Is it good or bad if we do?" he asked taking a sip of the coffee, which was better than any he had elsewhere.

"Good," Belle said grinning, "I like it because it's like fireworks, but nobody else does."

"Then I think you're going to be the happy one."

"You look troubled, Matt," Amos said. "Is something wrong? You don't come here without a reason."

"But we'd like that to change," Martha put in quickly. "You know you're welcome to eat with us anytime."

He sipped his coffee, delaying his need to find an answer for Amos. "Thank you, ma'am."

"Ma'am!" Martha retorted. "That's so formal. I know you and Amy aren't married yet, but you will be and in the meantime, I'd be honored if you called me ma or mama."

He looked up at her in surprise, his eyes wide with the emotions her words had unknowingly triggered.

310

"Unless Martha would be better," she said, instantly sensitive to his unsettled mood, "I mean because of your own mother."

"No, it's not that. I..." He stopped, tried to collect himself and managed to steady his voice enough to say, "That'd be fine." He looked then at Amos. "I am here for a reason. It's my brother, and you need to know." He stopped trying to think of words that would alert without causing possibly unnecessary fear. He rubbed his bristly jaw, wishing he had shaved, wishing he was prepared with words that explained Morey, but he didn't think those words would ever come to him.

"Morey has threatened, blustered, but tonight he said something about Amy. Something that worried me. To be honest, the farther west we've gone, the worse he's gotten."

"I don't like saying things against a man," Amos said. "Especially when he's not there to hear them, but I've never trusted your brother. There is something unsettling about him."

Matt nodded. "I shouldn't have brought him, or for that matter my pa, but that's not something I can change now. Tonight, I think he threatened more than me." He put his hand on hers.

Amos studied Matt for a long moment. "I don't know your brother so much as I know of him," he said, plainly choosing his words with care. "More than one man has come between him and an animal he was abusing. He's got a cruel streak. I think we should consider preventative steps to protect you as well as Amy."

Matt smiled, a sardonic twist to his thoughts. "Can't hang a man for what you think he might do—fortunately for me."

Amos laughed. "We might make an exception in Morey's case."

Matt gave a faint laugh. "I could wish. The thing is, if Morey thought he could hurt me most by hurting her, that's what he'd do--and that is how he'd hurt me most."

"And how would she feel if something happened to you?" Amos asked, obviously unwilling to back off from his concern that Matt exercise caution for himself.

Amy slipped up and onto Matt's lap, her arms around his neck. "You have to listen to Papa. You know he's right."

311

Matt looked at her parents' faces to see how they reacted to Amy's affectionate move. With a combination of relief and surprise, he saw they apparently considered it natural.

Amy brought him back to the reality he had to face. "I don't want you staying in that wagon with Morey or your father." The wind whipped up her hair, blowing it back across his face. He welcomed the scent, the touch of it, like a lifeline, a thing he could hold onto in a world that seemed filled with uncertainties.

"I haven't thought this through," he admitted. He was becoming increasingly incapable of reasoning it out, no longer certain of how sane his own reactions to Morey were.

"I have. I want you to take what's yours and leave."

Matt shook his head. "First off, it's all mine. I can't leave them out here without supplies, a wagon, a team."

"Then let it go. Nothing is worth you going back to be close to Morey. And while we're talking about it," Amy added bluntly, "I think it's time we quit delaying and set a date for our wedding."

Before Matt could make his confused brain respond to her quick twist of the conversation, Amos pulled Martha up. "The three of us are going to see how the Porters are faring tonight," he said, nodding to Belle, who'd been all ears. "That ought to give you two time to work through whatever you need. I've never believed in getting between a man and his woman when they're making decisions. That's even truer when she's my daughter."

In moments the three had left the circle, and Matt and Amy were as alone as anyone ever was on a wagon train. Matt forgot his concern over Morey and could only think with amazement what had just transpired. "I never thought they'd accept me. I figured when you climbed onto my lap, your pa'd kick me from here to St. Louis' wagon. Instead they go off and leave us to settle this-- ourselves."

Amy took hold of the scarf tied loosely around his neck and began pulling his head down. "Dare I say I told you?" Her mouth was so close to his, her breath like a teasing feather against his lips, more heady than wine.

He shifted a little to protect her from the increasing wind. "I know you did, but me--in their family? Not what they'd been hopin' for."

Amy shook her head with mock frustration and sent her question skyward. "What does it take to make this man see his worth?" She took his lower lip between her teeth and lightly nipped, freeing it to kiss first his lips, then his chin. When he would have pulled back, she kept the grip on his scarf, holding him a prisoner against her as she teased his lips, then the bridge of his nose.

"What's it going to take to make you see you're a man of worth, a man any family would be proud to have join them? Must I punish you further?"

"I might not mind that, ma'am." He reached out to try and kiss her, only to have her pull away.

"Ma'am! I don't like ma'am! How about another title for me too?" She kissed his eyes closed, then gave him feather light kisses down the side of his cheek to his jaw. She got hold of the thong that held his hair back and untied it, running her fingers through his hair as it fell over his shoulders.

"Uhhh, like darlin'? Dear?" His senses were enflamed by her fleeting touches. He tried to think, the words coming only with a concerted effort. "Baby?"

She pulled away, shaking her head. He smiled then, knowing what she wanted.

"How about--wife?" he asked. Taking control of the situation, he pulled her tightly against him, brooking no more games as he claimed her lips with his own, his tongue delving into the sweetness of her mouth. "How about Mrs. Matthew Kane?" he managed when he could.

"I like that. How soon can you put that Mrs. on there?"

"Pushy little thing, ain't you?" he drawled, between the kisses she showered on him.

"I can be." She pulled back a little. "Do you have any other complaints?"

"You change directions faster than a tornado. What're we talking about now?"

"I mean about today. Like have you had too little affection

from me... or too much?" She brushed her finger over his lips. "I just wanted to know how I've done?"

"I'm not so sure I want a wife who's always making fun of me." He took the leather thong from her fingers and tied back his hair.

"Was I doing that?" She snuggled deeper into his lap, her soft bottom now against his groin so that when she moved, she pressed against him intimately. He gritted his teeth, wondering if she knew what she was doing to him, the desires she was igniting. He could say only one good thing for it. He'd learned more about self-control from her over these last months than in all his sessions as a child with Morey.

"God," he groaned as she shifted slightly, the smile on her lips intimate and promising. "You're going to be the end of me."

"I won't but, Matthew, I will be there at the end for you."

She took his earlobe between her teeth, the sharp little pain leading to blood pulsing another place and his awareness he'd had all he could stand if he wasn't going to drag her into the shadows and give her that for which she was clearly asking. Standing up abruptly, Matt dumped her from his lap, keeping her from falling by his grasp on her arm.

"What did you do that for?" she asked, her eyes still slumberous.

"With the pressure you're putting on me," he retorted, his smile as suggestive as his innuendo, "I've got a few things to take care of."

"Is this good news or bad?" she asked, dusting off her skirt with an exaggerated effort.

"Depends."

"You're driving me crazy, Matthew."

"I'm driving you crazy!" he retorted, raising his eyebrows with mock disbelief.

"You know what I mean."

"I never know what you mean." He shook his head. "You just make sure you know what I mean—and be careful when I'm not with you."

"I promise," she agreed, reaching up to stroke his cheek. "I don't want to cause you more trouble with your brother."

"Sometimes it's hard to believe he's my brother. He's hated me as long as I can remember."

"You are different. Not just your size and hair color but that strong jaw line." Teasingly, she ran a fingertip along it. "Maybe you're like your mother's people. Have you ever seen a photograph of your mother or grandparents?"

"I doubt there were any. If there were Pa probably would've destroyed them. He's never wanted to talk about her." He didn't mention his own reluctance to ask questions because any reminder of her was a reminder of how she died.

Martha Stevens walked into the circle to pick up her shawl. "I knew your mother, Matthew." She tightly wrapped the shawl around her shoulders. "Laura was beautiful, blond. You resemble her in some ways but take after her father the most. Her father, George Adamson, was big, broad-shouldered and blond. The family was Scandinavian, I believe."

"Pa never even told me about them, not even her maiden name," Matt said.

"Perhaps it's still hurtful for him to think about her," Martha suggested.

Matt looked at her skeptically.

"We grew up on neighboring farms. Although she was two years older, I think you could say we were friends."

"What was she like?" He couldn't resist the first opportunity he'd ever had to learn about the woman who'd borne him.

"I think the best way to describe Laura was like a lily of the valley. There was something almost ethereal about her. I don't believe I ever heard her say a negative word about anyone."

"Hard to imagine someone like that marrying Nathan Kane," Amy commented acidly.

"Opposites attracting, I suppose," Martha said. "He had just moved to town, come up from Georgia, with that southern drawl. In his own way, I suppose he was attractive, even though he was undependable even back then. Perhaps Laura thought she could change him, or maybe she felt sorry for him. There had been a family tragedy." She hesitated and then said, "Whatever causes a woman to love a man, she did; and with Laura, love meant total commitment. Her folks gave them a nice farm, but Nathan wouldn't work at anything long enough to make a go of it. Even then, liquor had a hold on him. After her death, he let go of trying to do anything."

Matt gritted his teeth at the reminder of his mother's death.

"She'd been so excited about having you," he dimly heard Martha say. "It was such a tragedy the cholera took her before she could see you grow up. She'd have been so proud to see the man you've become."

The words penetrated but made no sense. "Cholera? She died in childbirth--my birth."

Martha shook her head. "No, Laura had you--hmmm you were born in March, so I guess you would have been four almost five months old when she took sick. Nathan sent for my mother. I took you and Morey home, and Mother stayed to do what she could, but it was hopeless. We kept you for a few months--until your father came to get you both and left to go back to Georgia where he said he had womenfolk to help with his children."

"I don't understand." Matt ran his fingers through his hair, trying to untangle his thoughts. "Why would they say--" He stopped unable to go on as he realized the truth.

"Who told you she died at your birth?" Martha asked.

"Morey. Pa. I don't know." He clenched his jaw. "It was just something that was always there... always. I killed my ma."

"Whoever said it lied." Martha bristled. "There were no problems with your birth, and I ought to know. My mother was Laura's mid-wife, and I was with her immediately after. Cholera took your mother months later. She breastfed you until she took sick. A sick woman can't breastfeed."

Matt's mind was tumbling over what she had said. Suddenly none of the words made sense. What kind of father would tell a child he murdered his mother? What purpose had it served? Why had his father allowed his brother to torment him with a lie... and worse all these years? Memories of other tortures, things he'd tried to forget came flooding into his mind. He needed to get away, had to have time to think.

He looked at Amy, saw her working to fight back tears. He could read her mind but she couldn't help him with this. He had to work it out—if it was possible. When she tried to touch him, he drew back. Arms wrapped around his chest, he muttered, "God, I'm sick of lies."

Amy's mother frowned. "You have a right to be. I don't understand why your father would have said such a thing, but you deserve the truth. If you've never had it, you need it all."

Matt's eyes were black when he turned to face her, his body tense. Would this be a killing blow, more than he could handle?

"No, Mama," Amy begged, "don't tell him more now. Surely it could wait until..."

"No, I need to know—whatever it is."

Amy's mother's gaze roamed over his face. "Yes, holding back pieces of the truth won't help now. There's been too much of that, and imagination only makes matters seem worse than they are. Before Nathan had met Laura, before he came to Missouri, his father shot and killed himself. Nathan found the body. According to Laura, he had nightmares about it, blamed himself, never really got over the horror. She believed it was why he drank. In some ways it's likely that depression was the problem for Nathan, why he drank and the same thing killed his father."

"What I also inherited."

Martha shook her head. "No, Matt. You have your mother in you far more than your father. She came from strong stock. It's a shame you never knew your grandfather, grandmother too but they both died before Nathan brought you back to Missouri. You know, Matt, it's not even your mother's people, but you... well you are a self-made man more than any I have ever known."

Matt ran his hand almost absently over his forehead; his jaw was clenched so tightly the muscle pulsed. He turned from Amy and her mother and looked into the darkness, a blackness whipped into motion by the increasingly cold wind. He felt defeated, as though he'd struggled forever, and it was all for nothing. Self-made? Self-made into what?

Amy's mother put out her hand to his shoulder. "Morey carries the burden of being like the Kanes but that's not who you are."

He took a deep breath. He had to find some peace on this,

317

and he had to find it alone. When he could master his voice, he said, "I know you want to help... both of you, but I need some time." He turned to Amy and tried not to see the tears in her eyes. "I'm sorry. I don't want to hurt you. I just need to think this through by myself."

CHAPTER 23

O blivious to anything around him, Matt stalked past the line of wagons out onto a high, rocky knoll. The wind was thunderous in his ears as he threw out his arms. Gusts of cold air cut through his thin shirt; he barely felt it. The moonlit sky was rapidly being covered with thunderclouds. In the distance he watched as lightning snaked from the sky, striking the hills, a roll of thunder filling the valley below.

Slumping to the ground, he drew his knees to his chest, trying to think about what he'd been told, about the truth of his life. Tears came unwanted, unwelcomed, tears for his mother and the love he'd never known, tears for all the lies. He slammed the ground with his fist, striking out in the only way he could.

He finally understood the truth he'd not faced before. The physical abuse, the lies, the hatred weren't the worst that had been done to him. He'd been branded by a sick family, marked with their ugliness, and there was more inside him than what anybody else knew. How could he ever get clean of it? He faced why he'd been afraid to commit to Amy, afraid of the happiness she seemed to promise. What if I am like my father, my brother? It wasn't just his father or Morey.

He closed his eyes, trying to shut out the thoughts. They tore through. He came from a long line of violent men, men who tortured and killed. He had feared he was already too much like his blood kin, too violent, too quick to react without thinking. Would it grow worse? Would something snap someday? Amy didn't need to be protected just from Morey but also from him.

Dried grass and hard earth under his body, he rolled onto his back, his arms outstretched as the storm moved overhead. The smell of sulfur was strong in the air. Thunder deafened as lighting struck across from the knoll on which he lay. The action of the storm was no more violent than his inner turmoil. He had no desire to escape the physical storm. He welcomed it. Rain was real, not twisted in lies and ugliness. It pelted down in large, heavy drops. He felt it soaking his clothing, drenching him.

Soon he was soaked to the skin, coldness creeping into the center of his being, and he didn't care. With an odd sense of detachment, he didn't care if the lightning struck him. He would have welcomed it as the ultimate cleansing.

All the campfires out, everyone under shelter from the storm, only the solitary night guard spoke as Matt walked past. At St. Louis' camp, a figure in a long coat stood beside the wagon. Drawing nearer, Matt knew it was St. Louis. Even though Matt didn't want to see him, it was too late to turn around. "Get in the wagon," St. Louis ordered.

Matt's teeth chattered with cold. "I'm soaked."

"We've had enough trouble doctorin' ya. Get inside." St. Louis' voice was brusque, brooking no argument. "Ya can't stay in those clothes, or ya'll get lung fever for sure."

Matt wanted to argue, but he had no resolve for it. He followed St. Louis into the dark wagon. The older man threw off his coat and lit the lantern. He helped Matt pull off his boots, then bent to find a dry quilt as Matt struggled to make numb fingers undo the buttons on his shirt. After a moment, St. Louis brushed Matt's hands aside and unbuttoned it then handed him the blanket. "Shuck yore clothes and wrap yoreself in this 'til ya warm up, then I reckon I can find ya something dry to wear."

Outside the rain beat heavily on the canvas cover, creating a discordant, violent symphony of its own. The warmth of the quilt was a dull reality, unrelated to Matt's physical self. Nothing seemed real. He looked up and saw that St. Louis was watching him. "Sorry...to trouble you," he managed, teeth still chattering.

"Ya done right comin' here. Amy said she thought ya might."

"I didn't know where I was going," he said through clenched teeth, trying to control the violent shivering. Gradually he felt the warmth begin to seep into his flesh. "Where are Adam and Clem?"

"Adam figured with the thunder and all, he'd sleep down by the stock. Didn't want 'em stampedin' and us have to spend all tomorrow running 'em down. Old man Collin's pleurisy's actin' up. They asked Clem to drive wagon and help out with the chores; he's sleepin' under their wagon tonight."

Matt stared at the floorboards. It took a moment for him to steady his nerves, for his shaking to abate enough to have control of his voice. If there was a way to lead into his story, he didn't know what it was. "My people are no good. You know that as much as you know anything."

"Wall I know your pa and brother are polecats."

Matt stared into the pouring rain, into the darkness, a darkness that had been with him seemingly forever. "Somehow or other you already figured out about the torture, didn't you?"

"Nobody knows the secret of the Sun Dance without somethin' teachin' them."

"You learn to endure what you have to. I didn't set out to do it with the whippin', but I guess my mind knew best and the habit was there."

"So long as ya were a child, they did what they wanted."

"It was Morey—or I thought it was." He was beginning to question that. Was it just his brother behind those years? "I don't honestly know right now, but finally, I got big enough to stop it. It's in the past-- except…"

"It's not for you."

"Not because of the pain back then, but something else. Their blood runs in my veins. I got a temper. Sometimes it rises up like a river in flood. I've seen men who beat their wives, arguin' they got the right. Before we left Georgia, I saw too much of how much fear and desperation a woman can feel. I'd kill myself rather than see that look on Amy's face, but what if..."

His voice was husky, the words pulled as though from a swollen throat. The pain he'd kept bottled up and the fear he now recognized as the wall between himself and Amy were revealed in every word. He could no longer hide the ugly truth from himself. "When I went into the other place, I didn't have control over it… not totally and it's like I stopped knowin' what was happenin' around me 'til I could come out of it."

St. Louis was silent a long time before he spoke. "Ya been walkin' a thin line, for a long time. I can't figure out yore people for you. I can tell ya this--ya're nothin' like those kin and yore reason for goin' somewhere else when ya were being tortured, that's not a bad thing but a strong one."

Matt swung around. A shaving mirror hung on a wooden support, and he caught a glimpse of himself in it. The light from the lantern shaded the planes of his face, shadowed the blond stubble on his cheeks, gave him a hollowed, gaunt look. Was that the face of a monster? He turned away from his image with a feeling akin to disgust.

"She talks of us having babies. What I know about families is nothin' like she knows. I've got nothin' back there to teach me —even putting aside my fear I might end up like them."

"I tried to tell you this awhile back. Do ya trust me?" St. Louis asked.

Matt looked up, surprised at the twist of the conversation but nodded.

"Why?"

"What do you mean why? I just do."

"No." St. Louis shook his head. "Ya don't just do. There's reasons why."

"I'm in no mood for games here," Matt snapped. "What are you getting at?"

"Ya answer my question first. Then I'll tell ya."

Matt thought a moment. "I know you, know how you treat people."

St. Louis smiled. "But ya trusted me from the beginnin' didn't ya?"

"I guess so. Yes."

"So it's a lot a gut feeling about how it was and would be with me, right? Where it comes to you, I had that gut-level feelin' right away. I knew ya were a man I could count on. Could be that gut feelin' woulda been wrong, but it wasn't, as we worked together, and it got tested. I seen how ya face trouble, the way ya think things through.

"Now I can tell ya both ways that ya ain't like yore father's people. I agree, there was bad blood in one side of your family, but it didn't taint yours. It won't taint that of your offspring because of how you'll be raising 'em. If ya really trust me like ya said, trust what I tell ya about yoreself."

"I'm too tired to think straight." Matt sat back on his haunches, suddenly so exhausted, it seemed he couldn't put two thoughts together.

St. Louis dug into a trunk. "Adam's clothes oughta fit ya good 'nuf, 'til yores dry." He handed Matt shirt and pants. "You need to get some sleep. Things'll look different in the morning."

The rain had stopped; it seemed the only sounds were their quiet voices and the drips from the canvas into puddles outside the wagon. Staring at the clothes in his hand as though he didn't know what they were, Matt had one more thing he had to say, one more doubt to express. "There's something in me--something mean that enjoys those fights once I get in them."

To his surprise, St. Louis chuckled. "You and every young buck on this train. A man gets older and some of that vinegar gets taken out of him, but when I was yore age, I felt the blood poundin' through my veins durin' and after a good fight." He smiled then and added, "Course I reckon, most women'd agree with ya it's bad blood, but I'm afeared it's bad blood all men share." He took the shirt from Matt's hands. "Ya want I should help ya dress."

Matt growled at him before quickly pulling the clothing on.

"Ya know what ya are doin', don't ya?" St. Louis asked.

"I expect you're going to tell me," Matt muttered.

"I am. Ya are tearin' apart all the normal things every man

does, lookin' at everythin' like it was a bug, tryin' to see some-thin' evil in it." St. Louis put his hand on Matt's shoulder. "Ya got a lot of things in yore life that'll make it different from yore brother or pa's. It's why ya don't never drink alcohol, ain't it?"

"Won't say I never have, but I saw too much bad comin' from it to want much of it in my life."

St. Louis nodded. "Well ya learned things younger than most ever do. That's rough but not all bad. But besides the kind of man I know ya are, ya got somethin' more goin' for you."

Matt loosened his hair and used the towel St. Louis handed him to dry it. He sat down then, feeling he'd expended all the energy he had.

"Ya got people who care about ya, a woman who can stand up with ya and to ya. If--and I don't believe it for a minute--ya did have somethin' come up later, somethin' that caused ya to get mean, why ya got a family now and friends like me to push ya back in line. Shoot, I plan on settlin' in the Willamette Valley myself this trip. I likely won't be that far from wherever you take up land."

"You don't think I'm mentally sick?" It was the hidden fear.

St. Louis snorted. "Matt, I seen Sioux do what you did that day, and they come out stronger for it. It's not sick. It's a tool most never learn to use, never need to learn, but the strong ones do when they need to."

"Except for Amy, I never had a friend--'til you." Matt's gaze met St. Louis'.

St. Louis smiled. He reached out and gripped Matt's shoul-der. "There's one thing more, then I want ya to go to sleep. Ya look plumb ready to keel over. There's a verse out of the Bible that come to me jest now. 'And I will restore to you the years that the locust hath eaten.' It's goin' to be that way for you. It's all yours now what ya never had before."

"Unless I wreck it."

St. Louis laughed. "Ya tried that already, and she stuck with ya. I don't say ya might not have some hard times ahead, maybe even some mountains to level or cross. That's the way life is. Up a hill, down a valley, but you can handle that."

"God, I want to believe it," Matt said with a groan.

"Than do. That family loves ya. They're your people now."

Matt felt as though a weight was being stripped from his shoulders as he considered St. Louis' last words. "They did stick by me."

"Damn right they did. Nursin' ya, lookin' out for ya. Those are folks it'll do to ride the river with."

Matt leaned back, half closing his eyes as he tried to think it all through. His eyes closed, seemingly too heavy to hold open any longer.

"Come mornin' thing's is goin' to look fresh washed, just like the desert after a rain. Ya remember this though."

Matt managed to open his eyes. "Yeah?"

"In the mornin' the sky's goin' to be blue. Then by afternoon it'll maybe storm. That's the way it goes. You got folks now that will stand beside ya. They'll be there through any storm."

Matt was almost asleep when he felt St. Louis lift him a little and lower him to a more comfortable sleeping position, then pull up the blanket that had fallen to his waist, tucking it around his shoulders. With a growing feeling of peace, Matt let go and let sleep claim him.

At first light, Amy found St. Louis sipping his coffee. "Matt's gettin' the mules." he told her as he poured her a cup of coffee.

"How is he?"

"A mite shaky, but he'll do."

"You're sure?" she asked anxiously, taking a sip of the coffee, only barely controlling the urge to grimace at the strong brew.

"Yep."

"He was so upset when he left, and I didn't understand all the why of it."

"He got a rough cut of the cards when it come to passin' out families," St. Louis observed, kneeling to turn a flapjack in the frypan.

She stared into her coffee cup, then back to St. Louis, meeting his shrewd gaze. "He looked like someone had dealt him a death blow last night."

"He'll be fine."

In the distance, Amy saw Matt's tall, straight form loom into view, mules behind him. His head was held high, his shoulders weren't slumped. Whatever devil he'd wrestled with last night, he hadn't been broken by it. The light blue shirt he wore was open at the neck, revealing the tanned column of muscular neck and the break of his shoulder. When his eyes met hers, the expression in them was open, not shuttered. She walked toward him, vaguely aware St. Louis had turned away from them as he reached for the coffee pot.

Matt tied the mules' lines to the wagon tongue, then put out his arms, and she dove into them like a bird to its nest. "You look tired," she whispered, her voice muffled against his chest.

"Some." He grinned as she pulled his head down, claiming his lips with her own. She felt his arms close around her, their bodies coming together. A little nervously, then with more sureness, she let her tongue play against his lips, then dive into his mouth, teasing his tongue. His arousal pressed against her as his arms tightened. Even though it was broad daylight with anyone watching who chose, she didn't care. She needed his kisses like the water she drank, the food she ate, and the sunshine that warmed her body.

When he stepped back a pace, she could see he was as shaken as she. As though trying to settle them both down, Matt asked, "How'd you like the storm last night?"

"Belle loved it, but you know how I like thunder and lightning," she retorted, not mentioning that the worst of this storm had been knowing he was out in it.

He smiled, taking hold of the mules' harnesses and pulling them around. She watched as his muscles tensed, moving the mules into their positions, tightening buckles and adjusting straps.

When he finished, he put his arm back around her, then went to eat the flapjacks St. Louis had set aside for him. Gulping his coffee, he and St. Louis spoke a little about the route they would take. "Maybe I'll have ya drive my wagon," St. Louis suggested with a canny smile. "Could be I'll ride out with Adam this mornin'."

"All right."

Matt's gaze didn't leave Amy's as he tipped his head back to finish his coffee. "How about if you ride with me today? We could talk."

"I'll tell Mama and get my bonnet." Amy frowned as she hurried back to her own wagon. What did he want to talk about? Were things finally going to be all right, or was something still holding him away from her? She felt a shiver of fear.

Sitting beside Matt on the wagon seat, Amy took pleasure in his actions as he brought the team around and pulled them into the line. In the first moments, his attention was of necessity on the mules. She watched the play of muscles under his shirt, the sure movements to control and direct the team; his concentration all centered on the job he was doing.

As the trail became established before them, he looked over and smiled apologetically at her. "I'm sorry if it seemed like I was cutting you out last night."

"I understood. At least I tried to."

"I don't know if I'd of been able to do that if it'd been the other way around, but I needed to work through some things. I had to do it by myself."

"Was it because of what Mama told you?"

"Some." He flicked the whip at the lead mule, pulling on the rein, then sitting back as the animal quit trying to kick his partner.

"It must have been hard hearing all of it--so cold, so quick."

"I think that was the best way. I couldn't have handled it if your mama'd held back anything." He took a deep breath, glancing over at her. "I've been afraid, baby."

"Afraid? You?" she retorted with disbelief. "I didn't know you knew the meaning of the word."

He smiled at her vehemence. "Lots of things scare me."

"You never show it."

"Maybe I'm not scared of things like other folks." He hesitated. Keeping his eyes straight ahead, he said, "I'm scared of you leaving me, scared of us having a family, of what kind of father I'd be, scared of counting on the future. I'm scared of what's inside me... of things I can't control. I'm probably scared of more than most."

Matt looked down at her, the way her forehead was wrinkled as she tried to think through his words to their meanings, and he smiled. "There are things I need to tell you. To explain," he said, leaning over and kissing her even though the lead mule took advantage of his laxity to kick his partner again. "I could start with Pa's drinkin'-- you already know about that, though I never wanted you to." He glanced at her with a smile. "Seems like no matter what, you've been a step or two ahead of me."

"Only on some things," she said with skepticism.

"I wish I could explain why things happened as they did. I can't." He didn't know how he kept his voice so level. It had always been a thing of shame for him. "I knew life shouldn't be like it was. I couldn't change it. Nothing I ever did changed it."

She held onto his arm, burying her head into the curve between shoulder and chest, but she said nothing. It was a risk to tell her everything, but he had to do it.

Her tears were on his shirt, soaking through to his skin. He made himself ignore them and kept going. "You know about Morey but not all of it. He'd grab me, wrestle me down, tie my hands behind my back, sometimes even gag or blindfold me, and Pa would be right there, seeing it all and doing nothing, like it was all fine with him. There was no help."

He grimaced, trying to keep his voice steady. If he didn't tell her now, he would never find the strength again. "I always tried to stop him, to fight back but for a long time, he was so much older, so much stronger." He didn't want her to believe he'd gone docilely, allowing Morey to do whatever he wanted without trying to fight back.

"He'd laugh, drag me off into the woods, and rope me to a tree." Even after so many years, he remembered vividly the feeling of the bark cutting into his skin, the ropes so tight he feared his hands would fall off. "Sometimes he'd string me up by the wrists. I think that was the worst, the pull on my arms, the ache, the knowing I had no control."

"Sometimes he'd strip me, leave me there alone. It'd get

dark. The brush would start to rustle, I'd hear a coyote howl, and I'd fight the ropes, try to undo the knots, but it was no use. The rope always held, and nobody ties a knot so good as Morey. I learned finally to stop fighting, to accept that if Morey didn't come back, I'd die there because nobody would've ever found me. Gagged, I couldn't have called for help if there'd been any around."

His breathing was coming with more difficulty, but he had to make sure she understood it all. "Sometimes Morey'd seem to forget about the games, then he'd start again. The things he did got worse. Tyin' me wasn't enough. He wanted to hurt me, and he was good at it." He clenched his jaw against memories that flooded through him. He wouldn't share those with Amy, wouldn't burden her with word pictures she couldn't do anything about.

"How did you bear it?"

He shrugged. "Well until I got some size to me, I didn't have much choice. I did get to seeing a look in his eyes that would be there when he was thinkin' that way, and then I'd stay away from the house, sleep in the woods. There was a lot of drinkin' with him and Pa. Sometimes Morey'd just fall asleep calling for me. When he caught me, that's when I learned to escape my body, like you saw with the whipping. Finally I was big enough to fight him and win. Morey didn't like pain so much when he was on the receiving end."

She drew his hand holding the reins to her mouth and kissed his fingers. "I'm so sorry."

"I don't want your pity, baby," he said sharply. "I didn't tell you so you'd feel sorry for me. I wanted you to understand, because you got to decide."

"Decide what?"

"The thing I finally faced square on. What's been scaring me about us being together is not what happened before, but what might. What if that bad blood's in me just like in them?" He swallowed, taking a deep breath before he gave her the choice that might set her free and in the process take away everything that made his life worth living. "Maybe deep down I'm like them. Maybe if we had a home, I'd go crazy like Morey someday. Start hitting you or one of our children. How could I know? How could you know? Remember how we talked that one day about men not treating their wives right. I know all too well how that can be."

"Oh love," she whispered, rising to her knees and kissing his jaw, her arms around his neck as she stroked his lean cheek. "I wasn't worried about you and me. I just wanted us to talk about it, to talk about marriage. I never thought my questions might hurt you or make you think I doubted you."

"I know you love me now, but you don't know what it's like to live with something like that. You don't know what it takes out of you. It can kill anything. Since you first said you loved me, I've been more scared than I ever knew it was possible to be-- scared of losing you because finally I had something to lose."

"You won't," she murmured, kissing him again. "I swear I will always be here for you. Sure you will hurt me. I will hurt you. That's part of loving. People aren't perfect. But you're not like your family--or at least not like that side. You have to be like your mother's people, like Mama said."

"The first time I even heard my grandparents' names was last night."

"I asked Mama for more. The Adamsons were Quakers. They were good people. Laura's mother died first, but her father lived until after your father took you to Georgia. He was a good, strong man who tilled the soil. Mama says you look a lot like him."

Matt frowned, flicking the whip at the truculent mule. "There's things in me. Last night St. Louis said they were normal, but I don't know. And I got an awful temper."

Amy laughed, tears running down her cheeks. "And which one of us hit the other?" she asked, caressing his cheek.

"I want you to spend some time thinking about what I've told you," he said, his voice somber, his eyes narrowed as he watched the road ahead. "Think about what Morey did. Do you really want to marry into something like that, have babies that could grow up like him?"

"I don't have to think," she said. He felt her tears soaking through his shirt onto his chest, her arms entwined around his neck. "I love you. Our children will be raised by us, not Nathan Kane. None of what happened before matters, except in how it hurt you. You're a part of me. I love you in ways I didn't even dream existed a year ago. If there is a problem someday--if there are demons you have to fight--I will be there with you. We'll fight them together."

Her felt her fingertips caressing his neck, smoothing back his hair. She kissed the side of his mouth, her tongue brushed his lower lip. He knew a raging frustration that because of driving the team, he couldn't take her into his arms.

"I want to be your wife, Matthew. And what's more, I don't want to wait until we get to the Willamette Valley to lie with you, to become yours in every way possible--with or without words being said over us. We are married in our hearts now, and you know it."

He thrust the reins into one hand, ignoring the antics of the lead mule. Reaching over, he pulled her against him, hungrily finding her lips with his own, tasting the tears and the promise of love. Their gazes locked. Shifting the reins back to regain control of the mules, pulling them back to the center of the ruts, Matt asked, "Are you that sure?"

"More than about anything else in my life."

With irritation at the combative lead mule, he forced his attention back to the surly animal. Stubborn cuss. It wanted to fight the other animals and seemed to live only for the moment, when Matt was distracted, to pull its tricks.

"Are you still trying to put me off?" she asked, her tone exasperated.

He smiled down at her, before he had to turn his attention to the mules that clearly recognized they had not only someone distracted, but an unfamiliar hand on their reins.

"You are the most distrustful gal. You know everything there is to know about me; if you'll take me that way, I got only one reason to think we oughta wait. Where would we sleep?"

"Wrapped in a blanket under a wagon or under the stars," she suggested. "I see us wrapped in soft, warm quilts--no make that one quilt. It's late at night, the stars are overhead, the moon just rising in the sky. There is just us, nothing between us, and I do mean nothing. Your arms are tight around me, I'm kissing you." She put her arms around his waist and nipped gently at his neck. "Doesn't that sound just a little tempting?"

He couldn't have lied if he'd wanted with the quick reaction of his body to the images her words painted, the touch of her lips seeming to brand his skin. He tried anyway. "Don't be distracting me from my driving. These stubborn critters know I got other things on my mind."

"Would I do that?" She began unbuttoning his shirt, pulled it apart to kiss the juncture of neck and shoulder before she moved to his chest. Her fingers skilled along his skin and took one nipple to roll between them, switching, as his breathing grew raspy, to the other.

"God, Amy, what do you think you're doing?" He fought the desire to pull the team to the side of the road and give her everything for which she was asking and his body was begging.

"What? Am I doing something?" Her tone was all innocence as she reached farther across his chest to stroke down his flexing biceps, her lips and tongue now on his collar bone. He felt the early morning sun on his bared skin as she pushed his shirt from his shoulders. He sucked in a breath as her lips moved down his chest. Of all the dreams he'd ever had about her, she was more woman than any he'd imagined.

"Enough," he gasped. "I want you so much now; it's like a fire in my belly."

"So, what are you going to do about it?" she asked tauntingly. She ducked under his arm and leaned across his lap. The wagon canvas mostly hiding her action, she took his nipple into her mouth, sucking on it before she nipped it lightly.

He took a deep breath, trying to keep control of himself and the mules. "I might have to throw you off this here wagon," he muttered.

"Well?" she asked, obviously not worried at his threat.

"I reckon I'll have to marry you."

"That's not a very romantic proposal," she murmured, as she purposely moved her hand down his belly. "You can do better."

"Not when you got me so crazy I can't think about anything except what you're going to do next."

"Then I'll do it for you," she said laughing. "Matthew Kane will you marry me?"

"Can I think about--" he started to say, until she leaned against him, his bare chest now against her well-covered breasts. Even through the cloth, he could feel the hardness of her nipples and knew her teasing had her as aroused as him. Even had he wanted, he was helpless to respond if he wanted to keep control of the troublesome mules. "All right, "he managed, "I'll marry you. Now cut that out."

"So, let's set a date while I have you in the mood," she teased but didn't move away. It was obvious his body was at her mercy, and she was taking full advantage of it.

"Next year at this time," he suggested huskily, knowing he could never hold out beyond a few days.

"Or?" she demanded, her eyes sparkling, she moved her hand along the edge of his belt, touching the skin it covered. How far was she willing to go with this?

He sucked in a breath, not wanting to look at her, knowing if he saw the softness of her eyes, the full, pouting lips, he'd lose all control, control that was tenuous at best. "Uhhh six months... Time to get a cabin up."

"It'd have to be a big cabin," she said, getting into the game. "Three rooms and a loft." Her lips teased his earlobe, stroking it lightly with her tongue, but her fingers were now well below his belt and heading to dangerous territory. God, she'd drive him crazy if she...

It took him a moment to master his voice. "Shore you wouldn't like to wait longer. Maybe give me time to put up a barn, get some livestock, a garden planted." The lessons of self-control under Morey's cruel hands served him well, even if the hands now tormenting him were loving as they moved closer to his groin. She wouldn't really do that.

"I don't think you can hold out that long, Mr. Kane," she said as she reached her destination. "You don't strike me as a man able to resist all that is about to befall you."

He sucked in a breath and wondered how much he could

really stand. He gave up. She had all the cards in this play. "All right... next week."

"Matthew, I--" She stopped, realizing what he'd said. "Do you mean that?"

"If you're willin' to sleep on the ground, wherever we can find a place, yeah, I mean it. Now let me go before I drive this wagon into a big rut and get it stuck."

She laughed. "I'd sleep anywhere with you. Even up a tree. You are a terrible tease, but I love you."

"I'm a tease!" he retorted with indignation. "Who's the one practically peelin' the shirt off my back, then making love to me, right here in front of God and everybody? You know anybody watching would figure I'm to blame."

"It is your fault. If you'd been reasonable and agreed to marry me back before we got to the Platte, I wouldn't have had to go to all the trouble of seducing you in broad daylight, thereby hopelessly compromising your honor." She giggled as she pulled his shirt back up to give him a modicum of modesty but left her hand on his belly, if a bit more modestly positioned.

"You are not safe to have around."

"I'm sorry," she said unrepentantly. Smiling, she rebuttoned his shirt. When she finished, she kissed his neck, the kiss light and tender.

She knows the worst, Matt thought, glancing at her contented smile. If she wanted him after what she'd heard, he had to believe in that love. He thought briefly then of St. Louis' words that a mountain might lie ahead, but he put them aside.

CHAPTER 24

A fter taking care of the stock and eating a light supper, Matt shaved, changed into a relatively clean shirt, and combed his hair but let it for once fall loose behind his shoulders. He and Amy had agreed he should be there when her parents were told of their plans for a simple trail wedding. Despite what Martha and Amos had said about accepting him, Matt still thought they might harbor a deep-seated hope that something would stop the wedding. He expected them to be less than pleased when faced with a definite date.

Walking into the Stevens circle, Matt grimaced when he saw Adam leaning against a wagon wheel, Loraine at his side. He had wanted to tell Adam alone, but there was no time for that now as Amy threw her arms around his waist, dragging him forward.

After everyone had settled back into places around the campfire, Matt said, "I reckon there's no way to say this easy. Amy and I would like to be married next week." He waited, braced for the objections.

"About time," Amos said with a broad grin. He rose, stretching out his hand. As though through a haze, Amos pumping his hand, Matt heard his future father-in-law saying, "We were wondering how long it'd take you two to work things out. Glad you have."

"I don't know," Martha Stevens said cautiously, frowning. "Do we really have time to get the dress fitted for Amy by next week-end, work out where they'll sleep, and plan everything?" She laughed then. "I'm teasing you." She pulled Matt's head down, kissed his cheek. "Welcome to the family, son."

Then the voices began to buzz. Speculations and proposals flew around the circle. Martha made fresh coffee while the women discussed dresses. Amy would wear her grandmother's wedding gown. It had been packed in the trunk, for just such times. Although the fabric was a little yellowed with age, the fit should be nearly perfect. Other voices questioned where the wedding should be held. Who would come? What time of day?

Matt's head whirled. He'd never been part of a family gathering like this where all talked at once, some with raised voices, yet none angry. He looked from face to face, seeing nothing but excitement and pleasure even from Belle.

"You could sleep under our wagon when the weather is inclement," Amos suggested, "or if it's really bad, the girls can sleep in the wagon with us, and you and Amy can have the tent." He grinned. "We'll find a way to give you privacy."

"Of course, you are welcome to take all your meals with us," Martha added. "We've been calculating since we thought this might happen. We have sufficient supplies."

"We can put up with each other in tight quarters for awhile."

"It'll be fine," Matt heard himself saying again and again. He felt his muscles relax and the tension ebb away.

"Where do you plan to homestead in Oregon?" asked Amos.

"I was thinking east of Oregon City. Heard there's good land still available there."

"We were thinking around there too."

"I know," Matt said, looking the older man in the eyes. "I figured Amy'd want to be near her kin."

"That's wonderful, Matt." Amos smiled with satisfaction. "We can help each other build our cabins. I know Martha'll like being close enough to see her daughter now and then. We'll try not to interfere, but if we do, you tell us."

"I'm not worried."

"I'm glad you're marrying my girl. You're a good man. I'm

glad for her, but I'm glad for me too. I never had a son. I knew one day though I'd get sons--through my daughters. I'm more than pleased you'll be the first."

Matt, choked with emotion, tried to think of a way to express what it meant to hear those words. There weren't words that covered it. He reached his hand out before Amos pulled him into his arms for a quick, manly embrace.

"Drop the sir. Pa or Amos, whichever is feels agreeable to you," Amos said as they stepped back.

Laughing, Adam shook his head as he stood up. "I've heard all the domestic bliss I can take. I got to get out of here before the marrying fever spreads to me."

Loraine shot him a glare, but he only laughed at her. "Walk with me a ways, Miss Loraine," he suggested with a broad grin.

"What for, Mr. Stone? You're afraid of the fever. Could be I'm already contagious!" she suggested, batting her eyes dramatically, her voice broadly mimicking Bernice when in full form.

He laughed and pulled her to her feet. "I'll take the risk."

"It will be slight, I promise," she retorted as they walked off.

Leaving the Stevens camp, heading for his own wagon, was for Matt leaving light for darkness. He had told Amy he had things to do, but didn't tell her one of them was notifying his family of the coming nuptials. She would have wanted to be with him, and he wanted her nowhere around Morey when his brother heard the news. Matt had even debated not telling his family, but they'd hear it from someone anyway.

His brother and father were slumped around a small campfire, each with a coffee cup, likely filled with rotgut whiskey they'd bought at the last fort.

"Where ya been?" his father asked.

Matt ignored the question as he dropped on his haunches across from them.

"Too good to sleep in your own wagon?" jibed Morey, his eyes narrowly watching each move Matt made. "Or maybe it wasn't St. Louis' you was sleepin' under. Maybe it was somebody else!"

Matt swallowed hard, forcing his muscles to unclench, as he fought against the urge to knock the smirk from Morey's face. He turned his gaze back on his father. "Amy and I are getting married next week," he said when he felt he had his voice under control.

"Probably needful." Morey laughed. "The way she's always pawin' you. Got a little one on the way, Matt?"

"That's nice," his father slurred. "Good to get married. Hope it works out better for you than me. Amy, huh? I kind of hoped it'd be that little blonde gal."

"How about us when you marry?" asked Morey. "We got hardly enough supplies as it is. How we goin' to feed another person?"

"Amy and I'll eat with the Stevens. There's enough here to get you to Oregon. The wagon and team is mine though, and I will be taking them when we get there. You'll have to figure out something else then."

"What about money?" his father asked, concerned for the first time. "When we get to The Dalles, we'll need to resupply... some things."

"There's enough of everything you need to get to Oregon," Matt retorted impatiently, anxious to get away from their selfish concerns and smirks. He stood up, stretching.

"I'll be needin' money for my rheumatism medicine," his father whined.

"Find another way. No more money from me," Matt snapped. He held back the rest of the words he wanted to say. It would do no good.

"High and mighty, self-righteous little brother. Always takin' care of hisself," Morey sneered, his narrow eyes unreadable in the darkness. "Thinkin' he's better'n others."

"Matt," his father pleaded, "I will need help... in Oregon. How will I live?"

"What you're doing isn't helping you to live. It's helping you to die."

"Goin' to give us a sermon now, little brother?" asked Morey, miming Matt's tones. "Tell us all about the evils of drink? Think you're better than us, but we know what you're doin' in the dark."

Matt hadn't come to fight, didn't want this to turn into a brawl, but if Morey kept making snide remarks about Amy, he would lose what semblance of control he had.

"About the money, son? Enough to get settled" His father's tone had gone beyond pleading to something else. Matt looked in his eyes but couldn't read the expression.

He felt his muscles tighten. "I'll think about it." He turned to leave.

"Yeah, you do that," Morey growled, walking to the wagon, rummaging around before he turned to face Matt. "You run to get out of here. Get yourself back to that woman. Amy's a pretty little thing. Don't dare leave her alone for long, or she'll find somebody else to give her loving."

Matt closed the distance between them with two long strides. "I told you I didn't want to hear her name from you-- ever."

Morey snickered as he brought forth a hammer from behind his back. Matt only glanced at it, laughing as he lunged. He dodged to the right as Morey raised the hammer, swinging hard with the obvious intent of braining Matt. Because of Matt's leap, the blow only grazed his cheek, glancing off his left shoulder.

Smiling savagely, Matt's right fist collided with Morey's chin, knocking him backward. Although his left arm hung numbly at his side, Matt reached out with his right, grabbed Morey's wrist and bent it backward, forcing the hammer from his grasp. Stepping back, he swung his good arm from the shoulder, connecting with Morey's jaw. A second blow to his brother's stomach doubled him, and he slumped to the ground, helplessly wheezing for air.

Matt stood above him, his own breath coming easily as he looked down. He felt neither sorrow nor regret. As if from a distance, he heard his pa saying', "Shouldn't fight. Brothers shouldn't fight."

Swinging around to face the man, Matt smiled coldly. "If the word has any meaning at all, Morey and I were never brothers." He barely resisted adding-- and you've been no father.

He reached into the wagon for his belt, holster and revolver. Belting them around his waist, he picked up his Sharps and left without a backward glance. His anger was almost gone by the time he got back to St. Louis' wagon. He recognized with relief something else was gone--the bitterness had been left behind when he had faced the full truth about father and brother. Rotating his shoulder to check its movement he walked into the camp.

St. Louis glanced up to see who it was, looked away, then quickly back. His gaze scanned Matt's face. "What happened?"

Matt grinned and sat down, moving carefully. "A disagreement."

St. Louis shook his head. "One that led to a pulled muscle durin' the disagreement."

"Possibly," Matt admitted. "Got any coffee?"

While St. Louis poured it, Matt gave him a shortened version of the confrontation. When he finished, St. Louis watched him as he reached out for the coffee, his eyes narrowing when Matt didn't bend forward without flinching.

"Let me see it."

"It's nothin'."

"Reckon I'll be the judge of that."

Resigned, Matt set down his up and pulled off his shirt, wincing as he moved his left arm. St. Louis stood over him, manipulating the joint and feeling of the rapidly swelling area. He shook his head . "Don't look like ya broke nothin, but it's gonna be some stiff, likely worse tomorrow. That's some bruise, gonna be real colorful."

Matt shrugged back into his shirt and sat to sip the hot coffee. "Want to hear some good news?" he asked with a grin.

"Always."

"If you'll do the deed, Amy and I are getting married next week."

St. Louis hooted. "It's about time ya made up yore mind to quit dawdlin'. For awhile I was scared ya was gonna let that little gal get away."

"That thought had crossed my mind."

"She's a real lady. Couldn't do no better. She's stuck by ya through thick and thin, even when ya didn't deserve it. You're a lucky man."

"I know that."

St. Louis nodded, smiling. "I'm goin' to take pleasure in this--real pleasure. I've married more than a few couples comin' across this trail, but this is gonna to be the one I'll enjoy most."

Matt sighed, leaning back with the first sense of relaxation he'd felt in what seemed weeks. He'd faced the truths of his family. Amy knew all there was to know. They could begin to put it all behind them now. There was only one more thing. "You said once I could bunk around here."

"No problem. Clem's gonna keep helpin' the Collins, while the old man takes it easy. It's just me and Adam. There's plenty of room."

Adam walked into the light and slumped down across from Matt and St. Louis, then looked steadily at Matt, his expression grim.

"What's got into you?" St. Louis asked.

"I kept hoping you would blow it," Adam said to Matt, his voice heavy with mock resignation.

"For awhile, it seemed a safe bet."

"That's what I thought."

"You want to mourn this for awhile?"

"I am not sure what deserves mourning but something seems called for."

"When you're through, I was wonderin' if you'd stand up with me, be my best man." Matt grinned at the surprise on Adam's face.

"You have got to be joking," Adam retorted. "When I am the best man?"

"Not arguing with you, but that's not the way she sees it."

"Well, if I can't be groom, I guess best man is next best." Adam chuckled and then put out his hand, which Matt took. "I am not going to say the best man won," Adam added.

Matt laughed. "I wouldn't ask it of you."

St. Louis shook his head. "I can't believe you two. Shore ya ain't gonna get into a fight over this?"

Matt shook his head. "I've had my fight for today."

"I haven't, but if I hit you and mess up your face, Amy'd mess up mine; so I have no choice but to be a good loser."

St. Louis shook his head and laughed. "Wait'll Clem hears this."

"We could make it a double wedding if you wanted to get married so bad. Loraine is a beautiful girl."

Adam stared into the fire. "It's there or it's not. Anyway I shouldn't hang around the family so much."

"Because of Amy?" Matt asked.

Adam shrugged his broad shoulders. "It doesn't matter why. I just don't think it's a good idea."

"You'd be lucky to have a woman like Loraine," Matt said. "Not that she'd be likely to have you anyway." He didn't like the way Adam seemed to be undervaluing the woman who would soon be his sister-in-law.

"I know that's true," Adam said. Then as though suddenly realizing what Matt was saying, yelped, "Man, isn't it enough to get yourself snared? Or are you bound to get me too?"

"Misery loves company," Matt said with a contented grin, stretching out his legs and crossing them at the ankle.

Adam hooted. "Oh, yeah. I've seen how miserable you are."

At dawn, Matt went back to his family wagon to gather up the rest of his personal possessions. It wouldn't take long; all he owned, except the wagon and team, fit in a small bag. When he got to Oregon, he'd arrange to sell or otherwise use the equipment. For now, his father and brother could use it.

His father watched as he stuffed a blanket into the bag with his shirts. "You really goin'?" he asked.

"I'll help if needed," Matt answered, "but I'm not staying here."

"Man belongs with his kin," his father said sullenly.

"Blood doesn't make for kin."

"You think you're important now. That them Stevens care for you. High and mighty like they are. It won't take long afore they'll be kickin' you out."

Matt stood back, looking at his father as though he'd never

seen him before. All his life he'd heard those warnings--Other folks will betray you. They don't think you're any good. Keep to your own kind. As a boy, every time Matt reached out to anyone, his father pulled him back with forewarnings, embellished with cutting remarks about Matt's own lack of worth.

Matt put his duffel over his good shoulder. "A man makes his life what it is."

"Don't say I didn't warn ya. Turn yore back on some, and you'll get it stabbed."

Matt looked back and saw his father's eyes, recognizing in them some of what he'd always seen in Morey's. His lips twisted. "Yeah, I do know that one."

"Just wait. Someday you'll need 'em, and they'll forget yore name."

"How'd you get to be so bitter, Pa?"

"Them kind lord it over others... Use church talk as an excuse to say they're better'n the rest. Pullin' out that black book and usin' it like a club over a man's head, condemnin' every little thing he does. All my life, no man's lifted a hand to help me."

"Amos Stevens tried to be a friend."

"Don't need pity."

Matt took a deep breath. "Why'd you tell me my birth killed my mother?"

"It was so."

"She died of cholera."

"Maybe that's what she had in the end, but if she hadn't been weak from havin' you, why she'd... Well, it was--"

"Cholera takes the strong and the weak. Martha Stevens said she'd come through the birth fine. You lied to me!"

His father turned away, leaving Matt to think he would never hear an answer. "It was better for you that way. Toughens a man up." The reedy voice was faint, almost inaudible. Matt shook his head. He heard the lie in his father's voice.

"Tough man can stand up against anythin'. That's the kind of man you are now. Oughta be thankin' me for what you are."

Matt looked at him with disbelief. "For lying to me? For trying to destroy me? For all the years you let Morey hit me or do whatever he wanted when I was too little to fight back? Who are you lying to, Pa? Me or yourself?"

"If yore ma'd lived, it'd been different."

"Or you'd have destroyed her as I think in the end, you tried to destroy me."

"That's a harsh thing to say," his father protested. "I tried to be a good pa. I tried to be a good father. I truly did. I just wasn't well, that's all."

"I won't be back," Matt said, working to suppress his feeling of disgust. "If you need anything, you know where to find me."

Amy was sitting with St. Louis, sipping a cup of coffee when Matt walked up. "What happened?" she asked after one look at his stony expression.

"Nothing."

"Well, there's something," she snapped a quick response to his gruff tone.

"Don't look for something hidden in everything, baby. It's going to wear us both out."

"Then don't lie to me."

"Don't put me in a spot where I have to." He looked at her irritated face and at the same moment realized what he'd said. "That didn't make much sense."

"You're shore right about that," St. Louis said. "I'm goin' to get out of here afore I get between the two of ya and end up beat up by ya both."

When he'd gone, Amy poured him coffee as he told her about the fight with Morey.

"You came to blows?"

"A few."

"Oh, Matt, I hate hearing that. He's such a vindictive man. If you shamed him, it might make everything worse."

"I doubt it could be worse," Matt said. The situation between them was as bad as it could get--with or without a fight. "Besides what was I supposed to do, let him brain me with a hammer?" As soon as the words were out of his mouth he regretted them. He'd never intended to mention the weapon Morey had used.

"He used a hammer on you?" Her voice rose as her eyes darkened, the pupils widening with shock.

"Tried to," Matt corrected in what he hoped was a neutral tone

Obviously not casual enough. She raised her voice another notch. "He hit you!"

"Barely grazed me."

"Where?"

"On the left shoulder." He felt a surge of frustration that it never seemed possible to keep anything from her.

In seconds she was at his side, unbuttoning his shirt despite his protest. Peeling it away from his shoulder, she exposed the livid bruises, which had gained ugly and intense coloring during the night.

"See," he grumbled at her gasp. Yanking his shirt back together, he began rebuttoning it. "It'll heal." They always did.

"Matt, it's awful looking. Are you sure your shoulder is all right, that nothing is broken?"

"St. Louis said it'd be stiff a day or two. That's all." He grinned at her wrinkled nose. "It's not that bad."

"Your whole shoulder is black and blue and--whatever that other color is. Does it hurt?" she asked, reaching up to stroke his cheek.

"What do you think?"

She frowned at his crooked smile. "You're taking this too lightly."

"It's over."

"It's not, and you know it."

"He can't stand up to me in a fight--not even with a hammer in his hand." Rocking back on his heels, he stared into the fire.

"But it's not a fair fight he'll try for."

"When we get to Oregon, he won't be near us."

She shook her head, walking away from him, looking off toward the mountains. "I wish I could believe you were taking this seriously."

"Don't do this, Amy," Matt murmured, coming to stand

behind her, putting his arms around her and drawing her back against him. "Don't ruin what's going right for us by borrowing trouble that isn't here yet and may never be."

"I can't help it. He walked past me yesterday. He looked at me. Just looked at me, didn't say a word, but my skin crawled. Matt, I really do I think he's crazy." She allowed herself to lean back against him as his arms encircled her.

"There's nothing I can do about it. It's not like I can just kill him because of what he might do," Matt said, uneasy at any mention that Morey took notice of Amy. He bent to kiss the indent between her neck and shoulder. Her sigh was soft as she turned her head to allow fuller access. He turned her around, claiming her lips with all the confidence of a lover soon to be a husband. "Not so long to wait," he murmured, kissing her again. "Think about that, lovely lady."

"I just wish--"

He cut her off with another kiss, his lips hungry and probing. His tongue plunged her mouth. He cupped her bottom with his hands as he pulled her against him, letting her feel his need. "Don't wish. You don't need to wish. It's all goin' to be ours in less than a week."

"But--"

"Amy," he ordered, "you're ruining my mood here."

"Sorry, but I can't turn off my worry like snuffing out a candle."

He shook his head. "What am I going to do with you? We're both going to be careful. But we're not letting him ruin things for us. You hear?"

"I hear."

"It'll be all right, baby. Maybe not right away, but soon."

Before Amy could argue with him or put up another concern, Bernice and Adam walked up. Matt turned Amy so she stood in front of him, leaning back against him, his hands resting lightly on her hips, the epitome of possession for both Bernice and Adam to see.

Amy noted with a twinge of irritation that Bernice was holding onto Adam's arm, just as she had once done Matt's. What about Raine?

"I hear congratulations are in order, Amy," Bernice said.

Amy tried to smile, finding it a hollow effort. "You usually congratulate the future groom, not the bride, Bernice."

"I heard that somewhere. It all depends, of course. I am so looking forward to your wedding, Amy. It should be... lovely." She looked at Matt as she spoke.

Amy's smile became frozen. The last thing she wanted was Bernice at their wedding, but she had no way to stop her.

"I love weddings," Bernice went on, "don't you love weddings, Adam?" She tugged on his arm.

"Oh yeah," he said unenthusiastically.

"Are you going to be at this one?" Bernice asked with another of her radiant, totally directed beams.

"Of course," Adam said with his first smile, "I'm standing up with him."

Amy looked at him in shock, then twisted her head to look up at Matt. "Best man?" she managed.

"We're still arguing that part out."

"That's... uh a surprise," Amy said in a small voice. She watched with amazement as Adam and Matt exchanged maddening expressions of male superiority.

When Adam and Bernice had gone, Amy looked up at Matt. "I can't believe this," she hissed. "I thought you two didn't like each other, and now he's going to stand up with you when we get married. And--and I can't believe Adam is so stupid as to be taken in by Bernice! What on earth is going on?"

"Nothing is my guess."

"Don't I get an explanation for any of it?"

"What part?"

"What could Adam possibly see in Bernice?" Amy asked crossly, looking toward the direction they had gone.

"He sees nothing in her."

"But…"

"Amy, you can't get everything you want. There's something more driving Adam than we know or he's going to say. You just keep your pretty, little nose out of it. You'll have enough on your hands managing one man."

"But--"

Matt shook his head. "Loraine's a fine woman, and if it's meant to be between her and Adam, it will."

"I don't like the idea of Bernice winning like that," Amy grumbled.

Matt grinned. "She is not winning anything."

"What do you mean?"

"I saw the look on Adam's face when they walked off. I recognized it because I've felt it myself around Miss Bernice. He was making excuses to get out of here and get her off him." He laughed as he remembered the expression of wry speculation he had seen in Adam's eyes as he'd looked down at Bernice's grip on his arm.

~

So tired she could hardly get undressed, Amy spent a few moments, before blowing out the lamp, writing in her journal. 'September 15--For months St. Louis has been telling us about the Blue Mountains and how important it was we cross them before the snow flies. We're finally in their midst. The steepness of the mountains through which we've passed is impossible to describe with words. At the end of a day I've seen heavily calloused hands bleeding from using the rope pulleys that keep the wagons from crashing to their destruction."

'It seems each day I see more treacherous ascents, followed by equally steep descents. Somehow the men and animals manage the impossible. We've been traveling from dawn to dusk. With fall nearly here, the nights are becoming bitterly cold and frost covers the ground in the morning.

'Things go wrong, but so far, no tragedies. An axle broke. That stopped everything while the wheels and all were replaced. They are making new spokes from whatever wood they find. In a descent yesterday, a rope broke, plummeting the Williams wagon to the floor of the valley. Goods had to be transferred to a sound wagon. The poor family will be temporarily housed with the Collins. Fortunately no one was injured. Primarily because no one is foolish enough to ride a wagon down the descents.'

She closed the journal. In two days, she and Matthew would be married, but she felt none of the joy she'd expected. Instead, fear over Morey left a dark feeling of dread in her stomach. She had seen again and again the ominous way Morey watched Matt, the threat in his eyes. She refused to write down those words, to put them down on paper might give them power.

CHAPTER 25

A my sucked in her breath as her mother fastened the small buttons at the waist of the wedding gown. Although the silk was somewhat yellowed with age, it had acquired a white-gold patina, seeming to glow against the background of crates and quilts under the canvas wagon cover.

"Be still, girl," her mother complained as Amy shifted her weight from one foot to the other, "if I'm going to get this last button, you can't so much as breathe."

"I'll try," Amy said with a wry smile, "but it's tight."

"Your grandmother was just a wee bit smaller than you in the bodice, but it looks lovely."

"You can breathe later," Loraine said as she brushed Amy's hair back and inserted two pearl inlaid combs to hold the front high, allowing the back to fall in a dark cascade down her back. "I think that looks good, but--" Loraine laid the lace mantilla over the long black hair, fastening it with two long pins. "That's it, the perfect touch."

"You make a beautiful bride, which is, of course, no more than we knew." Her mother smoothed the silk of the skirt one last time. "I'm so glad you're wearing Mama's dress, Amy. It's so right for you."

Belle, who had been running over the hills gathering what she could find for a bouquet, scampered into the wagon in time to add her own compliments regarding Amy's beauty and hand her the arrangement of dried flowers and grasses.

"It's lovely," Amy said admiringly. "Dried, I can keep it forever."

"Wait a minute, little sister." Loraine smiled and waved her finger admonishingly. "Aren't you supposed to throw it so somebody else gets to be a bride?"

"I don't know." Amy pretended to consider, "I like it awfully well, but I guess I'll have to--if you're ever going to become a bride."

"I'll probably never catch it anyway. Bernice will fly into the air like a vulture!"

"What about me?" Belle piped up. "Can't I catch it?"

"We don't want the real beauty of the family to be the next bride," Loraine explained with a grin. "That'd leave me to be the spinster. Not that that might not happen anyway."

Amy's mother looked at her and then her other daughters. "I think the bride needs a moment to herself." She kissed Amy's cheek. "We'll be waiting outside."

Grateful for her mother's insight, Amy stood looking in the small hand mirror. The neckline of the dress was lined with tiny seed pearls, the ivory color of the silk complemented her skin. The image reflected back was of thick black hair and golden skin. It would have been better, of course, if her skin had been pearly white-- nothing she could do about that. She had no time to lie around with an oatmeal face mask attempting to bleach it. Besides a tan, although not precisely considered beautiful, looked well with her dark hair. She bit her lips to add more color. She wanted to be beautiful for Matt, wanted this night to hold perfection for him, to match every dream he'd ever had. She thought of how little beauty and love Matt's life had held. It would all change after today.

Putting down the mirror, Amy's climbed down from the wagon. When her father saw her, he bent and kissed her cheek. "You look so much like your mother when I married her it's hard to believe I'm not stepping back in time."

Amy smiled up at him. Looking beyond his shoulder, she saw Matt coming from the other direction, Adam at his side.

Matt was wearing the white promise shirt she and her mother had sewn for him. Close fitting black pants hugged his narrow hips and muscular thighs. His blond hair was tied back making the angular planes of his face stand out. He was almost unbelievably handsome. When he saw her, his teeth flashed white against darkly tanned skin.

"So," she murmured sweetly, when he was near enough to hear, "I see you did not back out."

He laughed and bent to her ear. "I'll say something nice to you. You're beautiful," he whispered.

"You are too." Warmth filled her at his slow smile. He left her then to await her by the small stream where they would be wed. St. Louis, his beard neatly trimmed and a dark jacket giving him an air of authority, stood beside Matt, cottonwoods at their backs, the faint trickle of water came from the nearly dry streambed. Amy was vaguely aware of others--Adam at Matt's left, the Collins, Halls, Clem, the Porters to the other side, even Bernice, who stood alone, her eyes holding a wistful expression.

"Now then--" St. Louis began speaking the age old words. She knew he was continuing to talk but she felt her thoughts spinning away. She smiled up at Matt as she remembered her words of only months earlier. "I could never love you that way." How little she had understood of love that day.

St. Louis' request that she and Matt repeat their vows to one another brought her back to awareness. Then Matt was sliding a simple, gold band on her finger, a ring that had been her grandmother's. When St. Louis pronounced them man and wife, Matt eyes darkened as he bent and claimed her lips with his own.

"Better than I dreamed," he whispered his voice husky with emotion.

Amy turned to hug her mother and father, hearing all the voices wishing them well, telling them how happy they were for them.

"How about me?" A coarse, discordant yell came from above, on the opposite bank of the stream. At first she couldn't understand the words, but she knew who it was at the same instant Matt whirled to face his brother.

Amy reached out to Matt. At all cost he had to hold his temper, must not in anyway enrage Morey who sat on his horse, watching them. Only then did she realize Morey had a rifle pointed at Matt.

"You ain't been invited," St. Louis growled. "Get out!"

Morey only laughed. "In a bit."

"What do you want?" Matt grated out, his voice hard. When Amy came to stand at his side, he thrust her behind him.

"Just what any brother'd want. To see my little brother get hitched. Come on up for my congratulations."

Matt ignored Amy's attempts to hold onto him and took the streambed in a single step.

"Wait!" Morey yelled. "I need to congratulate the bride too, little brother."

"She stays with her family."

Morey kept his gun trained on Matt, but he glanced over at Amy. "It's up to you, Amy girl. You want to come up... or shall I blow a hole right through your brand new husband?" His voice was so emotionless she knew he meant it. She began working her way to the stream, then across it, holding her skirt high.

"No, Amy," Matt's voice was stern and calm. "Go back to your folks."

Morey looked back at Matt, "I could just as easy kill her as you. Might be even better."

Matt's eyes narrowed as he seemed to consider. Saying nothing more, he began rapidly striding up the bank as though if he reached Morey quickly enough, he could stop whatever his brother had in mind.

"Whoa," Morey yelled, a cunning smile on his face. "Stop right there and wait for your bride. Fancy dress like that, she's goin' to need help gettin' up the bank." He laughed as Matt halted, fists clenched in frustration.

Morey glanced back at the assembled people "Don't any of you move. I mean that Stone," he warned. "I saw you edgin' backward. You men put your hands in the air and keep 'em there. If you make a move, one of them's dead, and I'm not particular about which. Red on white, that'd be right purty." He looked back at Matt and chuckled. "Now, help your bride up the bank."

Matt's jaw was clenched, every muscle rigid, as he took Amy's hand in his own. She gripped him, not wanting to let go. Silently they climbed to the rise where Morey sat his horse, an unsaddled horse roped by a lead to his saddle. "Wal," Morey said, smiling again, "what do you think now, little brother?"

Amy clung to Matt's arm to prevent him from lunging at Morey and being killed instantly.

"You make a mighty pretty bride, Amy," Morey told her, his eyes making her feel unclean as his avid gaze raked up and down her body.

Matt tried again to push Amy behind him. She resisted, reasoning that with two of them to watch there might be a chance, even if it was a feeble one, that she could distract Morey long enough for Matt to get the rifle away from him.

Morey threw a strip of thin rawhide at Amy's feet. "Tie your lover's wrists together and make the knots tight."

Amy bent to pick up the rawhide, trying to find some way to avoid having to do this. She understood now what bondage meant to him. Tears came to her eyes as she looked up and into his gray eyes. The calmness in their depths gave her a strength she didn't feel. He nodded for her to obey and held out his wrists, allowing her to wind the rawhide around them. When she was finished, Matt held his wrists up. "You got what you want. Let her go."

"After you get on this horse."

Matt let out his breath in what sounded like a sigh of relief.

Shock had settled over Amy, nearly numbing her to what was happening, but at Morey's words, the truth shot through her. "No, you can't do this," she cried, trying to hold onto Matt before he could take a step away from her.

"It'll be all right," Matt said, taking hold of her arm with his bound hands. "It isn't our game--right now."

"Matt's right," Morey said, chuckling. "It's my game. Matt's gettin' on this horse, or one of you is goin' to die. And it's most likely going to be you, sweet thing."

Matt gave her a quick, hard kiss, then pushed her back as he strode to the horse, easily leaping on its back even with hands tied together.

"Don't cry, little sister-in-law," Morey said with a mocking laugh. "Don't you trust me to take care of him? After all, he's my brother."

He looked back down at the others, his gaze meeting Adam's, then St. Louis'. "If I see anybody followin', could be I'll do somethin' I'll be sorry for. You can know for sure Matt'll be sorry for it. I'll kill him before I start on anybody else. You know I mean it."

"Wait," Amy cried. "Take me too." She moved toward the horses.

"No!" Matt snapped.

Morey reached across and slapped him across the mouth, hard enough to jerk his head back. "That was rude," Morey scolded with another laugh. "Maybe the little lady just wants to see the last act of the play?"

"Yes, that's it." Amy said, trying to force a smile on her shaky lips. "I want to see the games."

Abruptly, Morey put out his hand, shaking his head. "No, can't do it. I'd like to, but just remembered I can't." His voice was frighteningly normal, as though he'd responded to her request for a drink of water.

"Whatever you have to do," she said to Matt, "do it. Come back to me." He managed a smile and nodded.

Morey glanced up at the sky, toward where the sun was edging below the horizon with a fiery show. "It's gettin' late. I reckon we got to be goin'." Without looking back, he wheeled his horse and spurring it viciously, set a rapid pace away from the wagons. Matt's mount, tied by a lead rope, had no choice but to follow.

Amy watched until they disappeared from sight. Her father had run up the bank and had his arms around her, but she barely felt them. She was unable to take her eyes from the horizon, from her last glimpse of Matt.

"Adam went for his gun and a horse," her father said, as the others reached them. "He'll trail them as soon as it's safe."

"Morey will kill Matt if he sees him. He meant it." Amy shuddered. Vivid images of what Matt had told her about Morey returned to haunt her. She gritted her teeth as she stared at the empty horizon. With sudden decision, she whirled, grabbing up the skirts of her wedding dress. "I have to talk to Adam before he leaves." She began to run. "I have to explain about Morey."

When she saw Adam saddling a horse, a hard expression on his face, she quickly told of the games Morey liked to play. "He'll be looking for a hole to hide in to do that."

"That's good then," Adam said.

"Good? How can you say good after what I just told you?"

"Delay, girl. We need time and that will give it to us. He doesn't want to kill him fast. That's to our and his advantage."

"You can't get too close to them," St. Louis said as he handed Adam a full canteen.

"Don't worry. I'll track out of sight and wait for full dark to make any move. With the clouds in the sky and the moon a crescent, that will help."

"Take me with you," Amy begged. "Please take me."

"I thought you wanted him back," Adam said checking the load in his gun. She knew the truth of his words and stood back.

"I'll start the wagons in the morning," St. Louis said. "You know where we're heading. Catch up when you can."

"I will."

"You will save him, won't you?" she asked as she watched Adam mount. His expression was grim as he kicked his horse in the side.

Riding away from the wagons, Matt fought to keep his balance on the rapidly moving horse. With bound wrists, horseman though he was, the ride bareback across the rocky plateau was anything but easy. He twisted his wrists against the tight rawhide thongs, but the effort gained him nothing. Already his hands were growing numb.

Briefly he considered letting go, taking his chances on the rough ground in a free fall, but at the pace they were moving, it would take a miracle to keep from breaking his neck. Morey would shoot him if he survived the fall. All he could do was stay balanced. He grasped the horse firmly with his knees and hoped for a chance, any chance.

As far as Matt could see across the darkening landscape, there was nothing but rolling hills, sagebrush, juniper, and dry grass. It was easily as barren as any country they had passed. There would be only the slimmest chance Morey and he would come across other people along this desolate ridge. As he rode, Matt faced what lay ahead. He was on his own. St. Louis would want to follow, want to do what he could, but he had the responsibility of the wagons.

If he could see one bright spot, it was that no one had been hurt. When Amy had said she wanted to come, Matt had felt his heart stop. An emotion of improbable gratitude had swept through him at Morey's refusal. Fortunately Morey had enough sense of self-preservation not to put his neck in that noose.

Futilely, Matt cursed himself. He should have expected Morey to strike at his wedding. It fit the pattern perfectly--wait for a moment of happiness and destroy it. He didn't think Morey wanted to kill him at least not right away. That would be too merciful. There had to be a chance to turn this thing around; and when it came, he'd grab it.

The miles passed; and Matt, the muscle in his previously injured thigh spasming, began to wonder wryly how long it would be before he had no choice about falling off. Morey veered to the left, heading toward a thicket of scrawny trees. Ahead loomed a narrow canyon, almost invisible from any distance. Morey maneuvered the horses into it. Stopping in front of a juniper, he dismounted.

With a twisted smile, Morey looked up at Matt, the growing darkness not hiding his expression of satisfaction nor the rifle in his hands. "Reckon nobody'll see us here, even if somebody followed. Not that I figure anybody would." He laughed. "Get down, little brother."

Matt slid from the horse, uncertain for a moment if his legs would support him. Leaning against the animal, he got his balance and stretched, loosening his muscles as best he could.

Morey watched his discomfort and chuckled. For a moment, Matt considered lunging for him, making an attempt--no matter how unlikely--to slam Morey in the face with his bound wrists. But the rifle edged down just a little, until it pointed at his belly.

"Gut shot's a hard way to go." Morey's finger seemed to tense on the trigger. "A man, layin' out here alone, could take days dying."

Maybe a gunshot death would be easiest. Then the thought of Amy came to him, the stricken expression on her face as he had turned to ride away. He would do what he could to survive as long as possible. He swallowed hard, forcing his muscles to relax.

"Now you obey me. Exactly like I tell you, and I won't shoot you. Get down on the ground." Morey gestured with the revolver.

"That's a boy. Take off them boots and socks. And don't get no idea about kickin' or throwin' 'em at me. I'll be watchin' like a hawk." He stepped back and watched.

Pulling off boots and socks with bound wrists was no easy task, but Matt managed and threw them toward the brush where Morey pointed.

"Now," Morey ordered, a smile on his lips, "Lay flat, arms over your head. Just make yourself comfortable." He laughed as Matt clenched his jaw but did as ordered.

When Matt felt the loop of rope tighten around his bare ankles, he instinctively tried to pull away, but Morey never took his eyes or muzzle of the rifle from him as he secured the half-hitch. When the end of the rope was secured around a juniper, Morey walked around him and with another length of rope looped his bound wrists to another tree, stretching Matt's body as taut as possible.

"Comfortable?"

Suddenly he was a little boy, the sounds of the night all around him. He fought those old feelings of terror. He couldn't do what he had done then or what he had done during the whipping. He had to keep his wits about him. He had to stay with it no matter what the cost. He'd make Morey work for this. Somewhere ahead, he would get a chance to turn this around. He had to believe in that. He swallowed hard, aware how little real hope he had.

Bending over, Morey smiled as he took hold of the front of Matt's white shirt. "She make this for you?" he asked, fingering the cloth. When Matt remained silent, he took hold of both sides of the collar and yanked, ripping open buttons, baring Matt's chest.

"Maybe I oughta take a closer look at it." Propping the rifle against a juniper a ten feet away, Morey returned with his knife and laid it against Matt's bare flesh. Quickly he sliced through the fabric, cutting the shirt to ribbons and stripping it away.

He held up the rags, pretending to study them. "Not much to it, was there?" Chuckling, he went off to tie the horses deeper in the little grove of trees.

Matt used the brief respite to rotate his wrists enough to get hold of the knot. Too soon Morey was back with a handful of twigs. He glanced down and almost gently kicked Matt in the ribs. "Won't do no good," he offered conversationally. "I bought this at the last post. Knew what I'd be doin' when the chance came. Rawhide was best. Wet, it shrinks as it dries. You won't be pulling out of those knots."

He scooped the twigs and pieces of Matt's shirt into a small pile and lit them. "I figure to keep the fire small. Don't expect nobody to come across us, sittin' down in a hollow like we are, but you never know." He laughed, a bizarre, unnerving little laugh. "Kind of funny--us endin' up like this again. Remember all the things we used to do? The fun we had?"

Matt stopped his useless struggle against the bindings and watched as Morey, sitting back on his heels, threw more pieces of his torn shirt onto the fire. Considering his situation, he knew it was foolish, but he mourned the loss of the promise shirt as Amy had called it. It had been the first made for him by love. Since the night she'd given it to him with eager kisses, he'd treasured the gift. Whatever the night held for him, and it'd not be good, he'd had that gift as a sign of her love.

"It's a good feelin' for me, I can tell you," Morey rambled

RAIN TRUEAX

on, glancing at Matt now and then. "I been all along figurin' what I'd do but then to be able to do it at your wedding, the last time you'd expect it, when you were so happy..." He chuckled. "It was so sweet and it worked so good."

"And what's this get you, Morey?" Matt asked. Getting his brother to talk might delay what he had in mind for the evening's entertainment. It wasn't over yet. In the past Morey had been satisfied with torture and then released him. It was a slim hope that he'd do such again, but he had to cling to that possibility.

Morey reached behind him for his saddle bag and pulled out a bottle of whiskey, taking a long swig before he answered. "It's going to prove it once and for all between us. All that muscle of yours didn't do you much good, did it? Not when I got the brains." He laughed, the bottle now held loosely in his left hand, in his right, his knife. He lifted the blade, studying its tip, then looked pointedly at Matt.

Matt shrugged as best he could. "So you kill me. You've ruined your life right along with mine."

Morey lowered the knife until the blade was cradled in the flickering flames. "Maybe so, but then, I'm not going to just kill you." He smiled.

CHAPTER 26

A my, having changed out of her wedding dress, stared into the darkness, seeing nothing. Behind her a large campfire burned. She didn't have to look to know that Mrs. Collins, Jennie, her sisters and Bernice sat around it, their voices little more than murmurs. Her mother moved between them, pouring coffee, saying soothing things that Amy couldn't and didn't want to hear.

In the distance a coyote howled. Amy wondered if any of those at the campfire had even heard the wail. She knew by the mournful sounds of their voices and the sad looks they cast her way that they had given up. She had not. Matt would not be killed. One way or another he would survive and come back to her.

Her mother put a cup of hot coffee into her hands. The cup warmed her hands as she sipped at the potent brew. Nothing could warm her inside. Nothing, that is, until Matt came riding back to her. She heard St. Louis' steps he reentered the circle. Unfortunately, right behind him was Nathan Kane.

"I am tryin' to understand what happened," he said sipping from a flask. "Where is my son?"

"Which one?" St. Louis asked.

"Well, Morey. He's my only true son."

Amy looked at him with amazement. "Matt is your son," she said."

"Never figured he was. I figured Laura had... well someone else."

"How dare you say that," Martha rose from her stool. "Laura was not that kind of woman."

"Boy not only killed her but never looked nothin' like me." He sipped again from the flask.

"That is insane," Martha snapped, looking as angry as Amy had seen her.

Nathan Kane shrugged. "Is it? Not be the first woman done somethin' like that."

"You never knew your wife at all, and you never appreciated the kind of man your son was," Martha said shaking her head with disgust.

"How long has it been since Mr. Stone left?" Mrs. Collins asked, her voice cracking with weariness.

"Over three hours," Amy's father replied.

Amy turned back toward the circle. She saw the exhaustion and tiredness in the eyes of the women, the frown on her father's face as he gazed into the distance, rubbing his hand absentmindedly over the butt of the pistol thrust into his belt. He looked up at Amy, his tired eyes meeting her gaze. "I should have gone with him."

"Adam was right. He'll travel faster by himself."

"What if he decides not to save him," Bernice said from where she had been sitting back against a wagon.

"What on earth are you talking about?" Amy retorted.

"Well, didn't he want you? He might decide this is the way."

"Adam Stone the one went after my boy? He better not hurt him," Nathan interrupted.

St. Louis snorted with disgust at them both. "Your son threatened Amy and kidnapped Matt. If he comes out of this alive, I'll be surprised." He looked then at Bernice. "And, little lady, you keep your mouth shut or you get out of here. If you even knew a mite of Adam Stone, you'd not say such a thing. If you had a good bone in your body, you wouldn't either."

"Just..."

"I need to be doing something," Amy's father said with frustration.

"You are," her mother said. "You're here in case Morey doubles back."

Bernice curled up by the fire. "Poor Matt."

"Poor Matt?" Nathan grumbled. "What about my son. Matt drove him to this."

Amy glared at him. "You knew all along what Morey did to Matt when he was small. Didn't you?"

Nathan looked away and then finally back when he saw she was waiting for him to answer. "Just games."

She swallowed back her rage. "Games? Mr. Kane, you are insane if that's what you think. Maybe as much as your crazy son—and you know which one I mean."

St. Louis poured himself coffee. "You figured he wasn't yores, that's about it, and from then on, ya let yore true son do what he wanted with him."

"Is that why you took them to Georgia?" Amos asked entering into the argument.

"I did that to get women to look after the boys."

"I think you did it so no one would know what Morey was doing to Matt," Amy said as she began to put the whole thing together. Matt had seen it as being his brother, but his father looked to have helped it happen, maybe had given Morey the idea in the beginning. She studied his narrow, wrinkled face and wondered how someone could do such a thing.

Nathan managed a laugh that was more like cackle. "Morey didn't really hurt him, which is more than I can say for what Matt did to him last week."

"After Morey attacked him with a hammer."

"It was just balancing things out."

Now Amy saw him for what he was—mentally ill. Maybe sicker than Morey. He had been the driving force to make Matt feel inferior, to make him feel he was responsible for the death of his mother—what a cruel man. She forced herself to stop thinking about this evil little man. She had to concentrate on Matt, on praying for his survival. She looked at St. Louis for reassurance. "If Adam had lost their trail, he'd be back, wouldn't he?"

"I saw fire in Adam's eyes when he rode off," he said. "He won't be back without Matt."

"He's just one man. He can't find them out there," Bernice moaned. "This land is too big, and now it's dark."

St. Louis grimaced. "Bernice, get back to your own wagon."

"I want to be with you all."

"But ya ain't. Ya are just here to stir trouble. Go before I take a switch to your bottom—which someone shoulda done years ago."

Bernice went on as though she hadn't heard him. "What do you suppose that monster is doing to Matt, I mean right now? Would he torture him, do you think?"

"My son ain't a monster," Nathan said swallowing again from the flask.

Amos walked over to him, took it out of his hands and emptied the contents onto the ground.

"Ya had no right to do that."

"More is coming if you don't get back to your wagon. We'll let you know when they get back."

Nathan glared at him but took his empty flask from him and stumbled back toward his wagon.

"I want to stay here, with you all," Bernice said. She sighed heavily before looking skyward. "Why do you suppose God would let something like this happen?"

St. Louis walked over to her, grabbed her arm and pulled her to her feet. "Go back to your wagon or heaven help me for what comes next."

Bernice glared at him. "I just want to help! I just can't bear the waiting, the not knowing what's happening."

Amy recalled the avid look she'd seen in Bernice's eyes the day Matt had been whipped, remembered her threat to have Matt hung, and suspicioned Bernice was enjoying all the drama, enjoying adding to everyone's horror and fear.

Amy placed her coffee cup on the back of the wagon. She walked to where Bernice had resumed whimpering. "Bernice, you are just like Mr. Kane and Morey."

Bernice stared up at her. She wiped her eyes, the expression in them hardening. "How could you say such a thing?"

"There would have been a time I'd have never dreamt it was possible, but..." Amy stopped and shook her head. "It's the truth isn't it?"

Bernice glared at her but said nothing

Amy's smile was cold, her heart even colder. "I know you want to hear all the details, listen in on every conversation, but for your own good, I suggest you follow St. Louis' advice. If you don't, so help me, your hair will be pulled from your head and what's left there, I'll slice off with a knife." Bernice looked at her, saw the determination in Amy's face and stalked off.

Amy walked to the edge of the camp. She had to believe Matt was alive. Adam wouldn't give up. Matt would walk away from this. She clasped her arms over her chest. She wanted to do something, anything. All she had was prayer. She wished she had been more faithful in it—or even believed more that it could protect Matt. She stared into the darkness. At the rim of the prairie a partial, golden moon edged into sight.

Matt looked into the blackness of the sky, gathering his strength for what would soon be a living hell. The moon was just rising, the stars shone like glittering diamonds on an almost crystal clear night. The same sky was looking down on Amy, on the wagons--the real world, the normal world. This canyon, all that might happen in it, was eerily unreal.

He wished it was a dream, like one of his nightmares. He couldn't deny the reality of the rough, abrasive ground under his bare back, the tiny rocks that dug into his skin, or the dryness of his mouth, the numbness in his hands. For a moment, he considered asking Morey for water. The only thing that stopped him was his certainty as to the answer. Morey wanted him to suffer in every way he knew to make it happen.

Whistling tunelessly, Morey kept his knife blade heating over the flames, occasionally taking a swig from a whiskey bottle and turning now and then to look at Matt.

Leaning over him, he held the bottle to his lips. "Want some?"

"No."

He laughed and move to pour it in Matt's mouth holding his chin brutally so he could not turn away. "Not too much. I want you to feel everything coming tonight." He set down the bottle and then using his finger traced a line down Matt's belly, brushing the skin lightly as he drew an imaginary design. His finger stopped at Matt's belt and hovered. "Remember the games we used to play, Matt? So much fun until you decided to quit."

"Fun for you."

"I took care of you afterward, didn't I? Sure I'd tie you up, but I'd let you go too."

"Is that what you are going to do this time? Let me go and leave me out here alone to die?"

"Not this time," Morey said with what almost sounded like a regretful tone. "You'd never let me do it again. I have to keep you this time... forever."

Matt kept his expression blank, his gaze coolly meeting Morey's. At all cost, he had to deny Morey the reaction he sought. If Morey saw fear in his eyes, it would only make the ordeal worse. He wasn't a little boy anymore and what Morey wanted most he could be denied.

Morey's eyes glittered with excitement, as his gaze moved slowly across Matt's torso. "I seen her cuddling up to you like a kitten nuzzling its mama." He stroked his hand down Matt's arm. "Must be these big muscles. Hear tell women like 'em." He drew his knife from the flame and poised it above Matt's underarm. Eyes staring at the red hot color of the blade, he brought it slowly down until Matt could feel its heat. Matt tightened his muscles and tried not to hear Morey's tittering laughter.

"Let's see how much you can take now, little brother," Morey said, still smiling as he laid the blade firmly onto Matt's skin. Matt twisted as far as the ropes would permit, gritting his teeth against the burning pain, pain made worse by the smell he recognized as his own flesh burning. He tightened all his muscles, trying to control his response. Maybe it would have been enough--if he had not seen the expression of avidity on Morey's face or had to listen to that droning whistle as he placed the blade back into the flames.

Watching numbly, he saw the blade returned from the fire. His mind demanded release. Go to the safe place. He couldn't do that. He had to stay, to use his wits. He made himself think of Amy, the feel of her skin, her lips, anything to keep himself where he was. The wonder of her touch turned into another pain as he realized he'd not be touching her again. The agony of that was almost equal to the vicious little burns and cuts Morey traced across his chest and down onto his belly.

In some remote corner of his brain, he wondered how long it would be before he was screaming. He had to distract himself, think about anything except what Morey was doing, what he was going to do.

"I feel sorry for you."

Morey sneered as he brought the knife up to hold it against Matt's throat. "You mean for yourself, don't you? I could slit your throat right now and nobody could stop me. So strong. What good did that do you against me?" He traced a fine line with the knife's tip from Matt's throat to his breast, leaving behind a thin trail of blood. Morey's eyes were wild with fervor, the lust for pain clearly overpowering him, driving him to a madness Matt had never seen before. Perhaps, Matt thought, trying to think past his pain, he could stoke that madness and spoil the almost sensual pleasure Morey was receiving. What that would gain him? Probably nothing, but he had to do some-thing. It seemed the only thing possible—his wits against Morey's insanity.

"Nothing you can do," he managed, "makes any difference." Morey took another drink and Matt thought maybe if his brother passed out, went to sleep, maybe he could free himself. "Nobody cares what happens to either of us in this little hell-hole. You are doing it all for nothing."

Morey sat back on his haunches and stared at him. "Got to be hurtin'," he muttered. Scratching his head in thought, he upended the whiskey bottle, gulping in a series of quick swallows. "I should've took her, too," he muttered, staring into the fire, then back at his brother. "That'd of broke you."

Matt tried to prevent his eyes from reflecting the truth of Morey's words.

Morey's face took on a look of frustration and anger. "So you figure you won after all by me not taking her, don't you? I could leave you here. You're not going nowhere and go back for her. Invite her to the party. She'd come willingly, wouldn't she? Anything to be with you."

Matt shut his eyes, closing out the sight of his brother's sneering face. The image of Morey's hands on Amy's smooth skin was enough to make him lose all control. "But it's too late now. You had your chance and blew it. Her pa, Adam, and St. Louis'll be watchin'. If you come within a mile of the wagons, they'd stomp you like the roach you are."

Morey swore, taking another swig from the bottle.

"You are losin' it all the way around. You can't even hurt me." Matt mustered up a laugh, but lost it on a groan as the knife came down. "That the best you got?" he asked when he could. It no longer mattered what happened to him, but he had to keep his brother angry, angry enough to forget Amy, to make him want more of the mind-numbing alcohol.

"We'll see who's laughin' when this is over," Morey muttered, leaning forward to reheat his blade. He watched glassily as the flames danced around the blade. He cast a wrathful glance at Matt as he rambled on, half the words unintelligible, the thoughts disconnected. "Things ain't right!" He nodded in agreement to a voice Matt couldn't hear. "Yeah, but if you took her, Morey, ole man, her people'd have come looking. Matt, nobody would care about, but her… Nah, couldn't have took her."

He leaned back over Matt, the whiskey bottle held loosely in one hand, the knife in the other. "I was just thinkin' about Adam with your woman." He made a sensuous circle with the bottle. "Comfortin' her'd be a pleasure. I can just see him, layin' his hands all over that lush, little body, touchin' them ripe breasts." He laughed at the anger Matt couldn't hide.

"Hey, Matt, this is your honeymoon. Only trouble is, Adam's

on it." He continued chuckling as he reheated the blade. "You know a knife's like a lover--slick and silky, caressin' your skin." His voice was slurred with the whiskey but the glitter in his eyes seemed as alert as ever. "Want me to let you go?" he asked abruptly.

Matt stared up into the sky. "You couldn't if you wanted to. You got no more control over what you're doing than I do."

"I can do what I want with you." He reached over, untied the leather thong that held Matt's hair back and then grabbed a length of it, yanking. "Could be there is one thing I could do that you wouldn't like so much. I could make it so you couldn't be with no woman again ever."

The flickering firelight eerily lit Morey's face into a demonic mask. A mask that smiled as Morey deliberately put down the bottle. Cradling the knife in his right hand, he reached for Matt's belt, fumbling with the buckle. Matt felt horror well up inside.

"Beg me not to do it," Morey rasped.

Matt clenched his jaw against the words that came to his lips. He might have begged, except it would have changed nothing. He saw the knife being lifted. Before it could descend, a shot rang out, shattering the blade.

Morey screamed an obscenity and dove for the cover of the brush. Matt barely had time to grasp the changing situation when Adam was at his side. His hand briefly was on Matt's shoulder before he sliced through the ropes at his wrists and then ankles. Matt felt an unreality to this abrupt shift that left his mind nearly as numb as his hands. He felt Adam slip the hilt of a knife into his right hand. He tried to grasp it and barely felt his fingers as they closed around it.

Adam shifted his revolver into his right hand. "Roll away from the fire so he can't see you. I'll collect him," he said with a hard smile, his teeth a white flash in the moonlight before he was gone. Matt rolled to one side but the brush and rocks blocked getting far until his circulation returned. He listened hard trying to determine what was happening.

After long moments, the rustling in dry grass was his only warning. He levered himself up on one elbow, to see Morey creeping toward him, moonlight flashing on the barrel of his rifle. Matt heaved himself to the side as a bullet struck where his body had been. Struggling to get a hold on the knife, he hurled it with all his strength toward his brother's chest. He heard the sound as it thudded home along with a shot, a scream and then silence.

Adam came out of the darkness and squatted besides Morey's body, feeling for a pulse. "He's dead." He rose then, his gun held loosely in his hand, the moonlight reflecting the tiredness on his face. "How are you?" His eyes scanned over Matt's body. Matt wanted to say something, but his mouth was so dry he didn't know if legible words would come out anyway.

"I could... use some water." His voice came out as little more than a croak. He still felt half numbed by the shock of the last hours and then Adam's abrupt arrival.

Adam went for a canteen. In a few moments he was back, handing it to Matt and then building up the campfire.

"How bad are you hurt?" Adam asked, as Matt drank.

"Considering," Matt said with a small smile, "I am good." He edged closer to the heat of the fire.

"God damn," Adam swore, his own voice none too steady. "I don't ever want to have another moment like that. Know you don't either. I got here just as... In time to see what he was doing. I had seconds to decide on the right shot. If I had shot him, not the knife, he might've gotten you on his way down."

Matt tried to stop shaking, but it seemed the more he tried, the worse it got.

"Where's your shirt?" Adam asked, frowning.

"He burnt it." Matt still regretted the loss of that shirt. "At least he didn't burn my boots. They're in the brush."

Adam took off his own jacket and put it over Matt's shoulders.

"How'd you find us?" Matt asked when the fire put out enough warmth that his teeth stopped chattering.

"I thought I'd lost the trail a couple times on that rocky ground. It made it hard, having to hang back. I really thought I'd lost you until morning." He stared into the fire. "I remembered what Amy said though, the kind of place he would look for." He fed a few more sticks into the fire. "What turned it was when I caught a whiff of smoke."

Matt began to feel the warmth from the fire seep into his muscles, the tight rigidity loosening. "You saved my life. I... Amy's all right, isn't she?" He massaged his hands to restore circulation.

"She would have come if I'd let her. What I can't believe," Adam said, "is how you managed to throw that knife. Your hands must've been nigh useless from being tied so long."

Matt smiled faintly and shook his head. He had no answer for how he'd done it. He waited a moment, then asked "Did I-- that is, which one of us killed him?"

Their eyes met as Adam said, "My bullet hit him in the head."

"I hit him too, didn't I?" No more lies and half-truths.

"Your aim was right to his heart."

"I can't say I'm sorry or glad. Just sick of what happened, that it had to happen, and grateful to you."

Adam shrugged.

"You didn't need to come after me... after us."

"Didn't I?"

"Thanks aren't enough."

"Forget it. Think you can ride back to camp?" Adam asked as he began searching through the bushes for Matt's boots.

"Not if you got an alternative," Matt said, only half joking. He ached in every muscle. He pulled on socks and boots as he grimaced.

"Back in camp, St. Louis will have that salve," Adam said with a laugh.

"Lord help me." Cautiously Matt stood, relieved his legs supported his weight-- even if he did feel like a hundred-year-old man. As he rotated the muscles in his shoulders, he tried to think of words to say what he was feeling. He looked at the ground, then up to Adam's clear gaze. "Morey didn't think anybody'd come. I didn't either."

Adam grinned putting his hand on Matt's shoulder before he went to get the horses. "Like you wouldn't have done the same if it had been me." He looked down at the still body at the edge of the light. "What should we do with that?"

"It'd be tempting to leave him for the buzzards," Matt said with a sigh, "but I guess he was loved by his pa. We should take him back and let him bury him." He would never again call that man his father.

CHAPTER 27

The sun was edging into the sky when they rode into camp. Matt wanted to get to Amy, hold her in his arms and finally know the nightmare was over. But he didn't need a mirror to know how he must look--dirty, bare-chested, with a myriad of small cuts and a couple of nasty burns. If he went to her this way, it would only frighten her; so he headed for St. Louis' wagon to clean up.

Stopping his horse in front of the wagon, he slowly dismounted. As his boots touched the ground, Amy flew from the front of the wagon and wrapped her arms around his waist, holding him tightly to her. Only at his wince did she pull back.

"I knowed it'd be all right," he could hear Clem chortling in the background. "I told her Adam'd bring ya back."

Ignoring the pain, Matt drew her against him, inhaling her clean, sweet fragrance.

"Are you all right?" Amy cried, kissing him and crying. "Are you really here? I've been so scared. Sometimes it seems, since I've known you, I'm always scared. Are you sure it's over? Tell me." Her hands touched him, ran lightly down his arms, and caressed his face.

"Give me a chance, baby," he retorted, smiling. He kissed her forehead.

"Was--is that Morey?" she asked, gesturing toward the burdened horse Adam was leading away.

Matt nodded.

"I'm glad. It sounds awful, but I'm glad. I know I'm babbling, but thank God, you're here. You are really here. Tell me you're all right. Even if you're not. Just tell me."

"I'm fine."

"What did he do to you?" She stepped back to scan his body. Swallowing back the urge to cry, she saw the evidence of the night he'd endured. "Where is your shirt?" she asked inanely, trying to keep control of herself. She was perilously close to breaking down.

"Enough of this lollygagging, Mrs. Kane," St. Louis interrupted, herbal tins in one hand, clean cloths in the other. "Let's find out just what did get done to this brand new, practically unused husband of yore'n."

Matt lowered himself carefully onto a stool and shrugged out of Adam's jacket. Amy felt her eyes fill again with tears as she saw the full extent of burns and cuts along his chest, belly, arms, and throat.

Clem grunted, shaking his head. "No good varmint! Glad ya done the little rat in." He put a pot of coffee onto the fire as he continued grumbling to himself about the worthlessness of some people. "Who finished off the buzzard?"

St. Louis unscrewed the liniment, then looked up at Adam who had just returned. "You tell Martha and Amos?"

"They saw us ride in. They said they'd wait a little before they come."

"Thank you," Amy said. "I knew you'd get there in time."

Adam smiled. "Wish I'd been so sure."

St. Louis frowned as he turned his attention back to Matt's injuries. "We're gonna have to disinfect these cuts."

Matt sighed, resigned to more pain. "Just do it."

The liniment burned as St. Louis wiped and cleansed the dirt from the open wounds. Matt clenched his jaw against the yowl of pain he wanted to make.

"Let it out," Amy said.

He panted. "What?"

"Damn it, I've had enough of your stoicism." Amy glared at him. "I want to hear you yelp when you hurt."

Matt stifled an expression more in keeping with his feelings before he gave her a faint smile. "Next time," he said, hissing as St. Louis' astringent bit into another wound.

She gave him one of the looks only she could give. "There better not be a next time."

St. Louis handed Amy a clean cloth to dry his skin. "This part'll be easier," he promised, opening up the tin of herbal ointment. Gently he anointed the burns and cuts. When he was done, Clem handed Matt a cup of coffee and a biscuit from the tin.

Gratefully Matt took a swallow of the strong coffee, barely restraining a grimace at the bitterness. He looked up and saw Adam watching him over the rim of his coffee cup. "Did you tell his pa?"

"I tried to. I'd say he was drunk as a skunk or playing possum. I asked Hall and Brick to dig a hole. When we throw the body in it, I'll try again to wake Mr. Kane."

Matt let out a breath. What did he owe to a man who had never treated him as a son, who had let his brother abuse him, who had turned his life into a hell, where Matt felt lucky to have emerged alive.

He shook his head finding comfort in Amy's hand as it rested lightly on his shoulder. Looking up he saw Martha, Amos, Belle, and others trailing behind as they walked into the camp. Their smiles were relieved.

"Glad to see you back, son," Amos said, putting his hand lightly on Matt's shoulder.

Matt managed a tired smile. Exhaustion was overtaking him as it was no longer overridden by adrenaline. He was relieved when everyone smiled, said how glad they were he was safe, but, except for Clem, asked no questions. Later it would be easier to talk about what had happened, but right now the mental wounds were deeper than the physical ones.

Bernice descended upon them, her questions coming so quickly Matt's dazed mind couldn't follow any of them.

"Bernice, can't you see the man is falling asleep on his feet,"

Loraine snapped, ending Bernice's monologue. "For once in your life, show some judgment and shut your mouth."

Bernice scowled but did shut her mouth.

"We got to get this show on the road," St. Louis said, "and Miss Loraine here, she's right about Matt. He ain't had no sleep for twenty-four hours." He paused for a moment. "Considerin' he was just hitched yesterday, he probably ain't had no sleep for forty-eight hours." There was a smattering of laughter.

"You sure we shouldn't have a shivaree for the bride and groom?" Adam asked with a chuckle that increased with the glare Matt sent his way. He innocently put up his hands. "It was just an idea."

"One that might get paid back someday," Matt warned.

"I got an idee too." St. Louis, ignoring the banter, looked from Matt to Amy, "I'll know Miss Amy didn't sleep at all last night. Why don't you two take my wagon today. I'll pull the front flap tight, and ya can sleep all day long. Unless o' course, ya think of somethin' ya'd rather do."

"My boy is dead?" Nathan Kane pushed his way into the circle, his eyes bleary and red.

"He is," Adam said. "I thought you were asleep."

"Jest didn't know what to say. You the one killed him?" He glared at Adam, a gun in his hand pointing at the scout.

"It was me," Matt said, rising to put himself in front of Adam. "Just before he would have killed me."

"I should have killed you the day you were born. I took one look at ya and knew ya weren't mine."

Matt shook his head. His exhaustion had fled. He walked toward his father. "Give me the gun."

"I ain't gonna."

"You are." Matt reached out and took it from his hand. "You'd get someone else to kill me, but you don't have the guts, do you Mr. Kane?"

The old man bent his head. "I done the best I could."

"You sure did and nearly had two sons killed," St. Louis said. "Now get out of here and back to your wagon afore I shoot you myself. I'll get you to The Dalles but no further."

Kane looked at Matt. "You owe me."

"And luckily for you, I won't hold a grudge. Now get out of here." He watched with no regrets as the old man turned and with defeat headed back to his wagon. Matt shook his head. He was surprised, after all he'd been through, to realize that for the first time he actually felt free.

As the wagon began its rocking journey, Amy lay in Matt's arms, careful as to what she touched and how she lay against him, grateful she could feel the beat of his heart under her fingertips. When she thought about how easily she might have lost him, she felt the tears well up and this time did nothing to stop them.

"It's all right, baby," Matt whispered. She knew he felt her tears. "It's behind us now. It really is over this time." He ran his finger lightly along her arm.

"What about your father?" she asked as she ran her fingers lightly along his wrist where the skin was torn in his attempt to get free.

"He's his own worse enemy and it appears always has been. I owe him nothing and am sure not going to let him turn me bitter when I have a life ahead of me."

"You said you killed Morey. Did you?" When he didn't immediately answer, she said, "I don't want you to think you have to tell me about it unless--I mean, I wish I understood men better. Is it going to be good for you to talk, or will it just be upsetting?"

"In other words," he drawled with a slow smile, "you want to know if you oughta kiss it, lance it, or cover it with salve."

"I suppose that's it. I don't need to hear something that causes you pain."

"Last night was hell for you too. You have a right to know the truth, or you'll be thinking it was worse than it was." He shuddered. He put his forearm under his head. Staring at the swaying canvas cover overhead, and with concise words, he related what had happened. As he talked, she lay beside him, stroked his arm, but remained silent.

"In the end, I guess you could say Adam and I both killed him."

Hearing the story, realizing the madness behind the words, the horror that had come so close to killing or maiming Matt forever, Amy swallowed back her tears, and tried to keep her voice in control as she asked the only question she could bear to. "Are you going to be able to live with that and with what you father was really like?"

She raised herself on one elbow so she could see his face. He looked up at her, his eyes a clear, blue-gray. The dark lashes thickly lining them gave him a little boy look at complete variance with the bristly jaw and the rawly masculine body which sprawled across the bed. She wished she could read the expression in those eyes.

"I can. How about you?"

"That I killed my brother?"

"The only way you'd ever be safe is with him dead. I wanted you to kill him. I prayed you would. If I could have, I would have myself." Sometimes evil had to be destroyed for life to go on.

"I am sorry for what it put you through."

She brushed the edge of his jaw with her fingertip. "It was worse for you."

"Sometimes worryin' is hardest."

"You mean that?" she asked, her lips nipping at his lower lip. He unbuttoned the top buttons of her blouse, pulling it apart to kiss the fullness of her breast. When he lifted his head to kiss her lips, he parted hers with his tongue, delving deeply into her mouth. His hand cupped her breast possessively, kneading the nipple. Smiling, she reached her hand down over his groin, feeling his erection.

"There is one more thing," he said with a sigh causing her to pull back. He lay quietly for a moment, and she waited for whatever he needed to say.

"It wasn't just that Morey tried to hurt me," he said finally.

"It looks like he succeeded in that." Amy's fingers lightly touched his lean cheek, brushing back his hair.

He shook his head. "He wanted to have power, but he didn't, not over any part of it. He was crazy, no more able to stop what was happening than I was. I just keep thinking maybe earlier I could have done something, something that would have changed all that happened if I had understood sooner that it was insanity, not just meanness."

Amy let her fingertip lightly caress his chest, drawing a light circle on his chest."And so you do want to try and help your father." It wasn't really a question.

"I don't know. Maybe it's the same sickness. I won't want him anywhere near us but maybe some money... I don't know. He's lost everything, and he sure doesn't have the ability to take care of himself."

"Whatever you believe is right. As for Morey, he made his own choices. I hope you don't blame yourself for not being able to turn him from them. We can't save everyone."

He smiled. "I know you're right—in my head."

She kissed his jaw, working toward his ear. She landed her kisses like a soft summer rain, working to tantalize each place she touched. From how his breath was coming faster, she thought she might've been succeeding. She stroked along the side of his chest.

"I'm sorry about your wedding getting spoiled," he whispered, as he pulled her against him at the same time he gave a little groan as she contacted one of the burns.

"Well, actually the wedding was lovely," she murmured as she leaned over him, kissing alongside a long narrow mark across his neck, not letting herself think how easily that could have taken him from her forever. "Belle was a little put out we didn't have the bouquet tossing, but the wedding was perfect."

Amy knew they couldn't do much. Matt wasn't going to be capable of consummating their marriage until he healed at least physically, but she couldn't stop her wayward hands from wanting to touch him. She needed the reassurance that he was with her and finally safe. She let her hands follow the route they had ached to take for so many months, down across his chest and belly avoiding the burns and cuts to where the thin line of hair dipped below his pants.

He lifted his head and claimed her lips, his kiss light, then deepening as his tongue delved into her mouth. She felt the familiar heat of desire throughout her body. Smiling, she lowered her head to his ear. "The wedding night left a little something to be desired," she teased. Her hand continued carefully exploring his torso, edging lower down his flat belly. She could feel him tense.

"A wedding night can actually go into the next day." His smile was sensuous as he kissed her.

"It can?" She let her lips follow the erotic path she had longed to take for months. She needed to feel more of him, touch him in places she'd only dreamed. Commonsense, waiting, all seemed words beyond her ability. "We don't have to do it all," she murmured, "except I'd really like to..." Her fingers began unfastening his pants. With them open, his erection sprang free. he sucked in a breath as she pulled his pants off.

She felt his fingers at the button of her blouse, pushing it off her shoulders and then her chemise down, leaving her breasts free to his fingers and lips. He laid her back, pulling off the rest of her clothing before he returned to her breasts. She groaned as he took her nipple in his mouth, sucking on it and then holding it lightly between his teeth. He stilled her cries with his mouth and tongue. She wanted his hands over her whole body, touching her all the places she had imagined. He pushed her legs apart and began to do as she had dreamed.

Nothing mattered but this. Not that Clem, driving the wagon, might hear them over the noise of the animals and the wagon or that someone could come into the wagon. They wouldn't. Amy's breath was coming unevenly as she moved down the cot, coming back up slowly tracing a path with her lips from his ankles, up his calves, the hard muscles of his thighs as she pushed his legs apart. She let her long hair brush him intimately, making him even harder.

"You're so perfect," he whispered as he stroked her breasts. He moved his hand then down her belly. Together they lay entwined, kissing and touching. She felt herself quiver as he touched her in places no one had ever done and where it made her writhe with feelings she'd only imagined existed. Hands and lips taught and learned until finally there was only the need to be one flesh.

He levered himself over her. "You know the first time it'll hurt," he whispered.

"I don't care. I need you in me." She rotated her hips upward to ease his entry. Groaning, he thrust deep, past the barrier. He was right it hurt. The pain was quickly replaced by other feelings, those that seemed to go through her whole body with ecstasy. Her flesh had found its other half.

It seemed only moments had passed when she threw her head back with what she realized was a climax. The feelings seemed to fill her whole body from head to toe. He followed her almost immediately. Afterward as they lay together, limbs entwined, their bare skin slick with sweat, Amy kissed his shoulder and chuckled.

"What?" he asked in a husky whisper.

"Just... I was never sure it'd be worth the waiting. So many times I wanted you, wanted you so badly, but then I'd tell myself to be practical. Maybe it would all be a disappointment." She felt more than saw his smile.

"You do know it was a first time for me too."

"You mean you hadn't had another woman?"

He stroked her cheek. "I met you when I was not even thirteen. I never wanted another woman from then on. I sure wasn't about to go to a whore."

"You're pretty good at it for not having done it before," she said a little skepticism in her voice.

"Because it's you. Only because it's you. I have had a lot of time to think about it. I thought I knew how it'd be... although I admit, if I'd totally known, maybe I wouldn't have been able to hold off either."

"I heard women talk about it, like it was a duty, not a joy. If it's a duty, I want you doing your duty over and over again."

His smile looked as satisfied as she felt. Then she heard him begin to chuckle.

"What?" It was her turn to ask.

He shook his head. "I can't believe it. I went through hell trying to keep from touching you, thought sometimes it'd just about kill me, wanting you so much and determined to wait, so's it'd be perfect when we finally did it, and--" He laughed again.

"I don't understand."

"So, here we are in a bumping, swaying wagon, the middle of the morning, Clem driving the rig, who knows who might take a notion to check on us. Everything I told you I didn't want."

"Except one thing."

"And that was?"

"You now have the right to do this," she whispered, her tongue circling his ear, her hand moving caressingly across his chest, "and it was perfect--for us."

Pulling her on top him, his fingers caressed her breast. His lips nuzzled the hollow at the base of her neck. She looked at him with surprise. "You mean we can do it again?"

He grinned and lifted his head to claim her mouth. "What do you think?"

EPILOGUE

November 1851, Oregon

"It's perfect, Matt," Amy said as she clasped her hands with delight. The log house stood at the head of a grove of towering fir trees. Along one side was a small stream with the remnants of dried wildflowers. The house had a front porch wide enough for a swing or bench. Two windows looked onto a meadow below. She knew the kitchen was to the back, with a smaller porch. One bedroom was to the east of the main room with a loft above.

Although, at Matt's insistence, she hadn't been inside since he hung the front door, she knew the main room had a large fireplace made of smooth, rounded river stones. A mantle of thick wood ran its width. The raised hearth was for sitting on with an iron hanger for cooking.

"I never imagined you could get a cabin up so fast," she said still finding it hard to believe." It was a little larger than the cabin her father, Matt, and St. Louis had built for her parents or the one St. Louis had planned for himself. They were less finished, as the priority her father had set was getting her and Matt into their own home.

She had expected to live in a cabin tent for their first winter.

Amazingly, the three men found their land, filed on it and got the basic cabins up-- even a lean-to for horses at her parents' home.

"Well, it's not really finished, but it'll get us through the winter for sure. Your father having the money to buy planed lumber and cedar shingles from Oregon City made the difference for how this went up so fast. I didn't know I'd married a woman with a rich family." He grinned

"Not that rich." She put her arms around his waist. "Anyway, it is theirs, not ours."

"Next spring I'll add on some rooms and build a barn." He smiled as he pulled her to his side.

"A nursery maybe too," she teased.

He managed a smile, but she already knew any talk of a baby made Matt uneasy. She so wanted a baby, but it hadn't happened as quickly as she had hoped. Matt being busy from dawn to dark hadn't helped.

"There is a tradition to be observed here," he said, reaching down and picking her up into his arms.

"Ah," she said as she kissed his neck. When they got to the door, she bent and opened the latch before he carried her over the threshold. "I love you so much," she whispered in his ear."

"If your parents and St. Louis weren't due in a few minutes, I'd put that to the test," he said with a laugh as he set her on her feet.

She twirled in the middle of the room. "It is perfect, Matt, just as I imagined it all those months ago. I can see two chairs over there by the window. You can make a table for the other wall." She then noticed a bookshelf. "How did you do that?" she asked.

"Took some boards left over from the floors. I knew you'd need a place for all those books." He smiled with that patient look he wore when discussing the literature she so dearly loved.

"I can read to you at night." She imagined it with a rug in front of the fireplace where they would lie on it as she read by candle and firelight.

"I'd like that. I wish the cook stoves had been in Oregon

City. They say more likely, with all the new arrivals, it'll be not 'til spring. They have to bring them 'round the Horn."

"It's all right. I learned to cook over the fire on the Trail. I can manage with the fireplace." It had a nice deep box to build a blazing fire. The mantle above would someday hold candles, cups, and a kerosene lantern. She had two tintypes of her grandparents; maybe those could be propped up there.

Arriving in early September, the deciduous trees down by the river had just begun to turn color. The beauty in this part of Oregon exceeded even her dreams. She thought of the garden they would start in the spring. Her own home! Of all the dreams she had imagined, this one had been borne on the trail west. It had been the one round the bend, the one she hadn't seen ahead of time. The best dream of all.

Matt heard Amy's family out front. Her mother's arms held a pile of quilts. Her father had a box full of food. Belle carried a few pots while Loraine had a box of glasses. "Come on back," Amy told them. "Help me put things away." In moments, they had disappeared into the kitchen, where Matt had built some counters and several cupboards. With the eventual iron stove, it would be a nice kitchen.

"I sure appreciate what you have done for us," Matt said to Amos. He looked around him. "All the help you gave me on the cabin. Helping me find the right place to file our claims. This land is going to be good for fruit trees, lumber, and even cattle with time."

Amos grinned. "I have to say, it's better than the books I'd read. I like this setting above the river where we can see it in the distance and no risk of flooding."

"Your research made it all work. It's all your doing, Pa." He was still trying out the words for his in-laws. Although he had come to love them, the words still came with difficulty.

"You're my son now. It's family," Amos said.

"Yeah... family," Matt said working to block the feeling of darkness that still descended, even now at the word.

"Thinking of your pa?" Amos asked. He didn't wait for an answer before he pulled a flask of brandy from his back pocket. "How about you take one of your rare drinks as we toast your new home?"

Matt smiled and nodded. Before Amos could go for the glasses that had been delivered to the kitchen, St. Louis was coming through the door. "Brought ya a cast iron dutch oven," he said. Clem won't be needing it now that he stayed in Portland to help the Collins get a store going. Don't know why the heck they'd stay there with it being smaller than Oregon City."

"Jacob said because of shipping, that it'll be the big city soon enough," Amos said. "He might be right. I just didn't want to live in a city and sure as heck didn't want to be a shopkeeper again." He grimaced.

Matt remembered Portland, which had been pretty much the stump town it was nicknamed. He agreed with Amos. He had a need to be out of town. This land, about fifteen miles from Oregon City suited him.

He remembered then the dark-haired man who had saved his life. He wished Adam had wanted to stay with them here. The scout had only laughed. "Rolling stones gather no moss," he had joked, as he waved and rode to the south where he'd been offered a job scouting for the military.

Amos put a comforting hand on his shoulder before he left to find three glasses. When he returned, he said, "Don't feel bad about your pa. He chose his bed." He set the glasses on the bookcase before filling and then handing one to each of them.

"To your new home, Matt."

St. Louis smiled. "I can drink to that one."

Matt took a sip trying to force the darkness from him. "I left my pa money. I suppose you know that."

"No, I didn't. You were more generous than most would be."

"I wanted him to have a start in The Dalles, but I told him to never show up on this land or I'd kill him. He glared at me but then I guess he saw I meant it as he nodded and left."

"Ya are a hard one," St. Louis said chuckling as he took another swig of the brandy.

"I won't let him hurt my family. You know... Amy wants a baby."

"And you don't?" St. Louis asked as he caught the tone of Matt's voice.

"I just... I can't get past thinking all those years that my ma died that way."

"It is true that women can die in childbirth," Amos said putting his hand again on Matt's shoulder. "A man does worry, but Martha knows about how the baby should be positioned. She will be here when it's time. There is a doctor in Oregon City." He smiled sheepishly when both men looked at him. "Hey, a father can worry some too. Amy will be fine. Martha had three with never a problem. Amy is built a lot like her."

Matt sighed. "Well, it's likely going to come one of these days—whether I want it or not."

"I'm kinda surprised ya gave your pa the money you had earned." St. Louis changed the subject. "Not likely he'll do more than drink it up."

Matt sat the barely touched brandy on the fireplace mantle. "It was half of what you paid me for working on the train. He's fifty-five. I wanted to give him a chance. It's up to him what he does with it. There are jobs to be had in The Dalles. I just didn't want to feel I left him no chance."

St. Louis grinned. "Ya are a good man."

"We agree," Amos said. "Let's rejoin the ladies, eat, and then, I think we have another job to finish here."

"And that is?" Matt asked as he followed his father-in-law.

"Make the two of you a bed. I am definitely in the mood for grandchildren."

. . . .

Book 1 of the Steven's family Saga.
Look for:
Where Dreams Go
Going Home
Love Waits

Thank you for reading 'Round The Bend'.

Join Rain online at Facebook and Twitter.
E-mail sign up at Rain's Blog
(rainydaythought.blogspot.com)